SECRETS OF THE
DEMON

DIANA ROWLAND

DAW BOOKS, INC.
DONALD A. WOLLHEIM, FOUNDER
375 Hudson Street, New York, NY 10014

ELIZABETH R. WOLLHEIM
SHEILA E. GILBERT
PUBLISHERS
http://www.dawbooks.com

First Printing, January 2011

1 2 3 4 5 6 7 8 9

**DAW TRADEMARK REGISTERED
U.S. PAT. AND TM. OFF. AND FOREIGN COUNTRIES
—MARCA REGISTRADA
HECHO EN U.S.A.**

PRINTED IN THE U.S.A.

To my sister, Sherry, for accepting and supporting
the nerds in her life.

ACKNOWLEDGMENTS

I tried to tell myself I didn't need to write a lengthy acknowledgment, but the truth is that every single book requires enormous help from a variety of sources and it would be a travesty if I didn't at least make the attempt to thank everyone who contributed to the creation of this book.

Therefore, huge thanks and appreciation go to:

Dr. Michael DeFatta, who continues to be an absolute goldmine of information on forensic pathology, and, amazingly, has not yet filed a restraining order to force me to stop texting questions to him.

Roman White, Michael Buckholtz, and Scott Gardner, for answering my numerous questions about the music industry with incredible detail and unwavering patience.

Sgt. Ben Eshleman and Detective Stefan Montgomery, for filling in the many gaps in my knowledge of financial crimes and the paperwork involved in investigating them.

Sgt. Roy McCann, for explaining the best way to shoot various things.

My kick-ass agent, Matt Bialer, and his lovely and awesome assistant, Lindsay Ribar, for not giving up on me or this series. I can't imagine being in this line of work without them.

Betsy Wollheim, my incredible editor, for *everything*.

Debbie Roma, for being such a great friend and fan.

Nicole Peeler, for helping me find the good stuff in the book.

And, of course, my mom, for the many varieties of support and motivation she's given me.

AUTHOR'S NOTE:

While I do my very best to ensure that all of the Kara Gillian books can be enjoyed as stand-alone novels, there is an overarching storyline to the series that I hope readers will enjoy as well. I advise those readers who are interested in earlier books to begin with *Mark of the Demon* and follow that with *Blood of the Demon*—both of which are available from fine booksellers everywhere. Thank you.

Chapter 1

The heavy music pounded through me, making my teeth vibrate and the muscles in my back tense in reaction. I leaned against the wall, as much as to have a good vantage to watch the seething mass of people in front of the stage as to ground myself from the incessant beat. Cigarette smoke burned the back of my throat and the stench of stale beer and sweat coiled around me in a noxious miasma. Every now and then I'd get a whiff of something putrid, letting me know me that I'd picked a spot too close to the bathrooms. I was in a good position to see the majority of the bar, but the raised alcove I'd claimed for my use suffered from a distinct lack of air flow—which probably explained why it was empty.

A few feet below me the dance floor was getting some vigorous use—its denizens clad in fishnets and corsets, PVC and leather, ball gowns and "Little Bo-Peep" outfits, and every possible combination thereof. Past the dance floor and through a broad brick archway I could see that the long bar was packed three deep. I was in serious need of some ice water, but I wasn't quite desperate enough to brave the crush at the bar.

<You do not enjoy this activity.>

I jerked in surprise at the feel of the demon's voice in my head. I'd summoned tenth-level demons before, but this particular *zhurn* was the only demon who had ever chosen to speak with me mind to mind. <This is not my preferred leisure activity,> I replied, tensing with the effort of communicating with the demon in this fashion. <I don't really care for crowds.> It wasn't as simple as merely *thinking* a sentence, which is what I'd always imagined it to be. Instead it felt as if I had to push the thought along the mental bindings that held the demon in this sphere. It was creepy and unsettling, and I couldn't help but be relieved that the *zhurn* were the only demons who ever chose to communicate this way.

I waited for a response from the demon, but my answer had apparently been sufficient. *Maybe it's bored?* Unfortunately, there really wasn't much for it to do. I'd only summoned Skalz as a contingency backup, even though I thought it very unlikely that we would need one. It had also been a while since I'd summoned a *zhurn* and this had been a convenient enough excuse.

"You're supposed to look like you're having fun," FBI Special Agent Ryan Kristoff said from beside me. It probably should have been a whisper, or at least *sotto voce*, but the music was so loud it ended up being more of a shout.

"Not true," I said/shouted back. "It's a goth bar. I'm supposed to look miserable!"

His eyes crinkled with humor. "It's good to see that you're embracing your undercover persona so thoroughly." I gave him a rude snort which only made him laugh. "So you don't like being on the 'financial crimes' task force?"

I had to smile at that. I was a homicide detective for the Beaulac, Louisiana, PD, and a few months ago I'd been the lead detective on the Symbol Man serial killer case. I'd met FBI Special Agents Ryan Kristoff and Zachary Garner during the investigation and had been surprised to discover that both agents were quite accepting of the existence of the supernatural and arcane. Later I'd been asked to join a multi-jurisdictional task force that dealt with white collar crimes and financial malfeasance—which had confused me until I'd discovered that this particular "financial crimes" task force also dealt with anything that had a supernatural or paranormal element.

"Okay, I'll admit that this is a thousand times better than slogging my way through financial statements." I knew what I was talking about, too. I'd paid my dues in white collar investigations before finally getting promoted to homicide. "But I still think the only reason we're here is because Zack wanted to meet Lida Moran."

Amusement flashed in Ryan's eyes. "Well, she *has* been receiving death threats, which makes it a Homeland Security issue, which technically we're a part of."

Ryan ignored my rude snort and continued. "And she's from Beaulac, so it makes sense for you to be in on the investigation, right?"

"And, since she's performing in New Orleans your little multi-jurisdictional task force fit the bill oh so perfectly," I said. Two days ago the manager for Ether Madhouse had notified the FBI that strange threats had been left on the fan forum of the band's website—messages stating that a "demon would consume Lida on stage" during one of her concerts. The IP address of the threats had been traced to a coffee shop in Beaulac with an open wireless connection, which meant that it could have been anyone. Hence the decision to go undercover at the concert.

I slid a glance to where Zack was "staking out" the area in front of the stage. To the average observer it probably looked like he was dancing with great enthusiasm. For that matter it looked like that to me as well. His tanned face, sun-bleached hair, and athletic build contrasted sharply with the pale faces around him, but he was so clearly enjoying the music that no one in their right mind would ever suspect him of being undercover. I couldn't help but smile. I never would have guessed in a million zillion years that the FBI agent who I'd mentally dubbed "Surfer Boy" had a thing for goth metal bands with female lead singers.

"Cognitive dissonance," I said with a shake of my head.

"And the threats did mention demons consuming her soul . . ."

I raised an eyebrow and Ryan raised his hands in surrender. "Okay, okay. It's true! My partner has a fanboy crush and was looking for any excuse to get close to Lida Moran." Then he laughed. "I still think you should have worn the outfit that Zack found for you."

I leveled a glare at him. "There is no way that I will ever wear a corset on duty."

Ryan summoned an innocent look. "But think of how well you would have blended in!"

"And think of how well I could manage in a foot pursuit wearing a leather miniskirt and red Mary Janes with five inch heels!" I shot back. Zack had enthusiastically produced the aforementioned "undercover" garb, and my reaction had been less than gracious. I'd very reluctantly allowed Zack to lace me into the corset, simply because I was curious to see if it could actually give me something resembling a figure. I tended to think of myself as shapeless—waist and hips damn near the same size, with the boobs barely edging them out. I wasn't fat by a long stretch, but I had zilcho muscle tone, and I wasn't going to be wearing midriff-revealing tops anytime soon. But the corset had given me a shitload more *figure* than I was prepared for. I'd taken one look at my corseted self in the mirror and then yanked it off, informing Zack that I couldn't possibly wear it since I couldn't breathe in the damn thing. But the truth was that I'd been stupidly and prudishly mortified at the thought of going out in public with my boobs shoved up and out like that—even though I was secretly tickled to see how I looked with actual cleavage and a defined waist.

I'd tried the shoes next. They were utterly lovely, but even though I'd enjoyed the sensation of being five foot ten, I was completely incapable of taking more than three steps in them without wobbling. And I'd flatly re- fused to try on the miniskirt, since there was no way in all of creation I was going to let the general public see my pale and out-of-shape legs.

Zack had finally exchanged everything for an outfit that I was far more willing to wear in public—a pretty nifty quasi-Victorian ensemble with ruffled blouse, fitted pants, and brocade jacket, along with a pair of gorgeous ass-kicking jack boots. My deeply buried inner goth had fallen madly in love with the boots, and was now trying to figure out some way to justify keeping them. For the rest of my "look," I'd layered on the eyeliner and at- tempted to tease my hair out into something somewhat wild, but my hair had stubbornly refused to stay teased or wild and had quickly fallen back into its usual boring straightness. I'd finally streaked red and pink through it, while praying that it really was as temporary a dye as the package claimed. I wasn't a huge fan of my natural hair color—I usually referred to it as "rat's ass brown"— but I'd yet to work up the nerve to permanently color or highlight it, and pink streaks were certainly not the direction I'd ever want to go with it. I'd been briefly tempted to buy some colored contact lenses—blue or green . . . anything but the current dull dark gray—but finally decided that would be going a bit overboard.

For his part, Ryan was decked out in a black T-shirt with buckles along the shoulders and black industrial pants with more buckles and rivets down the sides. The shirt was tight enough that I could see the ripple of his abs through it, and I had to admit—privately—that he looked awfully damn good in black. Every other woman apparently thought so too, judging by the gazes cast his way.

"It's too bad you can't pull off the goth look," I said with a shake of my head.

He looked down at what he was wearing and frowned. "What's wrong with this outfit?"

"Nothing's wrong," I said. "But no matter how hard you try to dress the part, you still carry yourself like a federal agent."

His mouth twitched in a smile and he slouched against the wall. "Better?"

I shook my head. "Now you look like a fed trying to look casual. I still think you could have shaved your head into a mohawk, like I'd suggested."

He gave a mock-shudder. "I'll take a lot of risks in this line of work, but that's one thing I don't plan to do."

"Chicken shit," I teased.

"My current style's not good enough for you?"

My gaze flicked up to his hair. His natural color was brown with hints of red-gold highlights, and he kept his hair short enough to comply with FBI regs but long enough that the barest hint of curl showed. I'd never admitted it out loud—and probably never would since we seemed to be locked in a sometimes awkward "just friends" mode—but there were times when I really wanted to run my fingers through his hair.

Now was *not* one of those times. He'd used a frightening amount of hair product in what looked like an attempt to make it spiky. Unfortunately his hair was too short for him to achieve the desired look. Or rather, I hoped that what he'd achieved was *not* the desired look. And then there was the color.

"Ryan," I said grimly. "Your head looks like a hairbrush that's been soaked in grape juice. What did you dye it with? Kool-Aid?"

"Now that was just plain mean," he said with a sad shake of his head.

I scanned the crowd, feeling a strange relief that tonight—so far—was turning out to have less than the usual amount of awkward tension between us. Ever since I'd saved Ryan's life by swearing myself to the demonic lord Rhyzkahl as his summoner, any feelings Ryan might have had for me were locked down pretty tight—not that I had any certainty there ever were. And, unfortunately, I couldn't blame him. The demons seemed to hold some sort of odd antipathy toward Ryan, calling him a *kiraknikahl,* or oathbreaker, though I had no idea why. And even though Rhyzkahl didn't *own* me, or anything like that, and the only service I'd sworn to perform was to summon him, nonetheless I was still bound to the demonic lord, and I could understand if Ryan wanted to keep me at arm's length.

I hated it, but I understood it.

My gaze was drawn to a black-clad figure smoking a cigarette against the wall near the bar. He wasn't dancing or even twitching to the music, and when my eyes rested on him he turned his head to give me a lazy smile, as if he could feel me looking at him. For all I knew he could. This was the fourth member of our little team tonight. Marco Knight was a detective with the New Orleans police department, and since we were in the city, we needed someone with local jurisdiction in case anything happened. He'd apparently worked with the team before, when they'd worked cases in the city. Ryan hadn't told me much about him, except to say that "he got it." And I hadn't picked up much more when I'd met him, though after he shook my hand in greeting I had the odd feeling that he knew a lot more about me.

One eyebrow lifted and then a sardonic smile crossed his face as he murmured, "Complicated," before releasing my hand.

Complicated? Yeah, that pretty much described my life.

I looked away, annoyed at myself for being ... unsettled? Intimidated? I couldn't really explain why, but I wasn't comfortable keeping my attention on him. Or vice versa.

I returned my attention to the stage. Lida Moran was the lead singer for Ether Madhouse as well as one hell of a guitar player. Her fingers flew over the strings as she threw herself around the stage with gusto, belting out something that might have been lyrics. I really couldn't tell, but the crowd didn't seem to care whether they understood what the words to the song were. She was good, though. I had to give her that. Nineteen years old, five foot ten, and with the kind of body that most of the guys I knew would dub "smokin' hot," she had a powerhouse voice that wowed everyone who heard her, whether they liked her style of music or not. The other three members of the band had some decent musical chops as well, though I wasn't much of a judge of that sort of thing. But I could tell that they didn't suck.

"Isn't she a little young for Zack?" I asked, casting a dubious glance at the singer. The purple streaks in her long, jet-black hair seemed to glow under the lights, and I could see the flash of metal from the numerous piercings in her ears, nose, and eyebrows. "How old is Zack anyway?"

Ryan's brow creased. "I have no idea. I guess late twenties or so? But don't worry. He's a fanboy, but that's as far as he'd ever take it."

I caught a snatch of lyric through the driving beat. *And the watchers on patrol / hunt the creatures in the night / until the demon eats your soul / and you have to leave the fight.*

"So, you're the big bad demon summoner," Ryan said. "Do you listen to this sort of music?"

I shook my head. "Not in the slightest! Give me some Faith Hill or Carrie Underwood any day."

"Country music and demon summoning," he said with a wince. "Now *that's* cognitive dissonance."

The driving beat ended and the lights dimmed. Lida set her guitar aside and the band shifted to a slower, almost sultry number. I let my breath out in relief at the cessation of the pounding. "Last set," I said with a nod toward the stage. "That's what the threat said, right?"

Ryan gave a nod, expression completely serious now. "See anything?" he asked. It was a twofold question. He was asking me if I saw anyone or anything suspicious, but he also wanted to know if I *felt* anything out of whack. Anything to do with the arcane.

I shifted into othersight, then shook my head. "Nah, just the usual background buzz you'd expect..." I paused, feeling the brush of *something.* I scanned the crowd again, eyes narrowing. *What the hell?* "Hang on, I think there's—"

My words choked off as a strange resonance slammed into me. I felt a sharp stab of pain at the base of my skull, and then the lights went out.

Chapter 2

"Kara!" I felt hands gripping my upper arms and I blinked to clear my vision. Then the emergency lights flickered on and I abruptly realized that the lights really had gone out. I had no idea if I'd actually lost consciousness, but if so it couldn't have been for more than a couple of seconds.

"The stage," I managed to gasp out through the dull pain that still throbbed in the back of my head. "Something's after Lida."

Ryan didn't seem to want to let go of me and I batted at his hands. "I'm fine! Go!"

He released me, then turned and jumped off the platform and into the milling crowd below. Shrieks and protests rose in his wake as he ruthlessly shoved people out of his way, but my attention was on the stage and Lida. She still held her microphone, a faintly bewildered smile on her face as if she was expecting the stage lights to pop back on any second now. I started to clamber after him, then stopped as another wave of the odd resonance washed over me. I shifted back into othersight, gritting my teeth as the strange feel of the resonance seemed to multiply with the increased perception. But it was worth it. The creature that leaped onto the back of the stage practically glowed in othersight. *Okay, so I was wrong about the arcane involvement!* "Zack! Get to Lida!" I shouted, pointing at the whatever-the-hell-it-was.

Zack snapped his head up to me, then quickly looked in the direction I was frantically gesturing. I shifted back out of othersight before another wave of resonance could flatten me, then watched in amazement as Zack made an incredible bounding leap onto the stage. In normal sight the creature looked like a vaguely man-shaped dark blob, and for a brief instant I was certain that Zack would be able to get to Lida before the thing did.

But the creature was shockingly fast, and before Zack could even take one step toward the singer, the thing grabbed her and jumped back down off the stage. Lida screamed as it took off toward the back door, scattering people in its wake like bowling pins. Zack made another leaping bound and hit the floor at a dead run, but the thing was already through the door and into the alley. I caught a glimpse of Knight moving swiftly and smoothly, but in the opposite direction—toward the front.

"Kara, what the hell is it?" Ryan yelled as he barreled through the crowd toward the back door.

"I have no idea!" I yelled back over the rising din.

Ryan burst through the back door, then took off down the alley after Zack. For about a tenth of a second I debated fighting my way through the crowd before quickly discarding the idea of running after them. Knight had the right idea. There was no way I'd be able to catch up to the agents. But then again, I wasn't expected to do a lot of running anyway.

There weren't many people between me and the front door, and I made it around the building and to the alley in less time than it would have taken me to get through the crush of bodies on the dance floor. The odor of stale beer and fresh urine assailed me as I entered the alley, and even though it had rained the day before, I had enough self-preservation going on to be wary about stepping in any puddles. There was no sign of Knight, but I didn't have time to worry about what he was or wasn't doing. "Skalz!" I shouted, also sending a mental urging along the bindings that held the demon in my control. I felt an answering surge, easily sensing the demon's excitement and barely restrained impatience. I'd told it to wait and hide on top of the building, not knowing if I would need to call on it. But the *zhurn* was bored and eager to join the chase. It needed no further encouragement.

I looked up as an oily shifting darkness seemed to pour over the edge of the roof, then heard a *snick* as its wings snapped open and it sailed down. But instead of chasing after Ryan and Zack like I'd expected, it swooped straight down at me. Before I could even blink in surprise it grabbed me by the upper arms and shot straight back up into the air.

I yelped in shock and my heart slammed in my chest as the demon skimmed the tops of the buildings—or rather my feet skimmed the tops. "A little higher, please?" I managed to gasp out, an unpleasant vision of my body ending up wrapped around an antenna that the demon hadn't seen filling my head.

The *zhurn* answered me with a growl that sounded like a stoking furnace, but it veered abruptly higher, causing me to clutch desperately at the claws holding me. I was more than a little surprised that the demon hadn't broken my skin with those wicked claws. Wasn't hurting me at all, in fact, other than scaring the absolute crap out of me. *Yeah, I probably should have specified that I wanted the damn thing to chase whatever had taken the girl,* I snarled at myself. But I had to admit that this was probably a better way to handle things. At least I'd be there at the end to control the demon.

<Look there,> Skalz sent through the bindings. I

looked down and saw the large figure running down Governor Nicholls Street with the screaming singer in its grasp—and being generally ignored by the few people in the area. This part of the French Quarter was far quieter and darker than the area closer to Bourbon Street, a ripe spot for muggers to prey on foolish tourists.

Ryan and Zack were about a hundred feet behind the thing. They were running all out, but the creature was just as fast and staying ahead of them. I still couldn't figure out what the hell it was. It looked big and lumbering—except that it sure as hell *wasn't* lumbering. As I watched from my superb vantage it crossed Decatur Street in two loping strides, then it raced past the French Market and toward the Moonwalk and the Mississippi River.

What the hell? Is it going to throw her in the river? Dread shot through me. The Mississippi was over a mile across and full of vicious currents, and going into the river, even near the bank, could be deadly. At night it would be damn near impossible to find her if she went in.

Ryan and Zack were beginning to close the distance, but I couldn't see any way that the agents would be able to stop the creature before it reached the river.

Skalz suddenly went into a steep dive, and I yelped and clutched tighter. We skimmed up over the levee and across the railroad tracks, then, in complete defiance of the laws of physics, the *zhurn* stopped dead about ten feet from the creature. I staggered briefly as the demon set me on my feet, and then I pulled my gun from the holster in the small of my back. I still couldn't tell what the thing was. Its face looked crude and half-formed— small depressions where eyes would be and a lump for a nose—like a sculpture that hadn't been finished.

"Let her go!" I commanded as I took careful aim at its head, not even sure if it would understand what I was saying. I wasn't even sure if it was something that was living at all. It glowed oddly in othersight, but it didn't seem to have any aura, or *feel* about it of something that lived.

I didn't have a chance to wonder about it for long. The thing opened its mouth and gave a weird and sound-less roar that vibrated through me, then it hoisted Lida high as if to throw her into the river. I gave a shout and started forward, but before I could take more than half a step a black oily blur struck the creature in the middle, sending both it and Lida into the water. Half a heartbeat later she and the creature disappeared beneath the roil-ing current.

Chapter 3

I frantically scanned the water as both Ryan and Zack pelted up alongside me. The miasma of the river surrounded me—a strange melding of mud and water and rot and the effluvia of every city upstream. It smelled a bit like death, and for the barest instant I felt the power beneath the muddy roiling surface—a deep and ancient force that had carved its way through a continent. I'd felt the barest touch of that raw elemental force once before, when I'd nearly died in the Kreeger River. But there was no comparing that trickle to this beast. There was no way I could tap the power of this river and survive.

Fortunately, I had other means at my disposal. "Get her out!" I commanded the *zhurn*.

But my order was unnecessary. Skalz had made a tight circle after tackling the pair and now made a silent dive into the water. Five heartbeats later it knifed back out of the river, with Lida in its grasp. It deposited her at my feet and then stepped back and melted into the shadow of a nearby wall so thoroughly that I could only see it because I knew to look for the two pinpricks of red light that were its partially closed eyes.

Okay. Totally worth the effort to summon a demon to use as backup! My pulse slammed in relief now that disaster had been averted, and I sent an impression of thanks to the demon along the mental bindings. I crouched by the coughing and shaking girl. "Lida, are you hurt?"

Ryan moved forward and handed me a small flashlight. I gave him a grateful smile and shined it quickly over her. Her makeup was streaked in chaotic patterns across her face and her hair was plastered to her skull in snaky tendrils, but I couldn't see any obvious injuries. "Are you hurt?" I repeated.

She shook her head. "No," she gasped. "I . . . I don't think so." She looked up at me, eyes wide, and for an instant I could see beyond the crazy makeup and hair and piercings to the scared and uncertain teenager. "Wh–who was it? What happened?" She looked around in confusion. "How did I get out of the river? Oh my god, I thought I was dead for sure!"

Crap. We were all quite obviously dry. "Another member of our team dragged you out," Ryan said quickly. "He's gone to see if we can find the, uh, guy who attacked you."

I had to hide a smile. Well, it was mostly true.

"Team?" The confusion in her face increased. "Who are you?"

"Police and FBI," I explained. "Your manager contacted us about the death threats, so we were staking out the concert."

"Oh," Lida said, her eyes wide and her voice small. "I didn't take those seriously at all!" She gulped. "Wow. Good thing that Adam did."

Knight chose that instant to pull up to the levee in his unmarked. He left the lights in his car flashing, then headed our way at an unhurried pace.

"I'm not much into running," he told me in a low drawl, giving another of his sardonic smiles. To my surprise his eyes flicked to where Skalz was hiding in the shadows, and then back to me as he gave a low snort of amusement.

Okay, so I didn't run either.

"There's rumors of all sorts of tunnels in this area," he continued as he pulled a pack of cigarettes out of his jacket pocket, voice still low and casual. "Gutter rats supposedly use 'em to move around the city." He shrugged. "Could be your bad boy ducked into one."

I gave him a slight nod. I'd ask Skalz as soon as I had the chance. I needed to get rid of all of these people around me first.

Knight's lips twitched. "How 'bout I get out of your way and go take care of those officers hoofing it this direction? And maybe Agent Garner can take Miss Lida over to one of those benches so she can have a chance to settle her nerves."

Okay, he was way too perceptive for me to be comfortable around him, though I couldn't bitch since I did need a couple of minutes alone. Knight winked at me, then turned and walked back in the direction of Decatur Street, holding his badge up to neatly intercept two approaching NOPD officers.

Zack took Lida's hand and gave her a smile. "Can you walk, hon'?"

"Yeah, I can walk," she replied, taking a deep breath to steady herself as she took his hand. The scared teenager was gone, covered by the same confidence that she'd shown on stage. Except for the fact that she was soaking wet, I'd never have known she'd been thrown into the river. I couldn't help but be a bit impressed. I hadn't possessed even a tenth of that much poise when I was that age.

"C'mon then," he said, gently tugging her to her feet. "Let's get you to where you can sit down more comfortably." Her gait was still pretty unsteady as he led her away, and she leaned on him slightly for support.

Okay, she's still freaked out, but she knows how to

cover it well. Then I saw her smile up at Zack and had to suppress a laugh. *Or maybe she's just trying to impress a cute guy.* I didn't miss that Zack returned the smile with a charming one of his own.

I glanced over at Ryan. He wasn't bothering to hide his grin. He also wasn't even breathing hard which was personally annoying to me. If I'd sprinted nine blocks I'd be gasping for someone to call 911. "He's a smooth one, isn't he," I remarked.

"He has those teen idol looks," he replied with a laugh. "The girls melt all over him."

"It's good that he can keep her distracted," I said, watching as Zack settled her on a bench about a hundred feet away. That was all the distance I needed.

"I'll go see if Knight needs any help," Ryan said abruptly, then spun away and headed toward Knight before I could question why. But the reason hit me as he walked away. He didn't want to be near the demon.

I stepped toward the shadow where the *zhurn* lurked. "Skalz, what of her attacker?" I murmured.

A tendril of shadow slid forward and I heard something fall at my feet with a wet plop. "I retrieved a portion of it." It spoke in a voice like crackling flame. I frowned and crouched, shining the flashlight down at what looked like an oozing clod of clay. I glanced back up at the demon. "Mud? She was attacked by mud?"

An odd noise came from Skalz as it straightened, and it took me about half a dozen heartbeats to realize it was laughing. I scowled, getting the unnerving feeling that it was laughing *at* me. "What?" I demanded, feeling rather petulant.

"It is a construct."

"A what?" I was missing something here.

"A creature of inanimate matter given a semblance of life through arcane means."

"You mean like a golem or something?"

"Yes," it hissed. "A very similar creature. An arcane construct."

"Oh." I looked again at the blob in front of me, trying to visualize it in man form. I didn't know diddly squat about golems other than what I'd read in the occasional storybook. *Time to do more research,* I thought with a mental sigh. "Okay, well, was it destroyed when it went into the river?"

"Such creations are durable, but it would likely sustain some damage," it answered. "Feel. Look deeply." Before I could move it seized my hand and plunged it into the depths of the yucky blob of mud.

Gross! was my first thought, but an instant later I could sense what the demon was talking about. The resonance I'd felt earlier washed over me so heavily I could almost taste it. <It will not affect you so deeply the next time you encounter it,> the demon sent along the mental bindings.

Skalz released its grip on me and I stood up, shaking my hand to get the clinging mud off it and wishing I had something to wipe it off with. I'd remember that resonance though.

I glanced quickly around. Zack still had Lida a good distance away, and facing the other direction as well. Ryan and Knight were down near the street and I didn't see anyone else nearby. Now was as good a time as any to send the demon back to its own sphere.

I drew in breath to begin the chant for the dismissal of the demon, then blew it right back out again in aggravation at the sound of more running footsteps. I looked back to see the keyboardist and bass player from the band hurrying over the railroad tracks toward us, along with Lida's manager, Adam Taylor, huffing his way a few hundred yards behind them. I'd met Taylor earlier in the day during the planning for the stakeout, but I'd never met any of the others.

Crap. "A few more minutes, Skalz. My apologies."

"I am in no rush, summoner," the demon replied, voice crackling deeply. I couldn't decide whether I preferred the mental voice or the spoken one. Both were incredibly unnerving. "I would discuss further matters with you before you return me to my sphere." With that the demon slid back into the shadow and closed its eyes, disappearing completely into the blackness.

I couldn't help but grimace. It never seemed to bode well when a demon had "matters" to discuss with me.

"Lida!" the keyboardist gasped, his face tear-streaked and contorted in anguish. Lida pulled away from Zack and nearly threw herself at the young man, but I realized she wasn't seeking her own comfort.

"It's okay, Michael," she said, holding him close. "I'm all right. See? I'm just wet." I gave Zack a questioning look and he silently mouthed *her brother*. Ah. Now his demeanor made a lot more sense.

"I . . . I should have done something—" Michael said, nearly hiccupping from his distress.

"Shh, no. Don't think like that." Lida spoke softly, reassurance thick in her voice as she tipped her head up to give her brother a comforting smile. She took him by the hand and led him to the bench, pushing him down to sit and then wrapping her arms around him again and pulling his head to her shoulder. "I'm all right."

He seemed to calm as she held him and finally took a deep shuddering breath. "I'm sorry."

"There's nothing you could have done," Lida said, then gestured toward Zack and me. "The cops did their job and protected me. You were playing your music. Everyone did what they're best at." She smiled at him and he lifted his head to return the smile, expression open and painfully innocent. He looked slightly older than Lida, but it was clear that she was his protector.

Zack stepped back and then glanced to me as I approached. "Did you finish?" he murmured when I reached him.

I shook my head. "No, but it's not like anyone can see it."

"I tried to get Michael to stay at the club," the bass player was saying to Lida, apology in his eyes. "But he wouldn't listen to me."

"It's all right, Trey," she said, sparing him a glance and a shaky smile. "I can't imagine any way you could have made him stay other than sitting on him."

Michael made a snorting sound. "I'm too big for him to sit on."

I had to silently agree with that. Michael was tall and thick, while Trey was lanky and lean.

Lida grinned at him. "Maybe Roger could have." She glanced up at Zack. "Roger's the drummer—total muscle-head," she explained. "Personal trainer, competes in local bodybuilding—"

"I'm too big for Roger too," Michael said with what looked almost like a pout. "I'm strong!"

"Of course, Michael," Lida said tiredly, patting his shoulder as if he was a child.

I sent another questioning glance to Zack, but this time he simply mouthed *later*, confirming my suspicion that Michael was somehow more challenged than most.

Her manager huffed up to us at that point, looking as if he was about to have the coronary I'd predicted earlier for myself. Adam Taylor's face was flushed and the front of his tailored white shirt was plastered to his torso with sweat, even though there was a touch of early October chill in the air. I had the feeling that he'd run those nine block as fast as he was able.

Before meeting him I'd expected her manager to be a weasely man with oily hair, perhaps with a weak chin and dark beady eyes. Instead, he was actually fairly good looking, and anything but oily and weasely. He was probably in his early fifties, a few inches taller than me, with ginger hair touched with gray at the temples— giving him that perfect "distinguished" look. He still didn't come anywhere close to touching the demonic lord Rhyzkahl in the looks department, but then again, there probably weren't any humans who could.

Lida stood as Adam came to a stop before the little group. "You're soaking wet!" he panted. "Are you all right?" He yanked his jacket off with shaking hands and hurriedly draped it around her shoulders, then turned to us, expression a mix of stark fear and naked relief. "What happened? Did you catch him? Who the hell was it?" He scrubbed a hand over his face as he swung back to Lida. "God almighty. I can't believe this happened. I can't believe you were thrown in the river. I never thought it would go this far. You could have died!"

"Adam!" Lida said, voice abruptly firm and hard. "I'm fine. It's cool." She flicked a glance toward Michael and I could clearly see the warning in her eyes that she didn't want Adam to say anything that would upset her brother—who already looked as if he was about to start crying again.

"Agent Kristoff can give you further details," I said in a lowered voice to Adam while Lida sat and put her arms around her brother again. "But her attacker fell into the river when he was attempting to throw her in. We were able to get Ms. Moran out, but we've yet to locate the other party."

Adam's face was a mask of worry as he looked to the river and then back to us. "So you didn't see him? You don't know who it was?"

"No, sir. Our primary concern was Ms. Moran's safety."

He blew out his breath, then gave a firm nod. "Yes. Yes, absolutely." He looked down at Lida. "You need to go to the hospital and get checked out."

I could see a flash of annoyance in her eyes as Michael tensed again. "Are you hurt?" her brother asked, eyes widening.

She gave him a smile and shook her head. "No, I'm fine. It's just procedure to make sure."

"That's right," Zack said, crouching by her brother and laying a hand on his. "She's not hurt at all, but that river water is pretty nasty and we don't want her getting sick. Right?"

The tension left Michael and he nodded. "Right. She can't get sick because then she can't sing."

Lida smiled back at Zack in relief, and once again I could see a quick flash of a normal nineteen-year-old. "And, it can wait until we get back to Beaulac," she insisted.

"That should be fine," Zack said.

"Detective Knight will want to get statements from all of you before you go," I said. "If you could all go and wait for him by his vehicle, that would speed things along." I gestured toward Knight's car. "Once that's taken care of, then you should be able to take her to get checked out." At this point all I wanted was to get them all *away*.

"Roger's not here," Michael said, frowning again.

"It's all right, Michael. Roger's probably making sure no one messes with our equipment." Lida grimaced. "At least I hope he is."

"He is," Trey said. "I told him to watch everything."

I gave Zack yet another questioning look. "Roger's also their tech guy," he said aloud with a mock-withering look as if to say, *How can you* not *know everything there is to know about this band?*

Somehow I managed to not roll my eyes. It took a few more minutes of reassurances, but finally Adam led his clients away. I let out a deep sigh of relief and headed back over to the shadow where Skalz waited.

Even though I couldn't see the demon, I could *feel* it there.

"Skalz, you said there was something you wished to discuss?"

The demon coiled out of the shadow with a chittering hiss. It turned its glowing red gaze upon me and I fought the automatic desire to shudder. "Yes," it said. "You are in need of a guardian. I would be honored to be considered."

Gooseflesh rippled along my arms. "Wait. What?"

It shifted, darkness oozing through darkness. "The arrangement that Lord Rhyzkahl has with you is an enviable one."

The gooseflesh continued its track down my spine and I could feel the hair on the back of my neck stand up. In exchange for Rhyzkahl's aid in defeating a soul-devouring threat, I'd sworn an oath to summon him to this sphere at least once a month. "Are there some who envy it?"

"There are some who would seek to remove Lord Rhyzkahl's advantage."

Okay, now I was getting freaked out. "Remove how?" It came out in more of a squeak than I'd intended.

It shifted again, black wings rustling like roaches skittering across a stone floor. "I do not know what means would be employed. I merely know that there has been . . . discussion."

Great. I'm the hot topic of conversation in the demon realm. I took a deep breath to settle the cold tightness in my stomach. "And you think I could use protection."

The demon turned its head to look off to my right. I followed its gaze and saw Zack standing silently about a dozen feet away from me, expression troubled.

Skalz turned its lava-red eyes back to me. "Yes. I would be willing to negotiate terms to serve as your guardian." Demons never did anything for free—not even submitting to being summoned. The offerings could vary widely depending on the demon and the task, but there was always a price to be paid.

"I'll have to think about it," I said. I'd definitely be thinking. And worrying. And fretting.

It lowered its head and I took a deep breath to begin the dismissal chant. At this point I didn't give a shit if anyone saw us or not. I simply wanted to dismiss the demon and get back to Beaulac. A sharp wind rose as I pulled potency to open the portal, swirling the musty stench of the river around me along with an acrid odor of sulfur. A thin slit of light formed behind Skalz, widening to perfectly silhouette the demon. Barely half a heartbeat later, a ripping *crack* echoed across the water and both the light and the demon were gone.

I bent over and put my hands on my knees, taking deep breaths until the brief spate of dizziness passed. Dismissals were a hundred times easier than summonings, but they still took effort. I felt a gentle hand on my back and I straightened to see Zack looking at me with worry.

"It's all right," I said with a reassuring smile. "I just needed to catch my breath."

But his expression didn't ease. "The demonic lord has put you at risk," he said, voice heavy with anger. "*He* should be the one to provide protection. You shouldn't have to negotiate terms."

"It's all right," I said again, though I wasn't as convinced of it this time. "I . . . I'll talk to him."

Zack's eyes dropped to my left forearm and I fought the urge to hide my arm behind my back. Rhyzkahl had left his Mark upon me there, an arcane tattoo visible only in othersight, as a reminder of our bargain. I tensed, waiting for Zack to say something about my arrangement with the demonic lord, but he remained silent. Finally he sighed and nodded, lifting his eyes back up to mine.

"He worries about you," he said quietly. "We both do."

I knew he was referring to Ryan, and a lump threatened to take up residence in my throat. "I know. And I appreciate it." I took a steadying breath and forced a smile. "But right now we need to figure out who attacked your new girlfriend."

He gave a soft snort of laughter. "Hardly. She's practically a zygote," he said, allowing me to change the subject. "But I do like her music. You think she'd sign a CD for me?"

I rolled my eyes as we started back toward the bar. "Zack, I think she'd sign your ass if you smiled at her."

He grinned. "And mar this perfection? I think not."

Chapter 4

By the time we gathered witness statements and dealt with the club owner it was nearly four A.M. At this point I was insanely glad that we'd driven to New Orleans in the same car—and not mine—because I was feeling too muddle-headed and fatigued to drive back to Beaulac. Ryan had obtained an SUV, since it had been necessary to transport Skalz from my summoning chamber to New Orleans. I'd taped black paper to the inside of the windows in the back and crossed my fingers that we wouldn't get involved in any accidents. Skalz had not seemed to care. He'd curled up in the back like a giant, nightmarish cat and had remained quiescent for the duration of the drive.

I was also glad that the three of us were in the car together, because it kept Zack from tattling to Ryan about what the *zhurn* had said before I'd dismissed it. I knew Zack would tell Ryan soon enough, but right now I was too tired to deal with his reaction. Hopefully, it would also save me from having to be anywhere near Ryan when he found out that there were some in the demon realm who might not be pleased me with me. I'd seen him angry and upset before. It wasn't pretty. Therefore, as a defensive measure, I closed my eyes and pretended to sleep.

And what would Ryan say when he found out? He sure as hell wasn't a fan of Rhyzkahl—he'd made that quite clear on several occasions, though he'd also failed to explain how he could possibly know enough about Rhyzkahl to form an opinion of him. But there was more to Ryan than met the eye. The demons seemed to know him, and the *reyza* Kehlirik not only recognized him, but had reacted to him with open hostility. And shortly after that Ryan and I had been attacked by a *kzak,* a creature from the demon realm used as a weapon or assassin.

Though we never had learned which of us that attack had been meant for.

Kehlirik had called Ryan a *kiraknikahl,* or oath-breaker. The creatures I summoned, though known as demons, were not creatures from "hell," nor were they inherently evil in any way. Instead, they lived within a complex social structure—they were utterly self-serving, yet they subscribed fully to a complex code of honor. Demons could be devious and calculating, but honor was key to every interaction and exchange, and breaking an oath was a damn big deal.

Yet I had absolutely no idea what kind of oath Ryan had broken—whether the demonkind had been involved, or if it had been related to something else entirely. And even though I was fairly sure that Rhyzkahl knew something about Ryan, so far I'd been unable to get the demonic lord to give me a straight answer. Rhyzkahl was obligated to answer two questions a month for me, but I had to be very careful as to how I asked the questions. I'd discovered that if Rhyzkahl didn't want to answer a question he would find a way to answer it while still evading it, and I'd wasted several questions that way.

Of course that was another source of tension between Ryan and me. In order to save Ryan from having his essence devoured, I'd struck a bargain with Rhyzkahl: I'd sworn to be his summoner—agreeing to summon him once a month for the next three years—and in return he would answer two questions for me to the best of his ability.

It had been three months since we'd struck that deal, and I was still waiting for the other shoe to drop. Rhyzkahl had some reason for wanting access to this sphere. I knew that. He hadn't pushed so hard for the bargain simply because he wanted to see the sights. But in the three summonings since then he'd done very little upon being summoned.

Well . . . other than the crazy sex.

I kept my eyes screwed shut, glad that it was dark in the car because I could feel myself flushing at the memories. Holy shit, but the demonic lord was *skilled.*

He stroked the back of his fingers across my cheek. "It has been long, dear one."

I leaned into the caress without thinking. "You are too impatient."

A smile curved his mouth. "What, do you not believe that I ache for your presence?"

I let out a bark of laughter. "You ache for what I can do for you."

He withdrew his hand. "You are skilled and clever, I will not deny that."

I waited a couple of heartbeats, then laughed again. "See, that's where you were supposed to add, 'But the sight of you fills my heart with joy' or some sappy crap like that."

"Is that what you wish to hear?" he asked, lifting an eyebrow.

I shook my head, grinning. "No, because I'd know you were full of shit. That's not your style."

A low chuckle escaped him. "You are more perceptive than most. You appreciate directness." He lowered his head slightly. "Then I will remind you that it has been long . . . twenty-six days since you last summoned me."

I jerked awake. Shit. Not only had I actually fallen asleep, but Rhyzkahl had seen fit to use the link he had to my dreams to remind me of my duty to him. I scowled. I didn't need the reminder. I had it circled on my calendar for each month—the last day I could summon him and be within the terms of the agreement.

"Nice nap?" Ryan asked from beside me.

I straightened, hoping I hadn't done anything obnoxious like drool or snore. "Sorry. I'm kinda wiped out." I glanced out the window, but it was still dark and I couldn't make out any landmarks. "Where are we?"

"About half a mile from your driveway. And don't feel bad. Zack slept the entire way as well."

I glanced back to see the blond agent with his eyes closed and head tipped back. His breathing seemed deep and regular, but I couldn't shake the feeling that he was completely alert.

Ryan blew his breath out. "I tell you, I'd have bet solid money that the threats Lida was receiving were pure bullshit."

"I know what you mean," I said with a weak laugh. "Shocked the shit out of me when that thing grabbed her."

He slowed to make the turn in to my driveway. "Any ideas what it was?"

"It wasn't a demon. I know that much. Skalz said it was an arcane construct."

"What, like a golem or something?"

"Yeah, that sort of thing. Inanimate matter controlled by 'magic' or arcane power to be animate. Unfortunately, that's about the extent of my knowledge." I glanced at him. "Do you know anything about them?"

Ryan shook his head. "Only what I've read in stories or seen in movies. So, someone has to be controlling it, right?"

"I would imagine so, but I don't really know how that works. I have a lot of research ahead of me." Maybe it was a good thing I hadn't yet summoned Rhyzkahl this month.

"I wonder if it's someone in the band," he said, mouth tightening slightly.

"You mean someone in the band who has it in for Lida?"

His shoulder lifted in a shrug. "I was thinking more along the lines of publicity stunt."

I considered it for a moment and couldn't find any reason to immediately discard it as a theory. "It's possible," I agreed, "though Lida sure looked terrified. Either she wasn't in on it, or she's one hell of an actress. But at this point anything's possible. Until I find out more about how those things are created and controlled, we're kinda in the dark."

"I foresee more interviews with Lida and her band mates."

I looked back at the supposedly sleeping Zack and chuckled. "Someone's gonna hate that."

"Sometimes our duty is tough," Ryan replied, mouth twitching in amusement as he pulled to a stop in front of my house. I lived nearly half an hour from Beaulac city limits, in a single-story Acadian-style house in the middle of ten acres of woods. The house was several years overdue for repainting, and the driveway would probably need a fresh load of gravel on it before the year was out, but I owned it outright, which helped make it possible for me to live on a cop's salary. But, more important, it sat on enough of a hill to allow me to have a basement—a rarity in south Louisiana—and that feature, coupled with the privacy the location afforded, made my house absolutely perfect for someone who enjoyed summoning demons in her spare time.

He shifted into park. "You're going to summon tomorrow night?" He made it sound like a question, but I
knew it wasn't.

"I have to," I said quietly.

"That's cool." He gave a curt nod. I knew he wasn't
cool with it, not in the slightest, but I had to give him
points for at least pretending to be all right with it.

He glanced at the clock on the dashboard. "At least
it's a Sunday and you can catch up on some sleep."

"Then back to the office grind on Monday." I wrinkled my nose, though I didn't really mean it. I enjoyed
being a part of the task force, but I had no desire to be
a full-time fed. I liked being a "small town" cop. Even
though Beaulac was the parish seat of St. Long Parish, it
was barely big enough to be called a city by census defi-
nitions, maintaining a small-town feel that managed to
be friendly and homey without being annoyingly insular.
The city of Beaulac curved around Lake Pearl and for
decades had survived primarily on an industry of sports-
men and weekend vacationers, but that was gradually
changing. The area was experiencing a few growing
pains as more and more people discovered the "rural
charm" of St. Long Parish, especially since the parish
was still within comfortable driving distance of New Orleans. But I figured that such things were inevitable, and
it would likely be decades yet before Beaulac and St.
Long Parish had to worry about the kind of issues that
plagued the immediate suburbs of New Orleans.

Besides, this was my home, and I liked being a part of
its protection, as corny as that might sound. Sometimes
the fact that I was on the task force put me in a bit of a
precarious position when it came to office politics, especially when there was a shift in the workload. But, then
again, I knew that some of the detectives would find a
reason to grumble no matter what I did. I tried to take
extra cases to make up for the times when I was busy

with task force things, which then earned me the grumbles that I was "sucking up and hogging the good cases." I'd pretty much reached the point of not giving a shit.

Ryan nodded. "Okay, then we'll starting figuring out strategy for this whole thing when we've all had some sleep."

I climbed out of the car, and he surprised me by getting out and walking me up to the porch. I almost made a smart-alec remark about how I didn't think I was in danger of getting mugged in the ten feet between the car and my door, but I restrained myself. We'd been doing a lot of "joking" back and forth lately, and it was beginning to feel forced, as if we were desperately clinging to the friendship portion of our relationship.

"Okay, you and Zack are hiding something from me," he said, but there was a smile in his eyes. "And I figure it has to be something that the demon told you, and the only reason for you two to hide it from me would be if it had to do with my favorite demonic lord. So I wanted you to know that I'm a big boy, and I don't want you to feel any more stress about any of this because of me." He put his hands on my shoulders, and this time his smile was tinged with something that might have been sadness or regret, though I couldn't tell if it was for himself or me. "I worry about you," he said, in an echo of what Zack had said earlier, "and I fucking hate that you're in this situation, but I also know that I have no business judging or make demands on you that will only make the whole thing harder on you."

I blinked at him, then returned the smile. "Wow. You're, like, being all mature and shit. That's kinda scary."

He laughed, then surprised me again by pulling me into a hug. "You are such a goddamn dork."

I recovered enough to give him a return squeeze, then he stepped back. He'd started with the "friend-hug that was a little more than a man-hug" shortly after I'd made my oath to Rhyzkahl. I really liked the hugs, but they confused the shit out of me at the same time. But I sure as hell wasn't going to tell him to stop. Ryan was solid and muscled, and he smelled damn nice as well.

"Hey, you're the one who chooses to hang out with me," I countered. "And I'm not the one who watches *Star Trek* and all that stuff."

He heaved a dramatic sigh. "One of these days I'm going to make you watch some quality television."

I glared at him. "I like my reality shows." One of my current addictions was a show about preschool beauty queens and their white trash mothers. It was like watching a train wreck. I loved it.

He shuddered. "The horror."

I poked a finger at his chest. "Right, and you want me to watch some show about a cheerleader who kills vampires."

"You have no idea what you're missing!"

I gave a derisive snort, but then I sobered. He knew something was up, so this was probably the best time to fill him in on what had happened. "Okay, so here's the deal. Skalz offered me protection."

All humor vanished from his face. "Tell me."

I did, tempted to skim over the part about my arrangement with Rhyzkahl being "enviable," but ruefully admitted to myself that it was better to get it all out in the open now. Besides, Zack would tell him eventually anyway.

"And so now you have the dilemma of whether to ask Rhyzkahl to provide protection for you instead," Ryan said, expression grim.

I exhaled in relief. He understood. "Yeah. Exactly. If I use another demon for protection, I'll have to negotiate terms. But if I accept it from Rhyzkahl, it seems . . ."

"Like another way for him to keep you under his thumb," he said, voice nearly a growl.

I nodded.

He started to run his fingers through his hair, then scowled as he realized that it was glued into place with a metric ton of hair product. He dropped his hand and sighed. "I'm glad you told me this."

I was too, suddenly. I liked feeling that I could trust him. There were times when I really wasn't sure.

"I don't know what to tell you," he said, "but don't rush into any decisions, all right?"

"I don't plan on it. I should be able to tell you more Monday."

His expression briefly tightened at the obscure reminder that I'd be summoning the demonic lord soon, but in the next breath he'd masked it and offered me a smile instead. "All right. Well, get some sleep."

For an instant I thought he was going to lean down and kiss me on the forehead, but instead he turned and walked back down the stairs to his car. I unlocked my front door, feeling the brush of my arcane protections, comforting and strange. I looked back to see the taillights of the SUV retreating down my driveway, then gave a pathetic soft sigh and stepped inside.

Chapter 5

I thought I'd have trouble falling asleep—that so-tired-I'm-wired feeling humming through me. But I barely remembered crawling into bed and the next thing I knew it was one in the afternoon.

I caffeinated myself, showered, and made myself reasonably presentable before heading over to my aunt Tessa's house. Tessa had been released from the neuro center a couple of months ago, after she'd mysteriously recovered from her even more mysterious coma. It hadn't been mysterious to me—I'd been fully aware that her essence had been pulled away from her body to fuel a powerful arcane ritual. She'd spent six weeks in a coma—without a mark on her body or anything that showed up on a CT scan or an MRI to explain it. With Rhyzkahl's help and instruction I'd created an arcane beacon to draw her essence back to her body—barely in time, too. Her body had been perilously close to losing its grip on life.

It had been another month before they'd allowed her to be released, but she'd finally convinced them—in her inimitable acerbic fashion—that she was in full possession of her faculties. After she was discharged I made sure to send a fruit basket to the nurses on her floor—as much of an apology as a thank you.

My aunt's house was in a historic district along the lakefront, full of century-old houses maintained or restored to immaculate condition. Gleaming white with elegant blue molding and pristine landscaping, Aunt Tessa's house fit the neighborhood perfectly. My aunt, not so much.

I knocked twice, then opened the door and stuck my head in. "Aunt Tessa?"

"Kitchen!"

I headed obligingly in that direction and found my aunt perched on a stool at her counter with the daily crossword in front of her. Her frizzy blond hair was pulled up into a twist on top of her head, and she had on billowing hakama pants that nearly overwhelmed her skinny frame and a gray T-shirt that said FRAK OFF—overall, a somewhat tame look for her. Unlike her personal style, her kitchen was as exquisite as the rest of her house—rose-colored tiled floors, lovely wallpaper with subtle patterns of climbing ivy, and dark granite countertops. Her one deviation from the original nature of the house was her appliances—stainless steel and thoroughly modern.

Well, there was one other deviation: the summoning chamber in the attic. I rather doubted the original owners had intended for the space to be used in that manner.

At the kitchen table sat Carl, with a mug of coffee beside his hand and a book in his other. He lifted his eyes briefly and gave me a small nod, then returned his attention to his book. I was still getting used to thinking of him as Tessa's boyfriend. To me he was Carl the Morgue Tech, quiet, somewhat emotionless, and—I'd discovered—impervious to arcane wards and who knew what else. And for him, that small nod was the equivalent of an exuberant greeting. Tall and lean with an athletic build, he had hazel-brown eyes set in a lightly tanned face and closely cropped hair that was more transparent than blond. He really didn't fit the stereotypical image of a lanky and pasty morgue worker, but his general demeanor made up for any deviation from the expected norm. I took a quick peek at the cover of the book he was reading. *Parasite Rex: Inside the Bizarre World of Nature's Most Dangerous Creatures.*

Yep, *more* than made up for not looking the part.

Tessa gave me a smile. "Hiya, sweets. You had a busy night last night?"

I pulled myself onto a stool opposite her. "Er, well yeah. Had a thing with the FBI task force. Woke up about an hour ago."

"So was it a demon?"

I blinked at her. "Huh?"

She pursed her lips. "The singer. The threats. Was it a demon that attacked her?"

"How on earth did you know about that?"

Tessa gave an exaggerated sigh and flipped her newspaper over to show me the front page. "I didn't lose *all* my brains cells while I was in that silly coma. The paper stated that Lida Moran was receiving threats that 'demons would take her soul,'" she said, making quote marks with her fingers. "You were working late last night with your FBI friends, and there was an incident during her concert." She gave me a smug smile. "So. Was it a demon?"

I chewed my lower lip as I scanned the article. It was a well-sanitized version of what had happened—no doubt thanks to the efforts of Ryan and Knight—with a few eyewitness accounts of audience members who, luckily, were skeptical enough to say that it was "some dude dressed up like a demon or something."

I began to set the paper down, then paused at another sight of the name Moran in a different article near the bottom of the page. LOCAL BUSINESSMAN BEN MORAN DONATES TO WOMEN'S SHELTER. I was usually completely clueless when it came to who The People were, but even I knew that Ben Moran was a major player in the local social and business scene. "Is Ben Moran related to Lida?" I asked.

"Her uncle," Carl said without lifting his eyes from his book. "He was her guardian too, after her dad died several years ago. They live on the other side of the lake."

"The *rich* side," Tessa added with a quirk of a smile. "Ben Moran is on the board of Lake Pearl Bank and owns Moran Debris Removal."

"Well, I'll get to see for myself," I said. "I'm going over there this afternoon to talk to Lida and see if I can find out anything more about what happened last night."

Tessa tapped the counter. "Which brings us back to my question: Was it a demon?"

"No," I said. "I'm not sure *what* it was, but I'm damn near positive that it wasn't anything from the demon sphere." I set the paper down, satisfied that there was no mention of me, and nothing that remotely implied that anything supernatural had occurred. Not that I expected the newspaper to say anything of that sort. "It had a strange resonance though," I continued, not concerned about Carl overhearing any of this. He was already clued in about the demon summoning, and he was also the last person I was worried about blabbing indiscreetly. "I'm pretty sure I'd know it again if I felt it. I had a *zhurn* with me, and it said that the thing was some sort of construct. Maybe a golem or something of that ilk."

Carl abruptly straightened and closed his book. "Time for me to leave," he said with a ghost of a smile. He stood and moved to Tessa, giving her a sweet kiss on the cheek before heading out. A few seconds later I heard the front door open and close.

I resisted the urge to comment on how strange he was. I didn't exactly have much room to talk. I returned my attention to Tessa. "Um, anyway, I don't really know too much about constructs or golems, so I'm probably going to be spending some time in your library doing research."

Her mouth drew down into a frown. "I'm not sure I want to allow you back in there after you ransacked it so terribly!"

I met her eyes with my own steely gaze born of too many weeks of uncertainty, stress, and feelings of betrayal. "If you'd been honest with me, there would have been no need to rearrange anything in that library."

I was shocked to see pain and sadness flicker across her face before she looked away. "I thought it was the right thing to do at the time," she said, voice suddenly quiet and hoarse. The capitulation and show of submission hit me like a blow. Tessa had always been the dominant one in our relationship—perfectly reasonable and logical since, not only had she been entrusted with raising me after my parents had died, but she'd also been my mentor in the art of summoning.

It wasn't the only change in her that left me somewhat unnerved. Somehow she'd known of my agreement to become Rhyzkahl's summoner, and in the weeks after she'd woken from the coma I kept expecting her to lay into me about it—to give me a full verbal flaying. Or to at least want to know more about the circumstances that had led to the agreement, or the terms of my oath. But neither argument nor conversation had ever materialized, and the couple of times that I'd tried to speak about it, she'd hurriedly changed the subject, as if the thought of even mentioning a demonic lord was anathema.

I shifted uncomfortably on the stool, suddenly insanely glad that Carl had left before he'd been forced to witness this. Or had he somehow known this was coming, and excused himself accordingly? Anything was possible. Especially with him. "Look, if you don't want me to use the library, I'll understand."

Tessa sighed and rubbed at her eyes. "No, go ahead and use it. I'm sorry I said that. Besides, you need it more than I do right now."

Something about her tone made me frown. "Aunt Tessa, have you summoned since . . . you came back?"

She gave a soft snort. "There've only been two full moons since I was released from the hospital. Give me a little time to adjust, all right?"

I schooled my expression into an understanding smile. I had yet to tell her about my discovery that potency could be stored—and without resorting to the kind of torture and murder that the Symbol Man had used. Summoners utilized the natural potency that flowed in the world to create the portal between the spheres through which the demons were summoned from their world to ours. Potency was also required to power the wards and bindings that protected the summoner from being torn to pieces—either by the forces of the portal, or by the summoned demon. Power was easiest to draw and control during the full moon, which was why summonings were almost always performed on—or very close to—the full moon. On rare occasions a summoner could perform a ritual when there was no moon, but only when calling a very low-level demon, for whom very little power would be required for the bindings and protections. During the waxing and the waning of the moon, the danger lay in the erratic inconsistency of available potency. A hiccup in the flow of power during the forming of a portal could mean an ugly and bloody death.

However, in an effort to "woo" me to become his summoner, Rhyzkahl had provided me with instructions for a ritual to help draw my aunt's essence back to her body. And I'd discovered that a portion of the diagram used in the process could be used as a means to store small quantities of power, and—more important—

release it in a smooth and steady flow. I still wasn't sure if Rhyzkahl had intended for me to discover this means of storing potency, but he certainly had yet to voice any objections to my use of it.

But I had absolutely no idea why I was holding back from telling my aunt about this. *Maybe it's because she doesn't seem like herself.* Was that it? The storage diagram was a huge discovery, and the more I learned about it, the more I realized that it had the potential to be dangerous as well. What could be done with a massive supply of stored potency?

I could summon other demonic lords. And bind them, with enough preparation. Not that I ever would. One demonic lord was enough for me, and such summonings were insanely dangerous. But what if another summoner—one with scruples similar to the Symbol Man—had this knowledge? What could someone like that do with a demonic lord at his command? I'd faced that possibility once already—even chosen to die rather than let it happen.

A chill swept through me. *What if that's why I might be in danger?* Not only did Rhyzkahl have the advantage of having a summoner bound to him, but he had one who wasn't limited to summoning during the full moon. There might be some who would seek to remove his advantage, or worse, there might be some who would seek to protect themselves by removing one who had knowledge that could make it easier to enslave them. *All the more reason for me to keep it to myself.* The last thing I wanted to do was put Tessa in any sort of danger again.

I jerked as Tessa put a hand on mine. "You look ill, sweets. What is it?"

I forced a smile. "Sorry. Lost in thought for a second. I think I'm still tired from last night."

She gave my hand a pat. "I'll make you some of that boring oversweetened tea that you tolerate, okay?"

I laughed. "That would be slightly delightful."

I expected her to turn and go to the sink, but her hand stayed on mine. Her gaze had gone distant, and I even glanced behind me to see if she was looking at something out the window.

"Aunt Tessa? Is something wrong?"

The barest hint of a frown furrowed her brow. "Do you ever wonder why Szerain was willing?"

I blinked. "Huh?"

She dropped her eyes to mine. "Szerain. The lord that my mother and Peter Cerise and the others were trying to summon . . ."

Even with her clarification it still took me a few seconds to figure out what she was referring to. "Right. When Rhyzkahl came through instead," I said, keeping my face immobile. Nearly thirty years ago Peter Cerise had gathered five other summoners together in a bold, ambitious, and shockingly dangerous attempt to summon the demonic lord Szerain. Cerise's wife was dying of breast cancer, and Szerain was—supposedly—amenable to being summoned for such a need. This was most assuredly not the case for any other demonic lord.

Perhaps the summoning would have proceeded without incident if Szerain had actually been the one to come through the portal, but Peter Cerise and the other summoners were unaware that the then-teenage Tessa was hiding in that basement that night. And though she'd yet to realize her potential as a summoner, her presence altered the forming of the portal. A different—and unwilling—demonic lord was pulled through instead: Rhyzkahl, one of the most powerful of the demonic lords.

The result was a slaughter. Rhyzkahl killed all the summoners except for one who later went on to plan another summoning of Rhyzkahl out of vengeance—becoming the serial killer known as the Symbol Man—

and who had tortured and murdered his victims in order to gather the power needed to make such a powerful summoning successful.

"Yes," Tessa said, expression strangely calm. "That's the one. Do you ever wonder why Szerain was willing to be summoned?"

The serene look on her face was beginning to seriously unnerve me, especially considering the topic of our conversation. Her mother—my grandmother—had been one of the summoners Rhyzkahl had slain. "I, uh, hadn't really thought about it."

"You should," she said, voice soft. "The demonic lords never do anything without motive." Then she patted my hand and looked back at me with a perfectly normal Tessa-smile. "Let me get that tea for you now."

I fled to the library after taking a few token sips of tea, but my mind was on Tessa's strange words—and her stranger mood shift.

Why *would* a demonic lord be willing to be summoned? I could think of an answer right off the top of my head: the demonic lord in question had an arrangement with a human summoner, much like the arrangement I had with Rhyzkahl. So perhaps Szerain had a summoner of his own at one time as well. Perhaps he still did. I knew next to nothing about the demonic lords except for Rhyzkahl, and I didn't exactly know a whole lot about him either—even if we did have crazy hot sex every time I summoned him.

But if some other summoner were to think that Rhyzkahl might be willing to be summoned simply because *I* was able to do so . . . well, that would most assuredly be a fatal mistake on their part. That, I was certain of. A summoning was considered a deep and terrible insult to a lord, a slight to their honor that could not go unanswered, else they risked losing yet more honor. It would be like yanking the pope out of his chair and setting him to clean your bathroom. But a thousand times worse, and with far more devastating repercussions. Honor was the bedrock of the demons' society.

There were twelve levels of demons: from the first-level *zrila* to the twelfth-level *reyza*. The higher level demons had more arcane skill and strength than the lower, but the demonic lords were above all of those. They were denizens of an alternate plane of existence, and I had the ability to open a portal between this world and theirs and summon them forth to serve me in exchange for a suitable offering. While it was an affront for any demon to be summoned, the demons gained status among their kind through knowledge gained in this sphere or the artifacts and offerings the summoner might exchange for the demon's service. Once the terms of a summoning were set—the offering and required service agreed upon—the demon's honor compelled it to complete the agreed upon task to the best of its ability, just as that same honor compelled the summoner to abide by the terms of the agreement. The demonic code of honor was a summoner's protection. Without it, any summoning would demand more power than one human could conceivably draw on his or her own, since it would be necessary to bind and enslave the demon and force it to the summoner's will. And, then, of course, that summoner would be living in constant fear that the demon might break its bindings and free itself. I had little doubt that the summoner's messy death would quickly follow.

I'd long been taught that it was impossible to summon a demonic lord and survive, though I knew now that there were exceptions to this. *And if I have an arrangement with a demonic lord, who's to say there aren't other summoners who do as well?*

I could feel the subtle brush of the protections pass over me as I entered my aunt's library, a mental prickling on the edge of my awareness. The arcane wards in the house and the library were now back to their previous strength, though when they were "installed" this time around I made sure that I had complete access. I'd received a rude surprise when Tessa was in the hospital and I'd found that her library and summoning chamber had been protected against me—with wards of deadly strength that I later discovered had been placed shortly after my first encounter with Rhyzkahl. It was an understatement to say that I'd felt terribly betrayed. I'd been unable to fathom why she hadn't said something to me, and even now I still didn't have a clear answer as to her motivations for doing it.

I checked that the portal in the corner was well warded. It wasn't an actual portal that a demon could be summoned through—more like a weak spot in the fabric between our world and the demon sphere. Or perhaps some sort of arcane pressure valve. I wasn't quite sure, to be honest. What I did know was that when I removed the wards in the library, some arcane beasties were able to come through—or, in at least one case, were pushed through from the other side—and had caused quite a bit of trouble. I had a feeling that portal was the reason she'd warded everything against me—and, I assumed, Rhyzkahl—but that precaution had backfired since I'd been forced to have all the protections removed after Tessa had been incapacitated.

I'd braced myself for a protest from Tessa when I had the wards restored to normal, but she'd stayed silent on the subject. It was yet another shift of power that made me uncomfortable. It was almost like a grown child who suddenly had the care of an elderly parent, though that was a weak analogy in a lot of ways. Tessa was only in her late forties and far from needing any sort of care. But there was definitely a strange fragility to her now that had never been there before.

And she was out of her body for weeks, I chided myself. *Give her some time to recover.* I was being unrealistic to expect her to bounce back to fully normal in the course of a couple of months.

Still, I didn't feel like lingering in the library, especially while Tessa was elsewhere in the house. The scattered books had been stacked in semi-neat piles, with as much system as there'd been before the incident with the portal. Or so it seemed to me, since I wasn't convinced that there'd ever been a system. But somehow I managed to find a number of books in the same general area that had stuff vaguely related to arcane constructs and golems.

Ryan called as I was stuffing the books into my bag. I knew this without looking because I'd actually assigned Ryan a ringtone of his own. Not that my phone rang so often that it was necessary. Pretty much the only calls I ever got were from Tessa, Ryan, Jill, or the dispatcher. My social life—a pathetic thing indeed.

"You awake yet?" he asked.

"Not only awake, but I've had a shower, coffee, and am finishing up at my aunt's library. So there."

I heard him chuckle. "In other words, you've solved the mystery and there's no need for us to go speak to Lida."

"Well, I wouldn't want to take all the fun out of it," I said. "I suppose we can still go through the motions."

"If you're still at your aunt's house, I'm only a few blocks away. Want me to pick you up?"

"Works for me. Meet you out front."

I disconnected, then ducked out of the house, calling out a "bye" to Tessa before she could challenge me as to what I was taking from the library.

Or not challenge me. I didn't want to face the possibility that she wouldn't even ask.

I snagged my gun and badge out of my car, and after

a brief debate, grabbed my jacket as well. I might as well look as official as possible, even if it was my day off. *And when was the last time I had a real day off?* I thought with a slight scowl.

About thirty seconds later a dark blue Crown Victoria pulled up to the curb. The passenger-side window slid down and Ryan gave me a mock leer. "Hey chicka chicka! You lookin' hot. You sellin' that?"

Groaning, I yanked the door open and slid in. "You are so weird."

He laughed. "Okay, the gun and badge does kill the sexy a little bit."

"Hey now, some guys would pay extra for that!"

"This is true," he said with a grin.

I buckled my seat belt, then grimaced. "Also, the stain on the jacket screams, 'Oh, do me, baby. Do me now.' " I swiped at the dark streak on the hem of my jacket, but only managed to make it a bigger dark streak. "It's so not fair. The cops on TV have awesome wardrobes."

"With terrific shoes," he added.

"Yes! High heels on crime scenes are an absolute must."

Ryan snickered. "I dare you to come out to your next crime scene wearing stilettos."

I made a hacking sound. "I'd be laughed out of the department. Especially after I fell on my face a few times trying to walk in them." I thought for a second. "I don't even think I own a pair of heels higher than about two inches." And I only owned one pair like that, I realized—the ones I wore for court or funerals.

He gave me a sidelong glance. "Please don't take this the wrong way, because god knows you'd have every right to take this the wrong way . . . But do you ever, um, dress up?"

I glowered at him.

"Okay, you're taking it the wrong way," he said with a

self-conscious chuckle. "I'm *not* saying you're not pretty and feminine and all that good stuff. Because you are." He flashed me a smile that mollified me somewhat. "But when was the last time you had a chance to dress up and go out and be fancy?"

My throat tightened up and I turned to look out the window so he couldn't see how deeply the question had affected me. "I dunno," I said as casually as I could, throwing in a shrug for good measure. "A while, I guess. I've had a lot going on." *Never,* I thought in sudden silent misery. *At least not since I was a kid. How fucked up is that?* I'd had two boyfriends, but neither relationship had lasted very long, and the dating had consisted of movies and crawfish boils and fishing trips. *And Rhyzkahl doesn't exactly take me out on the town.*

I heard Ryan swear under his breath. Obviously my attempt to hide my upset hadn't been very successful. "I'm sorry, Kara. I didn't mean to touch a nerve."

I schooled my face into a pleasant expression and looked over at him. "Ryan, it's okay. I just . . ." I shrugged. "My teen years were a mess, and then when I started training as a summoner I became pretty isolated." "A mess" was a mild description. My mother had died of cancer when I was eight, and then three years later my dad had been killed by a drunk driver. My aunt had been less than thrilled to be saddled with the care of a preteen, and by the time I was fourteen I was doing my best to destroy my life with drugs. The discovery that I had the potential and skill to become a summoner had given us both the impetus to get my life back on track, but the need to keep the demon summoning a secret had pretty much killed any chance of a social life.

"You never went out with your aunt for anything? Special occasions?"

I raised my eyebrow. "You've *met* my aunt, right?"

He winced, then gave me a rueful smile. "Yeah. Wow.

Sorry." He shook his head. "Look, as soon as this case gives us some breathing room, how about you and I dress up like people with actual lives, and go eat some-place where the staff has all their teeth and the napkins aren't made out of paper."

I could only stare at him for several heartbeats as my thoughts floundered. Was he asking me out on a date? *But he didn't say it was a date, and if I assume it's a date that could end up being totally awkward if he didn't mean it that way. But should I play it safe, or jump on the chance that he meant it as something more?* Though if I jumped and missed . . .

Uncertainty abruptly flickered in his eyes, and he reached over and gave my hand a squeeze. "I mean, just as friends, right? Two good friends going out and enjoying themselves."

I managed to nod, though my smile felt brittle. "It sounds great," I said, relief and disappointment doing the tango in my stomach. "For this I'll even buy a dress."

"Tight and slinky?" He gave me a comical leer again. "And stiletto heels?"

I smiled despite my inner turmoil, obscurely grateful for his attempt to break the tension. "Nah. Floor length. Long sleeves. Y'know: Amish."

"Wear the stiletto heels with it, and it's a deal."

I couldn't help but laugh. "Just drive."

Chapter 6

Lida Moran lived in a house on the lakefront, almost directly across the lake from my aunt's house. While my aunt's neighborhood was comprised of older museum-quality houses that had been carefully restored and were meticulously maintained, the other side of the lake was for the people who simply wanted a big horking expensive house on the lake.

And big it was, though it wasn't quite up to the level of some of the houses in Ruby Estates—the community for people with Too Much Money. Still, it was more house than I would ever live in. Two stories and sprawling, it took up at least three lots—and I knew that the price of land on the lakefront was nothing short of obscene. A mix of brick and stucco, it looked strangely like a scaled down ivy-league dormitory with a large central portion and two wings extending to either side along the lakefront.

I stood back and assessed the house. It had to be at least four hundred feet from one end of the house to the other.

"Weird-looking house," Ryan muttered as we walked up the driveway.

"Great minds think alike," I said with a low laugh. "They must *really* like living on the water."

He gave a derisive snort. "Sure hope so. The house takes up most of the damn lakefront."

Then we were at the door and had to carefully compose ourselves into a properly professional mien.

Lida met us at the door, barefoot and dressed in jeans and black T-shirt. She had little if any makeup on and about half her usual number of piercings, and my first thought was that she was absolutely stunning like this and why did she wear the crazy makeup and piercings when she was in public? Of course my second thought was that I was thinking like an old fuddy duddy and the makeup and piercings most likely had absolutely nothing to do with how "pretty" she wanted to appear and everything to do with her personal statement of style. Not to mention that the goth look was part of her persona as a performer.

"Ms. Moran, I hope you don't mind us stopping by, but we were in the neighborhood and figured we'd see how you were doing and if there've been any further incidents." I said it all with a smile, knowing full well that even though she was only nineteen she was sharp enough to know that we hadn't dropped by simply because we were in the neighborhood. But she seemed perfectly content to go along with the fiction.

"That's cool," she said and stepped back. "Nothing else has happened, but we haven't left the house either. C'mon in. We're being kinda lazy today, so please excuse the mess."

I had no idea what mess she was referring to. We followed her through a foyer and into an enormous living area, and the only things I could see that might be considered out of place were possibly the guitar on the couch or the shoes underneath the coffee table. Everything else was clean and orderly and about as far from the home of a singer of her "genre" as I could possibly imagine. Not a skull or black candle to be seen anywhere. Instead, the room had the unmistakable air of an interior decorator with too much budget. The furniture looked incredibly expensive and uncomfortable, and the few shelves on the wall held odd little decorative pieces that looked vastly overpriced instead of elegant. The art on the walls struck me as the sort of stuff that people murmured appreciative things over at galleries, but would never actually buy for their own home—colorful and intentionally abstract paintings that tried to be ever-so-slightly suggestive, but instead merely looked faintly sleazy.

I carefully hid my smile. I had an art history degree—an education that I'd always considered to be mostly useless, especially considering my line of work. *But I know crap art when I see it.* I also noted that I'd been right about the layout of the house. There were two hallways that led off to either side of the living room, and, oddly, two staircases that led to hallways on the second story. I couldn't figure out where the kitchen or bathrooms might be, unless they were hidden in one of the wings. Whoever the architect was, I wanted him drug tested.

I could hear piano music from the upstairs hallway on the right. I'd automatically dismissed it as coming from a CD player until I heard the player pause and then redo a section. *That must be Michael playing,* I realized. I hadn't heard any sort of flub or error, but I was no musician. However, even I could tell that he was phenomenally talented. I had no idea what the piece was that he was playing, but it was something classical, and it sounded complicated beyond belief.

Lida flopped onto the couch beside the guitar and I sat on the other couch with much less flopping involved. It was definitely as uncomfortable as it looked. Ryan remained standing, doing his best to look casual and relaxed. He looked about as casual as a Buckingham Palace guard.

"Is that Michael?" I asked, jerking my head in the direction of the music.

A proud smile spread across Lida's face. "Yeah, isn't he amazing?"

"Incredibly so," I agreed.

"You'd never know it from listening to our gigs, would you?" Lida said, sitting up into a less slouched position. "I mean, our stuff isn't very challenging. But Michael makes it all seem so effortless. It was pretty cool when the deal came through from the label and they wanted the rest of the band, which meant that Michael could keep playing with me."

"That's not guaranteed from the start?" Ryan asked.

"No way," she said, shaking her head for emphasis. "Man, there's so much about this business that no one ever really knows. People think that you get signed with a label and you're set for life, that you're guaranteed to be rich, a star." A grimace flickered across her face. "Trust me, it's nowhere near that easy."

"Few things ever are," Ryan put in with a wry smile.

"So how does it work?" I asked, curious. I counted myself in the camp of people who thought signing with a label equaled instant stardom.

"Well, usually bands are discovered by a manager or by a label person via clubs. Like if a manager spots a group or a singer, he'd approach and be all, 'I think you guys have a great sound. You being managed by anybody? I could easily get you a label meeting.' At that point, they'd make a demo and it would get sent to the label and the label would most likely want to meet them at one of their gigs or even call them in to play acoustically at their office. It all depends on the circumstance."

"Is that how it worked for you?"

She gave me a slightly rueful shrug. "Well, we had a bit of a leg up. Adam's a friend of my uncle, and when he realized I was serious about doing this—and after we were getting decent gigs on a regular basis—my uncle called up Adam and asked him to give us a listen. And Adam had some connections with Levee 9 Records and before we knew it we had a contract." She smiled, but there was a tightness around her mouth.

"But they're a pretty decent label, right?" Ryan asked.

"Well, Levee 9 is pretty good, though it isn't Sony or anything of that level. It's an indie, which has its pros and cons. They treat us pretty good and we have more control over the music. But, like I said, we're sure as hell not set for life or anything." Disappointment shadowed her face for a heartbeat, then she straightened. "With a bigger label an artist is signed for a certain number of albums and on their first outing the label foots the bill to pretty much turn the artist into what they need to be. Styling, dance lessons, photos, all that. This money kind of becomes a tab of sorts and the artist usually doesn't *make* any money until the tab has been paid back. The artist sometimes fails miserably and is let go, but if they're successful, the label gets their return on the money they spent on the artist."

"And you don't get any money until that tab is paid off?" I asked, incredulous.

She smiled wryly. "Well, there's usually some advance money, but we didn't *quite* get that sort of deal. I guess one of the advantages of being with a smaller label is that they didn't shell out a bunch of money on styling and choreography and stuff, so we don't have to pay that off." I could hear an edge of bitterness in her voice.

"And how does your manager get paid?" Ryan asked. "A percentage of what you make?"

Lida nodded. "It's pretty much a big gamble all the way around."

The sound of the front door interrupted any further questions, and we turned to see a man wearing a business suit enter. Lida brightened and bounced to her feet. "Uncle Ben! These are the cops who chased down the guy last night and got me out of the river."

I stood, fighting back a juvenile smirk. Uncle Ben?

Ben Moran dropped his coat on a chair by the door and strode forward with a warm smile. "I'm so delighted to meet you both. I'm Ben Moran, Lida's uncle, and I can't thank you enough for watching out for her last night." He looked to be in his early fifties, though his hair had completely gone to gray. His face was smooth and barely wrinkled, but a heartbeat later I realized that he'd obviously had a fair amount of plastic surgery to achieve that look.

Though why would anyone go through surgery to look younger and then not color his gray hair? I wondered silently. "It's a pleasure to meet you, sir," I said aloud, shaking his hand. "I'm Detective Kara Gillian with Beaulac Police Department, and this is Special Agent Ryan Kristoff with the FBI."

Ben Moran turned to grip Ryan's hand. "The pleasure is mine. Can I get either of you anything?"

Ryan shook his head. "We're just following up with your niece to see if there's anything else we can determine that might help us locate her attacker."

A frown somehow managed to crease Moran's forehead. "I thought the guy who grabbed her fell in the river. I figured he was gone and good riddance." He looked briefly abashed and shook his head. "I'm sorry if that sounds harsh, but I don't like it when people mess with my family."

"That's quite understandable, sir," I said. "We, uh, have reason to believe that whoever it was managed to climb out of the river." Might as well continue with the fiction that we'd come up with when it had happened. Even if the golem had been destroyed by its dunk in the river, whoever had created it was certainly still out there and possibly capable of making another. "Right now we're trying to determine what motivations the attacker might have had."

Lida let out a sigh. "Does it really matter?"

"We don't want it to happen again," Ryan replied.

Ben Moran shook his head. "No, we don't. But I'm more inclined to think it was a prank than a stalker. I mean, Lida's not exactly Beyonce." He shot his niece an apologetic look. "I don't mean that as an insult, Lida."

She shrugged. "No, I get it. I don't have the kind of fan base that would bring out the stalker type." She tugged at a lock of hair that hung across her face. "I mean, shit. Our tours are small venues, bars and stuff, maybe ten or twelve gigs total. The gig last night was the last one on this stretch. We don't play again for another two months. We thought we were going to get to open for Evanescence, but Adam wasn't able to nail it down." More disappointment darkened her eyes, but she covered it quickly. "But that's cool. It gives us time to work on new stuff for the next album." She tapped the guitar beside her.

I sat back down. "What about other members of the band?" I asked. "Has there been any friction?"

"No way," she said firmly and without hesitation. "I mean, you certainly can't worry about Michael. He doesn't have a mean bone in his body. And Trey's an absolute sweetie." An almost-shy smile filled her face. "He's my boyfriend. And I know that normally would mean he'd be at the top of the list of suspects, but I swear, he's the last person I'd ever need to worry about. He's beyond harmless. I've never seen anyone so laid back. He doesn't get upset about anything."

I carefully masked my dubious expression. I'd heard that before.

"Trey's a good kid," Ben Moran said firmly. "Though I guess I shouldn't call him a 'kid,' " he added wryly. "He recently graduated from LSU with a degree in finance."

I glanced down at my notebook. "What about Roger?" I asked Lida. "He's the drummer, right?"

"Uh-huh, and he also does all of our equipment setup when we have a gig." Then she shrugged. "But Roger would never get that bent out of shape over anything to do with the band."

I cocked my head. "Why do you say that?"

Ben made an irritated sound. "Because he has his fingers in so many pies that he can't focus on any of them."

Lida grimaced, but then she gave a reluctant nod. "Yeah. I hate to slam Roger, but that about covers him. He's a good drummer, and he likes being with the band, but we all know that eventually we'll need to find a new drummer. It's a hobby for him. And everyone's cool with that."

I wondered how cool "everyone" really was. "How's Michael handling all of this?"

"He's all right," she said with a smile, though there was a edge of worry to it. "He'll lose himself in his music for a while, which always calms him down."

Ben cleared his throat softly. "Michael has a difficult time processing emotional situations. He's come a long way since the accident, but there are times when he's very fragile."

"I'm sorry. What accident?" I asked, knowing that it was probably an insensitive question.

Lida took a steadying breath. "When Michael was twelve, he and I were out in the garage, helping our dad with one of his woodworking projects. It was a windy day . . . and the roof collapsed." Grief filled her eyes and she looked away. "Dad was killed instantly. I had a broken leg and Michael was pretty badly hurt with a head injury." She let out a shuddering breath. "He survived, but he suffered some brain damage as a result."

"I'm so sorry," I said quietly.

She tugged at her hair and looked back at us. "It's all

right. It was eight years ago—long enough that it's not so hard to talk about." She forced a small smile, but I'd seen the grief in her eyes.

She would have been eleven when she lost her father. The same age I'd been when mine was killed.

"But we're lucky," Lida continued. "Uncle Ben has taken really good care of us and made sure that Michael got the best care possible."

"I take care of my family," he said, giving her a warm smile. Then he looked up and past us. I glanced back to see Michael standing in the entrance to the upstairs hallway, gaze flicking rapidly over us and then to his sister as if begging for an explanation.

She rose and gestured to him. "C'mere, Michael," she said with an encouraging smile. "The cops who saved me yesterday came by to say hi."

His face cleared and he smiled broadly. "Hi!" he said with a wave. "I was playing piano."

"I heard." I gave him a smile as I stood. "It sounded beautiful."

He beamed in response. "Lida's writing new songs. I have to practice." He waved again and then pivoted and disappeared down the hallway. A few seconds later the sound of piano resumed.

Ben let out an amused snort. "Michael has the attention span of a gnat," he explained.

"Except when it comes to music," Lida corrected.

Ben inclined his head to her in acknowledgment. "Except when it comes to music," he agreed. "Then there's no budging him unless he's good and ready to be budged."

I wanted to say something like, *Well, at least he has that,* but couldn't think of a way to make it not sound stupid and patronizing.

"Well, we should probably leave you to enjoy your day," I said instead, ducking the moment completely. "If you think of something that might help, or if anything happens again—anything at all—please let us know." I pulled out a business card and handed it over to Lida.

Lida took it and tucked it into the front pocket of her jeans. "You bet. I really appreciate you coming by."

"The same goes for me," Ben Moran said with another warm smile as he accompanied us to the door. "And if the PD needs anything from me, be sure to have your chief give me a call."

The way he'd phrased that sounded odd, but I couldn't put my finger on what it was. I contented myself with a polite nod, then exited the house with Ryan. A dark green Lexus SUV was parked in the driveway beside Ryan's car now—Ben's, I assumed.

"Thoughts?" Ryan asked as soon as we were back in his car.

I opened my notebook and pulled a pen out of my bag. "She doesn't seem terribly upset about the whole thing. Not like someone who had an attempt made on her life."

"I noticed that too," he said, brows drawing together. "She was certainly shocked and scared when it happened."

"Maybe she simply wasn't expecting it?"

"So if it was a publicity stunt," he said, "then it's one that she had no prior knowledge of."

"And maybe she knows about it now, which would explain why she doesn't seem worried about a crazy stalker." I pondered that for a few seconds. "Or maybe she did know about it at the time, but she didn't expect it to go that far with the whole getting thrown in the river thing."

"That's possible too," he agreed. "Also, it's a little thing, but the last song was one that she didn't play guitar for."

"Ooohh, good point. A bit harder to snatch someone up if they're plugged in to an amp."

"And she might not want to risk getting the guitar banged up either." He drove quietly for a few minutes. I could see thoughts working behind his eyes, and I gave him the time to work through whatever he was trying to figure out.

"Yep," he finally said. "I'm fairly inclined to believe the publicity stunt angle. And if it was revealed now to be a stunt, that would be the wrong kind of publicity. Even if she wasn't involved, she'd want to keep it quiet since she'd be hurt by the revelation that it was a scheme."

"I like that theory," I said. "Only one problem."

He glanced at me. "The possibility that I'm wrong?"

I grinned. "Right. I mean, not that you're ever wrong."

"Never!"

"But, in that completely improbable circumstance when you were, then there'd still be a crazed stalker going after Lida."

He let out a heavy sigh. "So little faith you have in my baseless hunches."

"It's a character flaw of mine," I said with a shrug. "But, seriously, for all we know, Lida might currently be loaded to the gills with Xanax, which would help with the whole image of not being worried."

He snorted. "Better living through chemistry. All right then, Zack and I'll run down the threat posted on her website and see if our computer forensics people can get anything else to pop."

"And I'll drop by the station and do background checks on the band members and her manager."

"Sounds like a plan," he said. He turned onto the highway that led to my aunt's house. "So what's going on with your aunt's portal to hell?"

I shuddered. "The only hell in my aunt's house is the condition of her library."

"That's what I was referring to," he said dryly.

I exhaled. "It's all warded up and protected again, though I made sure that I was included in the wards this time."

"But has she ever explained what it *is?*"

Frustration welled. "No. Every time I try to pin her down about it she changes the subject, or gives me some vague answer that makes no sense."

He gave me a puzzled look. "Like how?"

Frowning, I fought to remember some of the stranger answers she'd given me. It didn't help that she'd given me several different varieties. "Let's see ... One time she told me it was a flower in a daisy chain. Another time she said it was a bar across a door. The best one was where she said that it's 'the butterfly on top of the rock.' "

"That makes no sense at all."

I smiled without humor. "Welcome to my world."

He pulled to a stop in front of my aunt's house. "Call me in the morning?"

"Will do," I replied. I started to get out of the car but he stopped me with a hand on my arm.

"Be careful tonight," he said, voice suddenly low and grave.

I opened my mouth to ask him what he was talking about, then shut it, chagrined. *Oh, yeah, I'm summoning Rhyzkahl tonight.*

"I will," I replied. I didn't know what else there was I could say.

He gave a tight nod and withdrew his hand. I shut the door and stepped to the curb, and resisted the urge to watch him drive off.

Chapter 7

The building that housed the Beaulac Police Department was on a street occupied almost completely by city and parish offices, which meant that on a Sunday afternoon it was damn near deserted. I half-expected to see a tumbleweed blow by. Not that I was complaining. At least this way I didn't have to search for a parking spot.

I entered through the back door that led to the Investigations Division and continued on down the wood-paneled hall to my office, intentionally walking loudly in an effort to cover the annoying buzz of the fluorescents. Unlocking my door, I flicked on the lights to reveal the not-very-spacious glory that was my closet-sized office. I didn't really mind the lack of space. It meant I didn't have to share it with anyone. And I'd finally managed to put something up to break the monotony of the stark white walls: a "Magic Eye" poster that wasn't really a "Magic Eye" poster at all. I'd quickly discovered that it was incredibly entertaining to watch people struggle to see a 3-D image that didn't exist.

I fired up my computer and started calling up basic background checks on everyone. The drummer, Roger Peeler, had been arrested for possession of steroids several years ago, but had avoided conviction. Trey Westin was clean as a whistle. Not even a parking ticket. I

ran Michael Moran as well, for the sake of thorough-
ness. *Who knows, maybe the whole brain damage thing
is a fake,* I thought with inappropriate and obnoxious
humor. But, no, Michael Moran wasn't even in the
system—not a surprise if he didn't have a driver's li-
cense or state-issued ID.

However, the manager, Adam Taylor, had several outstanding warrants for worthless checks. I allowed myself
a feral smile as I pulled up more info on the warrants.

I let out a low whistle. Now here was a guy who most
assuredly had a stake in whether or not Ether Madhouse made it big. Seven different warrants sworn out
by a variety of people, for a total of almost twenty thousand dollars. I wasn't terribly surprised that he hadn't
been arrested yet. There were a ridiculous number of
people with outstanding warrants for various offenses,
and the warrants divisions of the PD and the Sheriff's
Office were both understaffed and overworked. And
since check fraud was a decidedly nonviolent crime, of-
fenders seldom had to worry about getting a knock on
the door. Often they were only arrested after a traffic
stop, and that was only if the officer happened to run
them for warrants, which wasn't always the case, though
it was becoming more standard with the improvements
in the computer systems.

I leaned back in my chair, wincing as a spring dug its
way into my hip. *Well, if nothing else, I now have a ham-
mer to use on Mr. Taylor to get dirt on others involved in
the band.* I smiled in satisfaction and sent the info to the
printer. I ran checks on Lida and Ben Moran as well, but
both were as clean as Trey.

The printer seemed oddly loud in contrast to the deep
hush of the rest of the office. I glanced at the clock and
sighed. Almost five P.M. already. *Way to spend the day off.*

I retrieved the stack of paper from the printer, then
grabbed my bag and headed to my car, locking the door

to the bureau behind me. The sky had clouded over in the short time I'd been inside and a damp wind tugged at the sheaf of paper in my hands. A deep roll of thunder seemed to vibrate the air around me and I looked to the west, gulping at the sight of a rapidly approaching *wall* of rain. Thumbing the remote unlock on the key, I sprinted the rest of the way to my car, barely managing to get inside and the door closed just as the rain reached me and swallowed the car in a deluge.

I looked out at the pounding rain, unconsciously hunching my shoulders into a defensive posture. I gripped the steering wheel tightly, even though I hadn't even put the key into the ignition yet. Lightning struck in a blinding flash, followed so closely by a smack of thunder that I was pretty sure it had struck the car—or damn close to it. *It's normal Louisiana weather,* I reassured myself over the galloping of my pulse. *I'm safe in the car.*

I yelped as a bolt of lightning struck a few feet in front of the car, leaving my ears ringing and my eyes burning with the afterimage. My heart slammed in uneven tempo, oddly out of sync with the peals of thunder. *I'm safe in the car,* I told myself again, though at this point I wasn't so convinced that it was normal Louisiana weather.

And then, as suddenly as it had begun, it was over. I could see the wall of rain retreating to the east, sky still flickering with lightning. I let out a shaking breath and leaned my forehead against the steering wheel. The car still seemed to vibrate from the reverberations of the rapidly fading thunder, but I finally managed to slowly unpeel my fingers from the steering wheel. *Just normal Louisiana weather. That's all it was.*

But it was several minutes before I felt settled enough to drive away.

Chapter 8

A mile away from the station the ground went from soggy to bone dry, and even though it was dusk, I could see that the sky was cloudless. *This is Louisiana,* I repeated to myself. *Crazy weather is the norm.*

Somehow, I remained unconvinced.

I made it home before six, which normally would have given me time for a quick nap, but I was still stupidly unnerved by the freak thunderstorm. After twenty minutes of staring at the ceiling I gave up and started my preparations for the summoning. "Well rested" was the preferred state to be in when dealing with a demonic lord, but I reminded myself that I *had* slept until one this afternoon.

Actually, not dealing with a demonic lord at all was best, but that wasn't possible for me anymore. I'd first encountered the demonic lord Rhyzkahl by accident. I'd been attempting to summon a relatively tame fourth-level demon for help with finding the Symbol Man, and had instead produced a demonic lord—not a welcome state of affairs, since demonic lords were so averse to being summoned that they tended to slaughter anyone silly enough to make the attempt. However, I hadn't been slaughtered and had been seduced instead—a complete shock, and one that I didn't understand until much later. Almost half a year had gone by since then, and I was still trying to make heads or tails of my relationship with the demonic lord.

I'd summoned him three times since I'd sworn an oath to become his summoner, sticking to the terms of our agreement. The first time, he asked me what my two questions were, and I responded with a poorly phrased question about Ryan that Rhyzkahl managed to answer without actually telling me anything. Frustrated, I changed the subject and made my second question one about arcane techniques. Rhyzkahl was more than willing to teach me how to anchor a portal without closing it, and as soon as I mastered that, we did the hot and crazy sex thing in front of the fireplace.

And then he'd left. The second time he walked around my yard and my house for several hours, not saying much of anything at all, while I grew bored with watching him and dozed off in the swing on my back porch. He woke me up by doing interesting things to me, and we did the hot and nasty right there outside—a first for me. And I didn't ask about Ryan, because I had a more pressing need to find out a detail about the warding structure in my storage diagram.

But last month's had been the strangest and most surreal. I'd summoned him almost as soon as the sun set—as he'd requested. And then? We watched TV.

For two hours I flipped through channels, while he said almost nothing. Occasionally he'd lift his hand to indicate he wanted to see more of whatever was on. Everything from the local news and CNN to reality shows and HBO.

"You do realize," I finally said, "that all of this isn't really an accurate depiction of this world?"

He turned to me with a frown. "Truly? You are not forced to spend weeks on a remote island and engage in absurd competitions?"

I opened my mouth to explain, then I saw the amused gleam in his eye. Without thinking I grabbed a throw pillow and whacked him with it. "You ass!" I said with a laugh, then froze as shock coiled through me. *Oh, fuck. I did* not *just hit a demonic lord . . .*

The air in the room seemed to grow heavy as he lowered his head and regarded me. My mouth went dry as I dropped the pillow. But before I could stammer out an apology his hand shot out and seized the pillow.

And he whacked me right back.

I burst out laughing in a combination of surprise and relief. A slight smile curved his mouth and he carefully set the pillow back on the couch.

"Do not fear, dear one," he said. "I am able to discern entertainment from information."

I sat back and tucked my legs up beside me. "Okay, so why do you want to know all this?"

"Is this one of your questions?" he asked, eyes intent upon me.

I almost nodded, then I caught myself. "No," I said. "There's something else I want to know more."

He smiled and took hold of my ankles, then pulled so that I was abruptly lying with my lower half across his lap. He released my ankles then slipped his hand to the waistband of my silk pants and began to tug them lower. "You wish to know how many times I can make you release before I return to my demesne?"

A wonderful shudder raced through me. *Yes!* "No! I mean, well . . . that's not my question." I dropped my head back as his hand parted my legs, then couldn't speak for a few minutes.

"Ah," he said while I tried to catch my breath. "I will have to keep guessing since you refuse to speak it."

"Nice try," I managed as I pushed myself to sit. "I want to know if Ryan—" An instant later my words were cut off by his mouth on mine and his hand on my breast. I wanted to be angry, but I found myself laughing against his mouth instead. He was so clearly enjoying toying with me, plus I didn't exactly hate kissing him. He answered my laugh with a low chuckle, but didn't release my mouth for several marvelous minutes. And, when he suggested something else with which to occupy my mouth, I eagerly complied.

For a few precious seconds he was the breathless one, but I wasted time grinning smugly. As soon as I began to speak he was on his feet with me slung over his shoulder like a sack of potatoes. I let out a shriek of protest, and he gave me a light smack on my naked rear as he walked me to the kitchen. He was openly grinning when he set me on my feet, then he turned me to bend me over the kitchen table.

"This isn't fair," I protested as he proceeded to demonstrate the quick recovery time of a demonic lord.

"You have only to say the word and I will stop," he said as he thrust deeply.

I groaned and wiggled my hips. "Maybe in a bit."

"Good. Because I intend to fuck you in every room of your house." He stated it completely matter-of-factly and I couldn't help but laugh.

"I won't be able to walk tomorrow!"

But I didn't tell him to stop.

He lived up to his word, too. For the rest of the night we moved from room to room, always playful and laughing. My bedroom was the last to be christened, but instead of using the bed, he chose to press me against the wall, holding my wrists above my head while I wrapped my legs tightly around his waist as he drove into me. I twisted against his grasp and he tightened his grip, his azure eyes locked onto mine and a triumphant smile curving his mouth. But I wasn't afraid. Excited, aroused, and extremely well-fucked, yes, but not afraid.

"I will take you back to my realm someday," he

murmured, eyes still intent on mine. "And I will fuck you in every room of my palace. A different position in each room." His grip tightened very slightly and I let out a low moan. "And there are many many rooms in my palace," he added with a low chuckle.

"Yes," I gasped without thinking. But before I could say anything else his hand was over my mouth, and his eyes had gone dark and dangerous. Panic surged through me, and I struggled against him. Then I was coming, and screaming my release into his hand.

After it was done he carried me back to the living room and cradled me in his lap on the couch. I didn't know what to think about what he'd said. And what I'd said. After several moments of silence he spoke, voice low.

"Ask your questions, dearest."

I tipped my head up to look at him. For hours we'd been . . . lovers, and within the laughter and play I'd discovered a new dimension to the powerful lord.

I desperately wanted to know more about Ryan. I wanted to know why the demons called him a *ki-raknikahl,* and how he could change people's memories.

But I couldn't do it. I couldn't ask about another man. Not after the incredible night we'd just enjoyed.

I gave Rhyzkahl a small smile. "Tell me of the demon realm . . . and your palace. Please?"

He closed his eyes briefly, then kissed me lightly and began to speak.

I still had no idea why Rhyzkahl wanted to be summoned to this sphere, but if his goal was to confuse the ever-living hell out of me, he was succeeding admirably. And that was one of the reasons why I was waiting until practically the last minute this time. However, it had been twenty-seven days since I'd last summoned him, and I did *not* want to break my oath.

I descended into my basement as soon as the sun

dropped below the horizon. As large as my house, the basement had more than enough room for any arcane ritual I might ever want to perform. The southernmost third of the basement had long ago been converted into what I called a mini-office, but in reality was more of a relaxing/lounging area, with deep-red shag carpet, a large oak table, and a wingback chair. Somehow it managed to not look classy in the slightest, but since I had no intention of the general public ever seeing it, I didn't really care. There was even a fireplace set into the wall, complete with a fire that I'd lit earlier, since the basement had a tendency to get seriously chilly. The rest of the basement was smooth concrete floor, upon which was chalked a large and complicated design of circles and glyphs. Off to the side of the larger diagram was a much smaller and far more complex one.

The smaller circle was the one I was most proud of. I'd discovered the means to store potency somewhat by accident, but that discovery made summonings about a thousand times easier for me. I'd been funneling arcane potency into the storage diagram for the past week, which meant I now had plenty of power to draw from to complete my summoning—far preferable to when I'd been forced to limit my summonings to the full moon, when available power was most abundant and stable.

So why haven't I told Tessa about this? It was a question I'd asked myself before. She'd taught me how to summon and had frequently pointed out that the major limitation to summoning was the reliance on the phase of the moon. Yet that wasn't the case for me anymore. True, summonings were still insanely easier on the full moon, but I wasn't completely restricted because of a lack of available potency, as I'd been before.

I'm simply waiting for her to recover fully, I told myself, though it still felt like a hollow excuse.

I tried to avoid thinking about Tessa as I made the

needed changes to the large diagram—the one that would serve as the actual summoning circle. Each level of demon required a slightly different ritual and means of crafting the protections, and the last demon I'd summoned had been the *zhurn* Skalz. In some ways the summoning of Rhyzkahl would be easier, even though he was a far more powerful creature. Since I had an existing arrangement with him, I didn't have to maintain the wards and bindings that would normally keep me from being torn into ugly pieces by the demon before the terms were set. But the forming of the portal itself was trickier, and even though it didn't necessarily require more potency, my concentration had to be spot-on.

I pulled the arcane power to me, shaping it and feeding it into the diagram with the ease of far too much practice. It didn't feel natural to be so adept at summoning a demonic lord. *Then again, this is a demonic lord who* wants *to be summoned.* A summoning of an unwilling demonic lord would require several summoners and a helluva lot more power. I was insanely proud of my storage diagram, but I had serious doubts that it could hold enough power to summon an unwilling demonic lord. *Maybe have several diagrams?* But then the summoning would become even more complicated by the need to draw power smoothly and evenly from multiple sources ...

I scowled and shook my head, returning my full focus to what I doing. Now was not the time to allow my attention to wander. I could feel the portal as it formed, joining the two spheres, creating the slit in the universe. An icy wind rose from nowhere, whipping through the basement as the sigils in the diagram began to glow in arcane brilliance. The power surged through me with intoxicating surety as I spoke the demon's name.

"Rhyzkahl."

A heartbeat later the portal snapped closed, the wind and light gone as if they'd never been. My eyes adjusted to the sudden dark enough to see the crouched figure in the circle. As he straightened I dropped the wardings and protections around the diagram. They weren't meant to keep him contained anyway. I didn't have the means or power to create arcane bindings that could hold him.

He shook his white blond hair back to send it rippling in a perfect silken fall down his back. Holy shit, he was gorgeous. The sight of him took my breath away. Every. Single. Time. Angelic features—the kick-butt guardian angel kind, not the dorky cherub sort—coupled with broad shoulders and a narrow waist. Everything perfectly taut and muscled. His eyes were a sharp blue, full of carefully controlled power, deep and ancient. He was wearing a black silk shirt, unbuttoned and untucked, and black breeches and boots as well. And somehow he managed to still look like a complete badass instead of a romance novel cover model. No, the dangerous air about him wasn't a "bad boy" vibe. It was more of a "I have the power and the willingness to destroy you with the flick of my little finger" vibe.

"You grow more adept at handling the portal," he said with an approving nod, and I couldn't help but feel a smug pride. He had no problem giving me shit when I screwed something up, so a compliment from him about matters of the arcane was a legitimate reason to feel good.

He stepped to me and kissed me lightly—almost tenderly, then stroked the back of his fingers over my cheek. "You look well. Rested." He bent and kissed me again, and this time it wasn't tender at all. This was a "you're mine" kiss that sent my pulse slamming and heat surging down to my toes. His arms came around me as I molded myself against him. It was so much of a habit I hardly even thought about it anymore. Good thing, since rational thought was barely possible. His hands slipped under my shirt and within seconds he'd pulled it off. A heartbeat later I was on my back on the carpet as he deftly tugged my silk pants off and cast them aside.

"Wait, I—" I groaned as his mouth came down on my breast, tongue teasing my nipple even as one of his hands slid between my legs. Holy crap, he'd never been like this before—on me with barely any preamble or conversation. "Rhyzkahl, what—"

"Hush," he growled as he shifted lower, at which time I ceased to worry at all about silly things like conversation. It didn't take long for him to achieve the desired result, and while I was still struggling for breath from the one orgasm, he slid into me and quickly drove me headlong toward another.

I woke from a doze at the feel of him lightly caressing my thigh. I opened my eyes and gave him a sleepy smile. "Sorry. I guess I nodded off."

"No need for apology," he said. He was propped up on one elbow, looking down at me as he stroked his hand along my leg. "I had no fear that I had bored you."

My lips twitched. "Has anyone ever told you that you're kinda cocky?"

His crystal-blue eyes flashed with amusement, and I almost expected him to grin, but only a slight smile curved his mouth. "Never," he stated in a deep and ominous tone that made it clear that dire punishments would be visited upon anyone who dared speak with such disrespect to a creature of his power.

I raised an eyebrow. "Yeah? Well, you are."

He chuckled. "Ah, dear one, I do enjoy you," he said, leaning over to lightly kiss random spots on my torso.

I gave a slightly breathless laugh. "I'm glad you enjoy this. I'd hate to think you saw fucking me as a chore."

He lifted his head and fixed his gaze on me, eyes narrowed. "Do not slight yourself in such a manner."

I blinked at him in surprise.

"I said I enjoy *you*. I also enjoy giving you this pleasure."

I stared at him in even more surprise. This was the first time I'd heard the demonic lord express anything that could be interpreted as fondness or affection. Expressing a desire to fuck me didn't really count as the same thing in my book.

He traced a finger down my ribs. I could feel my skin ripple in gooseflesh in its wake. "So naive you are, in so many ways." He laughed low in his throat and I scowled. He glanced at me. "That was not meant as a slight, dear one. You have incredible depths yet to be discovered, and I look forward to discovering what desires you've not yet realized."

I controlled the shiver of reaction with effort and sat up, since I knew that if I continued lying next to him I'd probably grab him and do more nasty-nasty with him. I hadn't even intended to do this much with him, but he had a way of breaking down my willpower. Rhyzkahl might go on about how he enjoyed me or whatever, but I had a niggling feeling that part of the reason he enjoyed this was because it made me feel weird and confused about my feelings for Ryan. And Rhyzkahl had made it fairly clear before that he wasn't fond of Ryan. He knew something about the FBI agent—knew that there was more to him. Somehow every time I had the chance to ask Rhyzkahl about him, some reason came up that I couldn't do it. And, this month I had a far more pressing need for information about Skalz's strange offer.

"Okay, this has been very *enjoyable*," I said as I tugged my shirt on. "But you owe me two answers."

He stood and pulled his clothing back into place. Any other man would have looked silly or skeevy with his pants pushed down past his hips. Not Rhyzkahl.

Then again, he wasn't a man.

He sat in the armchair by the fireplace and gave me a slight smile. "Of course, dear one. What is it you wish to know this time?"

I slid my pants on and then hitched myself onto the table before fixing him with as steely a glare as I could manage. "Why does the demon Skalz believe that I'm in sufficient peril that he feels it appropriate to offer his services as a guardian?"

I never in a million years thought that I could have startled the lord, but he straightened in a way that let me know I'd definitely struck a nerve.

"Tell me what this demon said," Rhyzkahl growled, eyes narrowed.

I pulled my legs up to sit cross-legged. "Well, let's see. First he told me that I was in need of a guardian and that he wanted to be considered for the position."

Rhyzkahl's expression darkened, lip curling into a snarl, but I didn't give him a chance to speak. "Then, when I asked him what the fuck he was talking about," I continued, "he told me that your arrangement with me was an 'enviable one' and that there might be some who would like to remove your advantage." I glared at him, but he was no longer looking at me. His gaze was off into the distance, though his expression was still black. Normally I'd have been scared shitless to see him so angry, except that I had my own share of anger—a good measure of it directed at him. "You never mentioned that there might be any danger to me with all of this," I pointed out. "So, what's the deal? Is some other demonic lord going to try to kill me or something? Do I need to take Skalz up on his offer?"

"I will attend to the matter." Something about his tone made me wonder if his anger was directed at Skalz. He stood and began to walk toward the diagram.

"Whoa, wait!" I untangled my legs and hopped off the table to get between him and the diagram. I planted a hand in the middle of his chest, ignoring his snarl. "Don't keep me in the dark! I need to know what's going on, and you haven't answered my question!"

I had him there. He'd sworn to answer two questions, and so far he'd answered nothing.

I could feel the weight of his anger like a thick cloud. My stomach was a Gordian knot of tension, and common sense screamed at me to run and cower under the table, but somehow I forced myself to stand my ground, relying on the fact that he was honor-bound to answer me. Though I did drop my hand.

He folded his arms across his chest and stood, feet planted apart as he glared at me. "Very well. To answer your first question, there are some among the lords who envy the stature I hold by having a sworn summoner, and others who feel it is anathema that I allow myself to be summoned. In answer to your second, I have no way to scry the future or the intent of the other lords; however, since there is currently no other lord with direct access to this sphere, I rather doubt that any will be hunting you down in an attempt to do you harm."

He unfolded his arms, then inclined his head to me in a gesture that was damn near mocking. "Two questions answered," he said, but before I could speak he continued. "However, I will be benevolent and answer your third as well. Pay Skalz's price if you so desire, but I doubt his service will come cheaply—and there are others far more suited to giving protection. I have stated this before: I would be willing to assign you a protector. Think on it carefully."

And then he was gone.

I scowled at the empty space before me. Sure, he'd assign me a protector—someone who could also keep tabs on me. And how the hell would a demon be able to protect me at all times anyway? At least Skalz could blend into any shadow, but I still didn't think he'd be able to conceal himself during the day.

Rhyzkahl had stated once before that he didn't like the thought of me risking myself—which, considering my line of work, was tough luck on his part. I also didn't like the "big tough man will protect fragile female" implied in the offer.

But was this different? I was starting to get better at parsing his answers to my questions—even though I wasn't necessarily getting better at asking them. I had the feeling that—once again—I'd wasted both of my questions, which left me somewhat screwed since I'd also wanted to find out about the thing that had attacked Lida. But on reviewing his second answer, I was uncomfortably aware that he'd left out other possible ways that another demonic lord could come after me. My aunt had the portal in her library—a weak spot between the spheres that demons couldn't go through, but lower-sentience creatures could be pushed through. It was heavily warded and protected now, but if there was one, surely there could be others in the world.

And, of course, there was the chance that some other summoner could bring a demon through that would then attempt to carry out some sort of action against me. There weren't many summoners—perhaps only a hundred or so in the entire world, though I didn't think that anyone knew for certain. But again, it wasn't out of the realm of possibility.

I took a deep breath, forcing calm. Those were remote possibilities. Right now I couldn't see tying myself to Rhyzkahl any more than I needed to simply on the basis of Skalz's remark.

If I'd learned anything at all in the past six months, it was that nothing a demon said could ever be taken at face value.

Chapter 9

My alarm went off at six A.M., to my enormous annoyance. After slapping my clock to shut off the damn beeping, I glowered at it for several seconds as I tried to remember why the hell I had it set for so early, since I was on a ten-to-six shift this month.

Then I remembered. *Jill,* I thought, curling my lip. *My nemesis.*

I scowled and threw off the covers. Jill wasn't actually my nemesis, merely my running partner. However, the two were awfully similar in my mind, especially at this hour of the morning.

Jill Faciane was one of the few people I could call friend, and also one of the extremely few people who knew I summoned demons—something she'd discovered by accident after she'd come into my aunt's house and discovered a *reyza* in the hallway. Somehow I'd managed to convince her that the eight-foot-tall winged, horned monster in the house was friendly, which had led to me explaining how I could possibly know this.

It had been an interesting conversation, to say the least.

Shortly after I'd become sworn to Rhyzkahl, she and I had begun a Monday morning social hour—usually involving coffee and donuts. Then last month she got a wild hare up her ass and decided we needed to start running instead of being lazy slugs, pointing out that we had a PT test coming up. In theory I was heartily in favor of fitness as a requirement to be a police officer. In reality I hated running more than life itself, but at least it gave me time to indulge in all sorts of gossip with Jill. Not that I really had a choice. Jill had proven to be remarkably hard to budge on this, the stubborn bitch.

But first I intended to have my coffee. Nothing was going to happen until I had a caffeine infusion.

I loaded the coffeemaker with the appropriate quantities of grounds and water, then waited impatiently for enough to brew so that I could fill my mug. I glanced at the clock as I stirred in my usual insane amounts of sugar and creamer. I had barely enough time to check my email before I had to head out, which was convenient since I had an annoying tendency to forget to check it when I was at home. Not that I suffered from an overflowing inbox, but sometimes the penis-enlargement spam was worth a chuckle.

I sipped cautiously as I walked down the hall to the living room and my computer, humming in silly pleasure as the coffee worked its lovely stimulating magic on my nervous system. I set my mug on the desk, then went still.

Something's different. The thought skittered through my head. Something was out of place . . .

The chair. It was pushed all the way in. I never did that. A chill ran down my spine even as I tried to talk myself out of being freaked. *Okay, so it's more than possible that I actually did push it in after I used it last time.* Except that the keyboard tray was also pushed in. *Again, I never do that.* Pushing in the chair was like making the bed—they were both actions I considered to be totally pointless since I was merely going to undo it the next time I wanted to use the computer or sleep in the bed.

My gaze swept over the desk and computer, finding more things out of place. It was all little inconsequential things . . . the mouse was moved, the keyboard shifted. But taken together it was an unnerving whole. And, when I finally sat down at the computer, I realized that the monitor had been adjusted as well. For someone taller.

It's impossible. This house is warded to the teeth. I'd learned my lesson after dealing with the wards at my aunt's house and had spent several weeks summoning the demon Zhergalet to get my own house as secure as it could be.

I took a deep breath in an attempt to control my stupid paranoia. This was insane. Why the hell would someone break into my house to use my computer? Jiggling the mouse to clear the screensaver, I was relieved to see the familiar sight of my computer desktop. At least it still worked.

I leaned back in my chair, staring at the screen. *I dozed off for a few minutes, after Rhyzkahl and I . . .* Had it only been a few minutes? I hadn't bothered to check the clock or anything. Had he used that opportunity to come up here and . . . what, surf the Internet? It sounded insane. And how would he know how to use a computer? And why?

Unless he was simply trying to learn more about this world? That made a strange sort of sense. But why hide it from me?

I rubbed my arms, chilled by uncertainty. I didn't know whether I wanted to summon the lord immediately to confront him, or put off seeing him again as long as possible.

I scowled. I *couldn't* summon him again. It would be several days before I could store enough power to do so. Besides, what would it accomplish? What, I was going to accuse him of using my computer, and he would say, *Yes,*

I did, and I would say something like, *Oh, well, don't do it again?*

Yeah, that would be effective.

But the acceptance that I wasn't immediately going to summon the demonic lord didn't stop me from fretting about the whole thing pretty heavily while I drove over to Jill's house. I wanted badly to talk to someone about it, but it sure as hell wasn't going to be Ryan. And I didn't want to go anywhere near the subject of Rhyzkahl with my aunt.

I grinned wickedly. *My nemesis.* Jill wanted to drag me out of bed early? Then she could listen to all of my whining.

Jill lived about half a mile from my aunt Tessa, in a house that was within about two blocks of being in a rather crummy section of town. I always made sure to lock my car doors whenever I went over to her place. However, I loved her house. It was two stories, small and skinny, painted in a dusky blue that I adored, and raised a few feet off the ground. Somehow it reminded me of a really cool clubhouse.

"Let's go, you lazy bitch!" I yelled as I came through the front door.

"Bite me, you whore!" I heard the cheerful reply from the direction of the kitchen. I laughed and headed to the back. Her house couldn't have been more than about eight hundred square feet—and that was counting both floors, but it was all tucked together neatly and efficiently. The front of the house was the living area and the back was the kitchen. There was only one bedroom, which, along with a bathroom, took up the entire second floor. And, the only way to get upstairs was by way of an utterly charming wrought-iron spiral staircase. I was dying to put one of those in my house, except for the annoying fact that my house had only one story.

And I couldn't replace the basement stairs with a spiral staircase, since most of the demons I summoned would never be able to navigate it.

Thus I was reduced to lusting after Jill's.

Jill was perched on a stool with one foot on her counter as she tied the laces of her shoe, and I silently envied the muscle tone in her legs. Slender and petite, she had the sleek athletic build of someone who was always moving. Her red hair was cut into an adorable pixie style that I'd always wanted to try, but had long ago accepted could never pull off with my facial features. It totally worked on Jill, though she was far from "adorable." Fierce, determined, loyal, and caring—yes. Adorable? Not in this lifetime.

"I think I need new shoes," she said sourly. "I had to superglue the sole of this one back on last night. Why do they have to be so damn expensive?"

"Space age engineering," I replied. "Make you better runner. Faster. All that stuff."

"Ha. Make you broker runner."

"Y'know, if your shoe is falling apart, it might be safer to not run," I said, probably a little too hopefully.

She gave me a quelling look. "Nice try. You're not getting out of this." She laughed as I stuck my tongue out at her. "So I hear you had fun the other night!"

"Would have been a lot more fun without the whole chase-the arcane-creature-through-the-city part."

"You *chased* something?" she asked, skepticism heavy in her voice.

I planted my hands on my hips and tried to look offended. "Is it really that hard to believe?"

"Yes!" she said with a laugh. "I'm your running partner, remember? Or should I call it your wheezing shambling jogging partner?"

"You are such a bitch," I muttered, unable to keep from smiling.

"Yep, which is why I'll go ahead and remind you now that the PT test is in two weeks, and we're running again on Friday, and you need to have your butt over here by six A.M."

I scratched the side of my nose with my middle finger cocked in a rude gesture. "Seriously, you're really a bitch. I don't know why I bother with you." I took a dramatic breath. "Okay, so I *might* have hitched a ride with a demon while Ryan and Zack did the actual running part of the chase."

"Now that I can believe!" Her blue eyes were bright with amusement.

"Yeah, yeah, yeah." I planted myself on a stool. "Now, in the spirit of me putting off running as long as possible, I was hoping you could help me with something."

"Sure thing, as long as it doesn't take so long that you try to weasel out of running altogether."

I batted my eyes innocently. "Would I do that?" I ignored the rude noise she made. "Tell me everything you know about golems," I said.

She blinked at me. "Excuse me?"

"Ummm, aren't you Jewish?"

She gave the most withering look I'd ever experienced. "Okay, I like you," she said, "and so I'm not going to say something that I would probably go ahead and say to anyone else."

"Er, thanks?" I said tentatively.

She laughed. "Look, golems are part of Jewish lore, but I don't know much more about them than anyone else. Hell, most of what I know is from watching *The X-Files.*"

"Oh, no," I breathed in horror. "Don't tell me you're a nerd too!"

"Well, I can't hold a candle to Ryan and Zack, but yeah, I liked *X-Files* when it was on. Anyway, there was one episode about golems that was fairly true to legend."

I groaned. "Please don't make me go watch it. Can you sum up the legend stuff for me?"

"You are so damn pathetic," she said, eyes flashing with humor. "Well, all I really remember is that they're animated creatures made from inanimate matter. And there's usually something written on the forehead, or a piece of paper in the mouth. Erase the letters or remove the paper and the golem stops or falls apart."

"I don't remember seeing any letters on the thing's head," I said with a shrug. "Heck, I'm not even sure it was that sort of golem, but I know that a lot of legends have a seed of fact at their core." Inanimate creature animated by magic, or in this case some sort of arcane power I wasn't familiar with.

"So you think that's what grabbed Lida Moran off the stage?" Jill asked.

"It's a theory." I gave her the summarized version of what happened.

"Too weird," she said with a shake of her head after I finished. "And you've stalled long enough." She bent over in a stretch, placing her palms on the floor with her legs together and knees straight.

I winced. "Show-off. I can barely touch my toes."

She straightened with a grin. "I used to be a gymnast. Had a gymnastics scholarship and everything."

"I can't even do a cartwheel!"

"Yeah," she said as she headed to the door with me. "Not sure why I hang out with you."

"Because you can't have Pellini, so you settled for me."

Jill pulled the door shut behind us, then made a sound in her throat as if she was about to barf up a hairball. Pellini was one of the other Violent Crimes detectives at the PD, and Jill and I shared a dislike of the man— one that was fully reciprocated. "Oh, yes, I pine for that

big, disgusting, misogynistic, lazy idiot." She locked the
door and stuck the key in the pocket of her running
shorts. "Okay, usual route, or bump it up?" She eyed me
expectantly.

I sighed. "Bump it up."

"Ooo, studly!" she grinned as we walked to the road
and then started a easy jog, heading toward the lakefront area. "You'll be running ten-Ks before you know
it."

I scowled. "Y'know, you could at least *pretend* to
have a hard time running." I could believe she'd been
a gymnast. Her uniform hid it, but she wasn't just
slender—she was lean muscle. She ran like a graceful
deer, barely breathing hard, while I was already panting
by the quarter-mile mark.

"Nah, this is far more fun," she replied, tone annoyingly chipper. "Hey, you could always go running with
Ryan."

"And have him see my pale flabby legs and my red
sweaty face? I think not."

Her grin turned wicked. "I think he'd love to see you
all sweaty."

"You're a real pain in the ass, you know? Besides,
we're friends. That's it."

"Uh-huh," she replied, voice thick with disbelief.
"You're telling me that you don't want to snuggle up
with Fed Boy?"

I grimaced. "Things are too messed up right now for
that."

She flicked a glance at me. "Because of Rhyzkahl."

"I don't know what to do," I admitted. "I mean, what
the hell is wrong with me? Every time I summon him,
we end up fucking like rabbits in heat. And, then I get
all confused because I . . . well, I'm starting to really
like being around him. I mean, some of the time. Other
times he's totally the powerful arcane dude and I won-

der what the hell I'm doing even *thinking* about getting
emotionally involved with a demonic lord. And I *like*
Ryan, but there's no way that he's going to make any
sort of move on me, or accept any move from me, as
long as I'm sworn to the demonic lord." I had to pant for
breath after that long speech.

"Does Ryan know that you're still sleeping with demon dude?"

I gave a breathless laugh. "Ain't no sleeping involved,
darlin'. But, to answer your question, Ryan knows that
I slept with him that first time." I grimaced, remembering Ryan's reaction to that revelation. It had been ugly
and unpleasant, to put it mildly. Ryan had demanded
to know how I could have "fucked that thing." I'd retorted with something equally heated and nasty. We'd
managed to get past the incident for the most part, but it
wasn't an issue I cared to revisit with him. "I figure Ryan
assumes that I'm still sleeping with Rhyzkahl, now that
I'm sworn to him as his summoner." I abruptly realized
that this was the first time I'd spoken about all of this
openly to anyone.

"Seems to me that he'd probably assume you were
sleeping with Rhyzkahl even if you weren't," Jill pointed
out. "So, if you're gonna be suspected of something,
might as well do it!"

"You're not helping," I groaned.

She laughed. "I know, but I saw that drawing of Rhyzkahl in that comic. Holy shit, woman. I'd be on him like
white on rice!"

I sighed. "Even if I stop screwing Rhyzkahl, it won't
do any good. I think Ryan sees me as tainted goods
anyway." He definitely seemed determined to keep me
firmly in the "just friends" category.

Jill grabbed my arm and stopped dead, causing me to
flail for balance as she spun me to face her. "Now you listen to me, you stubborn hardheaded bitch," she snarled.

"I don't know if Ryan sees you that way or not—but if he does then he's a fucking moron who doesn't deserve you. And you'd better not see yourself that way, because the only thing you're tainted with is being a damn human who wants some good fucking every now and then."

I stared at her for several seconds before I finally recovered enough to give her a weak smile. "Okay."

She bared her teeth at me in a fierce smile. "I mean, seriously! Why is it that women get so damn angsty about having enjoyable sex?"

"I don't dislike enjoyable sex!" I protested.

"No? But you're sure determined to feel guilty about it. So, *do* you enjoy it?"

I actually blushed. "Well . . . yeah."

"Does Rhyzkahl make you feel good and sexy and special?"

I tried not to fidget. "Um. Yeah, but it's not that simple."

She narrowed her eyes. "Does he ever force you or coerce you into doing things you don't want to do?"

I shook my head. In fact I realized that I had absolutely zero fear that he would ever fail to back off if I ever wanted him to.

Jill shrugged. "Okay, so maybe you can't see yourself settling down with him as Mrs. Demonic Lord, but the way I see it, what you have with Rhyzkahl is the ultimate fuckbuddy. Hot, gorgeous, respects your limits, and makes you feel good. Am I missing anything?"

I stared at her, then began to giggle. "*Fuckbuddy.* Holy shit." I tried to picture myself explaining the concept to Rhyzkahl, which only made me laugh harder.

Jill grinned. "Exactly. So stop flailing around in puritanized guilt. If Ryan wants to be with you, then he needs to nut up and make a fucking move on you and fight for you."

I managed to get my laughter under control. "But he

hasn't made a move, Jill," I said. "Which means that he's *not* interested."

"Or he's completely thickheaded."

I snickered. "That's always possible."

"And what about you?" Jill said, fixing me with a piercing look.

"Um, what about me?"

"Have you made any sort of move on *him?*" she asked. "Have you made it clear to him that you'd like to try being more than BFFs?" The look on her face told me that she already knew my answer.

I grimaced and twisted the toe of my shoe onto the sidewalk. "Not *exactly.*"

She cleared her throat.

I sighed. "Okay, no. I haven't."

"Why not?"

I scowled. "Shit, Jill, because I'm scared to death that he'll say he doesn't want to be anything more than friends, and then things would be awkward and we wouldn't even have that."

She took me by the shoulders. "Yo, woman. It's not the nineteenth century anymore. You can't leave it all up to him." She gave me a shake. "Besides, how do you know he's not scared about the same thing?"

I regarded her sourly for several seconds. "I hate it when you make sense," I finally grumbled. "Okay, fine. You're right. I'm being stupid." I groaned. "When did I turn into a needy whiny angsty idiot who needed to be swept off her feet?"

She snorted then started running again, forcing me into a brief sprint to catch up. "We're conditioned from birth," she said. "I swear to god, if I ever have a daughter I'll ban all of the Disney princesses from the house. Except Mulan. She kicks ass."

I laughed, then had to save my breath for running.

* * *

I hated to admit it, but the jogging did seem to clear my
head a bit. Or maybe it was oxygen deprivation making
it difficult for my brain to concentrate on the various
things that were stressing me out. Like what I would do
if Ryan ever did make some sort of move. Would I have
the strength to keep Rhyzkahl at arm's length if that
ever happened? It wasn't as if I could simply stop seeing
him, not as long as I was oathbound to him. And even if
I did shift my relationship with Rhyzkahl to a platonic
one, I couldn't see Ryan being willing to endure the fact
that I had *any* contact with the demonic lord.

"I think you know way too much about me," I com-
plained after we made the turn to head back to the
house. "Obviously, I whine about my life too much."

She chuckled. "Or I'm simply a nosy bitch."

"Yeah, well, I'm going to start doing the nosy bitch
routine with you," I gave her a mock glare. "You keep
dropping these little snippets of enticing info."

"I'm boring," she insisted.

I rolled my eyes, and tried to resist the urge to actually *be* a nosy bitch. Jill had once revealed to me that
she was a widow, but hadn't said anything more other
than that it had been a short marriage and a long story. I
could respect that some memories could be painful, but
it shamed me that I knew very little about her in general. What kind of friend was I? Did I spend too much
time whining about my own issues?

Yes, I decided glumly. I was overly preoccupied with
myself and my own problems.

"Well, are you seeing anyone?" I asked. "Hot dates?
Cold dates?"

She shrugged, but there was a small smile on her face.
"A date here and there. Nothing much."

I'd been a detective long enough to know that she was
hiding something from me. "Anyone I know?" I pressed.

She kept her eyes on the road and shrugged again.

"Um, well it's a small town, so anything's possible." She abruptly veered to the right to take a side street, forcing me to quicken my pace to catch up with her. "Let's cut through here and run along the lakefront, okay?"

"Sure," I muttered, fairly sure that the change in direction was an excuse to change the subject as well.

"There's a five-K race next month," she said next, confirming my suspicion that she wanted to talk about something else.

Okay, so maybe she's simply a really private person. Or maybe she thinks I'd be upset if I knew who she'd been dating? The only possible way I'd be upset was if she was dating Ryan, but even though the jealous third grader in me wanted to rear its pigtailed head, I simply couldn't see the two of them dating. And why would she be encouraging me to make a move on him if that were the case?

Right?

I scowled and slapped my inner third grader down as we finally made the turn to head back to her house. I had enough drama in my life. I didn't need to fabricate any more.

Chapter 10

I showered and changed into my work clothes at Jill's house—a far more convenient option than making the thirty-minute drive back to my house to do so, where I would then have to make another thirty-minute drive to get to the station. My cell phone rang as I was toweling off after my shower, but since I recognized Ryan's ringtone, I finished drying off and getting dressed first. It felt a bit weird to think about talking to him on the phone when I was naked. Yes, I was that stupid.

"I figured you'd have called earlier," I said after I called him back.

"Don't you go running in the mornings with Jill now?"

I frowned. Had I told him about that? I couldn't remember. Not that it was a big secret or anything. "Yeah, my twice weekly dose of 'let's hang out with someone who makes me feel like an out-of-shape slob.' "

He laughed. "You're far from a slob."

"I notice you didn't say that I'm far from out of shape," I pointed out.

"You're far from a slob," he repeated.

"Asshole," I grumbled, but I was smiling.

"Don't compare yourself to Jill, fer crissakes. She was nearly an Olympian."

"Huh?"

"Didn't you know? She was a hotshot gymnast—expected to nail the trials and go to the Olympics . . . um, ten years ago or so. Then she had a bad fall, hit her head, and dropped out of competition."

"Oh," I said, feeling oddly hot and cold at the same time. "No, I didn't know that." *And how do you? I'm supposed to be her best friend, and yet you know these things?*

"Find anything in your research?" he asked, pulling me out of my stupid little pity spiral.

My lips twitched. This was his way of asking if I'd found out anything from Rhyzkahl, but I knew he had no intention of mentioning the demonic lord. "Nope. Yesterday was pretty much a bust for getting any sort of useful info." There. That covered the summoning, without saying it outright.

He muttered a curse. "Which means we're pretty much at a standstill with this now. Any other cases at work that you can sink your teeth into?"

"Not really. Things are pretty slow right now." Then I cringed.

There was a pause. "I can't believe you said that," Ryan said, voice low and ominous.

I laughed. "Me neither. Holy shit, I just totally jinxed myself."

"Dork," he said with a chuckle. "Okay, give me a call later on."

"I'll try to squeeze you into my busy schedule," I promised.

The biggest drawback to starting my shift at ten was a distinct lack of parking places in the detectives' parking lot. I scowled and circled the small lot twice in the misguided hope that a free space would magically appear, but my arcane powers failed me in spectacular fashion by refusing to vaporize any of the other vehicles in the lot and thus saving me the walk from the side parking lot.

Oh, whoopee. I could summon demons, but I couldn't get a parking space.

I grudgingly drove around to the side parking lot and walked the extra hundred feet, refusing to feel any sort of shame for being all *grudgingly* about the walk. I'd gone running that morning. I should be exempt from any sort of additional exertion. Right?

I paused before entering the bureau, my eyes drawn to a blackened patch about fifty feet away, in the detective's parking lot. *That's where the lightning struck the other day.* My fingers prickled, an odd sense of familiarity tugging at me unpleasantly as I started slowly toward the spot. *It wasn't just a storm,* the thought whispered through my head. I shifted into othersight as I reached it, even though I had a feeling I already knew what I would see.

I crouched, mouth dry as I looked at the star-shaped scar in the concrete and struggled to understand how my othersight could be showing me what were unmistakably arcane wards.

The lightning wasn't random. But, why on earth was part of the parking lot warded? That didn't make any sense. I wiped my sweating palms on the front of my pants as I deepened my sensing as far as I was able. A faint twinge of relief stole through me as I studied the wards. They were old and nothing I'd ever seen before, but the fact that they weren't recently placed made it slightly less ominous. There was no way I was going to start poking at them, but my assessment revealed something important. The parking lot wasn't warded. The lightning had broken through to the ground below the parking lot. *That's* what was warded.

Confusion and unease tightened my gut. Why would

the ground there have wards? And how long ago had they been placed? And had that lightning strike been directed, or had these wards somehow drawn it, like a lightning rod? And what did—

"Hey, Gillian, you lookin' for your lost virginity?" An unpleasant nasal voice jerked me out of my careening thoughts. I gritted my teeth and stood, then plastered a pleasant smile onto my face as I pivoted to see Boudreaux regarding me with a snide smirk, Pellini standing beside him with his thumbs tucked into his belt. Not that I could see his belt since his belly extended well over it, but that's where I assumed his thumbs were tucked. I didn't want to consider any other possibilities. Boudreaux didn't have to worry about large guts—he was about my height and so scrawny I had a suspicion I outweighed him. He looked like a meth-head to me, and I had a feeling that the only reason the Narcs didn't use him for undercover work was because they didn't trust him to not screw up.

"Hi, Boudreaux," I replied in an overly sweet tone. "Were you offering to help me look? Or were you going to loan me yours, since you still have it?" I grinned, then turned to walk inside, more than a little surprised to hear a guffaw of laughter from Pellini. The two detectives had always been somewhat annoying, though there'd been a time not too long ago that *annoying* had been more along the lines of *obnoxious, unpleasant, and insulting.* Until Ryan had done ... something. I still wasn't quite sure what, and I had zero proof that he had, but the two detectives had undergone an unbelievable change of attitude toward me in the span of a few minutes, going from openly hostile to warm and welcoming.

Seriously freaky.

The two hadn't remained full of warm fuzzies, to my strange relief. I wasn't sure I could handle the bizarro "nice" versions of Boudreaux and Pellini. However, they'd so far failed to completely revert back to the blistering assholes they'd once been, and had apparently settled into "annoying but not outright mean." I could handle that.

There was a note on the door of my office telling me to go see the chief when I got in. I dropped my bag on my desk and then headed to the chief's office, more curious than worried about the summons. Chief Robert Turnham had been the captain in charge of the Investigations Division before he'd been tapped to replace the previous chief of police. In fact, he'd been my supervisor during the Symbol Man investigation and had maintained a huge amount of faith in my ability to handle the case, for which I was still humbled and grateful.

His secretary gave me a smile as I entered the outer office. "Hi, Kara. You can go on in. He's expecting you."

Well, she wasn't acting as if I was about to get a reprimand. I thanked her and continued on through, pausing to tap on the doorframe instead of barging on in. Even with the secretary's go-ahead, I still wasn't quite nervy enough to enter the chief's office without permission.

Chief Turnham had worked for NOPD for fifteen years and had then spent the next ten years with Beaulac PD. A tall, slender black man with limbs that seemed too long for his torso, he gave an impression of being dour, but anyone who'd worked with him a while knew that he preferred to be a quiet observer until he knew precisely what he was facing. He was meticulous, and often anal-retentive, but he was also fair and dedicated. A far cry from his predecessor.

He looked up as I entered and gave me a warm smile. "Gillian. Come on in. Close the door behind you, please?"

The request to close the door sent a warning ping through me, but there was absolutely nothing in his expression or demeanor to indicate that anything untoward was about to happen. I complied, then took a seat in front of the desk. Little had changed in the office since I'd last been in here with the previous chief. The Beaulac PD seal was still painted on the wall behind his desk, and the shelves were still filled with books and various awards. But they were no longer arranged meticulously by height, and there were pictures of other people besides the chief. It was little things, but the general atmosphere seemed much less foreboding.

But some of my tension must have been evident. "Relax, Kara," he said. "You're not in any sort of trouble." He leaned back in his chair, as if to emphasize that this was a casual meeting.

Right. Like any meeting in the chief's office could ever be truly casual. But I forced down the sliver of worry and made myself relax into my chair. "Of course not, Chief. I never do anything that could get me into trouble."

He let out a dry laugh. "If it doesn't get caught on camera, it never happened, right?"

I maintained an innocent expression. He gave a soft snort of amusement, then leaned forward and laced his fingers loosely together on the desk in front of him. "I wanted to let you know that Ben Moran called me this morning."

I frowned. "Oh?"

He gave a slight nod. "He wanted to let me know that he was worried for his niece and to inform me that he believed that the incident Saturday night was little more than a prank that got out of control."

My frown deepened. "And why did he feel the need to call you with this theory?"

I could see his jaw tighten briefly. "He wanted to see if the investigation could be quietly dropped, and he expressed his concern that Lida would face possible fraud charges when it was discovered that the attack was merely a publicity stunt."

I digested this for several seconds. Chief Turnham remained silent as he allowed me time to consider what he'd told me.

"I see," I finally said, tamping down my annoyance at the entire situation. "What do you suggest I do, sir?" I steeled myself for the order to drop the case and look the other way.

"Do *you* believe it was a publicity stunt?" he asked, eyes intent upon me.

"It's one possibility, sir," I admitted. "But so is the possibility that Lida has a stalker. At this time I have nothing definitive to prove or disprove anything. Plus, the, uh, circumstances surrounding the incident in New Orleans were unusual enough that I wouldn't be comfortable simply letting the whole thing drop. Not without Lida coming forward to admit it was a prank."

He didn't ask me to explain what I meant about circumstances, merely gave a tight nod. "You should know that after I spoke to Ben Moran I received a call from the mayor, asking me to please accommodate Mr. Moran in any way I could." I could hear a trace of anger in the chief's voice now which told me that he was absolutely livid. He *never* showed anger. "But I want you to know that I expect you to do your job to the best of your ability and that you have my support."

I took a deep breath. "Sir, I appreciate that." I paused, unable to keep from smiling. "But the mayor and Mr. Moran are forgetting a fairly crucial detail."

Chief Turnham gave me a questioning look.

"She was attacked in *New Orleans,* sir."

A broad smile spread across his face and he began to chuckle. "And I take it you had a member of the NOPD on your task force?"

I matched his smile. "Yes, sir. Detective Marco Knight took the report, which means that Mr. Moran and the mayor will have a much harder time getting the whole thing dropped." I inclined my head to him slightly. "But, as far as this department is concerned, I think you can honestly state that the Beaulac Police Department has no active cases concerning an attack on Lida Moran."

He leaned back in his chair. "Detective Gillian, what I want to say at this moment would no doubt be considered extremely inappropriate and unprofessional, even though it would be meant as a compliment to you." Then he surprised me by laughing. "Screw it. You're a devious, clever bitch, and I'm glad you work for me."

"Thank you, sir," I said with a grin. "I think."

"Though I have to admit that I did wonder why a financial crimes task force was looking into a singer receiving death threats in the first place." He gave me a penetrating gaze, and I was reminded that he was quite shrewd, and I would be a fool to underestimate him.

"Well, sir, its primary focus is financial crimes, but it also deals with anything that doesn't quite fit anywhere else." Including anything related to the arcane or "magic" or strange creatures or ritual murders ... but I had no plans to explain all of that to him. "The whole thing is under the Homeland Security umbrella, which makes it kind of a catchall. When the complaint came in, our group was the one that was available."

"All right, well keep in mind that there's a lot of attention on you and that task force now. Make sure that you have justification for whatever you do."

"Yes, sir."

He gave me a wave of dismissal and I made my exit, mulling over what he'd said. I'd been a cop long enough to be unsurprised that someone with social or political clout would try to influence an ongoing investigation. Yet I could understand why Lida's uncle would try and do so. If his niece truly had participated in something as boneheaded as a publicity stunt—and, to make matters worse, one that got out of control—it was no surprise that he'd want to shield her from repercussions that would no doubt destroy her career and affect her future.

I'd also been a cop long enough to know that the world was *not* fair and just, and that people with money and influence often did not have to suffer the same tribulations that the "common" folk did. I still vividly remembered an incident from my days as a road cop. My sergeant had asked me to stay after roll call, and after everyone else had left, he'd handed me a speeding ticket that I'd written the day before. With a tight expression, he'd then asked me to please change it to a ticket for not wearing a seat belt.

"So, who is it?" I'd asked.

He'd sighed and shrugged. "Who knows. It came down from someone in the upper ranks. Someone they don't want to piss off."

And, I'd dutifully crossed out the speeding charge and written in the one for seat belt use. Sure, I could have made a stand against influence and the good ol' boy network. But I also knew you had to pick your battles, and I didn't want to stay a road cop forever.

The chief's comment about the task force bothered me, though. What if he was pressured to take me off it? A pang went through me at the thought. Even though I had no desire to leave Beaulac PD, working with the task force gave me—and my abilities—a feeling of legitimacy that I'd never had before. Now I summoned demons for good reasons—to find missing people and stop killers and protect potential victims. I liked that. A lot.

But he's not the type to bow to political pressure, right? The chief was good people. I had a huge amount of respect for him. *But the chief of police is an appointed position,* I reminded myself. If push came to shove, I doubted he'd be willing to sacrifice his job so that I could stay on the task force.

My gut was churning at the direction my thoughts

were taking. And when I returned to my office there was yet another note on the door, though this one told me to go see my sergeant, Cory Crawford. Continuing down the hall to where his door stood open, I looked in to see him reading what looked like a report, a baffled expression on his face. Crawford was a stout man engaged in a constant battle with a midsection that wanted to be more than stout. His hair had gone gray long ago, but he continued to dye it a dull brown—an almost perfect match to the color of his eyes. He was similarly unimaginative in his wardrobe—brown, brown, and more brown—except when it came to his ties. Those were always wild and psychedelic, in eye-bleeding colors and patterns. He'd recently grown his mustache back—which was, of course, also dyed. I'd never tell him, but I actually thought he looked better with the mustache. There weren't too many men who could pull it off, but he was definitely one of them.

I tapped on his door frame. "You wanted to see me? I can come back if you're in the middle of something."

He glanced up, then waved me in. "Nah, come on in. Glad for the break. I'm trying to decipher Pellini's report. Makes me wonder if English is really his first language."

I resisted the urge to snicker or make any other sort of commentary and dropped into the chair in front of the desk.

Crawford rubbed his eyes. "God, his reports give me headaches. You already went to see the chief?"

"Yes, he's recognized my innate brilliance and intends to promote me to deputy chief."

"Good, then you can approve my vacation time," Crawford said without missing a beat. I laughed and his eyes crinkled in a smile. "Funny, I figured it had more to do with the whole Lida Moran thing."

"Yeah, well, that might have come up too," I said with

a casual shrug. Then I made a face. "You know how it is. People with pull will pull."

Crawford's expression soured. "At least you understand. It sucks, but you're usually pretty good at keeping your head out of your ass." He turned and shuffled through papers on his desk. "Anyway, I need you to take some cases. I hate to throw you the boring shit, but it's your own damn fault for not being an incompetent fucktard."

"Sorry, Sarge. I'll have to work on that."

Crawford scowled as he handed two folders to me. "Spare me that, please. We already have our quota in this department. Now get out."

I gave him a sarcastic salute, then retreated to my own office with the folders.

I skimmed them quickly—one was a supposed burglary, but on closer reading it became clear that it was a property dispute related to a divorce and that the "burgling" wife still had legal access to the residence in question. That one was easily resolved—at least for now—with a few phone calls to the respective lawyers of the divorcing couple.

The other was a missing person report that had come in only about an hour ago. Victor Kerry, white male, fifty-six years old, hadn't shown up for his regular training session at his gym last Friday or this morning.

"You've *got* to be kidding me," I muttered. I started to toss the report back onto the desk, then paused as the name of the reporting person caught my attention. *Roger Peeler? That's the drummer from Lida's band.* I vaguely remembered Lida's comment about him being a personal trainer. I went back and read through his statement more carefully, though still with an admittedly jaundiced eye. Personally I saw absolutely nothing strange or suspicious about skipping out on a session with a personal trainer.

I finished reading the report, still far from convinced that there was anything to justify the complaint. From what I could determine, Victor Kerry was a financial planner and CPA with no family in the area. Roger Peeler had stated that Mr. Kerry was extraordinarily diligent about his workouts, and when he'd failed to show up for two sessions in a row Mr. Peeler had gone to Mr. Kerry's residence and his office, but had failed to locate him at either place.

"Wow, talk about your stalkers," I muttered. It seemed far more likely to me that Mr. Kerry had gone away for the weekend and had seen no reason to notify his personal trainer. *In other words, the probability is high that this is a bullshit case.*

On the other hand, the universe was gifting me with an opportunity to question one of the members of Ether Madhouse. I wasn't about to let that pass that by. Even if it did mean going to a gym.

Chapter 11

Magnolia Fitness Center was the largest gym in St. Long parish, and the only one of any decent quality in Beau-lac. I was a member there, though calling my attendance "sporadic" would have been generous. I tended to go through spasms of desire to get fit that usually lasted about two weeks and would then die down for several months. I was quite sure that Magnolia Fitness absolutely loved me, since I was kind enough to allow them to deduct the dues from my checking account every month, and I avoided adding any wear or tear to their equipment by the clever technique of remaining on my couch at home.

The front of the fitness center resembled a plantation, complete with a broad stairway, absurd columns, and rocking chairs on the "porch." However, the interior was more in line with what one would expect a fitness center to look like: shiny and chromey, with signs indicating directions to the spa, the hair salon, child care, or—amazingly—the weight room.

I'd called Roger and arranged to meet with him during a break in his training schedule. I had to ask for directions to the trainer offices, though, since I'd never had any desire to go there. The thought of paying someone to make me exercise made me whimper, both at the hit it would make on my budget and at the thought of being harassed and goaded to work and push and sweat.

It felt odd for me to walk through the gym in my detective-attire, and I found myself sucking my stomach in as I walked past the banks of mirrors. A couple of months ago I'd been accused of being too skinny—a result of being too stressed to eat properly because of worrying about my aunt. It hadn't taken long for my usual bad habits to assert themselves and for the "fleshy curves" to return. The running with Jill helped, but my fondness for ice cream before bed did not.

Roger was in the office when I arrived. He stood and shook my hand in a firm grip with no recognition in his eyes, not surprising since I was no longer dressed in gothy undercover garb. As Lida had said, Roger was definitely a ball of muscle. A damn good-looking one too, with dark blond hair and green eyes and a sharp little cleft in the middle of his chin. I had a feeling those good looks accounted for a fair number of the band's female fan base.

I debated briefly about *not* telling him that we'd met before when I'd taken his witness statement after the attack, then decided it would probably be more than a little awkward if he figured it out later.

"Oh, right!" he exclaimed after I mentioned the task force. He grinned, showing perfect teeth. "Man, that was some crazy shit, huh!"

"Yeah, sure was," I said as I settled myself carefully into one of the plastic chairs. Maybe they made the chairs deliberately uncomfortable so that people wouldn't want to sit for long and instead would eagerly rush out to exercise? "Seems kinda strange that Lida doesn't seem to be worried that it could happen again."

He shrugged. "Lida's a strange girl. I mean, she's cool and all, and super tough and driven, but at the same time she kinda does whatever her uncle and Adam say."

I desperately wanted to pursue that, but Roger didn't give me a chance. He plopped a chart down in front of me.

"So, I know that I'm not a family member or anything of Vic's," he began, expression earnest, "and I know he hasn't been missing very long, but if there's one thing he was super committed about it was his workouts. In the past three years he's only missed three appointments, and each time he made sure to let me know way in advance."

I obediently perused the chart, more than a little intimidated at the number of training sessions that Vic had scheduled. The man worked out five days a week—and that was just the sessions with Roger. I could also see that he was expected to do a fair amount of cardio on his own. "Wow, he must really be in shape," I said.

Roger gave a proud smile. "He's my star client. Three years ago he was close to four hundred pounds. Then he had a scare during a Christmas party—thought he was having a heart attack and was rushed to the hospital. Turned out it was only gastritis, but when they ran all the tests they found out that he was inches away from having a real one. He had a couple of stents put in, and as soon as he recovered, he decided he was going to change his life. He came here and signed up, and got serious." Roger pulled out two pictures and set them side by side for me to see—before and after pictures. I barely recognized that it was the same man in both pictures, and if Roger hadn't told me so, I might not have at all. The picture on the left showed a man dressed only in gray shorts—balding, morbidly obese, skin pasty and pale, and a deeply fatigued expression on a round and almost babyish face. The picture on the right had him in a white T-shirt and black shorts, and clearly about two hundred pounds lighter, but the differences went beyond the weight loss and the clothing. Vic Kerry was smiling, standing straighter with obvious muscle tone in his arms and legs. He'd gone and shaved his head and even though he still had a faintly cherubic roundness to his face, it was possible to see that he had cheekbones, and he no longer looked as if he never saw the light of day.

"Holy crap," I said, sincerely impressed.

"Isn't it amazing?" Roger said, nearly beaming. "Now he weighs one-ninety and his doctors say he'll probably outlive all of us." Then his smile slipped. "I went by his house and his office and he wasn't at either place. I have keys," he explained. "If Vic was busy he'd have me come to him so that he could still get a workout in." He scrubbed a hand over his face. "Vic's not just a training client. I mean, he's a friend as well. He's helped me out of some tough spots and given me some great financial advice, and . . . well, I'm really worried about him."

"I understand," I said in a reassuring tone. I asked a few questions about Vic and his family—of which there was practically none. Parents deceased, no spouse, no kids. A brother who lived in Seattle who Vic almost never spoke to—not out of any sort of antipathy, but more because they'd gone different directions with their lives, and their contact was now down to obligatory phone calls on birthdays and Christmas.

"Let me make some calls," I said. "I want to rule out the possibility that he had an accident and hasn't been able to get in touch with you."

He gave me a relieved smile. "I tried calling hospitals but they said that they weren't allowed to give patient information because of privacy rules."

"Right. I should be able to get more info." I'd also call the coroner's office to see if Mr. Kerry was in the morgue, but I wasn't going to tell Roger that. I was sure he knew that would be one of my calls, but that didn't mean I had to say it outright.

Roger excused himself to go tend to a client, and I used the opportunity to make the calls.

"Well, no one with his name or fitting his description is in any of the local hospitals. Or the morgue," I told him when he returned about ten minutes later.

He gave me an uneasy smile. "I don't know whether to be relieved or more worried."

"Sorry," I said. "But that's only the first step. Do you have time to take me by his office and house?" Since he had keys and—I assumed—permission to enter, that made my life a bit easier.

"Yeah, I just had my last client. I start at five A.M." He grinned at my involuntary shudder. "I'm free until about four-thirty this afternoon. Band rehearsal every night this week," he explained.

"Oh? Where do you rehearse?"

"Adam owns a studio in town—Sound Systems. It's convenient and *free*," he said, "which is nice since we're spending so much time practicing right now." A faint grimace flashed across his face. "Lida's putting together some new songs and it usually takes us some time to get all the instrumentation right."

I thought I could sense a touch of resentment about the amount of time the band demanded. "Lida writes all of the songs?"

"Most of them," he said, "though Trey's put together a few as well."

"What about Michael?"

Roger gave a small laugh. "Um, no. I mean, Michael's brilliant at playing existing stuff, but he doesn't do the creative stuff. At all."

"Does he read sheet music?"

He shook his head firmly. "No. Plays strictly by ear. I mean, don't get me wrong, he's absolutely amazing at it. He can hear something once and then play it damn near perfectly, but someone always has to play it for him first. Usually Lida does that." Then he smiled. "But she's incredibly patient with him. It's really cool."

"Sounds like it," I said, suddenly wishing I knew more about music and performance. I also wished I had more time to grill Roger about Lida and the other band members, but that would have to wait for another time. "Well, we're burning daylight. Let's go look for your client."

Taking separate cars, I followed Roger over to the City Towers, where Vic had his office. The City Towers building was a landmark in town, not only because it used to house the city offices, but it was also *the* skyscraper in Beaulac. If a seven story building could be called a skyscraper. But it was the tallest structure in town other than the water tower.

Unfortunately, the building had lost a number of its tenants in the last year due to newly constructed office complexes that were willing to price their rent competitively in order to fill their spaces. Judging by the almost empty parking lot, I didn't think there were more than a dozen occupied offices in all of City Towers. It looked as if any attempts at landscaping that were more complicated than cutting the grass had been abandoned. Bushes ringed the building, but they'd been allowed to grow so high and thick that the first-story windows were almost completely obscured. Walking into the building, I could see more reasons business owners would have left. The linoleum in the lobby was stained and cracked, and the walls probably hadn't seen a new coat of paint since the seventies. In fact it didn't look as if *anything* had been updated or maintained for a few decades.

Roger took me up to the sixth floor and unlocked the door to a very ordinary office. *Utilitarian* and *boring* were the words that first leaped to my mind. Black and white tile floor, metal desk, a row of metal filing cabinets, and a couple of slightly battered chairs. I had to wonder how successful an accountant and financial advisor he was if this was the best office he could afford. It certainly wasn't the sort of place I'd want to meet clients. As far as I could tell, Vic Kerry had the only occupied office on this floor. And, I didn't think the other floors were too much better.

Maybe he's simply frugal, I thought charitably. On the other hand, the view from his window was nothing short of spectacular. I could see down the entire length of Lake Pearl from here, and with binoculars I thought I'd probably be able to pick out my aunt's house on the lakefront.

"He has a little home gym set up through there," Roger said, gesturing to the another door. "Once he started to lose the weight he shelled out some serious bucks for really nice equipment." He opened the door and flipped on the lights. Still the same ugly tile floor, but this room was packed with weight benches and machines, and the far wall was taken up with a small kitchenette area with refrigerator. I didn't know a whole lot about exercise equipment, but even I could tell that this was gym-quality stuff—not the kind sold at Walmart. *Okay, so maybe he preferred to spend his money on stuff that actually mattered to him.*

"Actually, I work out here pretty often," Roger told me. "I gave Vic a discount on my training fee in exchange for being able to use the equipment here." He glanced at me with a wry smile. "Sometimes it's nice to get a totally uninterrupted workout. If I'm at Magnolia I'm kinda always on duty, and I get interrupted all the time by people wanting help or a spot or whatever."

"Trust me," I replied, "I totally sympathize with the 'always on duty' thing getting old."

He grinned. "Yeah, I guess cops get it all the time."

"You know it. So, was Vic dating anyone?" I asked.

"I don't think so," Roger said. "I'm pretty sure he would have mentioned it if he was."

"What about business dealings? Did he ever talk about that?"

"Um, sure, Vic mentioned some stuff sometimes," he said. "But he never gave details about the accounts he worked on. He knew his shit, though. He gave me some great advice."

"What sort of advice?" I asked.

"Investments. That sort of thing." He gave me a casual shrug that struck me as being a bit too casual. Maybe some of Vic's advice had been off the mark and Roger had retaliated? Just because Roger was reporting Vic missing didn't mean that he wasn't the cause.

I turned back to the front office and went to the desk. Neat and tidy, obsessively so. I riffled through a stack of papers on the desk, but didn't see anything that leaped out at me as a reason to go missing. No threatening letters from an ex-girlfriend. No blackmail notes.

I sighed and looked out at the view. A few sailboats were making their way across the lake in meandering patterns. I stepped closer to the window then stopped, frowning as a strange sensation rippled over me.

What the hell? I shifted into othersight, shocked as a familiar resonance washed over me. *Like the creature that grabbed Lida.*

Pulse quickening, I switched back to normal sight, then crouched and peered at the tiled floor. There was dirt there. Not much, but on the pristine floor it was noticeable. I straightened and looked at the window itself.

"Did you find something?" Roger asked.

I glanced back at him. "Do these windows open?"

"Yeah, they prop out," he said, stepping up to point to the latch mechanism at the bottom.

"This one isn't latched," I murmured. *Shit.* I knew I

needed to look, but I didn't want to. I had a sick and certain feeling that I knew where Vic was.

"Oh, god. Do you think . . ." He trailed off.

I took a piece of blank paper from the printer and put it against the window so that I could push it open without marring any possible prints too badly. I peered down, then looked at Roger.

"I think we found your client."

Chapter 12

I removed Roger from the room and secured the door, then parked him in the hallway while I started making calls. My first call was to dispatch, informing them of the situation and requesting a patrol unit to help secure the scene. My second call was to Sarge to let him know that I'd found the missing person—and not in the desired way.

"No such thing as a simple case with you, is there?" he grumbled after I gave him the rundown.

"I'm an overachiever," I said. "If I give you the particulars, can you get a search warrant for me so that I can go through the office? He's a financial advisor and I don't want to get flak later over privacy issues from client information I might run across."

"Always safer to get the warrant," Crawford agreed. "Text me the details."

I hung up with him and thumbed in the pertinent info, grateful that I had a sergeant willing to dig in and help with stuff like this. It was a basic boilerplate warrant, but if I had to take care of it myself it would be hours, since I'd have to wait for the scene to be secured and processed before I could leave to type it up and hunt down a judge.

Roger hadn't moved the entire time I'd been on the

phone. He wasn't freaking out or falling apart, but he did appear stunned. It didn't take much urging from me to get him to come downstairs. Fortunately, the body was deeply hidden in the bushes at the base of the building, so I wasn't too worried that anyone would disturb it while I waited for the patrol unit to arrive and get the area properly cordoned off. Right now I was more interested in watching Roger's reaction. I was convinced that Lida Moran had been attacked by the same sort of creature that had apparently tossed Vic out a window, and Roger Peeler was a big glowing link between the two incidents.

"I never thought Vic was the type to kill himself," he said in a rough voice, eyes hollow. He leaned up against the wall, looking stricken.

I knew that wasn't what had happened, but I figured I'd go along with that for a while to see what I could get out of Roger. "Well, you said yourself that he didn't have much family. Maybe he got tired of being lonely?" I offered, keeping my tone gentle.

He scrubbed a hand over his face. "I . . . I guess. But he had lots of friends. He was a super nice guy." He looked up at me. "Look, I can't see him committing suicide. His dad killed himself and Vic used to go on and on about how selfish and vicious suicide was to everyone left behind."

Well, that wasn't quite the response I'd have expected from someone who might have wanted to stage a murder as a suicide.

"All right," I said. "Had he mentioned anything about arguments or bad business deals he'd made recently?"

Roger shook his head slowly. "No. He was such a nice guy. Everyone liked him. He got along with everybody."

I nodded in response, but I remained skeptical. Nobody got along with *everybody*.

The marked unit pulled up then and I excused my-

self from Roger for a few minutes to get the scene secured. As soon as the tape was up and the crime scene
log started I returned to Roger. He didn't look as if he'd
moved—he was still in a stunned daze.

"Roger, I'm going to need to talk to you more a bit
later, but for now you're free to leave. Are you all right
to drive?

"Yeah. Yeah, I'll be okay." He took a deep breath and
straightened. "You'll let me know what you find out?"
The expression on his face was pleading.

"I promise," I said, then watched as he returned to
his car, those wide shoulders seemingly crushed under
a great weight. *If he's responsible, then he's also a fucking good actor,* I thought. I wasn't going to dismiss him
entirely as a suspect, because I'd definitely been snowed
before, but my gut instinct was leaning pretty far away
from him at the moment. *But if he's not the link, then
what is?*

Or maybe he was still the link. If Roger had a habit
of using the workout equipment here, maybe the golem
had been after *him,* and Vic had been in the wrong place
at the wrong time. Maybe someone had a beef with the
band, not just Lida.

I put Roger out of my mind for the moment and returned my attention to the crime scene here. I'd yet to
get a good look at the body and I hadn't wanted to do so
with Roger around.

The bushes ringing the building were high and deep,
and it wasn't easy getting to where I could even see the
body up close. It would have probably been another
week before the body had been found, and then only
if someone decided to investigate the smell. I didn't
want to mangle the bushes too badly, but I managed to
squeeze through enough so that I could get a peek. Not
that the effort and scratches were worth it. He was quite
clearly dead, and had been so for several days. He had on

dark blue pants and a leather bomber-style jacket over a dress shirt that had once been white, though blood and dirt now marred it. I could see a few maggots around the eyes and nose. A couple more days and his face would have been barely visible beneath the carpet of maggots.

I extricated myself from the hedge in time to see my sergeant get out of his car and head my way.

"Got your warrant. Search away. You do know this was supposed to be a simple do-nothing case?" Crawford said with a sour look as I brushed leaves off my pants.

"It's my own fault," I said with a sigh.

He regarded me with narrowed eyes.

"I made the mistake this morning of saying that things were pretty slow right now." I gave an apologetic shrug.

"God almighty, are you nuts?" He rolled his eyes. "So, do you figure he took a dive out the window?"

"He took a dive all right, but I think he was helped along."

He looked at me sharply. "Not a suicide?"

"I don't think so," I said. "Come on, I'll show you." Together we headed upstairs to the office. I unlocked the door with Roger's key, then walked to the window, carefully avoiding the thin smear of dirt on the floor.

"The windows prop open and have to be pulled shut," I said. "But it was shut—even though it wasn't latched. I doubt he climbed out, hovered for long enough to push it closed, and then plummeted down."

Crawford frowned. "No way the wind could have pushed it closed?"

"I don't think it's likely."

"Well then, we'll treat it like a homicide unless some other evidence to the contrary comes along."

I gave a slow nod as I stepped back out into the hallway. "It's a funny coincidence too . . ."

"What's that?"

I looked up as Jill exited the elevator with her case in her hand and camera slung around her neck.

"Bitch, you suck," she grumbled with a good-natured gleam in her eye. "Two scenes for the price of one?"

"I hate for you to get bored," I replied. "And can you please collect a sample of the dirt at the base of the window?"

She nodded and proceeded on in, too used to me to question any of my strange requests. But Crawford gave me a funny look.

"What's so special about the dirt?" he asked.

"I don't know if there is," I replied glibly. "But the rest of the floor seems pretty clean, so it might be from the attacker's shoes. Can't hurt to collect it."

He seemed content with the answer, to my relief. "So, what's a funny coincidence?" he asked, dragging me back to the subject from before Jill arrived.

"Oh, right. Well, the reporting person is Roger Peeler, who also happens to be the drummer in Lida Moran's band." Too bad I couldn't tell him about the fact that I was fairly positive that Lida and Vic were attacked by the same sort of creature.

"What about the victim? Any connection there?"

"Not that I know of," I replied. "But I haven't had a chance to look it into yet." I then explained how Roger was in the habit of using Vic's private gym.

"Hunh. That's interesting." He pursed his lips, silent for several heartbeats. "It looks like you have a lot of digging ahead of you."

"Yay. Woo," I replied, deadpan.

"Don't bitch about digging," Jill said from across the room as she snapped pictures. "I'm the one who was asked to pick up *dirt*."

Crawford glanced at me. "Is she always such a whiner?"

"Always," I said with a deep sigh. "It's embarrassing."

"I heard that!" Jill mock-snarled.

He chuckled. "I think I need to leave before this gets bloody."

"Smart man. I'm going to go through the office and see if anything leaps out as a motive," I said.

"Sounds good," he said. "I'll see about talking to others in the building."

"Can you check and see if there's any video surveillance?" I wasn't too confident that there would be. The building was old and decrepit, and I seriously doubted that any of the cameras still functioned properly.

"Will do." He turned to head out.

"Oh, and Sarge . . . ?"

He pivoted back to me while I put on my best hopeful/pleading expression.

"Kara, that expression doesn't work on you," he said with a glower. "It looks like you have gas. Just tell me how you want to add to my workload."

I snickered. "Well, I'd like to take a look through the victim's residence. But, at the rate I'm going here I might not be done until late, and I'd feel awful if I had to call you out in the middle of the night if I found something that needed your expertise."

"Yes, I'll take care of getting the search warrant," he grumbled, muttering dark invectives about worthless investigators under his breath as he left the room.

"Love you too, Sarge!" I called after him cheerily. I swung back to Jill. "You done with your pictures?"

She nodded as she unslung her camera. "Just finished. You need to do something?"

"Can you go ahead and collect the sample of dirt? I want to check something." I couldn't do this with Crawford in the room.

Jill pulled on gloves and scraped a portion of the dirt into an envelope, then stepped back. I crouched and placed my hand on the dirt that remained, shifting into othersight. Taking a steadying breath, I allowed the feel of the odd resonance to hum through me.

"It's the same as the thing that attacked Lida Moran," I murmured.

She crouched beside me. "A monster made of *dirt*. The golem."

"Or something similar." Shifting back to normal sight, I stood and pulled on gloves, then moved over to the desk and began opening drawers. Boring tax forms, boring letters, boring financial statements. I shuddered as a flashback from my time in white collar crimes washed over me. Too many hours spent poring over tedious paperwork . . .

"Whoa," I said, slowly pulling a paper from the top drawer

Jill glanced at me from where she was dusting the window for prints. "Got something?"

"Not sure," I admitted. "These are photocopies of checks written to Victor Kerry . . . and written by Adam Taylor, manager of Ether Madhouse."

She frowned and came over to peer at the paper. It showed the fronts and backs of three checks, each for five thousand dollars, and each stamped with NSF. I looked to see if there was any notation for what the checks had been for, but the lines on the checks were blank. However, the back of the paper had two brief lines of handwriting: A.T. $15,000. R.P. $15,000.

R.P? Roger Peeler?

"Adam Taylor already has several outstanding bad check warrants," I informed her.

"Hmm." Jill furrowed her brow in thought. "So maybe Adam came up here and they fought and he chucked ol' Vic here out the window with his trusty golem?"

"Quite possible," I said. "Though these checks are dated from only a few weeks ago, and I don't remember seeing any warrants for this amount. But that certainly doesn't rule out a confrontation." I set the paper aside and continued rifling through the drawers and file cabinets, but nothing else non-boring leaped out. A laptop case was propped against the desk, and I confirmed that there was actually a laptop within it. "Let's take this as well," I said.

"Sounds good. I'm finished up here," Jill announced as she gathered up her case and camera. "If you'll carry the laptop down, I'll take it to the lab and submit it for processing."

I pushed the desk drawers closed and picked up the laptop case. "Lemme give Ryan a call and tell him what's going on."

"Meet you downstairs."

I nodded to her then called Ryan. "So, get this," I said after he answered. "I think I have a homicide where the victim was thrown out a window by the same thing that attacked Lida. Or rather, the same type of thing." I gave him a quick synopsis of what I had and who the victim was. "At first I thought that maybe Vic was in the wrong place at the wrong time and that Roger was really the target since he often worked out up here, but then I found copies of some NSF checks from Adam Taylor to Mr. Kerry."

Ryan made a *hmmphing* noise. "You sure don't go for the simple cases, do you?"

I laughed. "Where's the fun in that? But it's also possible that the thing with the checks is totally unrelated, and that the entire band is being targeted, one by one. *But* even if there's no connection," I continued, "now we have a legitimate reason to go talk to Mr. Taylor."

"Did I miss something?" he said, sounding puzzled. "Why do we need a 'legitimate reason'?" I could hear the quote marks in his voice.

"Oh, that's right," I replied, a note of acid creeping

in. "I haven't spoken to you yet today to bring you up to speed on Ben Moran speaking to the chief and the mayor."

"Do tell," he growled.

I gave him the gist of my meeting with the chief.

"I like your chief," Ryan said gruffly after I finished.

I smiled. "Yeah, he's all right. But now that I have a possible homicide, all bets are off. Ether Madhouse is rehearsing at Adam's studio every night this week, and Ben Moran and the mayor can kiss my ass."

"You're becoming quite the rebel, aren't you?" he said with a laugh.

"You feds are rubbing off on me."

"About damn time. So did you want to hit the rehearsal tonight?"

Grimacing, I glanced at my watch. "Ugh. It's four already? I don't think I'll be able to tonight. I have no idea how much longer I'll be here. I want to run a search of the victim's residence tonight as well." Sleep? Who needed sleep?

"Stop being coy. I know how much you love all of that paperwork." I could hear the grin in his voice.

"Wow, we have a bad connection. I'll touch base with you later on, but I think that further harassment of Lida Moran and the band will have to wait until tomorrow."

"That's cool. Zack's in New Orleans right now anyway, picking up some paperwork from the bureau office there."

"Maybe we should sic Zack on Lida. She'll melt beneath his charms," I said, laughing.

"As if he needs any more reason to be cocky."

Chapter 13

I locked the office and returned downstairs right as the coroner's black van pulled up. I suppressed a laugh as I saw the driver exiting the van with a pair of lopping shears in his hand. Sarge had obviously tipped off the coroner's office as to the inaccessibility of the body.

Jill was finished with her pictures of the area, including shots of the exterior of the building. She retreated to give the van driver access to the hedge, but he hesitated, eyeing the thick bushes. He slid a hopeful glance to me.

"Any chance you have a chainsaw in your car?" he asked.

I had to grin. "Sorry!"

"Worth a try," he said with a rueful smile as he stepped forward, lopping shears at the ready. It took him several minutes to hack his way through the hedge, and I had to agree that a chainsaw would have been more efficient. The damage to the bushes would have been about the same.

Once the brush was cleared away, Jill stepped forward to take more pictures, and then I had the chance to take a decent look at the victim. Unfortunately my better view of the body didn't give me any new and fascinating insights. He was still bloated and maggoty. No previously unseen bullet wounds or arcane symbols. But

I took a mental note of the fact that he was still wearing his jacket. He'd probably been attacked as soon as he arrived at the office in the morning or right when he was leaving.

The coroner's personnel loaded the body into the body bag and onto the stretcher, then dutifully carted him off to the morgue.

"All right, chick," Jill said. "I'm done with my part, and I've seen you too much today. I'm gonna hit the road."

"Love you too, bitch," I replied, smiling.

She grinned and headed to her van. I helped the officer take the tape down, then made my way to the other side of the building where I'd left my car.

A chill wind hit me as I turned the corner, briefly robbing me of breath in shock at the abrupt change in temperature. It was a mild day, but that blast of air felt practically arctic. It faded as soon as it hit me, leaving behind an eerie calm that sent the hair on the back of my neck standing on end. *That feels like the wind from a summoning.* The thought snaked through my head even as a whisper of arcane brushed past me.

I turned slowly, completely unnerved. I sure as hell didn't see any summoning diagrams chalked out on the sidewalk. Maybe it was something else? Had to be. *Perhaps another portal like the one in my aunt's library?*

A nauseating ripple of menace passed through me and I edged toward the building, instinctively wanting something solid and real at my back. I shifted into othersight, scanning the area and the sky above me. There was nothing physical that I could see, but there was an odd cast to the surroundings, like a slow coiling of power—rapidly producing the effect of scaring the ever-living shit out of me. This was something that wanted me, and not in a nice way. I *knew* that viscerally.

Stucco dug into my back as I pressed against the

building. I could feel my pulse speeding as the odd coil of potency seemed to tighten and coalesce in front of me. Shit. *Is someone controlling this?* There was no one in sight. And what the hell was it anyway? I still couldn't see anything tangible.

Stop panicking and start doing something! I railed at myself. Pressed up against the building like this, I was an easy target for whatever was happening. Plus, I was pretty much powerless. *Too bad I don't have a portable version of the storage diagram.* I felt a lovely little ping at the thought, but I pushed it aside. Now wasn't the time to figure out how to accomplish something like that. If it was even possible.

I shoved off the wall and took off at a dead run for my car. I had no idea if I'd be any safer there, but visions raced through my head of other arcane dangers I'd faced, and the sanctuary of steel and plastic was better than nothing at all. I could sense the malevolence swirl behind me, as if snapping at my heels.

I heard the distant screech of tires on pavement and the thrum of an engine, and the thought flashed through my head that I might escape this unknown thing chasing me only to get hit by a car. But I also had the unshakeable sense that getting hit by a car would hurt less.

I heard a squeal of brakes, and suddenly a car slammed to a stop a few feet in front of me. The driver threw the passenger door open. "Get in!" he shouted unnecessarily as I practically dove into the car from sheer momentum. The instant I was mostly in, the driver slammed his foot down on the gas, and I had to yank my trailing foot quickly inside as the acceleration closed the car door.

I took a heaving gasp of relief, terror shifting to amazement that I'd somehow escaped the thing chasing me. Then I looked up and processed who my rescuer was.

Cory Crawford glanced first at me, then in the rear-view mirror, lips pressed together in a thin line beneath his mustache. "You okay?" he asked, words clipped.

I gulped and straightened in the seat, then fumbled for the seat belt. "Yeah." I busied myself with the belt while I racked my brain for some way to explain why the hell I'd been pelting across the parking lot.

But he'd somehow known that I needed a rescue.

"Did you see something behind me?" I blurted.

Uncertainty flickered in his eyes. "Not ... exactly." He slid a look toward me. "I was coming back to see if you wanted to go conduct that search warrant and I saw you running ..." He paused, skepticism and self-doubt warring in his face. "I ... I didn't see anything behind you." For an instant I thought he was going to add, *but I knew something was chasing you.* But he'd clamped down on whatever else he might have been tempted to say.

A tense and awkward silence descended upon the car as I resisted the urge to hug my knees to my chest. I glanced back once, using othersight to scan the road behind us, but I couldn't sense anything out of the ordinary.

Crawford slowed and then pulled into the parking lot of a convenience store. He parked, but left the car running. He kept his gaze straight ahead and his hands on the steering wheel. "Just give me some line of bullshit here, okay?" he said, voice tight and tense. "I'm not ready to hear anything else." Remorse shadowed his face, tinged with the barest trace of fear.

My chest tightened, a weary pity mingling with a nebulous sense of frustration. I wanted him to know, I realized. I wanted to stop having to lie to him and hold details back. But I also knew that forcing the truth onto him would make it all blow up in my face. Crawford had turned into an unexpected ally in the past few months, and I couldn't afford to lose that.

"It was a big dog," I heard myself saying, flat and expressionless. "Rottweiler, I think. I was trying to get to my car so that I wouldn't have to shoot it."

Some of the tension left his shoulders. "Yeah," he said. "That's what I thought too." He looked briefly disappointed, and I had the feeling it was directed at both of us. Silence fell for another moment, then he took a deep breath and turned to me with a tight, almost desperate smile. "Well, do you still want to do this search warrant?" he asked. "Or do you want to go see if . . . if the dog is still there?" I could almost see the thoughts whirling behind his eyes, praying that we could move on and forget that this strange and unexplainable moment had ever happened.

"You can take me back to my car," I said, fighting to keep from sounding anything other than normal and settled. If I still felt that odd sense of danger I'd tell him to clear out, and fuck the idea of shielding him from the truth. "And if everything's okay, then we can head over to do the search warrant." I needed to do the search anyway, and it would get my mind off what had just happened. Besides, that piece of paper with the initials had raised a number of questions.

"Sounds like a plan," he replied with a firm nod.

We returned to the City Towers building and cruised slowly through the parking lot. I had my senses extended as far as my little skills could manage, but there was no trace of the strange malevolence as far I could tell.

He pulled up right next to my car. "Vic lived in a condo near the lake—Emerald Heights. Unit number forty-three. I'll follow you over."

"Thanks, Cory," I said, meeting his eyes.

The smile he gave me in return was sad, and this time there was no doubt that he felt he was failing me. But I had no idea what I could say to reassure him that wouldn't make things worse.

I didn't linger in the parking lot and made tracks out of there as quickly as possible. I couldn't sense that strange menacing presence, but I wasn't about to take any chances.

It's not there anymore. So does that it mean it's gone, or did it merely relocate?

Either way I wanted to get the hell out of there.

The search of Vic Kerry's condo ended up being quite anticlimactic and mostly fruitless other than the picture it painted of a man living a mostly solitary existence. He had hundreds of books in damn near every genre, and enough DVDs to open his own rental store. But it was clear that he wanted far more out of his life, as evidenced by the number of brochures on the kitchen table for cars, houses, and vacation destinations. One room of the condo was fully occupied with exercise equipment similar to what was in his office, and I had to wonder if he'd thrown himself so thoroughly into fitness and working out more from a desperate need for a social outlet than from a desire to live longer.

There was also nothing work-related as far as we could see. After about forty-five minutes of digging through drawers and closets, we called it quits and left. An oddly morose fatigue dragged at me as we returned to our cars.

"Be careful out there," Crawford said as I opened my car door. I looked over at him to see that there was very real worry in his eyes.

I gave him as reassuring a smile as I could create. "Thanks. It's all good."

He dipped his head in a brief nod, then took a deep breath. "Look, Kara, I think you should know . . . there's a lot of chatter among the rank about the task force."

The frisson of worry returned. "What kind of chatter? They want to take me off it?"

He gave a shrug, which didn't exactly alleviate my

unease. "It's mostly stupid gossip." He slid an apologetic look toward me, which told me what most of the gossip probably entailed. I was growing used to the fairly open speculation that I was banging Ryan. Pretty damn funny, considering the truth.

"I know the chief's a supporter of you being on it, though," he continued. "And he's the one who really matters."

I nodded, but the simmering worry remained. The chief wasn't going to risk his job so that I could play around with the feds.

He grimaced. "I wasn't trying to upset you. I just thought you might want to know what's being said."

"I do," I said. "Thanks. Knowledge is power, right?"

He hesitated then gave me a weak smile. "Yeah. I guess it is." He licked his lips—a completely uncharacteristic gesture for him. "Watch out for those dogs, okay?" He tried to chuckle, but it fell flat. He sighed and shoved a hand through his hair. "You should tell Agent Kristoff . . ." He trailed off and I felt another wave of sympathy for him.

"I'll be careful," I said quietly. "Thanks for worrying."

He turned and climbed into his car without another word. I ducked into mine and watched him depart. One thing was for sure—I wasn't going to be telling Agent Kristoff anything, at least not for a while. Ryan would freak, and I wasn't sure I wanted to deal with that right now.

I drove without any real direction in mind at first, driven mostly by a need to simply get away. It annoyed me that I felt a twinge of guilt for not wanting to let Ryan know about what had happened. Why did I need to run and tell Ryan anytime something weird or strange happened to me? *Maybe because he's the one of the few people I know who understands "weird and strange,"* I reminded myself with a sigh.

But I couldn't face him right now. I needed to chill for a while before seeing him, otherwise he'd know something was up.

At the next stop light I sent a quick text to Ryan, telling him that the scene took longer than I'd expected and that we'd have to hit the studio tomorrow. I didn't want to get sucked into a phone convo with him. Too much chance that he might hear something in my voice, and then I'd end up explaining what happened and he'd be all worried and . . .

I sighed. And that was the problem. He acted worried and caring and all of that, like the absolute bestest of best friends. And I liked that we were such good friends, I really did. Or rather, I would like it more if I didn't want so much more, and if I could get rid of the niggling sense of uncertainty about him. *Aaaand we're back to me being whiny and neurotic!* Full circle on the emotional roller coaster.

Besides, as harsh as it might sound, there was little that Ryan could do if I told him, other than worry.

Rhyzkahl might be able to do something. Even as the thought whispered through my head I couldn't help but feel as if I was somehow betraying Ryan by even considering another summoning of Rhyzkahl. But the demonic lord would be far more able to tell me if it had been some sort of directed attack or simply some random ripple of arcane weirdness.

My thoughts continued to tumble in jagged discord for the entire drive home. Full night had descended by the time I pulled up to my house, with the waxing moon hanging above the trees, mocking me with its not-fullness. *Still, it's less than a week until the full,* I thought as I entered my house and locked the door behind me. And summonings of Rhyzkahl were always easier than traditional summonings since he was willing to be drawn through.

I descended the stairs to my basement and looked down at the storage diagram, uncertainty coiling through me. Unfortunately, I had no way to measure how much power was stored beyond a general sense of *full* or *not full*. I was fairly sure that I had enough to perform a summoning of Rhyzkahl.

But I'd been a summoner long enough to know that "fairly sure" was a good way to die a screaming death. If I ran out of power partway through the forming of the portal, it would latch onto the next closest source—me—and would then collapse in on itself while merrily reducing me to the smallest possible pieces.

I fought back the spurt of panic the mere thought of that had produced. No. It would be the height of idiocy to attempt a summoning without being absolutely positive that I had sufficient power. There was no such thing as screwing up a little when it came to that.

Not to mention I'm not exactly calm and focused right now.

I turned away from the diagram and returned upstairs. It looked like I was on my own for a little while longer.

Chapter 14

Needless to say, the next morning I was in the perfect state of mind to attend an autopsy.

As usual, the outer door of the morgue was propped open with a chunk of concrete. I stepped in, automatically breathing shallowly until I could get used to the odor—a strange combination of bleach and other sanitizers, with the faintest underlayer of rot. Carl kept the morgue as pristine as possible, but I'd seen the way bone dust and blood flew everywhere, and I knew there was no way to ever get the place truly clean.

Carl was already in the cutting room, setting out the equipment that would be needed for the autopsy. I went ahead and donned the plastic smock and gloves, earning me a slight smile and a raised eyebrow from him.

"So eager to dive into the gore today," he murmured as he headed off to the cooler.

"Are you referring to me or you?" I shot back.

"Either will do," he replied.

I grinned. I was used to Carl—or as used to him as anyone could get. He was quiet and dour—or at least that's how he came across to most people. I'd had the chance to get to know him a bit more personally in the past few weeks—due in no small part to the fact that he was dating my aunt.

Yeah, I was still getting used to that. My aunt had a boyfriend. The morgue tech. Not only that, there was something odd about Carl when it came to arcane powers. Protective wards didn't work on him. It was as if he didn't exist. Moreover, when he'd been attacked by a creature with the ability to eat souls, he'd been unaffected. *Does that mean he has no soul? Or does he simply have some sort of super-resistance to what we call magic?*

Either way, it was enough to make me treat him with newfound respect and caution. It helped that, as quiet and dour as Carl could be, he seemed to be a pretty nice guy, and my aunt was apparently quite happy to have him around.

And if he's with her, then I don't have to be around as much, the thought snaked through my head, and I felt a quick flash of guilt for thinking it. I loved my aunt. But sometimes lately it was a little creepy and unsettling to be around her.

I pulled my attention back to the present as Carl pushed a laden stretcher up next to the metal cutting table, then unzipped the body bag to reveal the body of Vic Kerry. "Another day out there and it would have been fairly disgusting," he commented, as if making note of the color of Vic's underwear.

I thought he was fairly disgusting anyway, with the bloated face and maggots crawling around his eyes and nose. Carl photographed the body while it was still dressed, then I gritted my teeth and helped Carl remove the man's clothing. Carl held out a bag for me to put the clothing in but I paused.

"Something wrong?" he asked.

"Sorry. I was looking at the dirt." Like handprints, as if someone with dirty hands had picked the man up. *Or with hands made of dirt.* The tiny bit of lingering doubt dissipated. Now if I could just figure out what exactly the golem-thing was.

Carl tilted his head. "I take it you feel this is unusual? He was lying in bushes for several days."

"It goes along with what I felt up in his office," I said, oddly relieved to know I could be more forthright with Carl. "There was a strange resonance there. I think Vic Kerry was murdered and I think it's connected to the attack on Lida."

"Interesting. Have you spoken to your aunt about it?"

I shook my head and went ahead and put the clothing into the bag. "Not yet. Haven't really had the chance." It hadn't even occurred to me to go talk to her after last night's incident. Had I lost that much faith in her? *No, I was simply preoccupied,* I tried to reassure myself. *That's all.*

Silence fell for a few minutes while we finished undressing the body and prepping it for autopsy.

"She's still your aunt," he said abruptly.

I grimaced. "I know. But—"

"She was changed. Subtly," he continued. "She was in the void for long enough that she absorbed aspects not of her original nature." Then he shocked me by saying, "Just as you were changed by your time in the void."

I stared at him, literally openmouthed. "I wasn't changed!" I finally managed. "I mean, I—"

"You were in the void for two weeks before you were called back," he said, eyes intent on me in a manner that was beginning to seriously creep me out. "The changes are subtle, but there for those who can sense them."

I could feel gooseflesh spring up on my arms. "Can you sense them?"

I expected him to confess to great arcane knowledge, or admit that he had othersight or some such thing. I didn't expect him to smile and shake his head. "No, but I see how the changes in you have affected those around you who can sense them. Whether they realize it or not." He shrugged. "Most don't realize it. But I listen and watch a lot."

"Ryan?" I said before I could think.

His smile widened very slightly. "He is one."

The banging of the outer door interrupted the odd conversation, and I wasn't sure if I was relieved or disappointed.

"Morning, boys and girls," Doc said with a cheerful grin as he strode into the cutting room. Dr. Jonathan Lanza was the forensic pathologist for the St. Long Parish Coroner's Office—a slender man about my own height, with dark hair and eyes, and a nose that betrayed his Italian heritage. He'd come to St. Long Parish after working in both Las Vegas and Houston, which meant that he had a wealth of knowledge that we were deeply fortunate to have access to.

"So, this is the guy who decided to try to fly?" he asked, gaze skimming over the body on the table.

"Yep," I said, "but I think he was helped along."

He picked up his clipboard and peered more closely. "Hunh. Well it definitely looks like he was attacked." He pointed to Vic's neck. "Carl, clean that dirt off please?"

Carl obligingly stepped forward with a wet towel and carefully wiped away the smears of clay.

"A bit easier to see now," Doc said, pointing to the marks on Vic's neck with the end of his pen. "Here you can see bruising—from the fingertips of whoever grabbed him by the throat." He frowned. "Looks deep too. His attacker was pretty damn strong."

I kept the interested look on my face and didn't offer any possibilities.

"And your boy here tried to escape," Doc continued, indicating several scratches. "Those look like fingernail marks—his own as he tried to get the attacker's hand off. I'll do scrapings from under his nails in case he managed to scratch the other guy as well."

"Sounds good," I replied. I'd be shocked if anyone else's flesh was found though. I glanced at Vic's hands and could easily see the dirt under his nails.

I watched as Doc and Carl took scrapings and clippings from the nails and sealed them in a small envelope. It would be forwarded to the DNA lab, but I felt no need to put any sort of rush request in.

They proceeded with the autopsy and Carl made his usual attempt to convince me to stick a needle in the eye to retrieve the vitreous fluid. Thanks but no thanks. There was a lot of gross I could handle, but that went way beyond my squick tolerance.

Doc began to peel the skin of Vic's neck back. "Good god, this was one strong son of a bitch!" He shook his head in amazement and when I looked I could see large clots of blood where the creature's fingers had dug in. "Carl, get pictures of this, please." He paused long enough for Carl to get the pictures, then continued peeling back the layers of muscle. He carefully palpated the throat area and let out a low whistle.

"Hyoid bone broken?" I asked. I didn't have much knowledge of pathology and anatomy, but I knew that the hyoid bone was often broken in cases of manual strangulation.

Doc snorted. "Broken? That's putting it mildly. The whole trachea is crushed, thyroid cartilage is broken." He shook his head again in disbelief. "This guy was dead—or at least well on his way there—before he was helped out the window."

I couldn't completely control the shudder. Poor guy.

Doc moved with careful efficiency through the rest of the autopsy—removing and examining organs and taking samples of blood and urine for toxicology testing. Finally he glanced up at Carl. "Let's get him sewn up. I'm going to want to do a posterior neck dissection to get a better look."

Carl removed the block beneath the body, then pulled out a thick, curved needle about three inches long and a ball of nylon string. He cut off about a yard of string and threaded the needle, then extended the needle to me.

"Care to help?" Carl asked, face impassive. "It will go faster with two of us sewing."

I reluctantly took the needle. "This is so disgusting."

His lips twitched. "Be careful," he said. "The needle can get slippery, and you don't want to poke yourself. And it doesn't have to be pretty or neat. The funeral home will take it out anyway."

I cringed as I pushed the needle into the flesh at the edge of the long incision. It didn't matter that I knew Vic Kerry couldn't feel anything anymore. It still sent a chill through me every time I pierced the skin. I definitely didn't have it in me to do the kind of ritual torture that the Symbol Man had performed.

I quickly discovered that "slippery" was an understatement. Even though Vic Kerry had lost massive quantities of weight and was fairly trim, he still had a thin layer of fat in his midsection. After a couple of passes through that fat, the needle was slick and damn near impossible to manage.

"Thanks for the help," Carl said. I looked up to see that he'd started from the other end, completely sewing up the rest of the incision in the time it had taken me to do three whole stitches.

I gave him a black scowl. "You did *not* need my help," I accused. "You only wanted me to do more gross stuff."

"Your perception astounds me," he replied with a dry chuckle. "But I *could* use your help turning the body over."

"I think I need to start filling out a time sheet for the coroner's office, Doc," I said over my shoulder.

The pathologist smiled and continued to jot notes. "It's not enough that you're my favorite detective?"

I hid my smile and made a rude noise. "Yeah, yeah," I said as I helped Carl flip Vic over. "I've heard that tune before. Money talks, Doc!"

Doc gave a low laugh. "Worth a try." He stepped up to the prone body and made a careful slit along the spine from the nape of the neck to a point between the shoulder blades.

"Unbelievable," he murmured after a moment of examination.

"Doc? What did you find?"

"Kara, whoever did this was unbelievably strong. You have shearing of discs of upper cervical vertebrae. Marked hemorrhage along vertebrae and into posterior neck muscles. Ligaments from vertebrae to base of skull are ruptured." He kept pointing at globs of blood that apparently meant a great deal to him, but simply looked like a gory mess to me. He straightened. "I mean, it's as if something grabbed this guy by the neck and just squeezed, breaking and ripping everything back here."

"And then threw him out the window in the hopes of making it look like a suicide," I said.

"There's no way that these injuries came from a fall," Doc said flatly. Then he gave me a wry smile. "My advice is to keep an eye out for a big, strong, dirty giant."

I gave him the chuckle he was expecting. *Good thing he doesn't know how close he is to the truth.*

Chapter 15

After leaving the morgue I called Roger, relieved to discover that it was his day off, which meant I could avoid walking through the gym again. I arranged to meet him at his apartment, then called Adam Taylor while I was on my way to Roger's. Adam seemed unruffled at my request to come talk to him, merely stating that he was in New Orleans in meetings with the band's label, and that he'd be more than happy to meet with me at the studio later in the day, perhaps five-thirty?

I agreed and disconnected, taking note of the fact that he'd been unsurprised at the request for an interview. It might mean nothing, or maybe Roger had given Adam a heads up about Vic Kerry's death. I sent a quick text to Ryan to update him and arrange to meet him at the studio at five, then headed out to see Roger.

Roger lived in a relatively new apartment complex on the north end of town, and about as far away from the lake as you could get and still be within Beaulac city limits. It looked like a decent enough place, though I was fairly sure I'd go nuts having neighbors on all sides. The complex was large—almost a dozen buildings—and each building had what I estimated to be about fifteen apartments. I had a hard time believing that there were that many people in the Beaulac area who needed rental space, but as far as I could tell the majority of the units had residents.

Roger answered the door with a wan smile. "Detective Gillian," he said. "Have you found out anything?"

"A few things," I replied. "I appreciate you taking the time to talk to me."

He stepped back to allow me to enter. "It's no problem." He closed the door behind me then led the way down a short hall and into the living room. Or perhaps it was the dining room, or an extension of the kitchen. It was a bit difficult to tell where one room ended and another began. It was tidy, though, and the furniture was arranged in what was probably the best way to take advantage of the strange floor plan. It felt comfortable and welcoming, and even the drum set in the corner seemed to fit into the flow of the room. I had only the barest knowledge of feng shui, but I somehow had a feeling that this room would be a perfect example of how to do it right.

Roger didn't seem very comforted at the moment though. He turned troubled eyes to me. "So, um, I'm guessing that the fact you want to talk to me means you don't think Vic committed suicide?"

"You're right," I said evenly. "It's been ruled a homicide."

He seemed to fold in on himself as he sank to sit on the couch. "That's so hard to believe," he said, voice hollow. "Vic was such a cool guy. Why would anyone want to kill him?"

"That's what I intend to find out." I pulled out my notebook and found the photocopy I'd made of the paper that had the initials and the dollar amounts. "Just so you know, I've already submitted subpoenas for Mr. Kerry's bank statements and financial information, but I found something during my search of the office, and I'm wondering if you can help me figure out what it means." I passed him the copy of the paper, watching him carefully for his reaction, but to my surprise he merely nodded.

"I can tell you exactly what this is. Well," he amended, "I can tell you what the 'R. P.' stuff is. I mean, that's me, as I'm sure you guessed." He looked back up at me. "And he loaned me fifteen thousand dollars."

"Can you tell me why?"

"I want to open my own gym," he said, leaning forward, suddenly earnest. "Not a fitness center like Magnolia, but a real gym for people serious about working out. No spa or any of that crap."

"Surely you need more than fifteen thousand dollars." Doubt colored my voice. "You have other investors?"

He sat back. "Not yet. No one's going to want to invest in a nobody without any seed money. But Vic really believed in me, which was why he loaned me the money. He put me on to some really good investments, and by the time I'm ready to go forward with the gym, I figure I'll have enough to be able to attract some serious investors."

"What kind of investments?" I asked.

He shrugged. "Honestly, I'm not really sure. Vic said he'd loan me the money and would take care of all the investment stuff. He had me sign some papers for him so that he could take care of everything."

I blinked. Was he truly this naive? "You mean a power of attorney?"

An expression of chagrin crossed his face. "Um, well, I guess it was kinda like that. I totally trusted Vic, though. And since it was his own money, it wasn't like I was worried about him taking it, y'know?"

"Did you ever get the feeling that anything about the situation wasn't completely legit?" I asked, doing my best to keep the dubious note out of my voice. It shrieked *not legit* to me, but then I was more cynical than most when it came to this sort of thing. Probably because I'd seen so many cases of fraud.

He shook his head firmly. "Never. Vic's known about my plans for the gym for close to a year now, and has always said he'd support me any way he could."

It was possible that there was nothing hinky about the whole deal, but now I was itching to find out more about these investments. "Roger, did Vic ever give you any paperwork showing you how he invested the money?"

The first shadow of doubt briefly clouded his face. "Well, no. But maybe he hadn't had a chance to do anything with the money yet. I mean, it was only a couple of weeks ago."

I nodded to let him think I accepted that as a possibility, even though I most certainly did not. "All right. One more question: Did you ask to borrow the money, or did he offer to loan it to you?"

"He . . . offered," Roger said slowly, then his face abruptly paled. He clearly wasn't stupid—simply completely unwilling to consider that Vic might have had anything but his best interests at heart. "Shit," he whispered. His eyes snapped up to mine in desperation. "Am I in trouble? Did Vic do something illegal in my name?" He groaned and dropped his head into his hands. "Oh my god. I trusted him."

He's not worried about being accused of murder, I noted. "I don't know, Roger. I'm looking into it." I paused. "But every bit of information you can give me will help me find his killer."

He gave a vigorous nod. "Anything. God. Just ask. I swear, I have nothing to hide."

"Would you be willing to allow me access to your bank and investment accounts?" I wasn't surprised to see him nod again. Good, that saved me the trouble of getting a subpoena.

"What do I need to do?"

I glanced at my watch. Where the hell had the day gone? "It would be easiest for me if you could go down to your bank and arrange for me to have full access. Then I can simply swing by and pick it all up when it's ready."

"I'll go down there right now." He paused, swallowed hard. "Am I a suspect?" he asked, a slight tremor in his voice.

I knew what I was supposed to say. I knew I should say that I hadn't ruled anyone out and that the investigation was ongoing.

"No," I said instead. The look of relief on his face was almost painful to see. I hated that I had to prick that bubble of relief. "Roger, I should tell you that I also haven't ruled out that Vic wasn't the intended victim."

Fear flickered in his eyes. "Oh, god. Because I work out there sometimes. And if he did something illegal in my name . . ." He ran a shaking hand through his hair.

I touched his arm. "Look, I'm not trying to spook you. But be careful, all right? Try to be with someone else at all times until I can find out more."

He took a deep breath. "Yeah. Okay. Watch my back." He still looked spooked, but I hoped that was better than him being oblivious.

"How well did Adam Taylor know Vic?" I asked, as much to distract him as to dig for more information.

He blinked, clearly surprised at the question. "I wasn't aware that they knew each other at all." Then his eyes dropped to the paper. "Ooohh, you think 'A. T.' is Adam Taylor."

I shrugged. "It's only a theory at this point." This was why I'd made a copy. I didn't want to have his answer influenced by seeing the copies of the returned checks that had been on the other side of the original.

Roger pursed his lips into a thoughtful frown. "Actually, that would make a lot of sense. Adam's been having a lot of financial problems. He owns the studio where we rehearse, and his business has kinda been sucking ass. I know he's been wanting to find someone to invest in it so that he can upgrade and attract more business."

Well, it looked like I was going to have a very interesting talk with Adam Taylor later today. I stood. "Roger, I appreciate you talking to me. You've been a huge help." I handed him my card. "Please call me if you think of anything else that might be of use."

He nodded as he took my card. I was pleased to see that he didn't look as freaked as he had before. He was tough and smart, even if he was more than a little naive. "I will. Thank you."

I gave him another reassuring smile and departed, thoughts churning as I returned to my car. Vic Kerry had been up to something dicey, and it had earned him a flight out the window.

Now I merely had to figure out what his scheme could have been. And how it could be connected to the attack on Lida Moran. And what the hell the creature was.

And while I was at it, I could go ahead and bring about world peace and end world hunger.

I returned to the station and headed straight to my office. After locking the door behind me, I plopped into my chair then winced as the damn spring poked my backside again. *You'd think my backside would have enough padding for that not to hurt,* I grumbled to myself as I logged on to my computer.

Google was going to be my best friend for a while I decided as I plugged in searches on Ether Madhouse, the band members, Adam Taylor, and Vic Kerry. As expected, the searches on the band and the members turned up a zillion results, with about half being websites with general information about the band, and the rest articles and blog entries about the incident at the concert. I skimmed a few of the blog entries, but the opinions and analysis of what had happened ran the gamut from "people are stupid and it was a crazy stalker fan" to "what a lame-ass and dangerous publicity stunt." There was nothing that even suggested that it might have actually been something demonic or arcane, which actually surprised me considering the level of Crazy that usually existed on the Internet.

The search on Adam Taylor pulled up some old biographical information. I was surprised to see that he'd once been a major player in the New Orleans music scene as musician, producer, and songwriter, and had even been appointed to the Louisiana Music Commission back in the nineties. But apparently he'd had a run of ventures gone sour, and then had lost his home and studio during Katrina. He'd dropped out of sight until about a year ago when he began promoting Ether Madhouse and had opened a studio in Beaulac.

He probably has everything pinned on this band making it, I realized. Sank all his money into the studio in the hopes of recapturing his former success.

I sent the page to the printer, then searched on Victor Kerry's name with meager results. A few scattered name mentions—usually connected to local social functions. Nothing that leaped out about financial misconduct or fraud. Oh, well. I couldn't have everything handed to me.

After making certain that my door was locked, I started searches on anything I could find related to golems or arcane constructs. I found a number of excellent websites with information about the golems of Jewish legend, but the more I read, the less I felt that the creature I'd encountered was that sort of golem. In the Jewish legend the creature was inscribed with magic or religious words to keep it animated—either with a holy word or name written on its forehead, or a word

or incantation written on paper and placed in the creature's mouth. I'd only seen the face of the thing that attacked Lida for a few seconds, but I was fairly positive
that there'd been nothing written on it, and there'd been
nothing in its mouth. But more than that, the golems of
legend were said to be clumsy and slow, and the one I'd
encountered had been anything but.

I spent close to an hour doing more searches and poring over websites. Oddly, it was a site catering to fantasy
role-playing games that gave me the first *ping* of possible recognition. A golem was listed in the pantheon
of monsters, but instead of being animated by religious
ritual, it was basically a statue of clay "possessed" by an
earth elemental.

I sat up straighter. There'd been something about
earth elementals in one of the books I'd taken from my
aunt's house, but I'd skimmed right over it since there'd
been no accompanying reference to golems or constructs. My knowledge of elementals was rudimentary
at best. I'd always assumed that such things didn't really
exist anymore, or if they did, there was no one left who
knew how to control them. Kind of a boneheaded assumption, now that I thought about it.

*For over a decade I've been operating under the con-
cept that the only "magic" in the world was the kind I
dealt with—using the natural power of the world to summon otherworldly creatures. And that's stupid.* I scowled
at my own rigid thinking. I was too used to automatically
assuming that the majority of the people who claimed to
have "powers" of some sort or another were full of shit.
And how was that attitude any different from someone
assuming that my skills and abilities were bullshit, or,
worse, due to some sort of evil pact with Satan?

And what about the essence eater? I reminded myself.
A few months ago I'd tracked down a murderer who'd
been consuming people's souls, or essences. In fact the

reason I was now sworn to Rhyzkahl was a direct result of the confrontation with the killer—the only way I'd known to save Ryan's essence from being consumed as well. That killer was hardly the sort of arcane practitioner I was used to.

I frowned, the memory of a conversation with Rhyzkahl suddenly bubbling to the surface.

"There are many humans with the ability to shape and manipulate potency," Rhyzkahl had told me. *"Some can open portals. Some can draw power from essence. A rare few are little more than parasites. You are all descended from the same source."*

There'd been no time to press him for more details, and then I'd forgotten all about it in the aftermath of everything that had happened.

So, perhaps calling and controlling an earth elemental was simply another way of manipulating potency. And what had Rhyzkahl meant about "the same source?"

The buzzing of the phone on my desk sent my train of thought crashing into a deep ravine and I barely managed to resist the urge to snatch up the receiver and yell, *"What?"* Instead, I took a deep breath and gently picked up the receiver.

"Detective Gillian," I said, tone nicely crisp and professional.

"This is Mayor Fussell, Detective Gillian. If you have a few minutes, could you come by my office? I have a matter I'd like to discuss with you."

Nonplussed, I actually stared at the phone for several heartbeats before returning it to my ear. "Mayor Fussell, I'm sure I can make time to meet with you. May I ask what this is about?"

"We can discuss that when you get here, Detective," was the curt reply.

I felt a muscle in my jaw twitch. "Certainly, sir. I'll be right on my way."

I hung up, fighting down anger by running through a few mental calming exercises. I had a damn good feeling I knew what this was about.

I shut down my computer and exited my office, then headed straight for my sergeant's. He looked up from his computer as I swung into his doorway, his eyes narrowing at the expression on my face. Okay, so maybe I wasn't controlling my anger as much as I'd hoped.

"What's going on?" he asked.

I took another deep breath. "I've been called to the mayor's office," I said. "Is the chief here?"

Crawford scowled blackly. "No, he's in Baton Rouge for a meeting." He pushed back his chair and stood. "And I'm sure the mayor knows it. Did he say why he wanted to meet with you?"

I shook my head. "No, but he didn't sound as if he wanted to give me a puppy and flowers. I'm pretty sure I know what this is about."

"Ben Moran," Crawford said, yanking his jacket on. "And yes, I'm coming with you. What a complete crock of shit." He glanced at me. "You have a voice recorder on your phone?"

I blinked, then smiled. "Yeah. I do."

He gave a curt nod. "Good, and I have one too. We're gonna nip this shit in the bud."

Chapter 16

The mayor's office was across the street from the station, and I had to resist the urge to skip and bounce on the way over. *Funny how knowing that someone has your back makes all the difference in the world.* But more than that, it was a relief to know that Crawford wasn't going to let the weirdness of the other day influence his support of me as one of his detectives. I could accept that he wanted to keep his head in the sand with regards to the bizarre stuff I was involved in. It was unrealistic for me to expect—or even hope—that everyone could be as readily accepting of the arcane as Jill was.

But my gut was still tight with nerves as we crossed the street. My job was *not* civil service, which meant that the mayor definitely had the pull to get me fired if he saw fit. *And my days with the task force might definitely be numbered,* I thought grimly.

On the way over I gave Crawford a summary of what was going on with my investigation—though I carefully censored out the not-so-normal aspects. An oddly pained expression crossed his face briefly after I finished, as if he knew I was holding something back, and I felt an unexpected wave of sympathy for the man. He truly did his best to be a good cop and an effective sergeant, and I'd unintentionally created a harsh dilemma for him.

And no way to take it all back now. I wonder if he regrets stopping to help me? A whisper of remembered fear curled through me at the thought. If he hadn't helped me, something *bad* would have happened. I knew that. Probably he did too. But I couldn't really blame him if he did harbor a measure of regret.

Entering the city administration building, I forced myself back to the here and now. Crawford and I rode the elevator in silence to the third floor where the mayor had his office. I gave the receptionist my name and advised her that the mayor was expecting me, and was completely not surprised when she replied that the mayor was on an important phone call and that it would be a few minutes.

"Keep me waiting," I murmured to Crawford as I took a seat in the waiting area. "Establish his control over the situation. I'm betting a beer that it'll be at least ten minutes."

He muttered something rude under his breath and dropped his eyes to his watch. "Fifteen."

"That's a bet."

At the ten minute mark he tipped his watch to me and tapped it, expression turning smug. Thirty seconds later the receptionist told us we could go in, and I had to bite back a laugh. "Beer's on you, Sarge," I whispered.

But I carefully wiped all traces of humor from my face as I entered, though I took a small amount of pleasure in the annoyance that flicked across the mayor's face at the sight of Crawford entering with me. Mayor Peter Fussell was a relative newcomer to the political game. The owner of a local chain of grocery stores, he'd made a run for mayor when the previous officeholder had to step down because of term limits and had won mostly because he'd poured a staggering amount of money into the campaign. In his late forties or so, with a trim build, brown hair, and blue eyes, he had the combination of looks and charm that had most assuming that Peter Fussell would be running for a higher office in the not-so-distant future.

"I requested to meet only with you, Detective Gillian," he said, gruffly. "There's no need to waste Sergeant Crawford's time."

"As her supervisor I'm electing to accompany her to any meeting where ongoing cases might be discussed," Crawford replied, just as gruffly. "Unless, of course, this has nothing to do with anything police related, in which case I'll excuse myself."

The mayor's expression hardened. "Fine. Have a seat then," he said. He paused as we did so, and I had a feeling he was mentally shifting what he'd been planning to say. When he turned the warm smile on me I knew that he'd decided to shift from *hard-ass* to *benevolent leader who merely needs your assistance to make the world a better place.*

"Detective Gillian," he began in tones laden with pure politician, "as I'm sure you're aware, we don't live in a perfect utopia where the good guys always win and the bad guys always pay for their misdeeds. Hence the need for fine officers such as you and Sergeant Crawford here." He paused, waiting for me to do my part and agree with him or nod or something. But I knew this was a game, and I had no desire to play it.

"Sir," I said, "does this have anything to do with the investigation into the attack on Lida Moran, the fact that Ben Moran is her uncle, and the fact that Lake Pearl Bank—of which he is a board member—holds the majority of the loans for the city of Beaulac?" I allowed a hint of impatience to creep into my voice, though I did my best to maintain a polite and pleasant smile.

His warm smile turned tight. "I see you're more into the direct approach, Detective. Very well. To answer your question, yes. Ben Moran has already expressed worry that his niece will suffer consequences for what is clearly a harmless prank that got out of hand. I'd already spoken to the chief about this matter and had thought it settled, but now I'm hearing that you're continuing to harass and annoy members of the band."

Harass and annoy? I resisted the urge to snort in derision and instead merely raised an eyebrow.

His response was to give me an oddly knowing look. "Detective Gillian," he said, voice dripping with what was probably meant to be sympathy and compassion. "I'd hoped that *you* would be more understanding of the mistakes that young people can make. I truly hate to see Lida's future thrown away because of charges related to the incident at the concert. *You of all people* should know that it's possible to turn your life around after a rough start and become a valuable addition to society."

I could feel the blood drain from my face, followed quickly by a white-hot surge of fury. The satisfaction that filled his eyes at my reaction wiped away any doubt that I might have misread what he'd said. How *dare* he attempt to manipulate me by bringing up my past issues with drugs? And how the fuck had he found out? I'd never been arrested, which meant that he'd have had to obtain access to medical records . . .

I started to rise from my chair, breathing harshly. "You—"

A hand clamped onto my arm in an iron vise and nearly slammed me down into the chair. I shot a look at Crawford, ready to yank my arm away from him, but he merely shook his head and held my gaze in a hard stare for several heartbeats.

I let out a long breath, forcing my anger to drain away. The mayor was playing me. The easiest way to get me to back off would be to goad me into doing something that would get me suspended or fired.

Well, fuck him.

Taking another steadying breath, I turned back to the mayor as Crawford slowly released my arm. "Mayor Fussell," I said, smiling so politely I thought my face would crack. "It's heart-warming to know that you have so much sympathy and compassion for our youth. Unfortunately, the attack on Lida Moran took place in New Orleans, which means that you'll need to direct your pressure and influence in that direction if you want it to go away." I took an instant to take pleasure in the annoyance that passed over his face at that bit of info. "Moreover," I continued, "any contact I've had with members of Ether Madhouse has been in the process of a murder investigation. Now then, sir, are you telling me that you want me to back off on that investigation as well?" I gave him an innocently questioning look.

His gaze flicked quickly to Crawford and then back to me, leaving me with an uncomfortable impression that if my sergeant hadn't been in here with me, the mayor *would* have tried to pressure me into doing just that. I filed that unpleasant little nugget away for future examination.

"Of course not," he said after a brief pause. "I had no idea. Though, of course I remain worried for Lida, and I do hope she's not a suspect. Why don't you give me a briefing on the case so that I can reassure Mr. Moran?"

I damn near sprained my eyeballs in my fight to not roll them. "That's not possible, sir," I replied, not adding, *and you know that, you asshat.* "I'm unable to release information on an ongoing case. However, I'll be sure to have our Public Information Officer forward any pertinent press releases to you."

His politician mask slipped just long enough for me to see the hint of desperation in his eyes. *He must be getting a lot of pressure from Moran. Does Moran really have that much influence?*

"I'm the mayor of this city, Detective," he said with a dark scowl, abandoning the pretense of polite conversation. "And I'm done playing games. You'll either have the case file on my desk in an hour, or I'll have your job." He shot a black look to Crawford. "And yours too."

I took a deep, slow breath as the threat hung in the air, oddly surprised to find that my pulse was racing. "Well," I said. I looked over at Crawford. "You good?"

He gave me a stiff nod. "I'm good." He stood and I followed suit, then he pulled his phone out of his pocket and pressed a button on it. "Glad that worked," he said casually, then he gave the mayor a friendly smile. "First time I ever used the voice recorder option on it."

The mayor sat frozen, staring at Crawford's phone, then he swallowed harshly. He looked as if he was about to speak, but I didn't want to hear what he had to say.

"Mayor Fussell, it's been a pleasure talking to you," I said with too-loud cheerfulness. "I'll be sure to take *everything* you said into consideration." I caught Crawford's eye and jerked my head toward the door. He turned and headed out, with me right behind him.

Somehow I managed to *not* turn and flip the mayor off on my way out.

I turned my own recorder off in the elevator, then let out a shaking breath. "Holy shit, am I ever glad you're my sergeant."

He let out a dry laugh as we reached the ground floor and stepped out. "Glad to know I'm appreciated." Then he shook his head. "Though, I gotta be honest, I didn't expect it to go that far. I'm glad we decided to use both phones. Between the two we should have enough recorded to cover our asses."

I fell silent as we crossed the street and headed to the station. "Do you intend to press charges of public intimidation on him?" I asked after a moment. Threatening a police officer's job was a criminal offense in Louisiana, whether you had the power and influence to do anything about it or not.

"No. Not at this time, at least," he replied. "But you should do what you feel is right for you."

I shook my head. "He's an asshole, but he's under pressure from Moran or someone else. I have the recording, which will keep him from coming up with some bullshit to fire us over." I flicked a glance at Crawford. "But did you notice that he never asked who had been murdered?"

He blinked, then gave me an approving smile. "You're right, he didn't. Good catch."

"He's getting pressure, which means I'm doing something right." Sure wished I knew what it was.

We reached the front door of the station, but Crawford paused before opening it, amusement dancing in his eyes. "Kara, I gotta ask. Is there a single official in this city who you haven't killed, arrested, or pissed off?"

I burst out laughing. "Give me time. I'll get to them all, I'm sure!"

Chapter 17

I stayed at the station only long enough to grab the printouts from my earlier Google searches, then took off. I still had an hour before I was supposed to meet Ryan at Adam Taylor's studio, but I needed to get away from people for a little while. Even though the situation with the mayor had been salvaged without the loss of my job, the whole fact that the incident had occurred in the first place still roiled my gut. I'd met the mayor a few times before, and even though he was known to be a hard-ass and a bit of a jerk, I figured he had to be getting some serious pressure to resort to outright threats. So what was Ben Moran's deal? What was his stake in all of this? Maybe I was being overly cynical, but I had a difficult time believing he was driven purely by concern for his niece's welfare.

I drove without any solid idea of where I wanted to go, though after a few minutes I found myself heading for the east end of the lake and Leland Park. The park occupied nearly a mile of the lakefront—a sprawling combination of sports fields, basketball and tennis courts, playgrounds, and picnic areas. It was late enough that school had been out for a couple of hours, and the ball fields were busy with youth football teams engaged in practice scrimmages. I parked near the boat launch and then got out of my car and sat on the hood, letting the warmth of the engine make up for the faint touch of chill in the air. This was the time of year that tricked people into moving to this area. In fall and spring the weather could almost rival southern California's. The winters were mild, with natives complaining any time the temps dipped below thirty, and I could count on one hand the times I'd seen snow here.

Today was one of those days, I decided as I leaned back on my elbows and listened to the distant shrieks of the kids in the playground. For most of the year the weather here was ideal. It was the summers that were nothing short of brutal. *But if I moved north, then I'd have to endure winters,* I reasoned with myself. Not that I could see myself ever moving.

The sound of a whistle pulled my attention to the football fields. The kids practicing on the field closest to me couldn't have been more than seven or eight, wearing huge pads that seemed to swallow them. Parents were scattered along the bleachers. A few were actively watching and cheering, but most seemed to be occupied with books or intent on their cell phones.

Will that ever be me? I frowned at the unexpected thought. I'd certainly wondered before about my chances of finding someone to settle down and have children with. And I'd always dismissed the idea as impractical and most likely impossible. How could I marry someone unless they knew about the demon summoning?

Except that now I had a number of friends who knew . . . and were still my friends. It wasn't out of the realm of possibility that I could meet someone worth settling down with who could handle it. And I was still young. I wasn't even thirty yet. Heck, I knew women who'd had their first kid when they were in their forties.

"Kara? What are you doing here?" A voice jerked me out of my reverie.

I turned to see my aunt standing beside my car, her head cocked in question. "Just chillin'," I said, strangely pleased to see her. "I had a crazy day at work and wanted to take in some fresh air. What are *you* doing here?" To my surprise she was dressed almost normally, in jeans, cowboy boots, and a T-shirt advertising something called Fruity Oaty Bars.

"Carl's nephew plays youth football." She gestured toward a field past the one I'd been watching where preteen kids were running drills. "Carl takes him to practice so that the boy's dad doesn't have to leave work early."

"Carl has relatives?" I blurted without thinking. Then I winced. "Sorry, that was stupid."

But Tessa let out a peal of laughter. "No, I totally understand. Actually, the nephew isn't really his nephew, at least not biologically. Carl grew up in foster homes, and this is the kid of one of his foster brothers."

My curiosity surged, but before I could say anything Tessa shook her head. "I don't know much more about him, sweets. He doesn't like to talk about his childhood." Her expression dimmed. "I get the impression it wasn't pleasant."

I forced back my questions and merely nodded. I'd only spent a couple of months in a foster home after my dad had died and before Tessa had been able to return from Japan. That had been more than enough.

Tessa hitched herself up onto the hood beside me. I shifted to make room. "The last time I was out here was for a crime scene," I said.

"Was that one of the Symbol Man victims?"

I nodded. "That baseball field way over there." I pointed in the general direction. It was empty of players right now. Wrong season for it, I guessed. "It's kinda neat coming out here when it's busy, though. Holy crap, but there're a lot of kids in this city!"

Tessa chuckled. "Scary, isn't it!"

I smiled. "I don't deal with kids very often. I think sometimes I forget they exist." I paused. "Y'know I was just thinking about kids. I mean, me having them someday."

She gave me a look filled with shock and horror. "Are you *pregnant?*"

"No!" I said quickly. "Holy shit, no. I was just thinking about . . . someday."

She relaxed, and I suddenly realized that the intensity of her reaction was most likely due to her fear that I could be pregnant with Rhyzkahl's baby. *Holy Yikes. Would that even be possible?* "Don't worry," I reassured her. "I'm still on the Pill." Even though my social life had always been heartily pathetic, I was prepared and cautious when it came to any thoughts of children. I'd been on the Pill since I was sixteen, at my aunt's encouragement. Okay, *insistence* was probably the better word, though considering the hash I'd made of my teen years I couldn't fault her for it. And even though it had been many years before I'd had my first sexual experience, I still appreciated the frank—and sometimes brutal—talking-to she'd given me about sex and the consequences of unplanned pregnancy.

Tessa patted my hand. "Good to know, sweets. Pregnancy is hard enough with a partner at your side, but going through it on your own is a tough haul that I wouldn't wish on anyone." She straightened and pushed off the hood of the car. "Looks like the practice is finishing up. I'd better go find Carl." And with that she trotted off without another word.

I stared after her, her last words tumbling around in my head like rocks in a dryer. If I hadn't know better, I'd have sworn that Tessa was speaking from personal experience.

Chapter 18

Leaving the park, I allowed my thoughts to explore the implications of what Tessa had said. *I'm leaping to insane conclusions,* I told myself. But . . . were they really all that insane? Tessa had left Beaulac when she was nineteen and had only returned when she'd been asked to become my guardian. That was eleven years. It was more than plausible that Tessa might have had a child during that time.

And in all the time since then, she's never spoken of it. Which either meant there was no baby and I was letting my imagination run wild, or that it was obviously a painful and/or touchy subject, and if she'd wanted me to know about it, she would have told me.

And, if nothing else, Tessa had managed to completely take my mind off of my other stress for a while.

My phone dinged with a text message as I drove, and at the next red light I clicked it to see a text from Roger telling me that the Lake Pearl Bank would have everything ready for me in the morning.

Nice to see at least one thing going right.

Then I gave myself a mental smack. *Watch it, Kara. You're going to jinx yourself again.*

Sound System Studio was situated near the middle of town, in the "gray" area between the well-maintained downtown and the shoddier older sections that had been allowed to fall into disrepair. The studio was housed in a two-story windowless metal building—the kind of prefab construction that can go up in a few weeks and was usually picked as an "after" shot during storm season when a tornado turned it into a freeform sculpture of twisted aluminum. A bright blue sign hung over the door with the name of the studio painted across it in a swirling font, though I noticed that there were a number of pitted marks in the sign, as if someone had been throwing rocks at it. Not too surprising considering the neighborhood. Probably a good thing there were no windows.

Ryan was exiting his car as I pulled in. I checked my watch as I parked, pleased to see that I'd managed to kill an hour exactly.

"Perfect timing," he said as I walked up.

"You had doubts?"

"Never." He grinned. He walked to the door and held it for me, then followed me into a cramped foyer that barely had room for a desk, a chair, and an artificial ficus tree in the corner.

There was no one in the foyer, but we could hear music coming from beyond a door on the far wall. It was unlocked, and so we entered to find ourselves near the back of a room about thirty feet by twenty, though at least half of it was taken up with various music equipment. There were double doors to the right and left—I assumed that the latter set led to the outside judging by the orientation of the room. Against the wall nearest us was a table with a variety of wrapped snacks scattered upon it. Beside the table was a battered white refrigerator, though it was barely recognizable as white since damn near every inch was covered with stickers and magnets from an impressive variety of music groups.

Lida, Michael, and Trey were at the other end of the

room amid their sound equipment, slowly playing something that I suspected was one of their new songs since I didn't recognize it from the concert.

Lida looked much like she did at her house, wearing low-cut jeans and a white tank-top, with only a few piercings and very little makeup. She caught sight of us and gave us a small nod but didn't stop playing. It didn't surprise me that Roger wasn't there. I could hardly blame him after the rough couple of days he'd had. I *was* surprised to hear Michael missing notes. After the third time he fumbled, Lida called a halt.

"I'm sorry, Lida," Michael said, clearly distressed

"It's cool," she replied gently. "It's a new song, and we're all trying to figure out how to make it sound right. That's the whole point of rehearsing, okay? Why don't you go get a Diet Coke or something." He stared morosely at his keyboard, then nodded and stood.

Trey set his instrument aside. "I'll take care of him, Lida. You go talk to the cops."

It was apparently the wrong thing to say. Michael jerked his head up, seeing us for the first time. "Roger didn't do anything wrong!" he announced loudly, features twisted in distress.

"Michael, they know that," Lida said with a tired patience. "Roger isn't in trouble, okay?" She gave us an apologetic look. "Give me a couple of minutes? I need to go take a walk with him and get him settled down."

"Take all the time you need," I replied.

The big man's shoulder's slumped and he allowed himself to be led outside, but not before shooting us another wary look.

Trey blew out his breath as they left. "Wow, the tension around here sucks ass."

"How long has it been like this?" I asked, walking up to him. "Tense, I mean."

He let out a dry bark of laughter. "Since we signed

with the label?" Then he winced and shook his head. "That's not really fair though. I was talking mostly about how things have been since Saturday night."

"Can you tell me again what you saw?" I asked. I'd taken his statement after the incident, but I knew how useful it was to do follow-up interviews to see what was remembered, forgotten, or outright changed.

Trey tugged at the collar of his shirt before dropping down to sit cross-legged on the floor. Of all the band members, he was the one who looked the most different in "regular" clothes. He'd been fairly gothed out at the concert, in a getup similar to what Ryan had been wearing. I was amused to see that Trey was now wearing khaki pants and an oxford-style shirt—again, similar to what Ryan had on.

"I hardly saw anything," Trey said. "The lights went out and something big shoved past me. Then I heard a bunch of screaming and yelling." He toyed with the end of his shoelace. "I stood still since it was so dark, and I didn't want to trip over anything and risk messing up my bass. About a minute later the lights came back on and Roger and Michael were all freaked out, yelling about someone grabbing Lida. Michael took off, so I ran after him. I didn't know what was going on, but right then I figured the best way I could help would be to make sure that Michael didn't get hurt or lost." He grimaced. "I love Michael, but I wanted to throttle him for taking off like that. I'm not supposed to do any running." Then he sighed. "But I can understand why he did. I've never seen anyone closer than those two."

"You're wearing running shoes," Ryan pointed out.

"Yeah, that's because I gotta wear them all the time," Trey replied. "I have plantar fasciitis. The doc told me to lay off the running for a while." He gave a morose sigh that at first made me think he was joking, then I realized he was truly upset about not being able to run. Then again, he had that lean lanky build of someone who probably ran a hundred miles a week without breaking a sweat. And enjoyed it.

Sick.

"And I don't wanna end up like Roger," Trey added, shaking his head.

I frowned. "What do you mean? What happened to Roger?"

"He used to do a lot of running too, coupla years ago." Trey looked at me, tragedy written all over his face. "Then he messed up his feet. He stopped running. Stopped! Never went back to it. Went with the weight training instead." He shuddered. "Man, I can't even imagine."

I stared at him, unable to come up with any sort of response that didn't include the words *Are you fucking kidding me?*

"How have things changed since you signed with the label?" Ryan asked, saving me.

A pained expression flashed across his face. "I don't know. I guess it's not what any of us expected, y'know? I mean, it used to be tons of fun, and now there's a bunch of pressure to earn back the money the label invested in us. And . . . well, it's not that great of a label, to be honest. We should have had a lot more distribution. So now we gotta think about making it big and getting noticed so that when our contract is up we can get signed with someone bigger. Plus, our concert schedule for the coming year is insane. But concerts are where we make money, not CD sales."

Ryan and I exchanged a quick glance at the *getting noticed*. "Has anyone in the band been talking about ways to get noticed?" I asked.

"Well, yeah," he said, lifting a shoulder in a shrug. "I mean we're always trying out new ways to do promo and stuff. Lida busts her hump writing new songs, and doing appearances and interviews. And I put together the website. But Adam's the one who's doing most of the regular promo. He works his ass off, but I think he has a lot riding on us really breaking out."

"Why is that?"

"Times have been tough, y'know? He owns the studio, but his business has been shit lately." Trey's gaze swept the room. "He's been trying to sell it, but no one's interested."

Well, that confirmed what Roger had said.

The side door opened and we all looked over to see Lida coming back in without Michael.

"Is he okay?" Trey asked her with what sounded like genuine concern.

Lida nodded, frustration and fatigue flashing briefly over her face. "I figured it was better to let him sit outside for a bit instead of bringing him back and risk him getting all upset again." She shot us a look of apology and I gave her a slight nod of understanding in response.

Trey stood. "You want me to go sit with him?" She gave him a grateful smile, but then he glanced back at us. "I mean, unless y'all need to talk to me some more."

"No, we're done," I said. "I know how to get in touch with you if I need to talk to you again." I handed him one of my cards. "And feel free to call if you think of anything that might be useful."

He tucked the card into the front pocket of his shirt. "Will do. Thanks." He moved to Lida and gave her a quick, sweet kiss, then strode to the door and left.

Lida let out a soft sigh that sounded like it was tinged with relief. "Trey is so good with Michael. Like his best friend and big brother all rolled into one." She sighed and rubbed her eyes. "Sorry about having to take him outside," she said. "Roger came by earlier and told us about his client, and unfortunately, Michael heard him. He's so sensitive that he gets really upset whenever he hears bad news. It's like he doesn't have the perspective to know that it wasn't someone he was close to." Sadness flickered across her face.

"Could Michael ever live on his own?" Ryan queried gently.

"No way," she said without any hesitation. "And I don't want him to go to a group home or anything like that either. He's my brother," she said, lifting her chin defiantly. "I can take care of him." She sounded defensive.

"Has anyone suggested you do that?" Ryan asked.

Her defiant stance wilted slightly. "Adam suggested it once. As talented as Michael is, Adam worried that the stress of being in the band would be too much for him, especially with our current schedule. And Uncle Ben agreed with him, though he said Michael wouldn't need to go to a home and said he'd hire someone to care for Michael at the house." The frustration returned to her face. "I mean, I know they're worried about me and think that I'm spreading myself too thin . . ." She paused, then rolled her eyes. "Okay, *my uncle* is worried about me. I think Adam's only worried that Michael will have a meltdown or something during a concert." Anger flared in her eyes, but then she took a deep breath and seemed to push it down. "But I could never do that to him. It would kill Michael if he was taken out of the band. He loves it."

"Follow your gut," Ryan advised.

Lida gave him a firm nod. "Yeah, I intend to. Screw the rest of them." She forced a smile onto her face. "Okay, I don't need to be dumping on y'all. Sorry about that. You need to talk to me some more?"

"Yes, if you have the time and don't mind," I said. "Though we mostly came by because we need to speak to Adam."

She frowned. "Adam's been upstairs for hours, working, ever since he came back from his meeting with the label. It's been a crazy day. It took over an hour to get Michael calmed down after Roger told us about Vic." She stepped behind us and snagged a candy bar off the table. "Sorry, I'm starving. It's probably a good thing Roger isn't here. He'd make me do an extra half hour on the bike if he saw me eating this," she said with a weak smile.

"He's your trainer?"

"Well, he sets up workouts for me and gets on my ass about my eating, but he's not officially my trainer or anything."

"Have you ever used the gym at Vic Kerry's office?"

She shook her head. "I didn't even know he had one there."

This next part was going to be more confrontational.

"This whole thing has generated a lot of publicity for you, hasn't it?"

I expected her to get indignant, but to my surprise she merely sighed, looking abruptly exhausted. "I know, and I know that you're wondering if this whole thing was staged. Uncle Ben grilled me hard about it the other day after you left." She met my eyes. "I swear, if it was set up, I had nothing to do with it."

"What about Adam?" Ryan asked.

She rubbed her eyes. "He's awesome. He really is. He knows the business inside and out, and he busts his ass for us."

I leaned forward. "And do you think he'd be capable of setting something like this attack up?"

Lida shook her head emphatically. "He would never do that." But I could see a flicker of doubt in her eyes. She seemed about to say more but then Michael came back into the room, closely followed by Trey.

"It's beginning to rain," Trey said with an apologetic grimace.

"And I'm hungry," Michael announced.

Lida gave a soft sigh. "If you need to talk to Adam, his office is upstairs," she said. "Go through the double doors, take a right at the end of the hall, and his office is at the top of the stairs. I'm sorry, but I need to take Michael home."

"I understand," I said. I watched as she returned to Michael and put her arms around him, speaking softly to him before leading him out.

"I hope she makes it big," Ryan murmured.

I exhaled. "Me too."

He scrubbed a hand through his hair. "All right, let's go see what Mr. Taylor has to add to all of this."

"Let's squeeze him nice and quick," I said, stifling a yawn. "I've already had an insanely long day and Sunday night wore me out. I haven't had a chance to catch up on my sleep yet."

He was silent as we walked to the double doors, but it wasn't until he stiff-armed through them like a tank that I realized he was upset. In the next instant I realized why. *Crap. And what happened Sunday night to wear me out? Or rather, who wore me out.* I sighed inwardly. *Nice move, Kara.*

He strode down the hall, forcing me to nearly run to catch up. Aggravation flared, pushing out the guilt. *The summoning was more exhausting than the sex, damn it.* So much for him being all mature and shit. But my annoyance vanished as a familiar sensation crawled over me. I reached out and grabbed Ryan's arm to stop him.

He whirled, nearly snarling at me, but then he saw my face and went still, giving me a more normal questioning look. I stared at him for a heartbeat, not wanting to believe I'd seen the earlier anger, but the resonance abruptly twined around me, fresh and disturbing. I sucked in my breath and looked away from Ryan as I shifted into othersight. I didn't think that whatever had left it behind was still nearby, but I pulled my gun anyway, relieved to see Ryan following my lead. Together we crept down the hall to the corner.

I took a quick peek, then let out a low curse. At the bottom of the stairs lay Adam Taylor, head twisted at an unnatural angle.

Chapter 19

The angle of Adam Taylor's neck had me fairly convinced that he was dead, but I still stooped and put my fingers to his throat to check for a pulse, while Ryan remained standing with his gun at the ready. I didn't think that the golem was still around, but best to play it safe. The body was faintly cool to the touch, which led me to the unscientific conclusion that he'd been lying there for a couple of hours at least.

I straightened and Ryan gave me a questioning look. I stood still for a moment, sensing. Ryan remained quiet, watching and waiting.

"The resonance feels stronger in that direction," I said softly, indicating the door at the end of the hall.

"That leads outside, to the rear of the building," he replied in a low voice. We moved to the door and opened it cautiously. A light drizzle fell on an empty parking lot. I stepped outside, but the trail of resonance ended at the edge of the lot, and I couldn't see any mundane clues such as tire marks or a conveniently dropped wallet.

"Whoever's controlling the thing must have driven it here," I said, returning inside and holstering my gun. "I doubt it's sophisticated enough to drive itself."

"Does it feel as if the golem was anywhere else in the building?"

I shook my head. "I can't really explain how it feels . . . but it's almost like a slime trail. I can sense it from a few feet away, and it's really obvious where the golem has been." I carefully stepped around Adam's body, then ascended the stairs. I paused when I reached the top. "It came up here," I called down to Ryan. Adam's office door stood open. I peered in and could see that the chair behind the desk was on its side. I stood silent and still for a dozen more heartbeats, assessing, then returned downstairs.

"As far as I can tell," I told him, "the golem came in that door, went upstairs, grabbed Adam out of his chair, and tossed him down the stairs. It might have given Adam's neck an extra twist to be sure he was dead, and then it walked right back out that door, where someone picked it up and took it away."

Ryan's gaze raked over the body and the stairs. "This certainly complicates things."

I crouched again, worrying my lower lip as I took in the feel of the resonance. After a moment Ryan crouched beside me.

"Any luck pinning down what it is?" he asked quietly.

I twitched a shoulder up in a shrug. "I have some theories. But I'm not sure it matters. It doesn't point to who might be controlling it, or how to stop it."

He laid a hand on my shoulder and gave it a gentle squeeze. "Well, then we'll simply have to resort to over-the-top violence."

I laughed and gave him a grateful smile for pulling me free of the funk before I could get into it.

He stood and I followed suit. "I'd better call Zack and fill him in," he said.

"And I need to call my rank." And how was I going to justify to Crawford that I knew this was connected to Vic Kerry's murder? I fought back a sigh. *Deal with that later. For now, follow procedure.*

Fortunately, there was no one else left in the building, which made it easy to secure the scene. Zack arrived about ten minutes later, with Jill pulling up in the crime scene van right behind him.

"You know what I love about working your scenes?" she asked after I filled her in on what I had. "The fact that I do all sorts of work and collect all sorts of evidence, and then I never have to actually process any of it since you then go off and solve the case using your *spooooky* demon powers." She wiggled her fingers at me and made an absurd face.

I had to laugh. "That's so not true, but I *will* say that I highly doubt that the perp in this one left behind any fingerprints."

She wrinkled her nose as she readied her camera. "Well, unfortunately I still have to check for prints, since it'll look pretty bad if I don't."

"And it's always possible that I'm wrong," I added.

"Well, I'm still not gonna waste my time hunting down matches for fingerprints on AFIS until you tell me to." She stepped past me and began photographing the scene. I grinned and stayed out of her way.

Crawford showed up as Jill was finishing up her pictures. He peered down at the crumpled body and then looked back up at me. He opened his mouth to say something then closed it again, clearly conflicted. He flicked a glance around, taking in the people present.

Finally he cleared his throat and returned his focus to me. "I take it you have some reason to believe this wasn't an accident?"

I nodded. Shit. How was I supposed to explain? This one wasn't as easy as saying a dog had been chasing me. "There are some, er, similarities to the Victor Kerry scene, as well as to the attack on Lida Moran in New Orleans."

His inner turmoil was painfully obvious. Even Ryan

and Zack seemed to be aware of it as they stood silently by, carefully pretending to be paying no attention to our conversation.

"Fuck," he muttered under his breath. Then he swept his gaze over the agents. "This is some kind of supernatural-type bullshit, isn't it?"

Ryan gave Crawford a grave nod. "In a way, yes. Our task force often handles cases that fall outside the commonly accepted norm."

Crawford gave a snort. " 'Commonly accepted norm.' I don't fucking believe this." He looked almost relieved, though, as if the fact that Ryan had admitted it helped to prove he hadn't lost his mind.

"Sarge," I began, but he held up his hand to stop me.

"Kara. It . . . it's okay." He still had a pained expression, but he didn't look miserably conflicted anymore. "So, are you some kind of psychic or witch or something?"

I fought the urge to smile. "Not exactly. I . . . um . . . have the ability to see arcane power and can shape it for certain purposes."

He blew out his breath. "Fucking shit, but that explains a lot about you."

I burst out laughing. He looked at me sharply, then joined in a second later. After a few seconds he regained control of himself and looked over at Jill. "And you're part of this *X-Files* crap too?"

She made a rude noise. "Look, just because I hang out with these weird peeps doesn't mean I'm one of them!"

That seemed to relieve Crawford more than anything. "All right. So, what do you really have here, Kara?"

"I have reason to believe that an inanimate creature controlled by supernatural means was involved in the attack on Lida Moran and in the two murders."

I could see him visible struggling to accept the otherworldly aspect to all of this. "Okay," he said slowly, voice perhaps a tiny bit shaky. "What do you do now?"

I spread my hands. "For now, treat it like any other investigation."

Relief filled his eyes. He knew how to handle "any other investigation."

"We have three victims," I continued. "Even though Lida survived going into the river, I'm still counting her as a victim."

"But how is Vic Kerry connected?" Crawford asked.

"Not sure yet," I said. "One theory is that it's possible Roger Peeler was the intended victim of Kerry's murder, since Roger was in the habit of using the workout equipment in Kerry's office." I chewed my lower lip in thought for a few heartbeats.

"That would imply that the band is being targeted," Crawford said, eyes narrowed. He was in his element now that we were talking about more mundane things.

"Yes, but I also found a copy of three NSF checks from Adam Taylor in Kerry's desk. And I also found this." I tugged the paper with the initials out of my notebook and passed it to him. "Roger Peeler confirmed that Kerry loaned him fifteen thousand dollars." I paused. "Or rather, Kerry loaned it to him, and then was nice enough to invest it for him. Plus, Kerry was a real sweet guy and approached Roger with the offer of the loan."

Crawford's expression turned dubious. "Real sweet. You have subpoenas out, I take it?"

"I do for Kerry's info," I said, "but I'll be shocked if I get the return back in less than a week." I couldn't help but scowl, even though I respected the privacy issues that delayed the release of information. "However, Roger went down to the bank and gave them permission to give me full access to his accounts. I'm going down to the bank in the morning to pick up copies. I'll also send out subpoenas for Taylor's financials." Ugh. I was going to be drowning in boring paperwork soon.

"Sounds like you have it covered. And with the bad checks there's a link between Taylor and Kerry," he said.

"Right, but I still have to determine if that link had anything to do with their deaths. I'd like to get a search warrant for Mr. Taylor's house."

"Do it," he agreed. He looked to Ryan. "Would you mind staying here with me while Kara takes care of that?"

"Not at all," Ryan replied. "Do you mind if Agent Garner accompanies Kara on the search warrant?"

"Not at all," Crawford replied.

I turned to leave, then stopped. *Crap.* I pivoted back and caught Crawford's eye, then gave him a narrow-eyed shake of my head.

He responded with a perplexed look. I scowled and gave my head a slight jerk in Ryan's direction, then shook my head again.

Crawford merely looked even more baffled. I rolled my eyes, then marched up to Crawford and took him by the arm to pull him a short distance away from Ryan. "Do *not* say anything about what happened out at the City Towers building to Ryan," I said in a low voice. "Please," I added belatedly.

Crawford made a sour noise. "Go do your damn search warrant."

I gave him a pleading look. "Sarge . . ."

He scowled at me. "I won't say anything. Now would you please get the hell out of here?"

I smiled and clapped him on the shoulder. "Thanks, Sarge!" I jerked my head at a bemused Zack. "C'mon, Surfer Boy," I said. "We're being kicked out."

Ryan turned to Crawford as I walked past. "How long has she been insane?"

"As long as I've known her, Agent Kristoff," Crawford replied with a dramatic sigh.

"I heard that!" I yelled.

The laughter of the two men followed me out.

This was the kind of search warrant that I preferred. Nobody home, no forced entry, and plenty of time to do what we needed to do.

Adam lived on the edge of town, in a bland little subdivision with only about fifty houses in it, all built from what looked to be a wide variety of four different house plans. There were no trees anywhere in the neighborhood, except for some scrawny twigs that had been stuck in the front yard of each house—one per residence. I assumed they were meant to someday grow into trees, but the tallest one I saw was only four feet high. It would be a long time before this subdivision saw anything resembling shade.

Adam's house was a single-story ranch, with brick on the front and vinyl siding on the back and sides. There were no cars in the cracked driveway, and the only concession to landscaping was a raggedly mown lawn and the aforementioned twig.

We'd snagged Adam's keys before heading out to get the search warrant, which meant that we didn't have to break any windows to get in. I drew my gun, then unlocked the door and pushed it open a couple of feet.

"Beaulac Police Department," I called into the silent house. "We're making entry on a search warrant." I was almost positive that Adam lived alone, however that didn't necessarily mean that the house was unoccupied.

The only response was the quiet hum of the refrigerator.

I flicked on the lights, then Zack and I went through the house with guns drawn to be absolutely sure there was nothing lurking. The interior looked about as exciting as the outside of the house. The living room held a dull beige sectional sofa and a flat screen television. The kitchen had dishes in the sink—remnants from breakfast it looked like—but the rest was generally tidy and neat. The bedroom had an overflowing laundry hamper and an unmade bed, but the carpet looked as if it had been vacuumed within the last day or so. There were no surprises waiting for us—no bodies splayed out on the kitchen floor or monsters leaping out of corners. We returned to the foyer and holstered our guns.

"You take the bedroom, I'll take the office?" I suggested.

Zack nodded. "Deal."

Compared to the rest of the house, the office was practically opulent. It looked like a record executive's office ought to look, with pictures of celebrities and framed CD covers on the walls. One of the largest pictures was of Adam and the members of Ether Madhouse standing on the Mississippi River levee with the muddy water behind them. All were grinning, with their arms linked around each other, and I had the feeling it had been taken shortly after they'd landed the deal with Levee 9 Records.

A lovely and large dark oak desk dominated the room, pristine except for one neat stack of papers atop it. There were two leather chairs in front of the desk and a luxuriously padded black leather executive chair behind it. I sat in the executive chair and ran my finger along the desk, then peered at the papers. Pursing my lips in thought, I tugged the middle drawer open.

Well, well . . . "Yo, Zack," I called. "Found something interesting." I pulled the papers out of the drawer and set them on top of the desk.

Zack came into the room. "What's up?"

I pushed the top paper to him. He picked it up and

frowned, then glanced over the other items I'd pulled out.

"Sooo," he drawled, "according to this, Taylor not only posted the threats on the band's website, but also paid some guy named Alvin five hundred dollars to dress all in black and grab Lida off the stage."

"It sure looks that way," I said. "Wow. That was easy. Case closed!"

Zack sat on the edge of the desk. "Awfully careless of him to leave it where it could be so easily found."

I let out a snort. "No shit. Especially in an office that he didn't use very often."

His gaze raked the room. "Right. His laptop is in his bedroom, as well as paperwork concerning gigs for the band. He probably only used this room if he had to meet with a potential client or some such thing."

I set my hands on the arms of the chair. "You wanna hear my theory?"

He grinned. "Do I have a choice?"

"Nope. You're a captive audience," I said with a laugh. "So here's the thing: I do think Adam knew that Lida was going to get grabbed off the stage, because after she was pulled out of the river, he said, 'I never thought it would go this far.' "

Zack nodded. "But obviously someone else was involved too. Someone who wanted to make it look like it was all Adam's idea. And then Adam has an unfortunate tumble down the stairs."

I leaned back in the chair, frowning. "Well, yeah. Someone else was definitely involved since I doubt Adam sicced the thing on himself and then drove it away from the studio. But I'm still wondering if the fact that Adam wrote some bad checks to Vic Kerry has anything to do with either murder." I chewed my lip in thought.

Zack skimmed the paper in his hand again. "If not for your ability to sense the golem, we wouldn't know that there was any possibility of a connection between the two murders." A frown furrowed his brow. "But why not stage Adam's death as a suicide?"

"I don't think the golem is sophisticated enough to do what that would entail. No windows to throw him out of at the studio. Maybe they were hoping it would look like an accident." Damn, but this chair was comfy. I needed to get something like this for my own office.

"Ah. That makes sense. All right, well let's say that the attack on Lida went too far. So maybe Adam started to get cold feet, and the golem was sent after him to keep him quiet."

"That makes sense, especially considering the amount of pressure that Ben Moran's been putting on the department to make it all go away." Then I grimaced. "Except for the murder of Vic who might have been mistaken for Roger, or the fact that Adam wrote bad checks to Vic, or for the fact that Vic might have loaned money to Adam ..." I pinched the bridge of my nose and grimaced. "Here comes the headache."

Zack continued to shuffle through the papers. "Let's focus on one scenario at a time."

"I'm more than willing to go with that for now," I agreed, then had to stifle a yawn. "Okay, I'm dying here. Let's finish this shit up. I've had a helluva full day." I stood and gathered up the papers.

We went through the rest of the house, not finding anything else interesting or incriminating, and nothing that would point us to who the other involved party was. We collected Adam's laptop and filled a box with papers and various documents to look at later, then headed out.

We exited into full night with the moon high in the sky. "I'm afraid to look at my watch," I said with a mock-whimper.

Zack grinned. "Why it's barely eight P.M."

"Liar," I replied as I shoved the box and the laptop into the trunk of my car. "But I appreciate the effort." I slammed the trunk closed. "I think I'm going to start sleeping every other night. This 'regular sleep cycle' thing is for wimps."

"There's a great science fiction series about people who've been genetically engineered to not need sleep," Zack said, looking up at the sky with a slight frown.

"That's what I need!"

A slight smile crossed his face. "The books or the not needing sleep?"

I made a rude noise. "If I didn't need to sleep I might have time to read a book occasionally. I mean, other than for research." He was still looking at the sky, and I followed his gaze. It was a clear night and the moon was almost three quarters full, but I couldn't see anything out of the ordinary. "Whatcha lookin' at?"

He dropped his gaze and shook his head. "Nothing. Just had a strange—"

A sharp cold wind slammed into us, cutting his words off and whipping dirt into our faces. *Good thing I already put the papers in the trunk,* was my first thought, quickly chased by a spasm of fear as the wind died.

That felt like the thing at the City Towers building . . .

"Zack," I gasped, "get in the car. There's something—"

He grabbed me by my arm, almost yanking it out of its socket as he took off at a run, near dragging me along. "No! Car's not safe. You need to get as far away as possible before it forms!"

I struggled to keep up with him, and only his fierce grip on my arm kept me from sprawling face first. "Before what forms?" I managed to ask. I expected him to veer between the houses, but he kept to the street. Apparently distance was more important than cover.

"It's a portal," he said through clenched teeth, pulling me along even though I was running as fast as I could—

which, admittedly, wasn't all that fast. "Can't you feel it? It's a summoning!"

I stumbled as his words penetrated, then my shock tripled as Zack hoisted me up onto his shoulders in a fireman's carry. "Hang on!" he ordered. And then *ran.*

I'd only *thought* he'd been running before. I clung for dear life as he nearly doubled his pace, sprinting flat-out like an Olympian, and as if he didn't have my not-so-light weight draped across his shoulders. Holy shit, the man had some seriously inhuman speed.

Oh, shit. The realization slammed home. *Zack's not human.*

A few seconds later—though it felt like a few hours—he slowed and stopped, then set me on my feet. He held me carefully to make sure I was steady before releasing me, then stepped back. He didn't say anything. He seemed to know what I was going to say.

Too bad *I* didn't know what I was going to say. "Are we far enough away?" I finally asked.

Zack nodded, eyes steady on me. He looked oddly expectant and bereft at the same time.

I swallowed and took a deep breath. "How did you know it was a summoning?"

"I've felt them before," he answered, voice low.

Them. More than one. "Was it directed at me or you?"

"I have no way to know that," he said, still terribly calm and quiet.

"If you were to guess," I prompted.

"I would guess that it was directed at you," he said with a slight nod, as if to congratulate me on the handling of the question.

A summoning of me. Someone from the demon realm was trying to pull me through a portal, the same way I pulled demons into this world. My knees wanted to shake at everything that implied, but I forced the panic down with every ounce of control I had and took another deep breath. "Are you human?" My voice cracked, but I didn't care.

He closed his eyes, naked pain on his face. "I cannot answer that."

"Can't or won't?"

"Both," he replied in little more than a whisper. "I'm bound by oath."

"You're a demon," I breathed. He didn't move or answer, but I didn't need him to. *What kind of demon can look like a human?* I'd never heard of a demon being able to shapeshift. Then again, there was a lot I didn't know about the demonkind.

"Is Ryan a demon?" I squeaked.

He opened his eyes and met my gaze. "No," he said, voice soft but firm. Relief swirled through me and for an instant I thought I saw a flash of pity in Zack's eyes, but then he looked away.

"Is he a summoner?" I was more than willing to keep asking questions as long as Zack would keep answering them, especially since it kept me from thinking about the extremely scary thought of someone trying to summon me.

He hesitated for so long I began to think he wasn't going to answer. "He has the ability to open a portal," he finally said, voice very low.

I could feel a knot in my chest relax ever so slightly. A summoner, though perhaps one who'd never been trained in the art. "The demons hate him," I persisted. "They call him a *kiraknikahl*. Why? What did he do?"

"I cannot say," Zack repeated, voice tight and pained. "Only that his punishment was dire. And just."

I took a step closer to Zack. "Please. I want to help him. He's my best friend."

Zack met my eyes. "I know. It's why I could risk revealing myself to save you from being drawn through the portal."

The way he phrased that struck me as strange, but before I could pursue it he put his hands on my shoulders. "Kara, I know this pains you deeply, but I am oathbound. I cannot tell you more, either about Ryan or about me."

I gave a shaky nod of understanding—even though I didn't. "Now you're even talking like a demon," I said in a lame attempt to find a shred of humor.

To my relief he grinned and slouched. "Sorry. Better?"

I mustered a smile. "Much." I glanced around. "How far are we from the car? Is it safe to go back?"

"We're a little over a half-mile away, and yes, it should be safe to go back. If you'd like I can run back and get the car and come get you."

"No!" I said quickly. "I'll walk it." Yeah, I was a cop, but that didn't mean I couldn't be completely freaked out and not want to be left alone.

He seemed to understand. "Nice night for a walk at least."

We stayed silent for most of the way back, though my thoughts were hideously turbulent.

"Does Ryan know?" I asked when the cars were in sight. "I mean, about you . . ."

"He is unaware," Zack replied. The he stopped and turned to me, expression bleak and worried. "He is unaware of many things. It is for the best. You must trust me in this." He paused. "Kara, you need to tell Lord Rhyzkahl of this incident the next time you summon him."

I scrubbed my hand over my face, suddenly feeling horribly defeated. I didn't want to have to run to the demonic lord for help and protection. Not when it was most likely *because* of him that I needed it in the first place. But I also knew that not running to him would be unbearably stupid. "I can't tonight. I'm exhausted." And shaken and stressed. Attempting to open a portal in this state of mind and at this energy level would be colossally stupid and most likely deadly. "I'll have to try tomorrow."

He began to nod then paused, brow furrowing in confusion. His gaze snapped up to the moon.

"Gods above and below," he whispered. "I am a blind fool. I knew you had summoned Skalz when the moon was but half full, yet I had assumed—" He bit off whatever he was going to say, then took a steadying breath as he shifted his gaze back to me. "But you've been summoning the demonic lord—no simple task, even with him amenable." Worry darkened his eyes. "You've found a way to store potency. No wonder you're a target."

Even though I'd already considered this, I still felt cold at hearing it from Zack. "It's not perfect," I said, feeling strangely defensive. "I mean, I couldn't summon an unwilling demonic lord or anything."

For an instant Zack looked as if he wanted to debate the matter with me, but then he seemed to take note of how close I was to totally losing it. "Let's get out of here," he said with a gentle smile. "Go home and get some sleep. There's nothing to be done now anyway." He draped an arm companionably over my shoulder and guided me to the driver's side door of my car.

I scraped together a smile for him. "Right. Um, thanks. For . . . everything."

Worry darkened his eyes, but he returned my smile and nodded. Then he turned and walked to his own car without another word.

Chapter 20

I stopped at the first Kwik-E Mart I saw. I was unsettled, freaked out, and still trying to process the mountain of shit that had just been dropped on me. I needed serious fortification for that.

Two carloads of teenagers pulled into the parking lot as I entered the store. I grabbed potato chips and chocolate, then headed back to the freezer to get the last ingredient for my comfort party. A kid who couldn't have been more than fifteen yanked open the door of the beer cooler and pulled out a six-pack, then froze as I gave him a black glare. His gaze flicked to my badge and gun, then he replaced the six-pack with a sheepish grin.

"Whoops! Thought that was the Diet Coke," he said, grin turning cheeky.

"Next door down," I said, doing my best to remain gruff.

His eyes dropped to the stash of junk food in my arms. "Whoa, someone's having a rough night."

I scowled as I retrieved a pint of cookie dough ice cream from the freezer. "You have no idea," I grumbled as I headed to the counter. Oh, well. At least I wasn't carrying donuts.

* * *

I lingered in the store until the kids left, even though I knew that if they really wanted to get booze they would. I'd managed to get my hands on plenty of contraband in my youth without too much trouble. But at least this one night would perhaps be alcohol-free for them.

I sighed and pulled out of the parking lot. The morose turnings of my thoughts were about to enter a death spiral at this rate. *Maybe Jill's still awake?* I glanced at the dashboard clock. Midnight. I sighed. Probably not. But I was right by her house. I could always check and see if any lights were on. And if there were, I had plenty of offerings in the bag beside me.

Cheered slightly by the thought of being able to unload on someone, I slowed as I approached her house. A whisper of relief stole through me as I saw that a light was on upstairs, in her bedroom. *Cool.* I thought with a smile. *I can bribe my way in with ice cream and . . .*

My smile faded as I suddenly took note of the car parked in the driveway next to her crime scene van. A dark Crown Victoria with public plates and an antenna farm on the back . . .

I accelerated past her house, thick knot suddenly making it hard to swallow or breathe. *Stop it. Be happy* for *her, for them,* I railed at myself without success. *Ryan and Jill are your best friends.*

I tore open the chocolate and took a big bite, then forced myself to see reason. I was being unbearably stupid. Lots of cops had unmarked cars. It could be anyone. Hell, even Cory Crawford drove an unmarked Crown Vic.

I almost snorted chocolate down the wrong tube at that thought, and in fact started coughing so hard I had to pull over. I managed to get the coughing under control, but by then I was laughing so hard at the image of Crawford and Jill together that tears ran down my face.

And then all of the events of the day flooded back in and I found myself crying for real. I clung to the steering wheel as if it was a lifeline, resting my forehead on it as I indulged in a few badly needed minutes of emotional release.

I finally lifted my head and took a deep breath, then continued on home.

But not before ripping the chips open.

By the time I made it to my house I'd managed to consume the chocolate and the chips, and my funk had been replaced by a queasiness in my belly. I shoved the ice cream into my freezer, then headed down to my basement.

I need to talk to Rhyzkahl, I told myself. It had nothing to do with a desperate need for comfort right now. Really.

Crouching by the partially full storage diagram, I took several settling breaths, then attempted to draw potency into it. But attempt was the correct word, because I couldn't draw anything. I was too unsettled and far too exhausted, and the power seemed to slip out of my control like an oiled eel.

I continued to try to pull power for at least fifteen minutes, then finally gave up and collapsed in a sweating and shaking heap in the chair by the fireplace. *And if I'd been attempting to open a portal, I'd be dead now,* I thought as fear and nausea twined in my gut. Even if I'd had power at my disposal, it would have been stupid to try to perform a summoning.

I crawled back upstairs, literally so for the last few steps, then stumbled to the bathroom and threw up the chocolate and chips. I knelt on the bathroom floor, head pounding as I fought the urge to cry. I'd done enough of that today.

I'm safe here, I told myself as I stumbled to my bedroom. *My house is warded and protected against living creatures and arcane power.*

But even as exhausted as I was, it was still a long time before I could get to sleep.

Chapter 21

I woke up feeling stupidly hungover—hardly fair since I'd thrown up all of the bad stuff I'd eaten. I felt marginally better after coffee, which restored a small measure of my faith in the universe. If coffee had failed me, I'd have been sorely tempted to go right back to bed and never get up again. But two cups of coffee and a toasted bagel later, I felt almost ready to face the world. *Bury myself in work* was part of my plan for the day. The other part was to try and forget about summonings and relationships and anything else that was stress inducing.

I had a feeling I was going to have more success with the first portion.

My first stop of the day was the crime lab to drop off the laptop we'd seized at Adam Taylor's house and to beg, plead, and whine to have it bumped to the top of the queue for forensic examination. As much as I itched to fire it up and see what files were on it, I knew that was a perfect way to destroy evidence. I wasn't a whiz at computers by any stretch, but I'd attended plenty of training sessions where it had been drilled into our thick little heads that doing anything to a computer—even turning it on—altered the data on it and could jeopardize the integrity of evidence.

Jill was in the front office of the crime lab when I entered. She was hunched over a table against the wall, peering through a fingerprint viewer at a latent print card. She glanced up at the sound of the door.

"Heya, chick!" she said with a broad smile. "You slumming?"

Curiosity about her visitor last night surged, but I smacked it down. I wasn't going to risk my friendship with Jill over *a guy*. Even if there was the slightest chance that it could be Ryan. Which it wasn't. I was sure of that. I was.

I forced myself to veer away from any thoughts related to Ryan. Last night's incident with Zack was still far too fresh in my mind, and thinking too hard about Ryan or what the hell he was being punished for, or the insane possibility that he could be seeing Jill, would easily tip me right over the edge. *Bury myself in work. Really, it's so much healthier, right?*

I gave Jill a teasing smile. "I figured I'd watch you pretend to work," I replied.

She rolled her eyes. "Riiiight. Because I'm merely killing time doing the work of three techs." She snorted and pushed the stack of fingerprint cards away from her. "One of these days I'm gonna go blind from looking at that crap. You know, most *real* departments have crime labs where people actually specialize in one area, instead of having to know how to do everything."

"Obviously, your rank recognizes your superior intelligence and wants to make sure you remain suitably challenged."

She made a hacking noise. "So, as much as I want to believe that you merely want to bask in my presence, I'm willing to bet that you need my help with something?"

"I love basking in your presence. But actually I'm here to drop this off for examination." I lifted the laptop case. "And, to find out if I can get it examined soooon?" I gave her a puppy-dog-eyes hopeful look.

She drew back in mock fear. "Stop making that face and I'll do anything you ask!"

I laughed. "Really? Cool!"

"Don't push it," she warned, eyes flashing with humor. "As it so happens, I convinced our resident nerd to run Mr. Kerry's laptop yesterday, so there's a very good chance he'll have something to show you today."

"I knew there was a reason I was friends with you!" I said.

"Nah, you love me for the running," she retorted. "C'mon, I'll take you to the computer lab."

She swiped her access card at the reader by the main lab door, and I dutifully followed her through. It didn't take long for me to be grateful for her role as a tour guide as we made our way through the winding corridors. We finally ended up on the second floor at the end of a long hallway, in front of a door with a sign taped to it with the dire warning, "Do NOT walk in to this lab without knocking first! Contraband material present. Knock first!"

"Most of what he does is search computers for child pornography," she explained, gesturing at the sign. She made a face which I echoed.

Jill knocked. I could hear movement inside, and then about half a minute later the door was pulled open by a man slightly taller than me with sandy blond hair and bright green eyes behind wire-rimmed glasses. He looked like he was in his mid-twenties, and he was slender to the point of being skinny, but even with all of the stereotypical physical attributes nailed, he somehow didn't look at all like a nerd.

He stood in the doorway as if guarding the gates of

hell. "Jill," he said, expression grave, "I've told you before that I simply *cannot* make any more porn DVDs for you."

Jill laughed and punched him lightly in the chest. "You are such an ass. I don't need your porn, I have plenty of my own. This is Kara Gillian. She's handling the Victor Kerry murder, and she has another computer for you as well. Kara, this is Brad, our computer forensics expert."

"Nice to meet you, Kara," he said, rubbing his chest. "I usually break out the pocket protector and taped-up glasses for newcomers, but you caught me out." He stepped back. "Come on in. Watch your step. There's crap and wires everywhere."

Everywhere was an understatement. The room was crowded with enough computer equipment that it looked as if he could be directing a space shuttle launch. It was almost as bad as my aunt's library, though with computers instead of books.

"I finished the laptop yesterday," he continued, "and pulled off copies of the files I figured you'd be most interested in—email, documents, spreadsheets, financial programs, that sort of thing." He handed me a CD in a plastic holder with the case number carefully printed on the front.

"That's fantastic," I said fervently. "I really appreciate you getting to it so quickly."

"Murders always take priority," he explained with a shrug. "Only thing that trumps them is missing kids." A pained expression flitted briefly across his face. "Anyway, I have the image of the hard drive, so if you think you need anything else, like Internet history, images, that sort of thing, let me know and I'll pull it out for you."

I cocked my head. "Internet history . . . you mean like what websites were visited?"

"That's it. Can even tell you how long they stayed

at each website and whether they typed the URL in or clicked on a link."

"So, if I think someone's been on my computer at home, I can find out what they did on it?"

"Sure can," he replied. "Though if you're worried about it happening again, you could always put a spy program on there that'll record everything that's done on the computer."

"I may get back to you on that spy program," I said. I could see Jill giving me a narrow-eyed look, and I could tell she'd figured out who I thought had been on my computer. It wasn't as if there were a lot of suspects. She knew how few people were allowed into my house. "Is there a way to find out the Internet history without going through all of this?" I gestured at the mass of equipment.

He leaned against the worktable and crossed his arms. "Uh-huh. It's not tough to do if they haven't cleared the cache. What kind of computer do you have?"

I hesitated. "You're going to laugh at me if I say 'a black one' aren't you."

Jill snickered but Brad managed to keep a straight face. "Not at all. I'll merely post it all over the Internet."

"Oh, well, that's all right then," I said with a roll of my eyes.

He grinned. "Okay, well is it a PC or a Mac?"

"PC. And I bought it about a year ago."

He turned and rummaged for paper and pen, then peppered me with a few more questions as he scribbled quickly. "Here," he said, passing the paper to me. "Instructions that even a non-geek should be able to follow."

"I owe you one," I said, deeply pleased. I tucked the instructions into my notebook and then lifted the laptop case. "Now I'm going to push your good will even farther. How long would it take you to examine this one?"

"Dunno. Let's see what we're up against." He took the case from me and slid the laptop from it, then flipped it over. A tiny screwdriver appeared in his hand, and a few seconds later he'd removed what I assumed was the hard drive. He pivoted to the table against the wall and hooked the drive into a gadget connected to one of the computers, then clicked a few buttons on the screen with the mouse. A gray box appeared on the screen with rapidly scrolling numbers. I waited patiently while he peered at the screen.

After less than a minute he straightened. "This won't take long at all."

"Great!" I said. "So you could finish it today perhaps?"

He shook his head. "I'm done now."

I looked at him blankly.

"It's been wiped," he said. "That drive is as clean as a whistle."

Chapter 22

After leaving the crime lab I headed to the main branch of Lake Pearl Bank, pausing only to zip through the drive-thru at Taco Hut in a carefully orchestrated effort to undo every bit of last night's unintended purge. I scarfed down two burritos while I drove, musing on the various revelations. Brad had gone on to explain that it was ridiculously easy to wipe a drive with the right kind of software, and that such programs were easily obtained online, with no special expertise needed.

So, if Adam Taylor and Vic Kerry were murdered for the same reason—whatever that was—why wasn't Kerry's computer wiped as well? Maybe the murderer didn't expect it to be pegged as a homicide. Or, since Vic Kerry was actually killed several days ago, perhaps the murderer hadn't yet realized that Adam needed to be killed too. *Or perhaps their murders really were for completely different reasons.* I grimaced. I had an ugly feeling I was going to be up late tonight looking at financial information. Woo boy.

As promised, the bank had copies of all Roger's financial information ready for me. The woman at the service desk smiled cheerily as she passed it over, chirping a "Have a nice day!" at me as I took the thick envelope from her. I thanked her in an equally chirpy tone and began to leave, then paused, looking past the woman at a sign on the wall behind her.

We're getting a new look! New name, new benefits, same wonderful service! Lake Pearl Bank will soon be Southern Regional National Bank of Louisiana!

"The bank is being bought out?" I asked her.

Her smile increased in radiance. "That's right! It's a terrific opportunity for our customers! SRNBL has branches all over, and we'll now be able to provide even more quality service for this community!"

I was slightly intimidated at how Very! Happy! She! Was! About! It!

I thanked her again and left. *Ben Moran has to be pleased about that,* I thought as I continued to the station. That would increase his status considerably.

Crawford's office door was open when I arrived, so I stuck my head in. He gave me a questioning look, then I realized that there was someone in the chair in front of the desk.

"Whoops. Sorry, Sarge, I'll get up with you in a bit," I said, then blinked as Detective Marco Knight turned to give me a smile.

"Oh, hey, how's it going?" I said. Then frowned. "What are you doing here?"

Knight chuckled. "Nice to see you, too."

Yeah, that had been real friendly. "Sorry. You took me by surprise. You're a long way from New Orleans." I paused. "So, what are you doing here?"

Crawford sighed and shook his head. "This is why she's not our public relations officer."

Somehow I resisted the urge to give Crawford the finger.

"Lida Moran filed a request to drop the investigation into her attack yesterday, but then I saw that her manager had died." Knight gave me a shrug, eyes on me. "I hate it when people try to drop cases after I've put work into them. Especially when there's a chance that it was a bullshit case to begin with."

I snorted and leaned up against the door frame. "Aw, where's your trust in human nature?"

"That died a long time ago," he said.

"Well, actually the whole thing may be a lot more complicated than a bullshit publicity stunt," I told Knight. "I have two murders, and I'm convinced they're connected, but I haven't pinned down the link yet."

"What makes you think they're connected?" Marco asked.

Crawford cleared his throat and flicked a glance from me to the door.

I took the hint and entered fully, closing the door behind me. "The thing that threw Lida in the river was a golem, or something similar," I explained in a low voice. "I could feel a weird resonance from it, and I felt that same resonance at the crime scenes for both of these victims. Plus, our pathologist said that whoever killed Vic Kerry was 'strong as shit' since he apparently crushed Kerry's neck." I flicked a quick glance at Crawford to see how he was handling this, but he merely looked slightly pained. It was progress.

Knight let out a low whistle. "So, how do you kill this golem thing?"

I had to shrug helplessly. "I'm not sure, mostly because I'm not really certain what it is. I'm only calling it a golem because it's easier to say than 'arcane construct', but it really doesn't quite fit with the stuff about the golems of legend. I didn't see any letters on its forehead, and it seems a bit too . . . nimble for that sort of thing." I shrugged again. "Not that I'm any sort of expert. My current theory is that maybe it's some sort of earth elemental that's being controlled and directed." I sighed. "And even that's a wild guess at best. I don't know a damn thing about elementals."

Crawford frowned. "Is there anything wrong with just shooting the ever-living shit out of the damn thing?"

I grinned. "Not as far as I know. Extreme violence, for the win!"

Crawford's phone rang, delaying any further speculation on the best way to destroy a creature I knew next to nothing about. He answered the phone, listened intently to the caller with a deepening frown, then gave me a penetrating look that didn't give me a warm fuzzy feeling. He muttered a thanks to the caller and hung up.

"Roger Peeler was found dead near his apartment," he said, voice tight. "It supposedly looks like an accidental death. A fall into a drainage culvert."

"Shit," I breathed. I knew it was no accident. Guilt rose in a choking wave. *I should have seen this coming. I should have done more to warn him, protect him.*

"It's not your fault, Kara," Knight murmured. "You don't even know what the connection is. How were you supposed to know for certain he was in danger? And you did warn him, didn't you?"

I scrubbed at my face, fiercely controlling the sudden desire to cry. "Yeah," I said hollowly. "I warned him." I shook my head. "Fuck. It *has* to have something to do with the money."

"You'll find it," Crawford stated so firmly that I had to smile a bit at his confidence in me. I only hoped it wasn't misplaced. "Now go," he said. "Get your ass out to the scene."

"Mind if I tag along?" Knight said.

"I don't mind," I replied, secretly relieved to have the company. "As long as it's okay with Sarge."

Crawford nodded. "Fine with me. I'll meet you out there as soon as I let the various rank know what's going on."

I exited Crawford's office and headed to the door, still trying to shed the clinging guilt.

"Yo, Kara."

I turned back to see who had called my name, surprised to see Pellini standing about twenty feet down the hall, frantically gesturing me over. I frowned, then glanced at Knight.

"Gimme a sec," I said. He tilted his head in acknowledgment, and I walked toward Pellini. He looked oddly agitated, which sent my natural distrust and suspicion into full alert.

"I need to talk to you before you leave," he said in an urgent whisper, gesturing again, this time to the copy room. "In private."

I scowled. "Pellini, if this is some kind of bullshit stunt—"

He actually looked pained. "It's not. I just need to talk to you. I swear I'm not pulling anything."

I gave him my best "I don't trust you farther than I can throw you" look, but went ahead and stepped into the copy room. He came in behind me and shut the door while I regarded him with narrowed eyes, but to my surprise his face held nothing but something that looked an awful lot like concern.

"What's up, Pellini?"

He licked his lips in a strange show of nervousness. "That guy you're with. How do you know him?"

"You mean Detective Knight? He's on the task force."

Pellini shifted uncomfortably from foot to foot. "Look, I know you and I have never really clicked," he said in a low urgent voice while I tried to keep my eyebrows from climbing up to my hairline. Clicked? That was putting it mildly. "But I gotta warn you about that guy. About Knight."

My bullshit defenses were in high gear at this point. "Go on."

"He's *weird*," Pellini said. "Seriously strange shit." He

paused. "I mean, you're weird too, but your weirdness is kinda entertaining, but his is seriously fucking creepy." He shuddered while I stared at him, at a complete loss for words. I was an *entertaining* weird?

"What ..." I tried. "Um ..." Nope. Couldn't think of a single coherent response.

"He *knows* shit," Pellini continued. "I worked with him at NOPD, and ..." He shook his head. "I know this sounds crazy, but I'm telling you, don't hang out with him too much. Trust me on this."

"Trust you on this," I echoed, unable to keep the disbelief out of my voice.

He looked briefly chagrined. "Yeah. I swear I'm not fucking with you. I've just ... well, I've seen him fuck people up bad, telling them things ..." He trailed off and scrubbed a hand over his face, then took a deep breath. "I know you got no reason to believe me or trust me. But, uh, I kinda get the feeling you got a lot of secrets. I'm just sayin' that sometimes secrets don't stay so secret around that guy."

"Okay," I managed after several heartbeats. "Why are you telling me this? I mean ... why do you give a fuck about me and ... my secrets."

For a second he looked puzzled at the question. "'Cuz you're a cop."

"So is Knight," I pointed out.

He frowned. "But I work with *you*," he said as if it was the most obvious thing in the world. "I'm not gonna let someone from outside fuck with a teammate."

"Oh. Right," I said, feeling as if the world was about to tilt and toss me off. "Then I, uh, appreciate the warning."

He gave me a jerky nod, looking almost relieved, as if he'd gotten something off his chest. Then he turned and yanked the door open and walked away without another word.

I stared at the open door for several heartbeats, then finally shook myself back to some semblance of reality.

"My life," I muttered to myself as I exited the copy room and returned to the waiting Knight. "It is never dull."

Chapter 23

Marco and I took separate cars to the scene, which was good since I needed some quiet to sort things out and regain my mental balance. Not only was I upset about Roger, but the strange conversation with Pellini had thrown me completely for a loop. I was far more stunned at the fact that Pellini would bother giving me any sort of warning than at the revelation that Knight was "weird." And I had absolutely no reason to believe that Pellini was being anything but sincere. In a way it was a bit comforting to know that I wasn't the only one who had the capacity to be unnerved by Knight at times. Not to mention I'd been braced for a confrontation with Pellini and I wasn't about to complain that it hadn't materialized. At this point, though, I'd spent enough time with Knight that, if he really was able to discern thoughts or secrets or whatever, he'd have a head full of them by now.

But I couldn't help but be stupidly warmed by the fact that—at least in this—Pellini had my back.

Who'da thunk it?

The emergency vehicles were clustered along the road a short distance past the apartment complex. I found a place to park behind an ambulance, then walked up to where a knot of people stood about a hundred yards from the road, on the edge of a drainage ditch. Marco dawdled a ways behind but I didn't worry about him. He seemed to be the type who preferred to observe from a distance as much as possible, which was fine with me, especially since I had the unerring feeling that he totally had my back. It was a comforting feeling, I realized. I'd gone for so long in my life without having anyone on "my side" other than my aunt. And the demons, of course, though any sort of dealings with demons came with its own price. So, yes, I was bemused at the whole concept of having a circle of friends and allies.

I really am *a dork, aren't I?*

Scott Glassman turned as I approached and gave me a nod and a slight smile. I'd worked on the same team with Scott back when I was a road cop. Bald and stout, he looked and acted like a hick, but he was a sharp and savvy cop with a gift for putting people at ease. He was a sergeant now, as well as a training officer, which I thought was an excellent use of his talents. With him was an officer I didn't recognize. Dark-skinned with angular features that reminded me deliciously of Denzel Washington, he stood almost a head taller than Scott. Probably his trainee, I realized.

"Looks like you're It," Scott said. "Thought it was an accident at first. Maybe the guy went running while it was still dark, decided to cut across the grass, then tripped and fell into the ditch, hit his head, and drowned."

I started to shake my head, but he held up his hand. "But it ain't no accident," he said firmly.

"What makes you say that?" I asked.

He gestured downward and I peered into the ditch. It was a decent six-foot drop down to the bottom where Roger Peeler lay, faceup, with mud streaked across his face and torso. The lower half of his body was still in the water, which didn't look to be more than a foot deep and only about three feet across at its widest spot.

"Dunno if you can see it from up here," he said, "but there's some blood on the back and side of his head."

I nodded. "I see it." Now I was interested to see where he was going with this. I had an enormous amount of respect for Scott and his experience. He'd have been a shitty detective, but he was one of the best street cops I'd ever known.

"Saw something like it on a body a buncha years back," he told me, tone still as conversational as if we'd been talking about whether the Saints would win the Super Bowl again this year. "Guy got jumped in the bathroom at Rosie's Roadhouse and after he got a good beatdown they shoved his head into the john and drowned his ass."

I had to shudder. I'd been in the women's bathroom at Rosie's before and had been completely grossed out. I doubted that the men's room was any classier.

"Dude put up a fight," Scott said, "but whoever was holding him had a solid grip. So solid that his scalp tore a bit during the struggle."

I breathed a curse, my eyes on the body of Roger. "Same thing here, right?" I asked. Scott nodded. "I told him to be careful," I muttered. "I told him to not go anywhere by himself."

"Then he shoulda listened to you better," Scott replied with a scowl. Then he shook his head. "But I know it's gonna eat you up for a while. I get it."

I gave him a small smile. This was why he was one of my favorite people. "Thanks, Scott. So, can you give me the gist?"

He jerked a thumb toward the other officer. "I'll let Gordon do the honors. He's my latest trainee, and I'm actually *not* worried that he's going to shoot me by accident. Can you believe it? We might have a keeper here!"

Officer Gordon gave me an amused smile and extended a hand. "Tracy Gordon. Pleasure to meet you,

Detective. Sergeant Glassman says you're not clueless, which I understand is one of his highest compliments."

I gave a low laugh and shook his hand. He had a lovely rich baritone that I could have listened to all day. "I have him thoroughly snowed. Good to meet you."

He winked, then released my hand and flipped open his notebook. "A Ms. Jeanne Henry, white female, forty-three years old, was out walking her dog at approximately oh-nine-thirty. Her dog, Scooper, a three-year-old Labradoodle, began to pull at the leash and bark and led her to this point where she saw the victim facedown in the ditch."

"I'm sorry," I interrupted. "What the hell is a Labradoodle, and how did you know it was three years old?" I asked, mildly incredulous.

His lips twitched. "A Labradoodle is a cross between a Labrador and a Poodle. I asked Ms. Henry how old the dog was—"

Scott interrupted with a snort. "No, Kara, I wish you could have seen this. Gordon here is the smoothest of the smooth talkers. This lady was spilling everything she knew about everything. In another couple minutes he coulda convinced her to give up her account numbers and passwords!"

Officer Gordon merely smiled and dropped his eyes back to his notebook. "Ms. Henry advised that she is an ER nurse, and that as soon as she saw the victim she climbed down and pulled him out of the water and attempted to resuscitate. However, she realized fairly quickly that rigor had begun to set in and ceased her resuscitation attempt. At this time she dialed nine-one-one on her cell phone and notified our agency. EMS responded at oh-nine-forty-seven and verified death. Sergeant Glassman and I arrived at oh-nine-fifty-four and secured the scene."

I shot a look to Scott. "What do you want to bet . . . a

year and a half before he's recruited to come to Investigations?"

"If that!" he replied sourly.

I gave Officer Gordon a nod. "You have contact info for the witness?"

In response he flipped to the next page in his little notebook and pulled a sheet out and handed it to me. On it was everything I could ever want to know about the witness and how to contact her, including home phone, cell phone, work phone, email, place of employment, and her work hours.

"I have no words," I stated. Holy shit, but I wanted a dozen more like him on the road.

I tucked the page into my notebook, then turned back to the ditch, taking in what I could of the scene. The bank of the ditch had numerous boot marks and shoe impressions, many of them probably from EMS when they'd run an EKG strip to confirm death. But I wasn't looking for footprints. Even without shifting into othersight the distinctive resonance hummed through me. The golem had done this.

"Has this been photographed?" I asked.

"Gordon here took pics," Scott said with a nod toward the other officer. "I called out the lab, but I figured we should get some pics before everyone and their brother got to traipsing around down there."

"And that's why you're the best," I said fervently.

He snorted. "Words mean nothing to me. Buy me a beer later."

"I'll do that." I gave him a friendly clout on the shoulder, then moved to where the majority of the scuff marks were and began to clamber down into the ditch. I wanted to get as much of a feel of the resonance as possible, and since some pics had already been taken I didn't feel too guilty for possibly disturbing evidence. *Besides, I doubt the golem was wearing shoes.*

Miraculously, I managed to reach the bottom without tripping and doing a face-plant into the water. I crouched beside Roger's body as the spasm of guilt tightened my chest again. Should I have done more to warn him that he could be in danger? But what else could I have done? *Something. Anything.*

I sighed and shifted into othersight, confirming what I'd felt from the top. I looked across the ditch. From my crouched position I could see gouges in the opposite bank. *He tried to climb out and was pulled back down.* I let my gaze travel over the body. He was wearing his Magnolia Fitness Center T-shirt with TRAINER on the chest, long athletic pants, and sneakers—on his way to work. *He came out of his apartment and went to his car,* I mused, *then saw the golem, took off running.* That would explain why he was so far away from the complex. But the golem could be fast. I'd seen that for myself. And Roger hadn't been running in a while, so he probably wasn't as fast as he might have once been. *It was dark and maybe Roger didn't see the ditch, or perhaps he thought he could gain some time by going through it?* Either way, the golem caught up with Roger and dragged him back down, then simply held his head under the water until he stopped struggling.

I swiped my finger across the mud on Roger's shoulder, then rubbed it between my thumb and finger. A faint flicker of the resonance seemed to prickle my fingertips. *It melted a bit as it held Roger under. But not all the way.* This mud had a clay-like consistency, and the dirt in the ditch seemed to be mostly sandy. There were a couple of glops of the mud scattered in the vicinity, but nowhere near enough to account for a whole golem. Or even a decent-sized piece of one.

"Fuck," I muttered, then stood and clambered back up the bank with help from Gordon and Scott. Brushing mud and dirt off my pants, I scanned the area for Knight.

I finally spotted him at the edge of the complex parking lot. He was crouching and looking at something on the ground and I headed his way.

"You find something?" I asked as I approached.

He pointed. "Keys. I'm betting they belong to your victim."

"That's his car." I indicated the dark blue Chevy Nova parked a few spaces away. "The golem was here," I said, feeling the by-now-familiar prickle of resonance. "Several hours ago, though, I think."

Knight stood. "It must have been waiting for him—came after him as he was coming out to his car."

"And Roger told me that he has a five A.M. client, which means it was still dark." I shoved my hand through my hair. "He probably didn't see it until it was right on top of him ... tried to outrun it, but he didn't have a chance."

We both remained silent for several heartbeats. Marco didn't say anything meant to be encouraging like *You'll catch whoever's doing this* or *I have faith in you.* I kinda appreciated that. Especially since I was pretty sure I wouldn't have believed him anyway.

Finally I turned and walked back toward the scene.

Jill had arrived while I'd been talking with Knight and was already down in the ditch taking pictures. There wasn't a whole lot to do other than take pictures, so I waited patiently by the side of the ditch and gave her a hand out once she was finished.

"Thanks, chick," she said. "Once the CO gets here I'll take more pics of the body."

"You rock, as always," I said.

"This one's like the others?" she asked, voice lower even though there was no one within a hundred yards. She started walking back to her van and I fell into step beside her.

"Yep," I replied. "And it's starting to piss me right the fuck off, too."

She gave me a sympathetic grimace. "Isn't there some way a demon can . . . I dunno, track it down or something so that you can find who's making it?"

"I have absolutely no idea if that's possible, but it's a hypothetical exercise at this point anyway, because I don't have enough power to do a summoning right now." And even if I did, I'd be using it to call Rhyzkahl so that I could tell him about the summoning attempts. But Jill didn't need to know about any of that. "Right now I'm forced to do my investigation using only *mundane* tactics." I gave a mock shudder and she laughed.

"Oh my god, the horror!" She cast a sideways glance at me. "Seriously, though, is anything popping?"

"Too much, if that makes sense." I made a sour face. "A bunch of strange little details and links, and I'm not sure what fits together or how. Plus, there's stuff that looks intriguing to me but might have absolutely nothing to do with why anyone was killed and is only managing to distract me."

To my surprise she wrapped an arm around me and gave me a companionable squeeze as we walked. "You'll figure it out," she reassured me. "You're too much of a bitch not to."

I jabbed my elbow lightly into her ribs. "Takes one to know one!"

She laughed then lifted her chin toward my car. "Who's that?"

I looked to see that Knight was leaning against the hood of my car, arms folded casually across his chest. "Oh, that's right, you haven't met him yet. He's part of the task force when we do New Orleans stuff." *And he freaks Pellini right out, which earns him extra points in my book,* I thought, masking a grin. By this time we were close to the car. "Jill this is Marco Knight. Marco, this is Jill Faciane, our crime scene goddess." I glanced at Marco. "Jill, um, *knows.*"

Jill snorted. "Yeah, I *know* that you're totally weird," she said to me, then she stuck her hand out to Knight. "Nice to meet you. I take it you're weird too?"

A lazy grin crossed his face. "Quite so," he said, taking her hand. To my surprise his grin abruptly slipped, an expression of shock and sadness flickering there before he released her hand and smiled normally again. "It's a pleasure to meet you," he said quietly.

Jill merely nodded, brow faintly furrowed, then she turned to me. "I'll be right back. I want to put my camera away and check the pictures."

"Sure thing," I said, then watched after her as she strode to her van at a brisk clip. I gave Knight a questioning look but his gaze was on her as well. After a few seconds he gave a soft sigh then looked back to me.

"Is everything all right?" I asked.

"Yeah," he said, giving me his usual lazy amused grin. I smiled back, but I'd seen that brief flash of . . . what had it been? Pain? Longing? Grief? It had been too quick to identify, but I knew the lazy grin to be a mask now.

But I felt no driving need to tear it away. I murmured something inconsequential and then moved off a short distance and pulled my cell phone out. I needed to let Ryan know what was going on . . .

I stared down at the phone, hesitating before dialing Ryan's number. I'd managed to forget the shock of last night for a while, but now it all came rushing back in. *Zack's not human. And Ryan can summon.* Though Zack hadn't said that Ryan was a summoner, merely that he had the ability to open portals. But if Ryan had never summoned before, what on earth could a human do to be labeled a *kiraknikahl?* Zack had said that his punishment was dire and just. And part of that punishment had to have been something that changed his memory or took it away. *But Ryan can do that,* I reminded myself. *I've seen him change people's memories.* Did he do something to a demon or a summoner? Maybe that was why—

I jumped and bit back a yelp at the touch on my arm. I whirled to see Marco standing beside me, a questioning look on his face. "Does it do tricks?" he asked.

I gave him my best stupid look in response. "Huh?"

His lips twitched with a whisper of amusement. "You've been staring at your phone for several minutes now. Figured you were waiting for it to do something."

I flushed and shook my head. "Sorry. Got lost in thought there."

He flicked a glance to where the coroner's office van was pulling up, directed to the ditch by Gordon. "Understandable. You got a lot to think about." He met my eyes. "You're caught right smack in the middle of some powerful forces."

I controlled the shiver that wanted to slide down my spine. "Pellini told me to watch out for you," I said before I could think about it. "Said you know shit," I lowered my voice in quasi-imitation of Pellini, "and that you fuck people up . . . telling them things."

The smile faded from his face and he looked away, into the distance. "I made some mistakes. Hurt people who didn't deserve the hurting they ended up with."

"Pellini?"

His head dipped in a whisper of a nod. "He was one."

"Do I need to watch out for you?"

His gaze returned to me. "I think maybe it's the other way around," he said, amusement brightening his eyes. He leaned against the car and pulled out a pack of cigarettes, then tilted the pack my way, smiling slightly when I shook my head. "You gonna go talk to Miss Lida now?"

I blinked, feeling as if I'd been in some sort of bizarre thrall. "Um, yeah. I want to let her know—"

"And see her reaction," Knight finished with a nod. He lit a cigarette and took a long draw on it. "I wouldn't mind tagging along again, especially if you don't want to bother the agents."

The shimmer of relief at his suggestion surprised me. "Yeah," I said slowly. "That would be cool." I lifted my phone again, then thumbed in a text message.

Adam Taylor's computer was wiped. Am out on another murder scene—Roger Peeler. Det. Knight is w/ me and we're going to talk to Lida. Will touch base w/ you after.

I hit the send and looked up to see Knight's eyes on me. I expected him to give me another amused or sardonic smile, laughing at me for ducking out of having to talk to Ryan, but he merely looked completely understanding. Was he telepathic? Or merely incredibly perceptive or understanding?

"I'm not telepathic," he said, then grinned when I raised an eyebrow at him. "I promise, I'm not, but I could tell you were wondering that."

"So what are you?" I challenged. Enough of being kept in the dark.

He shrugged. "I can sense things. It's hard to explain."

"Clairvoyant?"

He shook his head, then shrugged again. "I dunno. I get vibes from people sometimes. Can sense if something's eating at them or if they're grieving or missing something." He looked away again, and I wasn't sure if he was looking at the distant figure of Jill. "Sometimes I can tell what caused it."

"Sounds awful," I blurted before I could stop myself.

He turned back to me. "Yeah." He dropped the half-burned cigarette on the ground and twisted it out with his foot. "Shall we go talk to this singer of ours?"

Chapter 24

A complete stranger answered the door at the Moran house—a young woman about Lida's age who clearly shared similar tastes in clothing and style with the singer. She was short and petite with pale blond hair pulled up into a high ponytail, heavy makeup, and numerous piercings in both ears. Worry filled her eyes as she took in our badges and official bearing. "Y'all are here to talk to Lida?"

"Yes, ma'am," I replied. "And you are . . . ?"

"I'm Nikki. I'm a friend of Lida's." She stepped back and opened the door to allow us in. "She was super freaked out last night after she heard about Adam," the girl continued as we entered, closing the door behind us. "She called me up and asked if I could come stay the night with her since her uncle's out of town." Nikki shuddered. "I mean . . . she was *in the building* when her manager died and she never realized it."

"It was a tragedy," I said. "Is Lida here?"

The blond ponytail bobbed as she nodded. "She's upstairs. She's been crying most of the night. Kept saying that if she'd gone to check on him, maybe she could have helped." Nikki's lower lip quivered.

"You were here with her all night?" I asked.

"Yeah. I tried to keep her distracted . . . ordered pizza, watched pay-per-view, that sort of thing." She bit her lip. "You really gotta talk to her now? She's a bit of a mess."

"I'm sorry," I said gently, "but it's very important."

The worry in Nikki's eyes deepened as she searched our faces. "It's more bad news, isn't it? Should I . . . Can I stick around if it is? I don't think she should be by herself."

"It might be a good idea for you to stick around," I told her.

Her face fell. "God. The poor thing."

"It's only the two of you here?" Knight asked. "Where's her brother?"

"Trey came by and picked him up last night," Nikki said. "Michael doesn't know about Adam yet. He's gonna totally lose it when he does find out, but Lida didn't need to be dealing with that last night. Luckily Trey's really good with Michael." She let out a sad sigh. "I'll go get Lida."

She turned and climbed the stairs. A couple of minutes later Lida descended the stairs, with Nikki hovering anxiously behind her. I could believe that she'd been crying. Her face was puffy and blotchy, and her eyes were red and swollen as she turned them to me.

"Hi," she said, voice thin and wan. "I'm a mess. Sorry. I think I've been crying ever since the other two cops left last night."

That would have been Ryan and Crawford "It's understandable," I said. "Why don't you have a seat?"

She seemed to shrink in on herself, but obediently sank to sit on the couch. "You have more bad news, don't you," she stated, voice flat.

I hated giving death notifications. Hated them with every fiber of my being. But I knew that drawing it out or couching it in comfortable euphemisms only made it worse. "Roger Peeler is dead," I told her. "He was murdered sometime this morning."

She closed her eyes and clenched her hands together tightly. "Oh my god," she whispered. Nikki gave a soft cry of alarm and wrapped arms around her.

"Murdered?" Lida asked without opening her eyes. "You're sure?" Her voice cracked.

"Evidence at the scene points to that, yes," I stated. "We also believe Adam Taylor was murdered as well."

Her eyes snapped open at that and she gave me a look of pure shock. "But . . . but *why?* Why would anyone want to kill them?" Then she paled. "Oh, shit. Someone's going after the band. I could be next."

"That's a strong possibility," I admitted. "We have reason to believe that the same, um, person who attacked you at the concert is also responsible for these murders."

Luckily she didn't seem to notice my hesitation. "I . . . I need to call my uncle. I need security, bodyguards, right?" She gave me a bewildered look.

"We can't provide you with full-time protection here, though we could possibly arrange for you to stay in protective custody for a short while." I hoped I wasn't talking out of my ass, and that the FBI had some sort of safe house arrangement that might be available. I knew that little old Beaulac PD didn't have anything like that, nor did we have the budget to pay officers to protect her around the clock.

To my relief she shook her head. "No, Uncle Ben has a security company that he's used before. ATK Security. They do a bunch of high-profile stuff, rock stars and corporate execs." She gave a shaky smile. "I didn't think I'd need anything like that for a long time, if ever."

"I've heard of them," I told her. "They have a good reputation." They were also shockingly expensive, but I wasn't the one footing the bill. "Where's your uncle?"

"In New York, meeting with bank big shots about the buyout. He's helping with the whole transition." She pushed a hand through the mess of her hair. "I haven't told him about Adam yet. He'd want to fly right back, and I know these meetings are really important for his position on the board. But I guess I gotta now."

"I think he'd want to know," I said with what I hoped was quiet reassurance. I glanced to Nikki. "You'll stay with her?"

She hadn't budged from her arms-around-Lida position. "Damn straight," she said with a firm nod.

"All right." I stood. "Lida, get that security as soon as possible. For now, lock the doors, keep a cell phone on you at all times, and call at the absolute first suspicion that something might be wrong. I'll get a road officer to stay in the area until your security people can get here."

Lida managed to give me a brave smile. "Thanks. I appreciate everything you're doing."

I nodded. "Be careful," I said. Maybe with enough warnings and precautions I wouldn't be back here to investigate another murder.

I turned and left without another word, haunted by the mental image of the singer lying twisted at the bottom of those stairs.

I walked down the driveway feeling wrung out and exhausted.

"Can you tell when people are lying?" I asked Knight as I reached my car.

He paused with his hand on the door of his vehicle and shook his head. "Not really. Sometimes I can get a feel for what questions to ask, that's all."

Well, that explained why he'd asked about Michael.

"I do think that Lida was genuinely shocked," he continued, then he frowned. "But . . ."

"But?" I prompted after a few seconds of silence.

He shook his head. "Dunno. She's real worried about something or someone besides herself."

"Probably her brother," I offered.

He paused, still frowning. "Nah ... it was there when she was talking 'bout her uncle." He shrugged. "I dunno," he repeated. "It's more of a feeling than something specific. Sorry."

"It's cool," I assured him. "Thanks for coming with me today."

The smile he gave me was warm and genuine. "It was my pleasure." He paused and looked away over the lake. The sun shimmered across the water and I could hear the faraway buzz of a motorboat. "Sometimes it's tough to tell who the bad guys are," he said, voice oddly rich. "Evil is often a matter of perception."

Gooseflesh crawled over my skin as I watched him. I'd used those exact words before to describe the demonkind. He continued to gaze out over the water, but his eyes were completely unfocused. "Even the most powerful get screwed," he continued. "The world was at stake, and he had to make a terrible choice." Knight was only a few feet away from me but there was something about his voice that made me feel that I'd be able to hear him speaking to me even if I was on the other side of the lake.

"Sometimes the punishment fits the crime far too well," he said, then closed his eyes. An instant later he staggered, eyes flying open as he put a hand out to steady himself against his car.

His gaze snapped up to me, horror and shame warring in his features. "Kara ... I ..." He swallowed harshly. "I'm sorry if I said anything to—"

"What punishment?" I asked, blood pounding in my ears. "What did you mean? What was the crime?"

Agony rippled across his face. "I don't know. Kara, I don't even know what I said, I swear. I'm sorry. Please, believe me."

I wanted to grab him and shake the answers out of him. *He had to have been talking about Ryan.* What the fuck had all that meant? His words were seared into my mind. *Even the most powerful get screwed.* Ryan?

But Knight looked like he was a hairbreadth away from a complete freak-out. It was such a divergence from his usual calm that it pulled me out of my own shock. "It's all right," I made myself say. "It didn't really mean anything. It's all right."

Doubt shadowed his eyes, but the horror faded from his expression. He gave an uncertain nod. "I'm sorry. That hasn't happened in a long time."

"You okay now?"

He took a deep breath. "Yeah. I'm cool." He opened his car door and I could see him pulling his mask on, the lazy smile slipping into place, though not fitting quite as perfectly as before. "Y'all be sure to keep me posted on the case, all right?"

I gave him the relaxed smile he needed to see. "You got it. Be careful driving back to New Orleans."

He winked, then climbed into his car and drove off.

I waited a few seconds, then followed suit, his strange pronouncements still echoing in my head.

What the *hell* had all of that meant?

Chapter 25

Rain began to fall as I drove back to the other side of the lake, but to my relief this was a normal southern rainstorm—not an unnerving thunderstorm like the other day.

The traffic was down to one lane on part of the highway due to construction, and my phone rang as I waited in a long line of cars for my turn to proceed. Ryan, I noted absently without looking at the phone. I sighed. *I can't avoid talking to him any longer and have any shred of maturity left.*

"Hey, Ryan," I answered. "Sorry I haven't called you yet. I've been kinda slammed."

There was a heartbeat of silence. "It's cool," he said with an odd hitch in his voice. "So the drummer's death was a murder as well?"

"I'm positive. I don't know when Dr. Lanza will do the autopsy to officially rule it as a homicide, but that resonance was there."

I heard him make a frustrated noise. "Okay, so everything's more complicated. We need to all get together and see if we can come up with anything brilliant. Have you had lunch yet?"

Yeah, a nice public place would be best. "Nope. How about East Shore Diner?"

"Works for me. Meet you there in fifteen minutes."

* * *

East Shore Diner was a favored meal destination for law enforcement for three reasons: it was open twenty-four hours, it offered highly edible food at prices cops could afford, and it had two parking lots—one on the side where the majority of the customers parked, and a second one in the rear of the diner that couldn't be seen from the highway. It was the parking lot in the rear that was the most appealing feature, especially for cops working the night shift. Its location offered patrol officers the chance to eat at an unhurried pace and relax a bit—radio traffic permitting—without fear that some irate citizen would call the dispatcher and complain that a police car had been parked at the restaurant for at *least* half an hour, and why were tax dollars being wasted in such a fashion?

The diner itself was nothing special to look at. It had originally been a bait shop, and the exterior décor had been updated not one bit since its transformation to a diner, except for the addition of a deliciously garish neon sign that proclaimed EATS! complete with the flashing arrow that pointed to the building.

Ryan was already there in the side parking lot when I pulled up, a scowl on his face and his phone to his ear. "I'm trying to get Zack to answer his fucking phone," he explained after I got out of my car.

A sliver of worry intruded. "I haven't seen him since yesterday evening. Have you?"

Ryan gave a snort of laughter. "Yeah, he's fine. I know that much." He lowered the phone and pressed the end call button. "But apparently he's started seeing someone, and he's being really fucking tight-lipped about it. I sent him a text, and he acknowledged it, but he won't pick up the phone. Probably afraid I'll hear him doing things that involve wet slapping sounds."

I didn't hear what he said next as I closed my eyes,

beginning to laugh. *I am the biggest fucking moron who has ever walked the earth.* Yes, Kara, lots of cops drive dark-colored Crown Vics . . .

"Kara? What's so funny?"

You mean besides the fact that I'm an insecure idiot who needs to have a little more faith in her friends? "I think I know who he's seeing."

He raised an eyebrow at me in question.

"I, uh, was kinda bummed out last night and I was going to see if Jill was still awake and wanted ice cream. And, well, there was a Crown Vic in her driveway with government plates."

A slow grin spread across his face. "Ho-ly shit. Zack and . . ." He began to laugh.

"Oh, god, Zack and Jill." I joined his laughter. *But, does Jill know that Zack is . . . isn't human?*

After a moment he managed to control himself. "That's seriously funny." Then he gave me a more concerned look. "If you were having a tough time, why didn't you give me a call?"

"Well, um, for a second I actually thought that it was you at Jill's house." I tried to shrug and laugh it off. "I mean, it was only for a second, but y'know . . . And, besides, I kinda needed some girl talk." Wow, that sounded lame.

The look of shock on his face surprised me. "You thought that I would . . . with Jill?" Pain and disappointment flashed across his features, then he looked away and gave a laugh that sounded oddly forced. "Jill's not my type."

"What is your type, Ryan?" I said it before I could stop myself.

His gaze snapped back to me, spearing me. I wanted to take back the question, but I couldn't think of any way to do so that wouldn't have me sounding like a complete moron. Did I want to know the answer? *Only if it describes me,* I thought in stupid adolescent hope.

We were saved by the sound of tires screeching on asphalt. We both spun to see a Crown Vic—a black one—bounce over the curb and screech to a stop. Zack practically leaped out of the car and approached us with a wide smile. I noted with amusement that he had stubble on his chin.

"Dude," I said, shaking my head. "I know Jill's house is small, but I'm sure she could spare some space in her bathroom for you to leave a razor."

He stared at me in openmouthed shock for a heartbeat. "Are you a—" He stopped and then shifted his expression to a rueful grin. "Busted. Yeah, we've been seeing each other."

"Did you go up a hill?" I asked innocently.

He looked at me with a blank expression.

"To fetch a pail of water?" Ryan finished, grinning.

Zack groaned. "You two are a couple of assholes."

"It's why you love us," Ryan said, voice dry. "C'mon, let's get food. Kara has a bunch of shit to fill us in on."

We found a booth that was well away from any other customers. As soon as the waitress had taken our orders I filled them both in on the findings from the computer examinations, what I'd gleaned from Roger's murder scene, and the interview with Lida.

Zack frowned and pulled a small notebook out of his pocket. "So, with Roger's murder, we still have the possibility that Vic really was killed by mistake."

I grimaced. "No, I'm having a hard time buying that. Vic Kerry is still linked to both Adam and Roger financially. I just have to pin down how. Besides, if the thing was going after Roger, why go to the City Towers where there was no guarantee that Roger would even be there?" I shrugged. "And for that matter, why go to

City Towers if it *was* after Vic? Seems that there'd be more risk of it being seen."

Ryan tapped the table absently. "Where did Vic live?"

"Emerald Heights condominiums." I paused. "Which is gated and has security. Gold star to Ryan!"

He gave me a pleased nod. "Harder to get in, and surveillance video keeps track of cars coming and going."

Zack exhaled. "Which brings up back to believing that Vic truly was the intended target of that attack."

"I have all of Roger's financial information. I sent off subpoenas for Vic's and Adam's but it'll take weeks to get any returns from those. But I do have the info from Vic's computer and the books we seized at the crime scene." I tugged a hand through my hair, grimacing. "What I can't figure out is how the attack on Lida figures into any of this. If the intent had been to kill her, why do it in such a public way?"

We paused while the waitress delivered our food. Ryan looked askance at my entrée. "You're really having *fries* for lunch?"

"It's not just fries," I said. "It's cheese and gravy *on top* of fries. Three of the four food groups!"

He stared at me. "What the hell is your cholesterol level?"

"It's one!" I said, showing him my middle finger.

Zack grinned. "Don't get between a woman and her comfort food, Ryan."

I glared at him as I dug into my healthy repast. Was it that obvious I was in need of comfort food?

"Well, it looks like I'm in for an exciting evening of looking at financial information," I said after a few minutes of lubricating my arteries. "And I think that the rest of the Financial Crimes Task Force really needs to be helping me out with this!" I gave them both a hopeful grin.

"Sounds dangerous," Zack said with a mock frown. "I

think it would be much safer for us to hunt wild golems. Perhaps somewhere on the other side of the lake."

"Back off, fanboy," I said, pointing a gravy-and-cheese-laden fry at him. "I've already spoken to the object of your crush—"

"It is not a crush!" he insisted.

"—and Lida is arranging for private security, so your stalking services aren't needed."

"You wound me. My intentions are noble."

Ryan made a rude noise, then turned his attention to me. "So you warned her to watch her back?"

I nodded. "I told Roger to be careful, too, but . . . it wasn't enough."

His face tightened in a sympathetic grimace.

"And you need to watch your back as well, Kara," Zack said with a telling look.

Ryan spun to face me. "Why?" he asked, barely shy of demanding.

I glared at Zack, who gave a soft sigh. "I thought you'd told him already," he said.

"Tell me what?" Ryan said, and this time it was most certainly a demand.

I struggled to control my desire to fidget. "There was another, um, strange thing after we left the search at Adam Taylor's house."

His eyes narrowed. "Strange? Like what? And what do you mean another?"

Zack gave me a sharp look. "You didn't tell me it had happened before."

The worry on Ryan's face deepened. "What the fuck happened?"

I grimaced and rubbed my eyes. "Zack . . . er, I think it was a summoning."

Confusion flitted across Ryan's face. "Another summoner was trying to bring a demon through? Where? But it's not a full moon. I don't understand."

"No. A summoning of me."

He stared at me for several heartbeats, then the color drained from his face. "Summoning to bring *you* to the demon realm."

I shrugged, trying to be casual about it, but it was a pretty pathetic effort. "Well, I can't be certain of that, but that's the most logical conclusion."

He clenched and unclenched his hands. "And this has happened twice, and you didn't think this was something you needed to tell me." It wasn't a question.

I fumbled for a response. "No. I mean, yes. I knew you'd get upset, and it's not like there's anything that you could do—" Shit.

I knew I'd fucked up the instant the words were out of my mouth. His lips pressed together and he stood abruptly, jostling the table and nearly spilling the drinks. He was out the back door before I could do more than grab for my Diet Coke.

I stared after him, shocked at the depth of his reaction, and cursing myself at my own callousness. *Fucking shit, Kara. Why don't you just ask him to hand you his balls?*

"Go to him," Zack said quietly. I hesitated, then pushed up from the table and went after him.

The rear parking lot was empty of cars and people, or so I thought at first. I finally saw Ryan down near the corner of the building, head down. One hand was on the wall, the other clenched into a fist by his side. There was a huge part of me that did not want to go near him. I could *feel* the fury and hurt coming off of him.

But I was the one who'd fucked up. I moved toward him. "Ryan?" I said, more tentatively than I'd intended, but my resolve was wavering pretty badly in the face of his anger and distress. I didn't like that I was the one who'd caused this. If someone else had hurt him like this, I'd have been ready to kill them.

He straightened, pulling his hand from the wall but not turning to face me. "Go back and eat your lunch, Kara. I need a minute."

"Ryan, I'm sorry. That was a shit thing for me to have said."

"Yep. It was."

Well, damn. What the hell was I supposed to say to that? "I'm sorry."

"Why don't you trust me, Kara?" He turned now, gaze meeting mine.

"I do," I tried to insist, but even I could hear the hesitation in my voice.

Frustration swept across his features again. "I don't know what the hell else I can do, Kara. I'm not holding anything back from you that I know of."

"That you know of, Ryan?"

He jammed his fingers through his hair. "Fuck! Kara, I know I do and say strange stuff sometimes, but why can't you at least trust me enough to know that I would never hurt you, and that I give a fuck if you're in trouble?"

I took an involuntary step back from the vehemence in his tone. "I'm sorry. I didn't want to upset you."

His hands balled into fists. "But you'll summon Rhyzkahl—" He spat the name. "—and tell him?"

The words died on my tongue. *Yes. He might be able to help me.* "I don't have a choice, Ryan," I said softly.

I was ready for the rage that passed through his eyes this time and didn't step back.

"You asked me what my type was. I'll tell you," he growled, seizing me by my upper arms. I stiffened in surprise but didn't try and pull away. His grip was solid and firm, but he wasn't hurting me. Quite. "My *type,*" he sneered the word, "is someone who can fucking trust me. Not only trust that I won't screw other women, but trust me enough to tell me if she needs help, or just needs

someone to talk to. My type is someone who doesn't
reek of a demonic lord, who doesn't turn to him instead
of—" He released me abruptly and spun away. I staggered and had to reach to the wall to catch my balance.
My breath seized in my chest as I watched him storm off.
Half a minute later I saw his Crown Vic roar out of the
other parking lot in very un-Ryan-like fashion.

I felt frozen to the spot as his words seemed to clang
around in my skull, slicing at me. He was right. That was
the worst of it. Every word of it had been true. Now I
knew he was interested in me, wanted me as more than
"just friends," and I'd gone and fucked it up before I'd
ever given it a chance.

I barely felt the gentle hand on my shoulder. "Kara,"
Zack said softly. "He worries. He is frightened for you,
and he is lashing out with his pain. You did not deserve
that."

"Yes, I did, Zack." I turned to look at him in misery.
"Yes I did. Everything he said was the truth."

The gentleness and understanding in his eyes surprised me, until I realized that if he really was a demon
he was probably far older than the twenty-something
years that Special Agent Zack Garner supposedly had.
"Even if he spoke truth," he said, "he couched it in vile
terms and with vicious intent, designed to make you feel
pain equivalent to what he feels. You cause him pain,
but only with the intent to spare him such. Your bond
to Rhyzkahl exists only because you felt there was no
other choice save to allow Ryan to be consumed. Ryan
knows all of this, but knowledge and logic are easily
overshadowed by passion and pain."

I gazed up at him. "Zack?"

"Yes, Kara?"

"You're doing that 'talking like a demon' thing again."

He blinked, then gave me a wry smile. "Sorry." He
took a deep breath. "Look, I'll talk to him." He shook

his head. "He's going to be beating himself up right now anyway." He caught my eyes again. "Can you summon Rhyzkahl tonight?"

I hesitated. "I don't know. I couldn't store any more potency last night, and it's still a few days from the full moon."

He grimaced. "All right. I don't mean to be a nag about this, but I can't think of anyone else who could give you the help and protection you need."

I thought about the amount of power in my storage diagram and sighed. But maybe there was another option. *I could try calling him to my dreams.* A chill walked down my back at the memory of the last time I tried that, during the search for the Symbol Man. In a desperate move to glean information about one of the murders, I'd made a conscious effort to call the demonic lord to my dreams—a reasonable enough move considering that he'd visited my dreams before. Or so I'd foolishly assumed. But Rhyzkahl had not been pleased to be called forth in such a manner. For several nightmarish minutes he'd manipulated the dream state, teaching me in unforgettable fashion that he was a creature of more power than I could fathom, and that he did *not* serve me.

But this would be different, I told myself. This wouldn't be calling him to get him to serve me. Besides, I was fucking bound to him now.

I nodded morosely. "Yeah. I know. I promise, I will as soon as I possibly can."

Zack gave me a reassuring smile. "Hey, don't get bummed out. We'll get through this."

"Yeah." I didn't sound very convincing.

"It's going to be all right," he said firmly. "I'm gonna go chase Ryan down. I'll check in with you later on."

I mumbled something in the way of acknowledgment and watched him drive off, then returned inside and paid our bill. The most sensible thing for me to do now would be to go on home, hunker down with the financial information, and forget that this lunch ever happened.

But I found myself driving to my aunt's shop instead. It had been a quaint little natural food store before her coma, and I'd been forced to close it during her time at the neuro center. As soon as she recovered she reopened it, but bigger and better than before. It still had a section for the organics and natural food store stuff, but now there was also a small café and a yoga studio. And her business had never been better.

A subtle floral scent surrounded me as I walked in, paired with soft and soothing music that sounded faintly oriental. Tessa was behind the counter, barefoot, wearing purple leggings paired with a billowing white silk blouse, topped with yards of red beads draped around her neck. She looked up at the sound of the bell over the door and gave me a bright smile that managed to lift my spirits a few millimeters. Sketching a wave to her, I headed over to the cooler and snagged an iced tea, then found an unoccupied table in the corner. A few minutes later she plopped down into the chair across from me.

"You look wrung out, sweets," she said, eyeing me with worry.

"I feel wrung out," I admitted. "I'm working a big case that has me pretty baffled."

"You work too hard," she said, "but I know it's important to you."

I rubbed at my temples, still knotted up from the blowup with Ryan. "Yeah. My personal life is a fucking mess too. Or at least it feels that way."

She made a *tsking* noise. "You're simply unused to having a personal life."

"Well, this is true," I said with a tired smile. "Being a social isolate was easier in a lot of ways."

"I'm serious, Kara. Think about it. Six months ago

you were practically a hermit, without a single person you could call friend."

I fought the urge to scowl. "I wasn't quite that pathetic."

She gave me a dubious look. "You *didn't* have any friends, and you know it. Now stop being so defensive. I'm more responsible for that than you. But my point is that now you do have friends. And you don't know how much you can rely on them without scaring them off."

I wanted to protest, but unfortunately she'd managed to nail down a hefty portion of my current angst. "Yeah," I said slowly. "I guess so."

"So, enough psychoanalysis," she said brightly, as if she'd solved all of my ills in a few sentences. "You're investigating the murder of Vic Kerry?"

"Among others." I lowered my voice even though there was no one else in the café. "Someone has created a construct, like a golem, and is using it to kill."

Her expression darkened. "That's ugly stuff. I wish I could help you, but all I know about golems is in the library, and I think you already absconded with the pertinent books." She gave me a narrow-eyed look that made me grin.

"Vic and I went to high school together," she added in another wrenching change of subject.

"I didn't know you knew him," I said. "I'm sorry."

She shook her head. "Oh, I wasn't friends with him or anything. I didn't even realize I'd gone to school with him until last year. He was doing the taxes for the store and we happened to get into a conversation about how old we were. Turned out we were in the same graduating class, and even had the same senior English teacher. But I don't think we ever spoke a single word to each other. You know how that goes."

I gave a neutral shrug. I didn't like to think about my high school days.

"But, you know . . . He and Mike Moran were really tight," she said, with a slight frown.

"Huh? Mike Moran, the keyboardist for Lida's band?"

"Oh, no. He's actually a Michael Junior. Mike Moran was his father."

I straightened. "And he and Vic were good friends?"

"Best friends. Vic even stood in Mike's wedding, if I recall correctly. Mike and Audrey got married right out of high school. Everyone thought they were insane to rush into marriage like that, but then eight months later Mike Junior was born." She snorted. "Stupid reason to get married, but they seemed to be doing all right. Then Audrey got pregnant again."

"She died in childbirth with Lida, right?"

"Eclampsia," Tessa said with a nod. "Damn near lost the baby too. Hard to believe that happens anymore, but it does."

"Do you know how Mike Senior died?"

"Accident at the house, from what I understand. The roof collapsed in the garage. Mike was killed, and the kids were hurt—Michael quite seriously."

"Was it an old house?" I asked.

"Nope. New construction," she said. "He and the kids had only moved into it a few months earlier. Big two-story house with a huge yard. Mike and Ben had a debris removal business that was really taking off, thanks to a couple of big hurricanes and the need to clean up demolished houses. Those two grew up dirt poor, and Mike wanted to give the kids the kind of house he'd always dreamed of living in." She gave a sad little smile. "The builder was blamed for the collapse, but no one could ever prove fault."

The bell rang over the door as a couple entered the

shop, and Tessa patted my hand. "Lemme scoot and take care of them."

"That's all right, I need to run anyway." I stood and gave her a quick hug. "Thanks, Aunt Tessa."

She gave me a return squeeze, then turned to greet the customers. I watched her for a moment, smiling. No matter what else was fucked up in my life, Tessa was still the same person she used to be in all the ways that mattered.

Chapter 26

The pinch of my stomach reminded me that I hadn't eaten much of my lunch, and so, before driving home, I veered through the drive-thru of the coffee shop and ordered a muffin and a hot chocolate. There was a small part of me that both hoped and dreaded that Ryan would be at my house, waiting for me, but my driveway was silent and empty.

I pushed aside the desire to dissolve into angsty moping and headed inside, locking the door behind me. I dropped my bag by my desk, but paused after I did so, gaze lingering on my computer. Rhyzkahl had been on there. I knew he was up to something.

I dug the instructions from Brad out of my bag, then fired up my computer. Finding the Internet history was shockingly easy, but unfortunately the results didn't make a whole lot of sense. Six different searches in Google Earth for various locations in south Louisiana. One was in Leland Park. One was the Beaulac Police Department. Yet another was in Slidell in the middle of a subdivision.

I puzzled over the locations for several minutes, then sent it all to my printer. I knew that Rhyzkahl wanted more access to this sphere for a reason—not simply because he enjoyed my sparkling personality. As soon as things calmed down a bit, I needed to dig into the *why* a lot harder. And how did he know how to use a computer?

What if Rhyzkahl is behind this summoning thing, trying to make me feel threatened so that I'll call him more often? A sour taste filled my mouth as I pondered that possibility. I wanted badly to believe that the demonic lord wouldn't be that sneaky, but unfortunately I knew too well that the sense of honor that demons lived by was not one that prohibited devious shit like that.

I continued on down to my basement, oddly unsettled at the turn of my thoughts. Despite my knowledge of the deviousness of demons, I still had a hard time wrapping my head around the idea that Rhyzkahl would try and manipulate me like that. As much as I tried not to, I was growing to really like the demonic lord. *But I've been known to be colossally naive before.*

I crouched by the storage diagram. Rhyzkahl knew perfectly well that I had the ability to summon him at any time of the month. Could he be counting on that? Give me a bit of a scare so that I'd call him to me, thus giving him more opportunity to do whatever it was he was up to?

I shook my head. Either way, I needed to have power at my disposal. Even though I couldn't really measure the amount of potency the diagram contained, I could tell that it wasn't quite enough for a summoning, and I had no driving urge to risk running out of juice in the middle of opening a portal. I liked my molecules in their current configuration, thank you very much.

For the next twenty minutes I gradually siphoned power into the diagram, only stopping when I began to feel shaky and nauseated. Still not enough to risk a summoning of a demonic lord, but it was getting there. After I ate something I might be able to do a bit more, but still I knew that I wouldn't be doing any summonings tonight.

Tomorrow then. But even as I thought it I discarded it. No, I needed to try to call him to my dreams tonight. I could still ask him if he was involved in these attempted summonings, and even if I couldn't be guaranteed a straight answer from him, I could at least let him know it was happening.

I returned upstairs, unsettled at my decision. Unfortunately there really wasn't an easy answer. Calling him to my dreams was still risky because he had too much control over the setting and circumstance.

I dug something easy and microwaveable out of the freezer and set it to nuke as I pulled the envelope with Roger's financial information out of my bag. I poured a glass of wine, then sat at the kitchen table as I painstakingly made my way through the account summaries. Seriously boring shit, but my time working in white collar crimes had me fairly used to it.

Roger clearly made a decent living as a trainer, though he wasn't rich by any stretch. But he had modest savings and a fairly strong credit score.

Yeah, yeah. This wasn't what I wanted to know. I flipped through until I found his investment portfolio. All one page of it. There was only one investment. Puzzled, I skimmed through the rest of the information in the envelope to be sure I hadn't missed anything. But, no, there it was:

Fifteen thousand dollars worth of stock in Lake Pearl Bank.

What the hell? Why would Vic loan Roger money and then put it all into one investment? And had he done the same with the money he'd loaned Adam?

I relocated to my computer and stuck the CD with the info from Vic Kerry's computer in. But I couldn't find any reference to Roger or Adam or loans for fifteen thousand dollars. I did find information about vacation destinations and new cars, as well as a number of links to dating websites. Vic Kerry had definitely craved a better life for himself, and I was fairly sure he'd used Roger and Adam in his quest, but I couldn't make the whole thing click together.

I could feel an answer tickling at the back of my head, but I couldn't get it to behave and come out and play nice. *Screw this.* It was already late enough that I was going to be short on sleep. Too much had happened today for me to think straight.

I returned to the basement to pull a smidge more power into the diagram, then hauled my sorry, tired ass back up to my bedroom. Between the wine and the working with the arcane, I was asleep a heartbeat after my head hit the pillow, barely remembering as my eyes closed to dream of Rhyzkahl.

Chapter 27

I rested my hands on the stone of the battlement as I looked out over the deep canyon. A chill breeze teased my hair but I didn't want to go back inside. Morning mist shrouded the bottom of the abyss and I knew it would be hours yet before the sun would clear the high ridge and burn it off. A waterfall tumbled down the cliffs, descending into the depths with a muted roar.

I know this place. I looked up, oddly certain that I would see winged demons cavorting in the morning air, but the sky was empty of anything but a few small birds.

I took a deep breath, the crisp air tasting of green and mountains and snow. *I'm dreaming this, and . . . I'm aware that I'm dreaming.* That was a first.

Familiarity tickled at me. I'd been here before. Or rather, I'd dreamed this before, in sendings that Rhyzkahl had controlled. *Is this part of the demon realm?* I'd been to the demon realm once—albeit for only a couple of minutes—but even though my visit had been brief I couldn't shake the feeling that this was a different place. Maybe it was the light, or the air . . .

Frowning, I turned, familiarity continuing to tug annoyingly at me. I was on one tower of a massive fortress or keep that looked as if it had been carved out of the mountain. A dozen feet behind me a brass door set in a low stone structure stood ajar a few inches. To my right and left the battlements curved around and out of sight behind the structure. *Greg's comic,* I abruptly realized. *It looked the same.* Greg Cerise had been with my aunt when she'd first encountered Rhyzkahl—during the horrific slaughter of the summoners. He'd later gone on to create a rich and amazing graphic novel set in an amazing and fantastical setting. I'd read it from cover to cover, so surely this was simply my imagination creating an interesting dream-locale . . .

No. It goes deeper than that. I knew this place. Beyond the brass door were wide stairs going down. At the base of the stairs was a hallway and if I turned right—

I startled and let out a squawk at a touch on my shoulder. Heart pounding, I spun to see Rhyzkahl holding a fur-lined cloak. He calmly draped it over my shoulders even as I tried to make sense of what was going on. I was wearing a dress, I abruptly realized. A floor-length gown with an empire waist, slit sleeves, and a deep neckline, in a dark purple fabric that felt a bit like silk but somehow more luxurious. *I dress up in my dreams for Rhyzkahl,* I thought with an illogical twist of guilt.

"This is a dream, right?" I said, pulling the cloak close around me.

"It is," he replied. "You called to me."

I gave an unsteady nod. "Right. It's just . . ." I looked around again. "You've brought me here before in dreams, but, I know this place. Why?"

He remained silent for several heartbeats, expression betraying nothing. "This place was a favorite of mine once," he finally said. His face could have been carved from marble. "I prefer this locale to your bedroom."

"But—"

"You called to me," he repeated, cutting me off. "You have only done so once before, and thus I assume that this time your need is dire."

I hugged the cloak closer around me. "Some strange things have been happening. I think that someone is trying to summon me."

The rage that flashed through his eyes was unmistakable. So much for my theory that he was responsible. "Explain," he said, lips curling back from his teeth.

I did so, describing both incidents, though I left Zack out of it. I had no idea whether Rhyzkahl knew that Zack wasn't human, but I wasn't about to clue him in if he didn't. I was beginning to learn the value of information and discretion when it came to dealing with demons.

Rhyzkahl turned away when I finished and strode to the stone wall. I expected him to lean against it and look out over the canyon or something like that, but instead he crossed his arms over his chest and looked skyward. The light wind rippled his hair, and for a brief instant I found myself struck with the urge to step forward, wrap my arms around him from behind, and bury my face in that silken fall.

I shook my head sharply. No, that wasn't something I could ever see myself actually doing. Not to him. That sort of gesture implied a level of affection that we simply didn't have.

Did we?

"As soon as you are able, summon a *syraza* by the name of Eilahn," he said, voice breaking into my jumbled thoughts. He turned, ancient eyes piercing me. "This demon will serve as your guardian."

The near-savage look on his face stilled any protest I might have made. "Okay," I said meekly.

"I will deal with the matter as best I can in my own realm, but such issues are complicated." The anger in his expression retreated. "I regret that I have placed you in such a position, but I have good reasons."

"And you can't *tell* me those reasons?" I said, annoyance crowding out the confusion.

"To do so would imperil all I am seeking to do," he replied cryptically. "Summon Eilahn. The *syraza* will serve—" He jerked his head up abruptly as if an alarm had sounded, though I couldn't sense anything out of the ordinary.

"You have been careless," he hissed. "You will destroy yourself through carelessness!"

"What?"

"You are in dire threat. Wake up!" Rhyzkahl's face was contorted in fury and ... worry? But before I could fully process his words his hand came up to backhand me hard. I cried out as sharp pain exploded in the side of my face and I went crashing to the stone—

I let out a shocked yelp and sat upright in my bed, heart pounding. My bedroom was dark but enough moonlight filtered through the blinds that I could see it was empty. I put my hand to my face as I struggled to breathe normally. *What the fuck?* My cheek tingled oddly, though there was no pain—

I froze at a dull thump of sound in the hallway, cold shock knifing through me. *There's someone in my house.* Moving as silently as possible, I slid off the bed on the side away from the door, then tugged the nightstand drawer open and retrieved my gun. I stayed crouched behind the bed as I strained to hear any breath of noise over the mad pounding of my heart. *How can someone be in here? I have wards and aversions. Nothing living could possibly get through.*

The dull thump repeated itself, and with it a sickly familiar wash of arcane resonance. Footsteps. Slow and steady. Something heavy. *Nothing living. Fuck. Careless is right.* The thought sent a dark chill through me as I curled both hands around the butt of the gun. I wasn't exactly in a fantastic hiding place, but I had no idea what sort of intelligence the golem had, or how hard it was to destroy. But I *did* know how strong it was. Strong

enough to squeeze someone's neck into a pulp. And I'd
seen how fast it could be.

I heard the steps pause outside my door. *Shit.* I
scanned the room quickly in an effort to find more
weapons, but the desperately needed submachine guns
failed to materialize. However, there was a window. It
would be moronic to stay and fight. I shot to my feet
and tugged at the window, almost shocked when it slid
open with the barest whisper of effort. *Ha! If this had
been the movies it would have stayed stuck until the monster was in the room with me!* I popped the screen out
and shimmied out the window, then hopped down to the
ground and ran in a low crouch toward my car. Round-
ing the corner of the house, I could hear a low thumping
from the direction of my bedroom. *Okay, it's going to
be following me out real soon now.* But my car was right
in front of me. I grinned and resisted the urge to slide
across the hood in another movie move, and instead ran
to the door properly and slid in behind the wheel, glad
that I was in the terrible habit of forgetting to lock it at
night.

A split second later my grin disappeared. "Shit,"
I breathed. Yeah, I'd forgotten to lock it, but my keys
were in my bag, which was inside the house. *And this
isn't the movies, where the car keys are hidden under the
visor or some crap like that.*

I heard a sound of something heavy falling on the
side on the house. It was out of the window, I realized.
No time to think about this much more. I dove out of
the car and took off toward the front steps at a hard
sprint, seeing the hulking creature round the corner of
the house as I reached the door. The jamb was shattered,
but at that moment I could only be thrilled shitless that
it was, since otherwise I'd have been locked out of my
own house. And I wasn't athletic enough to be able to
leap back up through my open bedroom window. Bar-

reling through the door, I snatched up my bag. I heard
the clomping on the front steps and took off down the
hallway to the back door. *Please let there be only one!
And please let this one be really stupid!*

I reached the back door and glanced back in time
to see a hulking humanoid creature fill the front doorway. This one seemed bigger than the one I'd seen at
the concert, or maybe that was simply my terror talking.
Its features were far from sophisticated—dull pits for
eyes and crudely shaped features that would never be
able to pass for a human. Its mouth opened in a silent
snarl—far more unnerving than if it had actually been
able to make sound. It started to run toward me, hands
outstretched and crude thick fingers grasping in my direction. I had sixteen rounds in my Glock, and I didn't
think that would be anywhere near enough.

But I just needed to slow it down at this point. I took
aim at its lower half and started firing as fast as I could
pull the trigger. Dust flew from its legs as several rounds
found their mark, and it stumbled against the wall, leaving an ugly dent in my drywall. I snarled and took better aim, this time concentrating my fire on one leg. The
slide locked back on the Glock, telling me I was out of
ammo. The thing took another step toward me, but the
leg crumbled as the golem set weight on it and the creature tumbled to the floor.

My hopes that it would give up were dashed in the
next instant as it pushed itself up and continued to
clump toward me, this time on one knee and the other
now-truncated leg.

I turned and yanked the back door open, then jumped
down the back stairs. *Let that slow it down!* I prayed to
whoever might want to listen to me. I ran around the
house as I dug in the bag for the keys, vaguely relieved
to hear the thumping continuing toward the back. At
least it wasn't smart enough to double back. The car

door was still open and I threw my bag and myself into the car in one motion, yanking the keys out while I slammed the door and locked it with the other hand. I could see the creature shambling around the house as I jammed the key into the ignition. Even on its knees it was still damn near my height and moved more quickly than I was happy with.

The engine cranked first try, and I jammed it into drive and stomped on the accelerator. The golem was still coming at me, and I made a split-second decision— based on movie-influenced instinct—and aimed the car right at the thing.

The car struck the golem with an impact that felt like hitting a tree. And, just as if I'd struck a tree, the airbag exploded in my face, nearly knocking the wind out of me and completely obscuring my view.

"Shit!" I shrieked as I fought to get the bag down to where I could see. An acrid smell and a thin smoke filled the inside of the car; however, I could see a lump on the ground about ten feet in front of the car. It was down, at least. But a heartbeat later I could see the limbs move as it tried to right itself.

"Oh, no, you fucker!" Thankfully the car was still running, though it had an unpleasant rattle that hadn't been there before. I threw the stupid car into reverse, nearly careening into an actual tree, then shoved it into drive—this time going *around* the slowly stand-ing golem—spitting gravel and dust at it as I sped down my driveway. Glancing quickly in my rearview mirror, I could see it break into an ungainly lope, following my car. I reached the end of the driveway, gave the briefest of glances to make sure an oncoming car wasn't about to plow into me, and then I hit the smooth asphalt and left my house and the golem far behind.

Chapter 28

I clenched the ragged steering wheel tightly in an effort to keep my hands from shaking. If Rhyzkahl hadn't woken me, I'd have been killed in my sleep. I didn't bother worrying about how the demonic lord had known I was in danger. He'd saved my life, no doubt about it.

I didn't even know where I was going, where I was driving. I glanced down and groaned. *And wearing nothing but a T-shirt and undies. Niiiice.* And my phone . . . I groaned again. Still plugged into the charger by my bed. *Oh, extra nice.*

And, because bad things come in threes, the red coolant light flickered on as the car began to shudder. I pulled to the shoulder and turned my emergency flashers on, desperately trying to think of anything I might have in my car that was wearable. I needed a tow, and I needed a phone. Because obviously I'd stumbled onto something bad enough to make it worth sending the golem after me. *And if one was sent after me, then Zack and Ryan could be targets as well.*

I radioed the dispatcher to notify them that I needed a tow and to please have an available unit swing my way. Then, after making sure that there were no cars coming down the highway, I went digging through the trunk of my car for something to preserve what little dignity I had left.

About ten minutes later Scott Glassman pulled up behind my car and got out, frowning at me as I leaned on the trunk of my car. A second later Officer Gordon stepped out of the passenger side, looking at me dubiously. Great, now even the new guy would get to experience Weird Kara.

"Why the hell are you wearing your rain gear?" Scott asked as his gaze swept over the knee-length yellow slicker that I clutched around me.

I gave him a dark glare. "It's a really long story," I said, knowing well that I needed to come up with something plausible to explain the extensive damage to the car. And why I was half-naked, barefoot, and forced to dress in a damn rain slicker. "Right now I really need to use your phone."

He chuckled and passed his cell over to me while I struggled to remember Ryan's number. I had it stored on my phone, not memorized. "Shit. Do you happen to have Jill's number?"

Scott had begun walking toward the front of my car. "Yeah, it's under *J* for Jill. What the hell did you hit? A concrete post?"

"Something like that," I muttered as I dialed Jill's number. A few seconds later I heard her sleepy "hello."

"Jill, it's Kara. Yeah, I know it's two A.M., but I need Zack's number. And, yes, I know about you two."

"Yeah," she said after a couple of seconds. "He told me you knew. Here, talk to him." I heard a rustling sound then heard, *Wake your butt up, Kara sounds freaked.*

I did? Great.

"Kara? What's wrong?" Zack asked.

I lowered my voice and checked to make sure that the two officers were still examining the front of my car. "The golem attacked me at my house. I ran it down with my car and got away, but I broke down on the side of the road. I wanted to warn you and Ryan in case there's more than one."

I heard him curse. "Where are you?"

"Highway 1792. I can get a ride over there, though. Make sure Ryan knows, all right?"

"Will do. We'll talk more when you get here."

"Why the hell are you wearing a raincoat?" Zack asked when I climbed out of Scott's car.

Unfortunately, since Officer Gordon had the passenger seat in front, that meant I'd had to ride in the back—usually reserved for prisoners. I could only imagine what Jill's neighbors were thinking as Gordon opened the back door to release a raincoat-clad woman into their neighborhood.

I thanked the two officers for the ride, then turned back to Zack as Scott drove off.

"Because I was asleep when the damn thing attacked me," I grumbled, stalking to the door where Jill was waiting. "And apparently my wards only work against living creatures. And I didn't have time to grab clothing on my way out my bedroom window. And the only options that were in my car to cover my girly parts were my rain gear or a strategically placed gun belt."

Zack grinned. "I vote for the gun belt," he said, then laughed as Jill thwapped him on the back of the head. "What?" He put on an innocent expression. "I was merely thinking that she might need her gun to defend herself!"

Jill snickered. "Oh, yes. Always thinking of others!" She turned to head back into the house just as a screech of tires from down the street caught our attention. A heartbeat later a dark blue Crown Victoria hurtled into the driveway, slamming to a stop millimeters from Zack's car. I stared as Ryan practically flew out of the car and toward me, dressed only in running shorts, a T-shirt, and untied sneakers with no socks.

He stopped and raked a gaze over me, expression relaxing once he determined that I was in one piece. Then he frowned. "Why the fuck are you wearing a raincoat?"

Zack burst out laughing. I turned to Jill with a pleading look. She draped an arm over my shoulder and gave me a comforting squeeze. "Poor Kara. C'mon, I'm sure I have something you can wear that doesn't make you look like a sex offender."

"I'm still voting for the gun belt!" Zack called after us as we headed inside.

Chapter 29

Even though Jill and I could never fit into the same size jeans, she had T-shirts and stretchy-type pants that were suitable for my current needs. And even better, she had a stretchy-type sports bra that fit well enough to keep me from revealing the room temperature. I dressed quickly in the loaner clothing, then returned downstairs.

"First things first," I said. "I don't know if that thing found me because whoever's controlling it drove it to my house, or if it somehow has the 'scent' of me. So, we need to be cautious."

"Tell us what happened," Ryan said, his voice and gaze cool and professional. I did so, even telling the part about Rhyzkahl waking me up. I expected Ryan to react to that in some way, but his face was an iron mask. Oddly, his control bothered me more than if he'd been upset or relieved. I kinda wanted to see *some* sort of reaction.

Zack had remained standing near the window during my recitation, occasionally peeking out. I didn't miss that he was careful to maintain cover. "You touched a nerve with someone somewhere."

"Yeah, well, maybe y'all can help me figure out what nerve." I scrubbed a hand through my hair, wincing as I found tangles. Crap, I was probably an utterly lovely sight. I had yet to look in a mirror. At this point I was afraid to. Sleep-tangled hair, no makeup, and borrowed clothing. Sigh. Maybe it was a good thing that Ryan didn't seem to want to look at me.

"Right now most of the attacks seem connected, but it still doesn't make any sense," I continued. "Vic Kerry was thrown out a window, Adam Taylor was tossed down a flight of stairs, and Roger Peeler was chased down and drowned. And Vic loaned money to both Adam and Roger . . ." I frowned. The stock purchase. That meant something, but I was too frazzled to figure it out. "The attack on Lida is the one that doesn't fit."

"I'm still inclined to believe that Lida's attack was a publicity stunt that went too far," Ryan said.

"Okay," I said. "So we're down to who might be controlling it. Adam and Roger are out, obviously. Trey doesn't seem to give a shit about publicity. And Michael only wants to be left alone to play piano."

"But Vic and Ben Moran were pals," Jill piped up, shuffling through newspapers.

I frowned. "My aunt told me that Vic and Mike Moran Senior were good friends. Ben and Vic were too? How do you know that?"

Jill lifted a shoulder in a shrug. "I freelance for the local paper—go to society events and take pictures." She smiled. "It's a pretty sweet gig. Free ticket to the events. Only downside is the mingling with the snobs. Though luckily most people aren't snobby at all."

"How about Moran?"

She snorted. "Wanted to be sure his picture was taken any time there was a camera. Loved being popular. But people kissed his ass too."

"Because he's on the board of Lake Pearl Bank," Zack said with a nod. "He has some pull when it comes to loans and business dealings."

Jill nodded. "And he'll have even more now that

they're being bought out. He made a lot of stockholders *very* happy with this deal."

It hit me. "That's it," I murmured. "Vic and Ben were pals? How close?"

Jill cocked her head. "They hung together a fair amount, or at least every time I saw them at a function."

I stood, excited. "That's it. All of that time I suffered in white collar crime is finally paying off!"

Zack raised an eyebrow. "Would you be so kind as to share with us?"

I grinned, beginning to pace. "Okay, Moran is on the board of Lake Pearl Bank. He loves being on the board of LPB because it makes him popular and powerful. People kiss his ass and do shit for him. He fucking loves that shit."

"We've noticed this," Ryan remarked, tone dry.

"So, getting kicked off the board would be about the worst thing that could happen to him, in his mind. He wouldn't be invited to any of these events and parties anymore. People wouldn't be kissing his ass."

Zack and Ryan exchanged a baffled glance and I rolled my eyes. "Okay, if you two are going to try and pass your task force off as a financial crimes unit, you need to be up on the financial world." I stopped pacing. "Though, to give Moran credit, he didn't actually break any laws. I mean, until he started murdering people. Though he'd probably be in deep shit with the SEC."

"Kara," Ryan said tightly. "Would you please get to the point?"

I took a deep breath. "In the banking world, if Bank A is interested in buying Bank B, then, assuming Bank B wants to be bought, Bank B has to disclose all sorts of information, open their books up, that sort of thing. But the catch is that it's completely secret until the deal goes through. If a member of the bank board lets it slip that the deal is in progress, they can be kicked off the board."

Jill's brows drew together. "Why? What's the deal?"

"Because, if people found out that a bank was in trouble and possibly needed buying out, it could cause a run on the bank. But also, if someone knew that a small bank was going to be bought out—especially if it was by a large bank with more valuable stock—he could conceivably buy up a big chunk of stock in advance of the sale—"

"Insider trading," she finished with a nod. "Okay. Got it. So Vic found out and started buying stock?"

I shook my head. "Not quite. Moran and Vic were buddies, and I think that Moran let it slip to Vic that Lake Pearl Bank was about to be bought out. And, Vic—nice, charming, wonderful Vic—decided he could make a bundle. But he knew better than to make any purchases himself since it was known that he was friends with Ben, so Vic very *nicely* offered Roger a loan and the chance to make a huge profit. And Adam Taylor owed Vic money—probably for stuff related to the studio—so Vic convinced Adam to let him make some investments in his name as well."

Jill made a sour face. "What a sweetheart. Throw everyone else under the bus. He knew perfectly well what he was doing, and I'm sure that after he sold the revalued stock for his 'clients' he would have skimmed off a hefty portion of the profit."

"I'm sure you're right," I told Jill.

Zack let out a low whistle. "So Moran found out about the big stock purchase and realized that people knew."

"And by then it was too late," I said. "An investigation into insider trading wouldn't be far behind."

"It's nothing illegal," Ryan said, musing. "But for a guy like Moran, losing that social position would be as bad as going to jail."

"Right," I said. "That's why I don't think that Moran

was complicit in the insider trading, other than being indiscreet. He values that position too much. And somehow Moran can control this golem and sent it to take care of Vic, and then Adam and Roger, in an attempt to clean up the mess. With them dead, there's no way for anyone to prove that Moran was the one to leak the info about the sale."

Silence fell for a few ticking heartbeats.

"So," Jill said finally. "How are you going to prove Moran killed them?"

I looked at her. "I have no fucking idea."

Zack stood. "And, how does this connect to the attack on Lida?"

I set my hands on my hips. "I have no fucking idea about that either, but can you people at least allow me to feel smug about figuring the murders out? Jeez!"

Jill laughed. "Oh. Yes," she said in robotic deadpan. "You are so brilliant."

"Bite me, bitch." I stuck my tongue out at her.

Zack rubbed a hand over his face. "So what do we do about it?"

I sighed. "You mean, how do we prove that Moran sent a magic creature to kill three people? Let's all say it together: No fucking idea."

The room grew quiet. A faint scent of vanilla hung in the air from a reed diffuser on one of Jill's bookshelves. In the other room I could hear her refrigerator cycle on.

"We need him to confess," Ryan finally broke the silence. He kept his gaze straight ahead.

A chill washed over me. I'd seen Ryan change people's memories. Only a few months ago we'd been attacked by a demonic dog-like thing at a restaurant, and he'd done something to the people working there— somehow taking away their awareness of the incident. *Can you do that?* I wanted desperately to ask. *Can you make him confess?* No, I didn't want to ask. I didn't want to know if he could do that. "Can you read minds?" I found myself asking instead.

His eyes lifted to mine. I expected to see pain or angst or regret or something in them, but he was as controlled as stone. Nothing was leaking through. "No," he said evenly. "Many things would be easier if I could." Then he looked away and lifted one shoulder in a shrug. "Or perhaps not."

My gut tightened at the subtle jab. Zack cleared his throat in an obvious attempt to cut the sudden tension. "Arrange a meeting with him," Zack said. "Maybe something will shake loose."

"This is so cliché," I groaned, flopping onto the couch. "So we confront him, or set up a trap or sting or something, and he does the mustache-twirling villain and reveals all? No way. He's too smart and he has too much at stake."

"But you have the bank records showing the insider trading. That should give him pause," Zack insisted.

"Except that we have no proof that he was involved," I replied, frustration seeping into my voice. "Nothing that we could go to the Securities and Exchange Commission with."

"What about Lida?" Jill suggested. "You think she's clueless? Or is she too loyal to her uncle to be willing to share any useful information?"

I hesitated before answering. "I don't know," I admitted. "And at this point I have no choice but to pressure her. Maybe that will shake something loose with Uncle Ben." But even as I said it, I knew it wasn't true. Ben looked out for Ben.

I stood, thoughts tumbling. "I need to go back to my house. I, um, have something I have to take care of before I do anything else."

"Let me guess, you're going to summon Rhyzkahl,"

Ryan practically growled. "You've already summoned him for the month. What if that golem's still there?"

Anger flared red hot. This was bullshit. It wasn't as if I'd set out to insult or hurt Ryan. Fuck him and the way he assumed I was summoning Rhyzkahl. And so what if I was? "You know what, Ryan?" I shot back. "*Fuck you.* I'm sorry if this pisses you off, but Rhyzkahl saved my fucking life tonight. And yeah, he probably didn't do it because of some deep and abiding love for me, but he did."

I didn't wait to see or hear his reaction. I snatched up my bag and left the house, not quite storming out, but doing my best to give a firm impression of *So Fucking There.*

I was halfway to the sidewalk when I heard the door slam behind me. "Kara! Where are you going?" Ryan demanded.

"To my aunt's house," I said over my shoulder, not stopping. "I'm going to borrow her car. Now leave me alone."

A heartbeat later his hand was on my arm, turning me around. Fury blazed again and I brought my hand up as he spun me, turning it into a slap instead of a punch at the last instant. I knew I hadn't hit him very hard, but his head jerked to the side at the blow, and the sound seemed to reverberate down the empty street. I tensed for some sort of retaliation, shocked at myself that I'd struck him. But I wasn't going to back down from this now.

"Give it a rest, Ryan!" I said, struggling to keep from shouting. "I'm sick to death of tiptoeing around you! I'm sorry if you don't like the fact that I'm fucking the demonic lord—" I took a deep breath, trying to keep from shaking. "Y'know what? No, I'm not sorry. I'm a grown-up. I can sleep with who I want, and I'm sick of being made to feel like some kind of sleazy whore simply because you don't approve of him! This is *your* problem, not mine!"

He simply stared at me in shock. I began to turn to walk away but he caught my arm again. "Wait, please," he said, putting his other hand up as a block in case I tried to hit him again. Smart move on his part, because I was more than ready to do so, and this time it wasn't going to be a slap. I was no expert in hand-to-hand, but anger was making up for the lack.

"Kara, I followed you out to tell you that I'm sorry," he said, voice gruff. "I'm being a dick."

I pulled my arm out of his grip. "Not gonna argue with you there," I retorted, scowling.

He sighed. "It's just that . . ." He scrubbed a hand over his face. "You matter to me. Your friendship matters to me."

My anger shifted to annoyance. "Fine. You want to be friends? Then act like a friend! Stop making me feel like shit all the time!"

Surprise flickered in his eyes, then he abruptly pulled me into a hug, wrapping arms around me before I could react or try to pull away. Though I suddenly had no desire to pull away from him. "I'm sorry," he said again. "You're in a shitty position, and I'm only making it harder for you."

"Yup," I said against his chest, anger beginning to trickle away. He was making it awfully tough to stay mad at him. He smelled like all sorts of nice manly stuff and I could hear the calm and steady beat of his heart.

He gave me a light squeeze. "Do I have any redeeming qualities left?"

I sighed and tilted my head back to look at him, not breaking away from his hold. "Well, you still give a fuck. So that's nice."

He gave me a soft smile, then surprised me by kissing me lightly on the forehead. A thrill raced through me, followed by a massive tsunami of confusion. A kiss on the forehead? What the hell was that? Should I do something? Should I try to kiss him? Was that a "we're great friends" kiss? Or was he holding back because he didn't want to get burned?

He tightened the hug briefly, then stepped back, making the tsunami of confusion somewhat moot—at least as far as the "should I kiss him" part went. "I do give a fuck," he said, still lightly gripping my shoulders.

"I appreciate that. I'm sorry I slapped you."

He frowned. "You slapped me? I thought that a mosquito had landed—" He ducked and laughed as I swung at him again.

"You are such a jerk," I said, trying to glare without much success.

"I think that's been well established. C'mon, I'll give you a ride home."

I hesitated. "Ryan, when I get there, I'm going to—"

"I know," he said. "You're going to summon Rhyzkahl." He gave my shoulders a squeeze. "It's okay. I know you need to do this."

I searched his face for any flicker of regret or pain or angst or anything, but if he was feeling it, he was keeping it under unspeakably tight control. "Thank you."

"I'm trying," he said, voice low and rough.

"I know," I said, hiding a smile. "And you have no idea how much that means to me. Which makes what I have to say next even harder."

His brows drew together in a frown. "What?"

My lips twitched. "I'm actually *not* summoning Rhyzkahl. You totally wasted all of that control and maturity."

He smiled. "Well, damn!" he said, though there was relief in his eyes.

"But I still appreciate the sentiment."

"Good thing," he said. "I don't have a whole lot of

control and maturity to waste on false alarms like that. So, if you're not summoning the lord, then why do you need to go back to your house?"

"Well, you were close. I *am* going to summon, just not the demonic lord. But, I know that you um . . ."

"Don't care to be insulted and growled at by demons?" he offered.

"Well, yeah. I know you're a real weenie like that."

He laughed. "You're definitely hanging out with me way too much. You're becoming an asshole."

"I'm learning from the best!"

Chapter 30

Despite our earlier banter, neither of us said much on the drive back to my house. Even though I wasn't summoning Rhyzkahl, it was guaranteed to be an odd and tense situation with Ryan present, which was why I didn't intend for him to be in the basement for the actual ritual. This summoning was a bit too crucial and I didn't want to risk something going wrong because I was distracted by worry over Ryan's safety.

Dawn was sending pink fingers creeping across the sky by the time he pulled into my driveway. I'd grabbed the extra ammo out of my own car before leaving it to be towed and had reloaded on the drive back to my house. We both scanned my yard cautiously before getting out of the car. I gripped my Glock, extending every sense possible in the hope that I'd be able to sense an imminent threat. It didn't escape my notice that Ryan's gun was in his hand as well.

My front door was ajar and slightly askew in its shattered jamb. *What if it's in the house?* I'd damaged it, but I had no idea if it was capable of repairing itself or if it could only stay active for a set amount of time. We moved up the porch and through the house, guns at the ready, silently clearing it and checking for threats.

Crumbles of clay littered the hallway—remnants of the creature's leg—but no other sign remained.

I holstered my gun after we finished searching the house from top to bottom. "It creeps me out that the wards didn't affect it at all," I admitted to Ryan. "Do you mind staying up here while I do the summoning?"

"I was going to suggest it."

I glanced at him and could see that, again, he understood. *Great, he's capable of being all understanding about the demonic lord and the summoning and all of that. So why can't he be more understanding that I want to know where he and I stand?* Or maybe by keeping me at "just friends" he *was* letting me know.

Now was a bad time to start getting all moody about that particular emotional train wreck. I did my best to shove it from my mind. "Okay, well, lemme go get ready."

He gave a short nod. "And I'll go raid your fridge."

"I bought a new brick of cheese yesterday. Go wild."

I grinned as his groan of despair followed me down the hall.

I quickly showered and wrapped my bathrobe around me, then sent Ryan into my bedroom to wait and count to fifty while I did my superstitious little routine of going down to the basement naked.

You're so stupid, I chided myself as I pulled my summoning garb off the hook at the bottom of the stairs. *You have no problem at all letting Rhyzkahl see you without a stitch on, but you freak the fuck out at the thought that Ryan might catch a sight of tit.* Maybe my subconscious was telling me I really did want Ryan as a friend and nothing more? Or maybe Ryan's opinion of a naked me mattered more.

I gritted my teeth and yanked on the silk pants and shirt. *Stop thinking about this!* My wayward emotions were going to get me killed at this rate.

I carefully made the changes in the diagram for the calling of a *syraza*. I didn't summon them very often, and so I pulled out my heavily warded, well-hidden, and barely-legibly-written summoning notebook to be sure I was doing it right. Usually I summoned a *reyza* if I needed a higher demon. *Syraza* weren't known for skill in warding or other arcane areas that I might want information or instruction in. They weren't big and scary-impressive like the *reyza,* or even unnerving like the *zhurn* Skalz.

But obviously Rhyzkahl felt this demon would be a competent guardian for me. *Maybe this one owes him a favor or something.* That made more sense. *But I'm going to have to buy an SUV or something to carry it around,* I thought with a sigh. How the hell was this going to work?

I reviewed my notes one more time, then tucked the little book back into its hiding place.

The power flowed smoothly from the storage diagram into my control as I set the bindings and protections. The glyphs and sigils around the summoning circle began to glow in my othersight. Carefully manipulating the potency, I began the weaving of the portal itself. The icy wind swirled through the room as the light from the diagram increased to near-blinding incandescence. I felt the portal widen as the wind whipped my hair about my face, and I spoke the demon's name.

"Eilahn."

The wind dropped to nothing as the light vanished. I held the arcane bindings, waiting for my vision to adjust. A few seconds later I could see a figure on one knee in the middle of the diagram. Its skin was a pearlescent white that caught the light from the fireplace and shimmered with hints of orange and red and pink. It was slender, almost birdlike, with long graceful limbs. Its head was smooth and hairless, with large and slanted violet eyes set in a delicate, almost human, face. Its wings looked as fragile as tissue paper, but I'd once had the chance to see *syraza* in flight, so I knew that somehow those wings really were strong enough to support the creature.

I paused, suddenly uncertain what to say. Usually there were forms to be followed for setting terms and bargaining for service, but this was different. I wasn't the one who would be paying the price.

At least, not in the usual manner.

"I am Kara Gillian," I finally said. "Lord Rhyzkahl bade me summon you and said that you could provide me with protection." It ended up sounding more like a question than I'd meant. But how could this creature—who looked like a strong breeze could carry it away—offer me protection . . .

My thoughts trailed off even as the *syraza* lifted its head. *Kara, you're awfully dense sometimes.* I was pretty sure that Zack was a demon, and he sure as hell didn't look like one.

"I am Eilahn," it replied in a voice that sounded like birds singing and bells chiming all at once. "I have given my oath to Lord Rhyzkahl to give you protection and support."

I lowered the wards and bindings. "I am grateful for your service." I paused. "Please forgive me if I give offense, but are you able to, um, shapechange? I mean, your current form is quite pleasing," I added hastily, realizing that it sounded as if I didn't like the demon form. "But I wonder how you'll be able to give me protection without revealing yourself as a demon."

It rose with sinuous grace to its feet. "Yes, I am able to shift my form, though it is not simple. I will require your assistance."

I nodded, feeling surreal. *I was right. Zack is a demon. Ha!* "Just tell me what I need to do."

It inclined its head, though its violet eyes stayed on

me. "First we must complete the bond so that I may re-main in this sphere."

A bond? A wave of uneasiness passed through me. "I performed an adjustment to bindings once before so that the *reyza* Kehlirik could remain past sunrise," I said. "Is it the same sort of thing?"

"Similar," it replied and stepped to me. "But this will go deeper. I will guide you in the process."

I didn't have a chance to ask *how* deep. Eilahn slipped a hand to the back of my head in a lightning-fast move and placed the other hand on my face, touching my fore-head and cheeks with the tips of its fingers. A brief fris-son of shock and fear surged through me, amplified by the fact that I could feel the strength of the grip that held me in place. Eilahn looked wispy and delicate and its fingertips seemed to be barely touching me, but I sud-denly couldn't move my head a millimeter. My survival instinct screamed at me to struggle, but before I could twitch I felt a jab of potency spear through me, freezing me in place. *It was a trap!* I thought in sudden panic. Rhyzkahl hadn't sent this demon to me. *This is a demon sent to kill me or capture me—*

A wave of calm and peace flowed through me and my desire to struggle faded. A small part of me tried to insist that this was part of the attack, but the flow of se-renity pushed it down with barely a ripple. A soundless tone vibrated through me and for an instant I thought it would shake me apart, my molecules flying apart from the force of it. Suddenly I could *feel* the *syraza* as if I was inside its skin. I could see the shock on my face, taste the moisture on my breath, yet I was still looking up at the demon in a bizarre double-vision. But more unsettling were the shimmers of completely alien emotion that swept through me, too quickly for me to understand, and leaving behind only the awareness that I was some-how feeling what the demon felt.

And then it was gone, and my senses were my own. Eilahn slowly released me and stepped back, a smile on its delicate face. "Forgive me for using force. There was no way to fully prepare you, and it was vital that the process not be interrupted once begun."

I blinked a few times as I tried to shake the sensation that I still wasn't quite inside my head. "Um. Yeah. It's cool." I took a breath, slowly beginning to feel more normal. "Wow. That was . . ."

" 'Intense' is a word that is often used to describe the experience," the *syraza* offered, still smiling.

I gave a weak laugh. "Yeah, that about covers it." I scrubbed my hands through my hair, the last vestiges of the not-in-my-body sensation finally fading. Seriously weird. I didn't agree with Eilahn's statement that there was no way to prepare me—a simple "This is going to make you feel way funky" would have been good. I had the niggling suspicion that the *syraza* had enjoyed weirding me out like that.

Great, there was a good chance that I was now bound to a demon with an evil streak.

"Okay, so . . . how do I help you shift your form?"

In answer the *syraza* dropped down to a crouch, folding its wings tightly across its back as it wrapped its arms around its legs. I felt another soundless tone shimmer through me, though not even a hundredth as powerful as the first had been. But this time it didn't fade away and continued to resonate. I could feel the demon again, could sense a slow shifting. It wasn't a morphing like in the movies, but more as if the demon was being redrawn, a flickering of reality like falling rain. The resonance shifted to a series of alternating tones as the flickering increased and I found myself shaking from the effort of holding onto the resonance. Somehow I knew that if I didn't keep it in check it would take over and shake us both apart from some sort of arcane vibration. I gritted my teeth as the flickering and resonance built to a shrieking crescendo.

And then it was gone.

Dizziness slammed into me, and I sagged and crumpled to the floor, barely catching myself from smacking my face on the stone. I took several deep breaths until the spots faded from my vision, then looked over at the demon.

Or rather, I looked at the naked woman shakily pressing herself up from the floor.

Chapter 31

My hands still had a bit of a tremble to them as I went through the motions of making coffee, even though it had been over half an hour since I'd come up from the basement with a hot chick in tow. I was definitely way too tired for this shit.

And Eilahn *was* a hot chick. There was no doubting that. Eilahn-the-demon might have appeared gender neutral, but Eilahn-the-human was *quite* female. Dark-skinned and tall, with sleek black hair that flowed past her shoulders, she still had a violet cast to her eyes, though nowhere near as deep and intense as when she'd been in her demon form. She looked like a perfect multiethnic mix of damn near every continent, with the build and muscle tone of one of the Cardio Barbies who haunted my gym, but without any of the artificial enhancements that so many of them employed. She didn't need them.

Right now she was wrapped up in my bathrobe, sitting across from Ryan at my kitchen table. Glaring at him. Ryan merely looked baffled and amused, seeming to take the whole demon-in-human form thing in stride. He was certainly handling it a whole lot better than I. Here I was, the accomplished summoner, and I'd had no idea that *syraza* could shapeshift. Could other demons?

And could the *syraza* shift to other forms besides human? Curiosity pounded at me, but I knew I'd have to wait until later to satisfy it.

I dumped the water into the top of the coffeemaker, then turned to face the two. "Eilahn, please stop giving Ryan nasty looks," I said wearily. "He's under my protection." *And, Ryan, you can stop looking at her at all,* I thought with stupid, jealous annoyance.

The *syraza* slid her gaze to me, then gave a slight nod of acknowledgment. "Lord Rhyzkahl warned me of your association with the *kiraknikahl.* Forgive me. I should have guarded my reaction with more discretion. I assure you that I meant no insult to your judgment."

Great. Now I was deemed a poor judge of character among the demonkind because I hung around with Ryan. This was getting better and better. "Well, you'd better get used to him and learn to get along with him, because he's my friend." I flicked a glance to Ryan and was surprised to see him looking at me with a pleased and grateful smile on his face. I found myself returning the smile. Yeah, I had his back.

I ran my hands through my hair. "Okay, so, I guess I need to get you something to wear." There wasn't a whole lot of my clothing that would fit her, except for sweats and stuff like that.

"Clothing would be appreciated," Eilahn replied.

Shit. This would get expensive if I had to provide her with an entire wardrobe. And no doubt she'd be living with me, too. Fuck. I was so not ready for this. If Zack was a *syraza* as well, was he bonded to Ryan the way Eilahn was to me? I had to assume that, if he was, Ryan was completely unaware of it.

I looked at the clock above the sink. Almost five A.M. And me with about two hours of sleep in me. This was going to be a fun day. "Well we're going to have to find a store that opens early, because we need to get moving on figuring out how to stop the golem before it's sent after one of us again." *Or sent after someone close to us,* I thought with a sudden rush of worry. Tessa's wards wouldn't keep the creature out any more than mine had.

"Hang on," I said, grabbing my phone and going to the living room. I quickly dialed my aunt's cell phone number, fidgeting as it continued to ring. She picked up on the fifth ring.

"Mmmph?"

"Aunt Tessa? I'm sorry I woke you up," I said in a rush, "but I need you to go somewhere else for a little while. I'll explain it all later."

"Somewhere else? What are you talking about?"

So much for "I'll explain it all later." I should have known that Tessa wouldn't blindly submit to my request. "The construct I told you about isn't stopped by wards," I told her. "It came after me at my house, walked right through the wards, but I managed to get away from it. We're pretty sure we know who's controlling it, but until we stop him and destroy the thing I don't want to run the risk that you might be a target simply because you . . . you matter to me."

"Oh, sweetling, that's such a nice thing to say," Tessa said, voice still fuzzy from sleep. "But don't you worry about me. I'm not at home anyway."

Fear pierced through me as I flashed back to the hideous moment when I'd discovered that the Symbol Man had taken my aunt. "Where are you?" I asked, voice shaking despite my desire to remain calm. "Are you all right?"

She let out a low laugh. "I'm quite fine, Kara. I'm at Carl's house."

Relief mixed with embarrassment washed over me. "Oh. Oh, well that's good." I smiled weakly. "Okay, well, be careful anyway, all right?"

"We've been quite careful, sweetheart. You know I

haven't hit menopause yet, so I make sure Carl uses a condom—"

"AUNT TESSA!" I screeched as she burst into laughter. "You are a horrible evil woman, and you know perfectly well what I meant. Eww!"

"I know, I know," she said, still laughing. "I couldn't resist. You've been far too tense lately."

I snorted. "Yeah, well, there've been a lot of things to make me tense."

She was silent for a few heartbeats, and I expected her to say something reassuring such as, *That's all over now. It's going to be all right now.*

"You have a heavy load," she said instead. She sounded tired but this time not because I'd woken her. "I'm so sorry. This is my fault in so many ways."

"No, it's not your fault. It's going to be fine," I said, a little off-balance that I was the one doing the reassuring now.

"The demons are not . . ." she trailed off.

"Aunt Tessa? The demons aren't what?"

"The demons are not demonic. You know that."

I frowned. "Um, yeah. I know." We'd had these conversations before about how the demons we summoned were not the evil demonic creatures of religious mythos.

"It applies in reverse as well."

"Huh?" I scowled. I was too tired to sort through verbal games. "What are you talking about?"

"The demons are not demonic. The demonic are not demons."

I bit back a whimper of frustration and slowly counted to five. "Aunt Tessa, I love you dearly, but you're driving me batshit crazy at this moment."

I heard her yawn. "I'm sorry. It's not important right now. I'm going to go back to sleep, sweets. You'll let me know when I can go back home?"

"Um, yeah," I muttered, feeling off-balance again.

"You're a good girl. I'm so proud of you. I'll talk to you later." And with that she disconnected.

I let my hand fall to my side and let out a low groan. *She's going to drive me absolutely crazy.* Well, that much was back to normal.

I returned to the kitchen. At least Eilahn was no longer glaring at Ryan.

"Okay, I don't have a car," I said. "So, Ryan, you're stuck driving me. Us." I fought back a yawn. I wanted to go through the financial info again, but I knew that it wouldn't help at this point. Showing that Vic had used Roger to participate in a little insider trading didn't provide any proof that Ben Moran was responsible for the murders. I didn't even have proof that he was the one who let slip the information about the sale of the bank. "But we need to relocate. I don't know how safe it is to stay here."

"If you were attacked here once, it could happen again, and with more force and preparation," Eilahn pointed out.

"I think it's time to take the fight to our opponent," Ryan said, eyes narrowing.

"With what?" I said, frustration rising. "We have nothing. No proof. No probable cause for a warrant."

"Fuck warrants," he growled. "This asshole tried to kill you in your sleep. I don't know about you, but that kinda pisses me off."

I snorted softly. "Yeah, well, it didn't exactly give me warm fuzzies."

He stood up. "This has gone beyond what our legal system can deal with. Think about it, Kara. There's *no way* we'll ever be able to put together a case that could go to court. Ben Moran isn't strong enough to crush someone's spine, and we can't exactly present his accomplice in trial." He leaned forward and planted his hands on the table. "You said it yourself. We have no proof."

My mouth felt dry. Ryan was voicing things I'd been

reluctant to consider. "But then we're nothing more than vigilantes, Ryan. And what are we supposed to do? Go kill Ben Moran?"

"If that's what it takes to eliminate the threat, then yes." He straightened, never taking his eyes from me. "He brought this on himself, Kara. If he hadn't brought the fight to us by attacking you, then he probably would have gotten away with this."

"But what if we're wrong?" I said. I rubbed my arms, unsettled at the turn the conversation had taken. "What if he's not the one doing this? Ryan, I couldn't live with myself if we did something drastic and he wasn't the bad guy."

Frustration and anger swept across his face. "Then we'll make sure we're not wrong. We'll get proof, or a confession, or whatever it takes. It won't be anything we can take to court, but it'll be enough to let us know we're doing the right thing."

I gave a shaky nod, but I still felt horribly conflicted, which, frankly, surprised me. I'd always kind of assumed that in a truly dire situation I'd be able to do the whole superhero thing and Do What Needed To Be Done—no matter what—to save the world. After all, I knew without a doubt that, as a police officer, I could pull the trigger in a life-or-death situation. I'd carefully examined that moral issue when I'd first entered law enforcement. But what Ryan was talking about was different—taking the fight to the bad guy and eliminating the threat in a preemptive strike. Crossing heavily into that grey area, and edging dangerously close to the darker edge, if not going over.

I guess I had more faith and support for our legal system than I ever imagined.

"I took an oath, Ryan," I said, stomach oddly tight. "I'm supposed to uphold the law. Not commit ... murder."

Ryan came around the table and took me by the shoulders. "Kara. I know this is tough for you. You're a cop. I'm a cop. You're passionate about your work and you believe in justice and what's right. But this has gone beyond the laws of the mundane world. He's using *magic*. And that's how we have to fight back. You swore an oath to uphold the law, but that oath also includes protecting the public."

I looked over at Eilahn, hoping for some sort of signal or advice or solution or something from her, but she was silent and still, watching us. This was *my* moral dilemma.

I could feel tears snaking down my cheeks, but I made no move to wipe them away. Why was this so hard for me?

Because I'm normal, I told myself. *It shouldn't be easy.* Back when I was a road cop one of my teammates had revealed to me that he'd shot and killed a man in the line of duty when he'd worked for NOPD.

"It was a good shoot," he'd told me. *"The guy had a gun and woulda killed me. There was never any question that my actions weren't justified."* He'd paused. *"But it still ate me alive that I'd killed a man. I saw the counselor for a long time, and you know what? That's the way it should be. It shouldn't be easy to deal with killing some- one, especially if you're a cop. We do it when we have to, but if it doesn't hurt, then you're a sick fucker."*

And now I was being asked to take it to another level. I looked back at Ryan. "Have you . . . ?"

His expression grew very remote. "I have. But only when there was no other choice. Kara, I'm not going to give you some bullshit line about how you were given a gift and how you should use it for the benefit of man- kind, or some crap like that."

"But that's what this is about, isn't it?" I retorted. "I have arcane abilities. I can do things other people can't."

"So what? It's not about your abilities. It's about

you and your moral base." He lifted a hand and wiped a tear away form my face, a move that damn near un-did me. I was too exhausted to be dealing with this right now. "Kara, I know what you're going through. I went through it too. You swore to uphold the law and protect the public. I'm not trying to tell you what to do—"

I held up a hand to stop him. "Enough." I pulled away from him. "Yes, you *are* trying to tell me what to do. I know you mean well and you're worried about me and everyone else, but ... I need a few minutes." I started toward the kitchen door.

"We don't have much time, Kara," Ryan said, begin-ning to follow me. I turned back to say something sharp and unpleasant, but before I could open my mouth, Ei-lahn stepped in front of him, barring his way.

"You will give her the time she needs," the demon said, tone low and even. I watched in mild shock as anger swept across Ryan's face, clearly directed at the demon. But I had the unerring feeling that there wasn't a damn thing he could say or do that would move her. "Do not push her to an action that could destroy her later."

She's protecting me, I realized in a burst of clarity. She was a guardian in all ways, not just physically.

Fatigue and regret replaced the anger as Ryan shifted his gaze to me. "I would never do anything to hurt you, Kara."

I nodded, a lump in my throat. "I know. Ryan, I just need to think and figure this out on my own." I said qui-etly. I turned and headed down the hallway to my bed-room. I didn't look back again, but I knew that Ryan wouldn't try to follow me again.

I changed out of the borrowed clothing, not think-ing of anything in particular, but allowing the thoughts and emotions of everything that had happened in the past year to swirl freely through my mind. Six months ago, my life had changed irrevocably, when Rhyzkahl had come through my summoning portal instead of the fourth-level demon I'd intended. I was a full summoner, with the power and knowledge to call forth demons—creatures of incredible strength and arcane power. Moreover, I was oathbound to the most powerful demonic creature of all—a demonic lord.

This wasn't about me wasting my gifts, I realized as I pulled jeans on. This was about me using every weapon and tactic at my disposal. One of those weapons was my ability to see if arcane power was being used, and if not for that, no one would have even known that the deaths of Vic and Roger and Adam had been anything but accidental.

I hesitated with my hands on the button of my jeans, then shucked them off and dug my fatigue pants out instead, pulling on boots and topping it all with a black T-shirt. I belted on my holster, as well as my ankle holster and my backup piece, then grabbed a clean set of sweats and headed back to the kitchen. Eilahn stood in the doorway, casually leaning against the jamb. Ryan sat at the kitchen table, looking oddly morose.

Eilahn straightened and stepped aside to allow me to enter. Ryan lifted his head but didn't say anything.

"We're facing someone who's committed several acts of murder," I said, "and will no doubt commit more if he's not stopped. My job—my oath—compels me to do all I can to stop a murderer." I took a deep breath. "And, failing to act would be a greater violation of my oath. We're not going outside the law. We're going beyond what the law can handle."

I thought Ryan would look pleased at that admission, but he merely gave a small nod, a haunted expression passing briefly over his face.

"That being said," I continued, "we have to bear in mind that if we decide to do what needs to be done, there may be ramifications, such as, oh, being arrested for murder. Therefore, we need to think hard and long about what we do, and then plan and be careful."

I turned and handed the sweats to Eilahn. "Put these on, please. We need to relocate to someplace safer, then we can figure out what we're going to do and see about getting you proper clothing." Good thing I'd recently paid off my credit card. It was about to get a workout.

She accepted the clothing with a gracious nod, then, without a blink of hesitation, dropped the robe from her shoulders, standing unashamedly naked in my kitchen before pulling the sweats on.

"We can go to my place," Ryan said. I flicked a glance to him to see his reaction to Eilahn, but he was very carefully looking at the opposite wall. Smart man. "I highly doubt Moran knows where that is. I'll call Zack and let him know."

I nodded, suddenly realizing that I had no idea where he lived either. He'd mentioned something a while back about renting a house in the area, but I'd never asked where it was. Good thing he was driving.

"Then let's roll," I said, feeling like a badass.

Chapter 32

My badass attitude lasted as long as it took for me to get into the car, put my head back against the headrest, and close my eyes. The next thing I knew someone was gently shaking my shoulder.

"Kara," a vaguely familiar voice said. "You have rested long enough now. It is time for you to wake."

I opened my eyes, instantly confused to see that I was in bed—and not my own. I rolled over to see Eilahn standing beside the bed. Behind her Ryan stood in the bedroom doorway, scowling darkly. I sat up and scrubbed at my face. I had the vaguest whisper of memory of being carried from the car to inside a house. I was pretty sure it was Eilahn who had carried me, too, which might have possibly explained why Ryan looked pissed.

"How long have I been asleep?" Sunlight streamed through the blinds covering the window, but I couldn't see a clock anywhere in the room. Or anything else that wasn't an absolutely necessary piece of furniture. Bed, nightstand, dresser, and armoire—all in a very sturdy-looking blond wood. The bedding was in muted autumn tones and the walls were a dusky blue. It looked *exactly* as I would have expected Ryan's room to look.

"It is midday," Eilahn replied.

I grimaced. "Shit. I wish you hadn't let me sleep so long." Small wonder that I'd crashed so hard, though, between the scant sleep and the normal exhaustion of performing a summoning. I tried to run a hand through my hair, but the tangles made that impossible.

"I tried to wake you a couple of hours ago," Ryan said sourly. "She wouldn't let me."

Eilahn inclined her head slightly. "It is truth. You were in dire need of rest, and those few hours would have been insufficient."

I stood up, feeling as if I'd slept in one position the entire time. Someone had been kind enough to remove my boots and gun at least. "That's great," I said as I tried to get my vertebrae to behave and line up properly. "But there's too much that needs to be done."

"And you need to be clear-headed and at your peak performance for such tasks," Eilahn replied, slight smile curving her lips. "The *kiraknikahl* briefed me on the nature of the threat you are facing in this construct, and I concluded that it was highly probable that you would need to employ your arcane abilities in order to thwart it. Thus your need for further rest."

I glanced again to Ryan. I didn't think anyone could look more annoyed at the moment. I sighed. "Eilahn, his name is Ryan. Please cease referring to him as 'the *kiraknikahl*.' "

"As you wish," she replied.

I suddenly realized that Eilahn was dressed in something other than sweats—black jeans, form-fitting gray T-shirt, and boots. She looked like a fashion magazine version of How to Look Fabulous in Urban Casual. "Did you two go shopping?"

Ryan's scowl deepened, if that was even possible. "No," he gritted out. "She refused to leave, and made me go shopping. For her."

I tried to picture the tough FBI agent shopping for

women's clothing and failed. "How on earth did you know her size?"

He folded his arms across his chest and glowered at the demon. "I estimated and bought a bunch of shit in a bunch of sizes, and tomorrow I'll go and return all the shit that doesn't fit."

"Oh. Thanks for taking care of that. I'll pay you back."

"No, you won't." He smiled tightly. "*She* owes me, not you."

I looked doubtfully between the two. I wasn't so sure it worked like that since Eilahn was here to serve *me*, but to my surprise she merely gave Ryan a slight nod coupled with a faintly amused smile.

I heard a door open and close somewhere in the house. Ryan glanced down the hall. "That'd be Zack. I told him to bring food. C'mon and eat, lazybones."

My gun and bag were on the nightstand and my boots were on the floor beside the bed. I quickly donned boots and gun, then grabbed my bag. But I paused before following Ryan out of the room.

I turned to Eilahn after Ryan was out of earshot. "Did Lord Rhyzkahl tell you why I needed protection?"

She dipped her head in a brief nod. "He advised that there had been attempts to interfere with you, and that you might be at risk for being summoned to the demon realm."

"What would happen if I was summoned?" I asked, gut tightening.

"It is the same as when you summon demons to this sphere. There are bindings, and terms are negotiated. Save for one difference." She paused, and whether she intended it to be or not, it was seriously ominous. "Only a demonic lord would be capable of opening a portal to summon you to the demon realm. And a lord would have more than sufficient potency available to bind you against your will, negating any need for your willingness to set terms."

My throat was completely dry. "Like the Symbol Man was going to do to Rhyzkahl." I croaked. A slave.

"Yes," she said quietly. "And with far less effort."

Fear sliced at me, and for a moment I had trouble getting breath. Then Eilahn put a hand on my chin and gently forced me to meet her eyes.

"I will protect you," she said with such utter conviction that it was impossible not to believe her. My terror faded to apprehension and wary caution. I could handle that.

She dropped her hand and gave me a warm smile. "Come. You need to eat." She turned and exited the room. After a heartbeat I followed her out and down a short hallway. It opened out into living room where Ryan was waiting for us. From what I could see, the rest of the house was more of the same as the bedroom. Somewhat spare, incredibly neat, sturdy-but-nice furniture, autumnal tones. There were blinds over the windows, but they were open enough for me to see that Ryan lived in a subdivision—a somewhat older one to judge by the number of trees visible. I realized I still had no idea *where* Ryan lived.

Off to the left I could see into a spotless kitchen, where Zack was standing at the counter with his back to me and a number of grease-stained paper bags before him.

Zack turned as I came into the living room. "Hey, Kara," he said with a smile. "I didn't know what you liked on your burgers, so I asked for . . ." He trailed off and went still as he caught sight of Eilahn. She froze as well, eyes locked on Zack. Any doubts I'd harbored about whether or not Zack was a demon were suddenly gone as an electric tension filled the room. Neither made a move, but I had the unswerving feeling that both were milliseconds away from doing something blindingly fast and vicious.

"Zack, this is Eilahn," I said, shattering the strange tension as surely as if I'd thrown a rock at a window. "Rhyzkahl sent her to protect me."

He remained silent and still for another three heartbeats, then abruptly smiled a normal Zack-smile as he grabbed several bags and came into the living room. "Nice to meet you, Eilahn," he said with a cheerfulness that felt jarring after the tableau of seconds before. "Hope you like burgers!"

Ryan took one of the bags from Zack, apparently unaware of the brief tension. But then again it hadn't lasted very long. I'd probably only noticed because I knew about Zack.

"Love them," Eilahn replied with a bright smile that was just as jarring as Zack's cheerfulness. "Thanks!"

Zack passed me a wrapped burger, meeting my eyes and giving a slight nod that I took as a sign of approval. I felt a weird surge of relief. At least if I had to have a demon dogging my every move, it was one that apparently met Zack's standards.

"I need to call my sergeant," I said after inhaling half a burger. The last food I'd had was a piece of cheese right before summoning Eilahn, and I was feeling it. "Since he's pretty much on board with the whole 'magic' thing, it'll be damn useful to have him along." I glanced at Ryan. "Another witness for our side, so to speak."

"And what's your cover story going to be for Eilahn here?" Zack asked with a nod toward the demon.

Crap. I hadn't thought about that. "Um, a visiting cousin or something."

"If I might make a suggestion?" Zack said. "If she's here to protect you, then she'll need to be in a position to be near you fairly often."

I set my half-eaten burger down. "So she needs to be a cop or something." Maybe Crawford could figure out a way to get her hired? But then how would she get through the background check? I'd have to get a whole identity forged for her, and I had only the barest idea of how to go about doing that. I could probably scrounge up some contacts, but it would take time and be risky.

"It'll be too difficult to get her hired on with your department," Zack continued in an echo of my thoughts. "With any department, for that matter, and you don't have the luxury of time to do anything that requires detailed work. The easiest thing to do would be to have her be another member of our task force."

I glanced at Eilahn to see how she was handling being talked about, but she seemed unconcerned, leaning against the wall with her thumbs tucked into the pockets of her jeans. Apparently she recognized that Zack had been through this before and was willing to benefit from his experience. Or least that was my assumption. At some point I *was* going to pin Zack down and squeeze more info from him.

"Great," I said, "so she'll be another FBI agent."

But Zack shook his head. "No, still too easy to check that. Easier to make her foreign—here on an exchange program, or that sort of thing." He flicked a glance at the silent demon. "That will also help cover any slips she makes with regards to culture or social stuff."

I slid a look to Ryan. He was focused on Zack, and he had an odd expression on his face as if he was trying to remember something. Zack suddenly grinned cheekily. "I knew all those suspense thrillers would pay off!"

The confusion cleared from Ryan's eyes as he smiled. A strange chill crawled down my back. *So, if Zack is also Ryan's guardian, is part of his duty making sure that Ryan doesn't remember whatever it is he's not supposed to remember? Is he a guardian or a prison guard? Or was* the line between guard and guardian a fine one? Like a reverse Stockholm syndrome.

My appetite had disappeared, so I left the rest of my burger and excused myself to the hallway to call Crawford. When I pulled my phone out I realized that I'd several missed calls from him, and I groaned. Great, I wrecked my car *and* didn't show up for work. Nice way to earn points with the rank.

"Goddamn it, Kara!" he said when he answered, in lieu of *hello* or anything of that ilk. "What the fuck is going on? Are you all right?"

"I'm sorry, Sarge. I'm okay. Had an unwelcome visitor last night." I paused. "Ten-twelve?" Ten-twelve was the code for "Can you talk freely/are you alone?"

I heard a shuffling and then the closing of a door. "Okay, go ahead," he said.

I gave him a quick rundown of what happened at my house last night, leaving out the part about being woken up by a demonic lord. Crawford was handling the woo-woo stuff all right so far, but I didn't think he was quite ready for the bit about me summoning demons.

He muttered something foul. "All right, we'll come up with something to explain what happened to your car. Do you know who sent that thing after you?"

"We have a pretty strong theory, but, well, we've run into a snag."

"Go on."

"I have no idea how to get a warrant that accuses someone of committing murder using an arcane construct," I said sourly.

"Well, shit."

"We're trying to put together a plan," I continued. "It would help if you were a part of it, but it might not, um, follow procedure."

He was silent for several heartbeats. "Then it sounds like you might have need for me."

I breathed a silent sigh of relief. "We're holed up at Ryan's place. I'll text you the address."

"I'll be on my way as soon as I get it."

I disconnected and walked back to the living room. "Sarge is on board. Where the fuck are we?"

Ryan laughed and rattled off an address that I recognized as being even more out in the boonies than my own house. I quickly sent the text to Crawford, then plopped back down on the couch and concentrated on eating. No matter what course of action we decided on, I had a feeling I was going to need all available energy.

Crawford arrived about twenty minutes later, which gave me enough time to finish my burger and even finally pull a brush through the snarled mess that was my hair.

I introduced Eilahn and Crawford, quickly glossing over where she was from and why she was here. He gave her a gruff greeting, shook her hand, and then ignored her so studiously and carefully that it would have been insulting in any other circumstance. However, I was pretty sure that Crawford had somehow figured out that he didn't really want to know too much more about her. Crawford's tenuous acceptance of my weirdness seemed to include an instinct to not ask questions unless it was absolutely necessary.

Probably a damn smart move on his part.

"I think the first thing we have to do is find the golem and destroy it," I said, once we'd all settled in the living room. "Then we can deal with Ben Moran without worrying about silly things like getting smacked by a giant clay monster."

"It would have to be somewhere at the house, right?" Zack suggested.

I started to agree, then paused. "No. I've been to the house twice and never felt any resonance. I think if it was being kept there, I'd have felt something." I considered for a few seconds. "And not at the studio, either. Or rather, I only felt resonance there in certain places, where the golem would have been to kill Adam Taylor."

Silence fell.

"You said this thing is made out of clay?" Crawford asked after a moment.

I nodded. "That's what it looked like to me. Dirt, dried clay, held together and animated by some sort of arcane means."

"And it's pretty big, right?" he continued. "Which means that whoever made it would need a fair amount of clay."

I nodded again.

He pushed off the wall. "I know where to start looking."

We looked at him expectantly.

"C'mon, boys and girls," Crawford said with a cheery smile. "We're going to the dump."

Chapter 33

Ben Moran had made his money in debris removal, or so Crawford reminded us after we'd looked at him like he was insane. One of the reasons Moran had enjoyed such success wasn't simply because he had trucks to haul debris, but also because he owned a decent-sized tract of land in the north end of the parish which he was able to use as a place to dump said debris. And one of the reasons that the site was so ideal for a landfill was the fact that the ground was mostly clay—which had saved him a great deal of trouble and expense, since the landfill permits required a significant clay barrier to be placed before debris could be dumped.

Unfortunately, the landfill was a shit location as far as tactics went. It was in the middle of dense woods, there was only one road leading to it, and it was surrounded by a high chain-link fence and higher dirt berm. We'd scouted the location as best we could using the Internet, but we knew that the satellite images we found were probably months old. Eventually we grudgingly decided that there was nothing to do but go.

We went in two vehicles—Ryan, Eilahn, and me in one car, and Zack and Crawford in the other. As a concession to tactics we parked beyond the last curve of the road before the landfill, less than a quarter mile from the entrance. This area of the parish was hilly enough that we couldn't see the landfill from where we were, which we hoped meant that anyone—or anything—at the landfill couldn't see us either.

I stepped out of the Ryan's car, then slung the strap of my shotgun over my shoulder. I had it loaded with double-aught buckshot and slugs, and I hoped like hell that I wouldn't have to use it. I hated firing slugs. The last time I'd been forced to qualify with the shotgun I'd ended up with a bruise the size of a dinner plate on my shoulder that had taken weeks to fade completely.

But I had more faith in the ability of the shotgun to stop a golem than my 9mm. And, since we didn't have access to grenades or rocket launchers, this was the next best thing for destroying the thing. I hoped.

"Doesn't smell like a dump," I remarked to Crawford as he walked up. He'd changed into fatigue pants and boots as well, and he held his shotgun down by his side.

"That's 'cuz it's not for regular garbage," he replied. "Almost entirely for construction debris, and I don't think it's used much anymore. Moran made a killing after the last hurricane, when the local governments were desperate to find a place to dump storm debris, but this site's a bit too remote for regular use."

"Which makes it the most likely place to store a magic monster," I said.

Ryan peered up at the berm that blocked our view of the landfill. It was at least twenty feet high and unnervingly steep. "Zack, you're a nimble little fucker. You wanna reconnoiter?"

The blond agent smiled. "Thought you'd never ask." A second later he was scrambling up the side of the steep hill, barely disturbing a single clod of dirt. We watched as he edged up to the crest and pulled out a small pair of binoculars. He remained still and silent for a couple of minutes, then scrambled back down.

"I'm not seeing any surveillance cameras," he reported, brushing dirt from his pants. "Chain-link fence around the perimeter, with the one gate at the road. Gate's open, and there's a dark green Lexus SUV parked in front of a small metal building—about a hundred yards beyond the gate. And there ain't shit for cover between the gate and the building. Lots of low hills of dirt, that's all."

"So he's here then. He's likely repairing the golem," I said.

"We have bolt cutters, right?" Crawford asked. Ryan nodded. "Agent Garner and I can work our way around to the left and approach that way," he continued. "I don't like the thought of all of us marching up the road."

"Do it," Ryan said. "Take a radio." We were using FBI-issue radios for this since we sure as hell didn't want to have any chatter related to this on the police channel. The FBI radios looked a lot like walkie-talkies I could buy at Radio Shack, but I wasn't going to complain.

Zack shouldered his rifle and gave me a significant look that I couldn't interpret, then he and Crawford and Ryan loped off along the edge of the berm.

I watched them go, feelings the first flutters of nerves begin. *There are five of us and we have plenty of firepower,* I reassured myself. *We can take out a golem, even if it's back to full strength.*

Then why did I feel like I was overlooking something?

Ryan glanced back at Eilahn and me, then started up the road at a slow jog. I bit back a groan and broke into a run, relieved when he slowed as soon as we rounded the curve and came in sight of the gate. As Zack had reported, the gate stood open. Beyond it was a squat metal building with an SUV parked in front. There were no other vehicles that we could see.

"That's Ben Moran's vehicle," I murmured. A strange frisson of relief swept through me. I'd been right. The lack of tangible proof had caused me more doubt than I'd realized until that moment.

We moved forward cautiously through the gate. As soon as we passed through it I had even more confirmation. "Hold on," I said in a low voice as a wave of resonance washed over me. "Golem's definitely here."

Ryan flicked an acknowledging glance at me, then I heard him mutter low into the radio as he passed the info to Zack.

"Foul," Eilahn muttered. I glanced at her to see her nose wrinkled as if she smelled something disgusting.

"Have you ever seen one before?" I asked.

She shook her head, keeping her eyes in a constant scan of the area. "It is a different sort of power, but it makes my nose itch." She didn't have a gun, since she'd pointed out that she had yet to have any sort of training with such a weapon. Instead she had a goddamn sword strapped to her side. The sword was Zack's and he insisted it was merely a high-quality costume piece that he used for Renaissance fairs, but there was something about the weapon that made me think that this sword was not only very real, but had also seen actual battle.

The door to the building opened when we were about twenty yards away, and we raised our weapons. Or rather, Ryan and I raised our shotguns, and Eilahn drew her sword.

I expected to see Ben Moran step out.

I was shocked as shit to see Trey step out. *What the hell? Is he working with Moran?*

Trey didn't seem very surprised to see us, though he did give Eilahn and her sword a brief "what the fuck?" look before returning his attention to me. He no longer looked harmless. He stood straighter now, more focused, but his smile had a nervous edge to it. We might not have surprised him, but he wasn't looking forward to this confrontation.

"Keep watch for the golem," I murmured to Eilahn, probably unnecessarily. I held my shotgun leveled at Trey. "Keep your hands where I can see them," I called out, "and step forward slowly."

He lifted his hands slowly and spread them to show that they were empty, though he didn't move from the doorway. "Detective Gillian, what on earth is going on?" he asked, trying to look puzzled.

"Where's Ben Moran?" I demanded.

His shoulders twitched in a shrug. "I'm not sure." Then his smile turned more confident. "Most likely in a stockholder meeting, accepting the appointment to the new board of the bank."

I scowled, rethinking my theories. "So, he had you do his dirty work?"

Trey cocked his head. "Detective Gillian, what do you think you're going to do here? Do you have a warrant? I really think you should leave and forget all this."

"We're beyond warrants, Trey," I said, slowly stepping forward. I could feel the resonance grow stronger, like a buzzing in the back of my teeth. I saw a shift of movement behind him, but I couldn't tell if it was the golem. "You and Moran shouldn't have sent your creature to try and kill me last night. We're here to destroy the golem. Maybe then we can talk about warrants and murder charges."

He shook his head. "I haven't murdered anyone."

"Semantics," I retorted. This was stupid. I didn't want to get involved in conversation. I simply wanted to get this over with. My hands were beginning to sweat and I had to fight the urge to wipe them on my pants. "Where is the golem?"

He took a slow step forward as I tightened my grip on the shotgun. "Which one?" he said mildly.

Resonance slammed into me as Ryan let out a curse. Shit! My heart began to slam in my chest. That's what I was overlooking. If he made one, he could make more.

Eilahn give a soft hiss. "Five . . . no, six that I can see. We are flanked."

I risked a quick glance and confirmed Eilahn's info for myself. Crude and shambling, they rose out of the dirt piles we'd passed like zombies rising from graves and terrifying me about as much.

I stepped forward and lifted the shotgun, training it on Trey's chest. "Call them off!" I shouted. "Make them stop, or I'll fucking drop you right here!" I didn't know if killing him would make them stop, but it seemed like a fucking good start to me.

He let out a nasty laugh. "But I can't. I'm not the one controlling them." He stepped to the side. "Michael? These are the people who are trying to ruin everything."

My gut tightened as the young man stepped through the doorway, his face contorted into a bewildered anger. *Shit!*

"Tell your clay men to take them away, Michael," Trey said, gaze never leaving us. "Take them away so that they can't take your nice house away."

"Michael, don't believe him!" I shouted. "We're not here to ruin anything. Your uncle and Trey have been killing people with your clay men. You know that's not right!"

Doubt flickered across Michael's face. Out of the corner of my eye I could see the shambling advance of the golems slow. Trey gave a sigh. "Now she's accusing your uncle of being bad, and you *know* that's not true. You can't trust anything she says." He met my eyes and the look of smug satisfaction in them told me more than any confession could have.

What if that was true? What if Moran wasn't involved at all? *It doesn't matter right now,* I told myself. *Get him to stop the golems!*

"Michael! You're not a murderer." I tried to keep my voice strong and steady, which wasn't easy considering how scared I was. At least these golems were moving nice and slowly. Maybe it was because he was controlling so many instead of only one. "Trey wants your men to take us away to kill us. He already had one of your men kill Adam and Roger!" Where the hell were Crawford and Zack?

Michael shook his head slowly. "Roger and Adam weren't nice. They were bad for the band. They were ruining everything. Them and Mr. Vic. They were gonna take our house away, and all our money. They were gonna put me in a home, and I'd never see my sister and uncle again."

Fuck. I didn't have time to debate this crap. I turned and fired at the golem on my right while it was still a dozen feet away. The blast from the shotgun took a portion of its right shoulder off, but I felt as if it had taken off a portion of mine as well. I heard a cry of dismay from Michael, even as Ryan unloaded on the golem coming up on his side. I didn't have time to spare him a glance, but judging by the satisfied *"Take that, fucker!"* I heard from Ryan I had a feeling his aim had been better than mine.

Eilahn let out a strange piercing battle cry, and out of the corner of my eye I saw her leap toward a golem coming up on our rear, swinging her sword in a broad arc. But my golem was still moving in inexorable advance, as were the other three. I pumped another round into the shotgun and fired again, this time with more success as the creature's head exploded in a cloud of dirt.

"Nice shooting!" Ryan shouted. I wasn't about to tell him that I'd been aiming for the middle of the thing's body.

I took aim at another golem. "Michael, call them off! Think of Lida! What would your sister think if she knew what you were doing?"

My chest tightened at the sound of a feminine laugh.

"She'd think he was finally being useful," I heard Lida call out. I looked with dismay to see Lida step out of the doorway behind Michael and put a comforting hand on his shoulder. But her expression was anything but comforting.

I scowled and snapped my attention back to the approaching golem. "So what's the deal, Lida? You afraid of losing your comfy lifestyle? You're on your way to being a big star. Why do you care if your uncle loses his position on the bank board?"

She let out an ugly bark of laughter. "I don't give a fuck about my uncle, but I do so love his money and influence. I wasn't going to let it all disappear because he couldn't keep his stupid mouth shut around his friends. And, besides, I was ready to kill Adam anyway for how much he'd fucked up the band. But Trey knew about Michael's cool little talent and organized a little damage control." She cocked her head. "But you knew, somehow. You can speak to the elementals?"

So, I'd been right about the golems actually being earth elementals. *But I was wrong about Ben Moran.* Later I'd have a small freak-out about how close I came to murdering an innocent man. First I had to get out of this situation intact.

I tried holding the shotgun down by my hip in the hope of giving my throbbing shoulder a break, but instead damn near broke my thumb when I fired at the golem. Plus, I missed. "We know that the attack at the concert was a publicity stunt," I said, ignoring her question. "That was gutsy to have it throw you in the river. Or stupid." I raised the hated shotgun to my shoulder and fired again, this time blowing the leg off the thing and dropping it. I was glad to have stopped the thing, even though, once again, I'd been aiming for the middle of its torso. I looked around, near sagging in relief to see that all six of the creatures had been dispatched.

My ears rang in the sudden silence after the shooting and my shoulder was so numb I could barely hold the shotgun.

Lida slipped an arm around Trey, looking quite unconcerned that the golems had been destroyed, which didn't give me a warm fuzzy feeling. "The river wasn't part of the plan," she replied with a shrug. "Michael fucked that up."

Her brother's face crumpled as fury surged through me. But his face lit up again when she put her hand on his shoulder. "Don't get upset, little brother, you redeemed yourself with Adam and Roger."

Michael gave her a tentative smile, then looked to me. "They were p–pussies who didn't have the stomach for the business," he said as if reciting a script.

I was only paying him the barest of attention. Lida and Trey were too relaxed, too confident. Something else was coming. I kept every sense I had extended, scanning. Eilahn and Ryan could sense it too; we stood with our backs to each other, weapons at the ready.

"So, Lida," I called out, "how long before you ditch Trey? Now that you've wiped out half the band, you can probably get out of your contract and go solo, right? That's what you've always wanted." I could see doubt flicker across Trey's face, and I wondered if I was saying something he'd refused to admit to himself. "Trey doesn't want to be a full-time musician. He wants money and stability. He's doing this for you because he wants your uncle to get him a nice high-paying white-collar job."

"Or, for that matter," I continued, "how long before you get sick of caring for Michael and put him in a home?" I heard Michael's swift intake of breath and pressed on. "It's not like you're going to keep up this pretense of caring for him if you don't have to, and you're not going to take him with you when you leave

Trey and Beaulac behind. You don't want him in your band, do you? Not when you have to stop and coddle him every time he gets upset." I looked her way, seeing the truth of it in her eyes. "Or will you even bother putting him in a home? Once you've taken care of us, you won't need him anymore. In fact you won't be able to risk him blabbing, will you?"

Trey took a shocked step back from her. Yet another truth he hadn't wanted to consider.

"Shut up!" Lida screamed. She was losing control and knew it. "Michael, shut them up! Call the rest!"

Confusion warred with misery in the young man's face. There was a part of him that understood, but he'd been loyal to his sister for too long to want to believe it.

But Trey wasn't giving up that easily, and apparently had a bigger stick than sibling love. "Detective Gillian, did you know that Michael killed his father?" His tone was conversational, but there was a vicious gleam in his eye. He *had* to win this now and get rid of us.

Michael gave a strangled cry of horror. "You promised you'd keep it secret!"

Trey's hands tightened into fists. "Michael, if you don't take care of these people, they'll take you to jail and keep you there forever."

Michael looked at us in sudden terror. "I didn't mean to! He was teaching me! I lost control! I'm sorry!"

A wave of pity nearly overwhelmed me as I realized how Trey had managed to control the young man. "Michael, don't believe him," I said as gently as I could. "You were just a boy, right? It was an accident. We don't put little boys in jail for accidents." I felt a vibration under my feet. *Not an earthquake,* I realized, mouth going dry. *But a lot of dirt moving.*

"You can't trust her, Michael," Trey said, eyes not leaving us. "She wants you to put your men away so that she can arrest you."

I felt as much as heard a low rumble. Shit. How many more of them are there? "Michael!" I yelled. "You have to stop this! They're going to kill you as soon as your men have killed us! They won't need you anymore!"

"See, Michael?" Trey said, turning a comforting smile on the man. "She'll say anything to get to you. You can't believe anything she says. I love your sister, so that makes us family, right? And family would never hurt you."

Michael looked into Trey's oh-so-earnest face, then nodded and turned back to us.

And an army of golems descended upon us.

Chapter 34

They came from all around us like a slow wave, with more coming from behind, cutting off our retreat. I couldn't take the time to count them, but I estimated that there were more than twenty and less than fifty. I hoped.

I barely noticed Trey and the others retreating inside the building. I was almost grateful for that since it meant I didn't have to worry about accidentally shooting Michael. At this point I didn't have a problem shooting Trey or Lida, but my *do whatever it takes* attitude wasn't quite ready to cut down someone who'd only been a pawn. I wasn't so sure that Eilahn or Ryan would share that attitude.

But I didn't have time for that particular moral dilemma. "Eilahn, you keep our backs safe!" I shouted as I quickly reloaded. I chambered a new round into the shotgun, then held it tight against my miserably sore shoulder, gritting my teeth as I fired at the approaching golems. At least my lousy aim didn't matter so much. With so many of them coming at us, I was guaranteed to hit one of them.

I breathed raggedly as I fired again and again. I couldn't hear anything but a low buzzing, a combination of the gunfire and my own stress response of blocking out all sound. I dropped five or six of them, but the line kept advancing, closing in on us like a giant claw. I could only trust that Eilahn was keeping our rear safe.

I chambered another round and squeezed the trigger, but there was no violent kick of the shotgun this time. *I'm out.* I slapped my hand onto the side pocket where I had extra shells, but it was empty. In my peripheral vision I could see Ryan swinging his shotgun like a club, taking off the head of one of the golems. I could barely hold the shotgun at all; I doubted I'd be playing T-ball with golem heads.

I let the shotgun drop from my hand and drew my Glock. My right arm was so numb that I nearly dropped it, and I quickly transferred it to my left and started firing. I could see puffs of dirt rising where my rounds struck the golems, but they weren't very impressive. We'd taken out over half of them, but the rest still marched in devastating silence toward us.

I felt another rumble beneath my feet. *No,* I thought in dismay. *Not more. We can't even handle these.* I looked past the golems, braced to see another wave of the creatures come around the building.

I sure as shit didn't expect to see a big yellow bulldozer come around the corner. Crawford was at the controls, while Zack stood atop the canopy, keeping his footing with inhuman balance. He squeezed rounds off from his rifle, sighting down it and blowing off golem heads even as Crawford mowed down a good dozen of the creatures with the bulldozer. Crawford was shouting something incomprehensible, face stretched into an exultant grin that I never expected to see on my sergeant.

Zack suddenly swiveled the rifle toward me. No, not at me—

I whirled to my left in time to see Zack's shot take a chunk off the head of the golem there, but it apparently wasn't enough to slow the thing down. I yanked my gun up, but I could see its fist coming at me . . .

White light exploded behind my eyes and I crumpled to the ground. *I'm dead,* I thought through the haze and pain. I struggled to focus only to see the golem standing over me, raising its blocky fist for a blow that would no doubt crush my skull like a melon.

Not dead yet. About to be. I couldn't make my body move, could only stare at the impending blow. And I could hear again. I could hear everything.

Eilahn screamed something. It wasn't Ryan's name, but he whipped his head around, his face filling with horror and shock as he took in the sight of me on the ground and the golem about to brain me.

In the span between one heartbeat and the next he straightened, expression smoothing to ice, with only his eyes showing a devastating rage. He raised his hands before him, and in the next heartbeat the space between his hands filled with white-blue potency. He lowered his head, lip curling as he unleashed the power into the golem above me.

Then his eyes rolled up into his head and he collapsed as dirt rained down around me.

I felt frozen as I stared at Ryan's motionless form. I distantly heard Zack let out a cry of horror. He leaped off the bulldozer and swiftly moved to Ryan, cradling him in his arms like a child. I felt Eilahn's arms around me and I was distantly aware that she was holding me in similar fashion, but I couldn't look away from Ryan.

A hand on my chin did it for me as Eilahn turned my face up to hers. "What did you yell to him?" I asked. It came out in little more than a cracked whisper, but I knew she'd heard me.

"It matters not. How badly are you injured?"

"The golems?"

A flicker of annoyance passed over her face. "They have all been defeated. How badly are you injured?"

I put a hand up to the side of my head. I could feel the lump there, but I didn't have double vision or anything. Yet. I was probably mildly concussed, but the fact that I was able to realize it was probably a sign that it wasn't too bad. "Help me stand," I said. "This isn't finished."

She nodded and helped me up. I swayed briefly but she kept a hand on my arm to steady me. I couldn't look at Zack and Ryan. Instead I focused on the scene by the building.

Trey stood in front of the building door, shielding himself behind a weeping Michael. I could see Lida still inside the building, staying mostly behind the doorjamb. Crawford had come down from the bulldozer and had his gun trained on Trey. I couldn't see the gun that Trey was holding to the back of Michael's head, but I knew it was there from the level of tension in everyone involved.

"It's over, Trey," Crawford growled. "The golems have all been destroyed. Killing Michael won't give you a way out."

I knew what Trey was going to do. Crawford probably did too. I could see the decision click into place in the man's eyes, chasing away the anger and defeat for the few seconds before Trey pulled the gun away and stuck it in his own mouth.

I didn't even twitch at the sound of the gunshot, but Michael jerked violently, no doubt thinking that he'd been the one shot. He fell to his knees, clutching his head in his hands as Trey's body crumpled to the floor.

"You stupid fucks!" Lida screamed. Her face twisted in fury as she reached down and yanked the gun from Trey's limp hand.

She's not *going to kill herself,* I thought in a flash. But my gun wasn't in my hand. I'd dropped it when the golem hit me. I could only watch in numb horror as she lifted the gun to aim at her brother's head, hatred suffusing her features. "Crawford! Shoot her!" I yelled.

Lida's whole body jerked before the words were out of my mouth, and a red spot bloomed on her forehead. An instant later the gun fell from her hand, and she dropped to the ground.

I blinked in surprise at Crawford, but he was looking at the crumpled form of Lida with a perplexed expression on his face. He turned to me. "Kara, did you . . . ?"

I lifted my empty hands. "Not me, Sarge."

Eilahn cleared her throat, then held my gun out to me. "You dropped this," she said. Then she gave a light shrug. "They are not so hard to use after all."

She turned to walk away, smugness radiating from her every move. I rolled my eyes and started to retort, but the words died away at the sight of Zack still cradling the motionless Ryan.

He blasted that golem with arcane power. The image I'd pushed aside came flooding back in. *I've seen that done once before,* I thought, hands beginning to tremble slightly. And the expression on Ryan's face had been . . . inhuman.

I took an uncertain step toward them. "Zack? Is he all right?"

He jerked his head up, then shocked me by baring his teeth and growling deep in his throat. I froze, then took a slow step back.

A shudder seemed to crawl over Zack, then he seemed to regain himself. "I will tend to him," he said in a low, hoarse voice. He stood, still cradling Ryan, then started walking down the road.

"Zack?" I couldn't keep the desperate note out of my voice. "Is he going to be all right?"

He paused. "I will tend to him," he repeated. I expected him to continue walking, but he remained still. "Kara, you must trust me," he said without turning. His back was stiff and straight. One of Ryan's hands dangled at Zack's side, and I could see the top of his head by Zack's shoulder. I didn't know whether I wanted to rush to Ryan and put my arms around him or run as far away from him as I could.

He blasted that golem with arcane power.

"He will be as he was, Kara," Zack said after another several heartbeats of silence. "You have my oath on that."

As he was . . . when I knew him? Or before? A chill shimmered through me.

I watched him walk down the road until he rounded the curve and was out of sight. Then I returned to the others and the rest of our mess.

Chapter 35

"What are we going to do about Michael, Sarge?" I asked quietly.

Crawford scrubbed at his face with both hands before letting them drop to his side. "Fuck if I know, Kara." Somehow we both understood that we weren't talking about who would take care of him. There was still a great deal of investigating before us, but from everything that had been revealed by Lida and Trey, I now doubted that Ben Moran had known of the murders. So, yes, his uncle would remain his guardian, but . . . "What if he does something like this again?" Crawford said with a sigh.

I echoed his sigh. Evening was falling and the mosquitoes were beginning to come out. The moon was barely visible through the trees. A couple more days and it would be full, and summoners all over the world would be inscribing circles and preparing offerings and making bargains.

The subject of our conversation was sitting on the ground on the opposite side of the bulldozer from where the bodies of his sister and Trey still lay. Michael hadn't spoken a word since the shooting had ended and had acquiesced numbly to being led to sit by the bulldozer. He stared off into the distance, his arms wrapped around his legs and his chin resting on his knees.

"He's broken," I said. "His best friend blackmailed him into using his talent to kill, and the sister he adored actually hated his guts."

"Fuckers," Crawford muttered. "What happened to the father?"

I shrugged. "I can only guess from what was said. It sounds like their dad also had the ability to control earth elementals and was teaching Michael Junior how to make the golems. Something happened and it got out of control. Michael Senior was killed and Michael Junior and Lida were badly injured." I shook my head. "I guess we'll never know." Lida had probably blamed him for their father's death—in an accident that was most likely Michael Senior's own fault.

"The uncle is his only family, yes?" Eilahn said, startling me slightly. She moved so damn quietly, and I'd half-forgotten she was with us.

I nodded.

"Send him to the demon realm then," she said, folding her arms over her chest, her gaze on the young man. "He would be cared for there, and his skills treasured and guarded."

I could only stare at the demon in surprise at the suggestion. Send him to live there? Was that even possible?

"Send him to the *what?*" Crawford asked, abruptly jerking me out of my own thoughts.

Oh, yeah, I thought with a grimace. *I never did tell Crawford about the whole demon summoning thing.* I cleared my throat uncertainly. "Um, it's not what you think, Crawford. I mean, she's not talking about hell."

He slowly turned his head to look at me, expression so incredulous that I almost burst out laughing.

"Let me explain," I began.

Crawford listened to my explanation about the demons in stony silence. I left out the little detail about Zack and Eilahn being demons, but I told him about me being a summoner, and what that entailed. At the end of he simply gave a long sigh. "Why couldn't you simply be an alcoholic like all the other detectives?"

I grinned. "Demon summoning has less vomiting!"

"What kind of life would Michael have in the demon realm?" I asked Eilahn after Crawford had moved away to start making phone calls.

"What kind of life would he have here?" she replied evenly.

I shook my head. "Nope. That's not good enough. His life wouldn't be unbearable here, he wouldn't be a slave or anything like that—"

"Michelle Cleland," Eilahn interrupted. I struggled to place the name. A few heartbeats later I remembered, ashamed that I'd forgotten it at all. Michelle Cleland had been a victim of the Symbol Man, offered up as a sacrifice to the demonic lord Rhyzkahl by the serial killer. After the Symbol Man had been killed, Rhyzkahl had returned to his realm and Michelle had vanished at the same time.

"I thought she was dead," I said finally, brow furrowed. "Rhyzkahl took her back to the demon realm after the summoning, and I assumed that . . ." I trailed off. I'd assumed that he'd killed her in retaliation for being summoned, but now that I made myself actually think about it, that didn't fit with what I'd come to learn about Rhyzkahl and the demon's code of honor. Michelle had *not* been the one to summon him, in fact had been a victim herself. Killing her would have been a pointless act of misplaced vengeance, which was most certainly not the demon way.

"Why would Lord Rhyzkahl slay her?" Eilahn asked, in line with my thoughts. "She has some small arcane skill and has proven to be useful." The demon tilted her head to look up at the sky, where the moon was beginning to clear the trees. "She is free of her addiction and seems content." She flicked a glance at me. "Happy, even."

"Is she free?" I asked, still dubious.

A smile briefly curved her mouth. "As free as any of us are."

Well, that could certainly be taken many ways, but I didn't have the energy to get into that sort of discussion. I sighed and rubbed my eyes. I felt dirty and gritty all over. "He'll be cared for? He's so . . . broken."

"They can care for him as none here can," Eilahn said with quiet reassurance. "He will be treasured."

In the end we agreed that Michael was simply too dangerous to go back to stay with his uncle. Moreover, if Michael went missing, it allowed us to spin a more plausible cover story for what happened at the landfill. After much careful consultation, Sarge and I came up with a scenario that was as close to the truth as possible, leaving out the bit about the golems. Instead we stated that Michael had been the one to kill the three men—coerced into doing so by Trey and his sister. Michael had then been murdered by the pair—body dumped somewhere in the swamp—and when we confronted them, Trey suicided, and Lida had been shot when she'd tried to fire on officers.

I'd learned that deviating from the actual circumstances as little as possible made it easier to stick to a consistent story. I was getting pretty good at the whole fictional police report thing.

That night Eilahn and I returned to my house with Michael in tow. I still wasn't certain about sending him to the demon realm. *But what other option did we have?* I reminded myself. Killing him was absolutely out of the question. I was relieved to see that even Eilahn agreed with that completely.

Michael sat against the wall near the fireplace, fingers plucking absently at the fabric of his jeans. He'd retreated deep inside himself, numbly obeying our requests to *sit*, and *walk*, and *sit* again. Eilahn leaned against the wall near him, almost protectively.

I still felt dirty, even though I'd taken a long shower after we'd returned to the house. I wanted to ask the *syraza* more about what would happen to Michael, but at the same time I knew it was pointless. There really was no other choice.

I finished making the changes to the diagram, then stood and began the summoning. When Rhyzkahl appeared in the circle, Eilahn sank to one knee, keeping her head lowered in a position of obeisance. I remained standing. I was oathbound to Rhyzkahl. I didn't serve him. Or so I told myself.

The demonic lord stood with his hands clasped lightly behind his back, not moving from the center of the diagram. His eyes stayed on me, but I had no doubt that he was completely aware of every living creature in this basement.

"Lord Rhyzkahl, this is Michael Moran," I said without any preamble. "He has significant arcane skills, but he is ... damaged. Eilahn made the suggestion that he could go to the demon realm." It sounded like more of a question than I'd intended, but it got the point across.

Rhyzkahl's eyes shifted first to the *syraza*—still kneeling with her head lowered—and then to Michael. The young man seemed completely oblivious to what was happening in front of him. "Interesting," he murmured, then stepped out of the circle. I expected him to go to Michael, but instead he moved to me. He put a hand beneath my chin and gently tipped my head up, then very lightly touched the lump on the side of my head. I winced, but a soft warmth quickly replaced the slight pain and my barely-perceptible headache faded.

"I sent Eilahn here to protect you, and yet you are injured," he said, voice low and rich.

"I'd be dead if not for her," I replied. *And Ryan,* the thought whispered and I quickly shoved it aside. I didn't want to think about that right now.

"Then I am well pleased with her service," he murmured. His fingers traveled to stroke my cheek and brush my lips lightly. "I do not wish to lose you."

Lose me as his sworn summoner? I found myself wondering. *Or something more?*

He bent and kissed me, not deeply or passionately, but with a strange and unexpected tenderness which only served to deepen my sudden confusion. Then he straightened abruptly and moved to Michael.

The demonic lord crouched before the young man, regarding him silently for several heartbeats before lifting a hand to Michael's cheek. He remained motionless in that position for what had to have been several minutes, while I stood as quiet and still as possible, not wanting to do anything that could interrupt whatever was going on.

Michael suddenly took a ragged breath as if he'd woken up, then focused on the face of the demonic lord. He stared in astonishment for several heartbeats, then smiled tentatively.

Tension coiled through me as I watched the exchange. There was something different about Michael's expression now, as if he was more aware than he'd ever been before. *Could Rhyzkahl heal his brain damage?* I thought in sudden shock. I had no idea if that was within the realm of possibility or not, but I knew firsthand that the demonic lord had the power to heal. The no-longer-hurting lump on my head was evidence of that.

Rhyzkahl dropped his hand from Michael's face, then turned and walked back to the diagram. A second later Michael scrambled to his feet and followed. Rhyzkahl set his hand on the young man's shoulder, and in the next heartbeat they were gone.

I exhaled softly. "Wow. That was . . ." I trailed off.

Eilahn lifted her head and stood in a smooth motion. "Heartening? Enlightening?"

I gave a light shrug, unsettled at the strange twist of envy and longing in my gut. I'd been to the demon realm once, albeit only for a couple of minutes. *But do I envy Michael because he gets to stay in the demon realm, or because he'll be with Rhyzkahl?*

I didn't want to think about that right now.

"I was thinking 'touchy feely bullshit,' " I said with a deliberately snarky grin, "but yeah, I'll go with heartening and enlightening." I headed for the stairs. "So, Eilahn, do you drink alcohol?"

Her low laugh told me all I needed to know.

Chapter 36

I picked at my pancakes and tried not to keep sneaking glances at Ryan. At least he *looked* like he'd been through hell. If he'd been acting perfectly fine and chipper, I'd have been completely freaked.

But, no, he seemed as normal as I could have expected. Or as normal as I'd ever known him to be.

We were at Ryan's house, and it had been a week since the incident at the landfill. The reports had been filed, the cases closed, and the bodies buried. Ben Moran had resigned from the board without any prompting or pressure, citing grief and shock after the machinations of Lida and Trey had been revealed. I remained convinced that he'd known nothing of the schemes.

I'd heard nothing from Ryan or Zack in all that time until this morning, when Zack had called to invite us over for a pancake-fest. But the atmosphere was remarkably non-fest-like, and the silence at the breakfast table was brittle and awkward. Zack had pulled me aside and told me that everything was all right, and that Ryan was recovering well from his "concussion," yet had refused to give me any further hint or clue as to what was going on, or what might happen next.

He's still Ryan, I tried to tell myself. Except . . . I wasn't so sure of that anymore.

Finally Zack threw down his napkin. "Eilahn, care to take a walk with me?"

Eilahn gave him a grave nod in return and stood. Neither looked back at us as they strode out of the house.

"God, those two are subtle," Ryan remarked dryly. He met my eyes and gave me an unsteady smile. "I'm glad you're all right."

"Ditto," I replied. "I was really worried about you." I poked at my pancake for a few seconds. "What do you remember, Ryan?"

He looked off into the distance, brow drawing down into a frown. "I remember swinging at the golems, then Eilahn screamed my name. I turned and saw that you were down, and . . ." He swallowed hard. "And then I woke up back at the house. I don't remember anything else."

Except that it wasn't "Ryan" that she screamed, I thought. *It was a different name. A name I've heard before.*

The pain in Ryan's face was so clear that I put my hand on his before I could think about it. He looked down at my hand. "When I woke up, all I could think was that I'd failed you," he said, voice unsteady. "I thought you'd died and that the reason I couldn't remember was because there was no way I'd ever want to remember seeing . . ." His voice broke, and he bowed his head, unable to go on. I squeezed his hand even as the tightness I'd been harboring in my chest began to loosen. I didn't have all the answers, but at least I truly knew how he felt about me.

"You saved me, Ryan," I said softly.

He gave a jerky nod without looking up. "Zack told me that." He took a ragged breath, then straightened. I could see him consciously regaining his composure, and after a few seconds he gave me a more normal Ryan-smile. "Sorry."

I cocked my head at him. "For saving me?"

He snorted. "You are such a dork. No, for being . . ."

"Human?"

"God forbid," he muttered, shuddering in mock horror.

"Now who's the dork?"

He grinned and fell to eating.

"I'll be right back," I said after a moment. "I need to talk to Zack."

I found Zack on the porch, leaning against a post with his hands wrapped around a cup of coffee. I moved up to the post and leaned on the other side of it.

"So, Ryan had some sort of blackout, huh?"

"Moments of great stress will sometimes do that, I've heard," he replied evenly.

"Uh-huh. Y'know, I asked you once if Ryan was a demon."

"I told you then that he is not. Nothing has changed."

I nodded. "Right. I get that. And I know you wouldn't lie to me." I pursed my lips. "My aunt said something strange to me the other day."

I heard him take a sip of his coffee. "From what I gather, your aunt says many strange things."

I gave him a chuckle. "True! But this time she was talking about demons and things that were and weren't demonic, and vice versa," I continued conversationally. "It didn't make any sense at the time. But I think now it does. 'The demons are not demonic, and the demonic are not demons.' "

Even though I wasn't looking at him, I could feel Zack tense.

"Is Ryan a demonic lord?" I asked, pleased that the question came out calmly and smoothly, and that none of my inner turmoil had been revealed.

I felt his shudder. "Kara, I am oathbound," he replied, barely above a whisper. "I cannot answer that."

I pushed off the post, blood roaring in my ears as I walked back inside. "It's all right, Zack. You just did."